Based on the novels by Nancy Springer

Enola HOLMES

The Graphic Novels

Book Two

Serena Blasco

Translated by Tanya Gold

Andrews McMeel
PUBLISHING®

Andrews McMeel Publishing
a division of Andrews McMeel Universal
1130 Walnut Street, Kansas City, Missouri 64106
www.andrewsmcmeel.com

Adapted from the series of novels entitled "The Enola Holmes Mysteries,"
written by Nancy Springer and first published by Philomel Books
(The Penguin Group, New York, USA) and by éditions Nathan in French

Volume 4
Copyright © 2008 by Nancy Springer
Graphic adaptation © Jungle! 2017, by Serena Blasco

Volume 5
Copyright © 2009 by Nancy Springer
Graphic adaptation © Jungle! 2018, by Serena Blasco

Volume 6
Copyright © 2010 by Nancy Springer
Graphic adaptation © Jungle! 2019, by Serena Blasco

22 23 24 25 26 SDB 10 9 8 7 6 5 4 3 2 1
ISBN: 978-1-5248-7135-2
Library of Congress Control Number: 2021948436

Made by:
King Yip (Dongguan) Printing & Packaging Factory Ltd.
Address and location of production:
Daning Administrative District, Humen Town
Dongguan Guangdong, China 523930
1st Printing— 6/27/22

ATTENTION: SCHOOLS AND BUSINESSES

Andrews McMeel books are available at quantity discounts with bulk purchase
for educational, business, or sales promotional use. For information, please e-mail
the Andrews McMeel Publishing Special Sales Department:
specialsales@amuniversal.com.

Enola HOLMES

1. The Case of the Peculiar Pink Fan

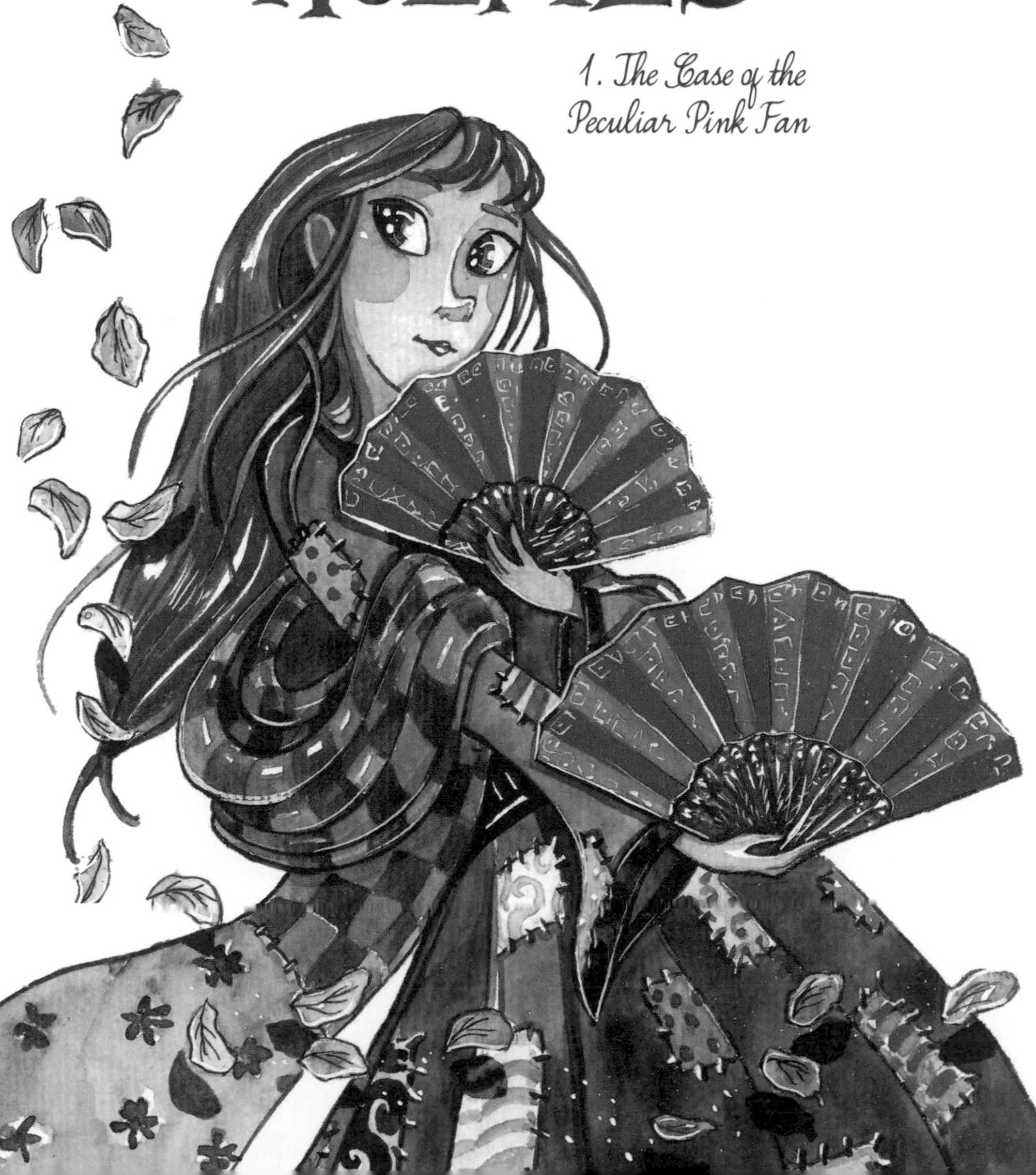

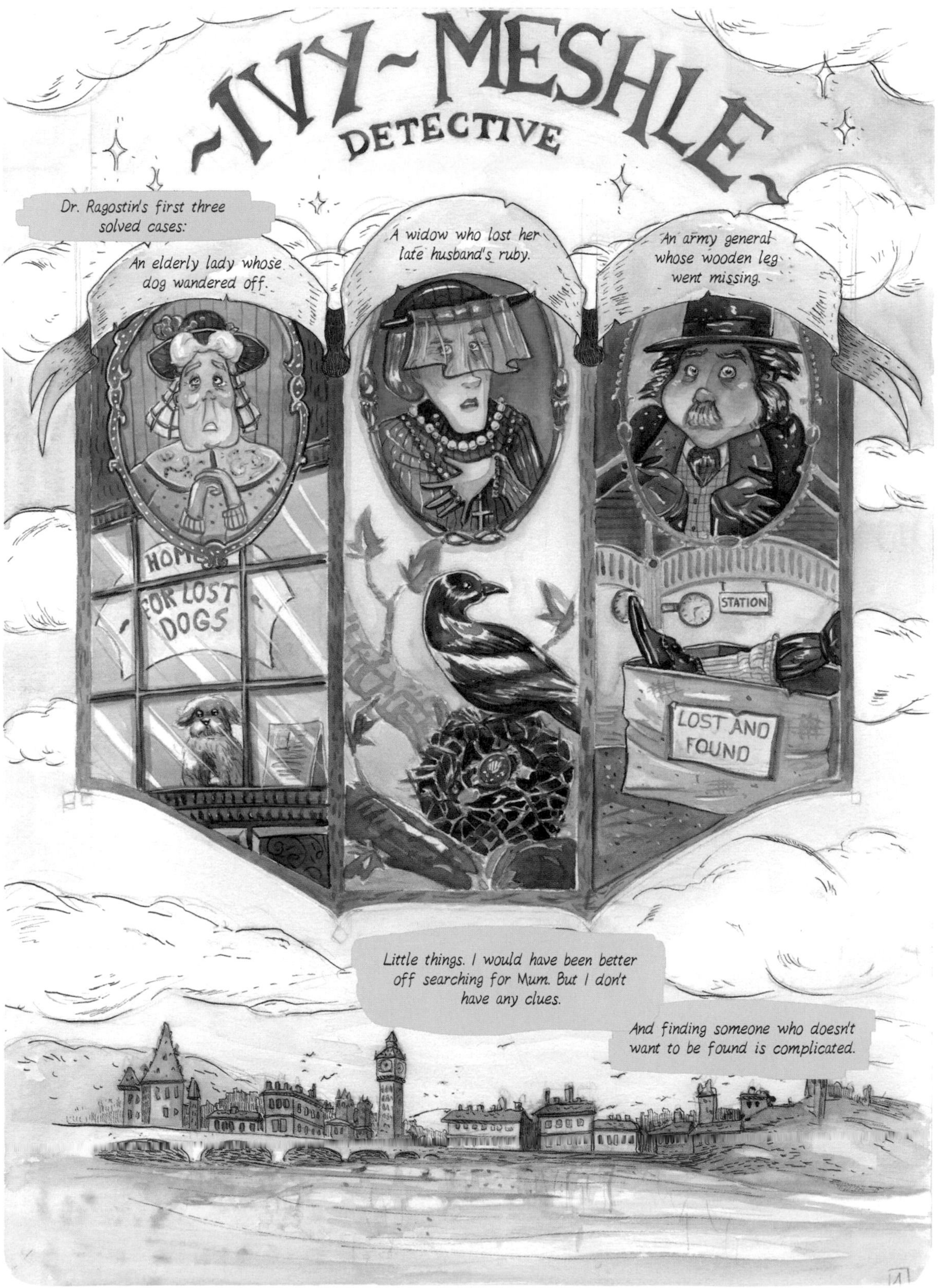
IVY MESHLE
DETECTIVE
Dr. Ragostin's first three solved cases:
An elderly lady whose dog wandered off.
A widow who lost her late husband's ruby.
An army general whose wooden leg went missing.
HOME FOR LOST DOGS
STATION
LOST AND FOUND
Little things. I would have been better off searching for Mum. But I don't have any clues.
And finding someone who doesn't want to be found is complicated.

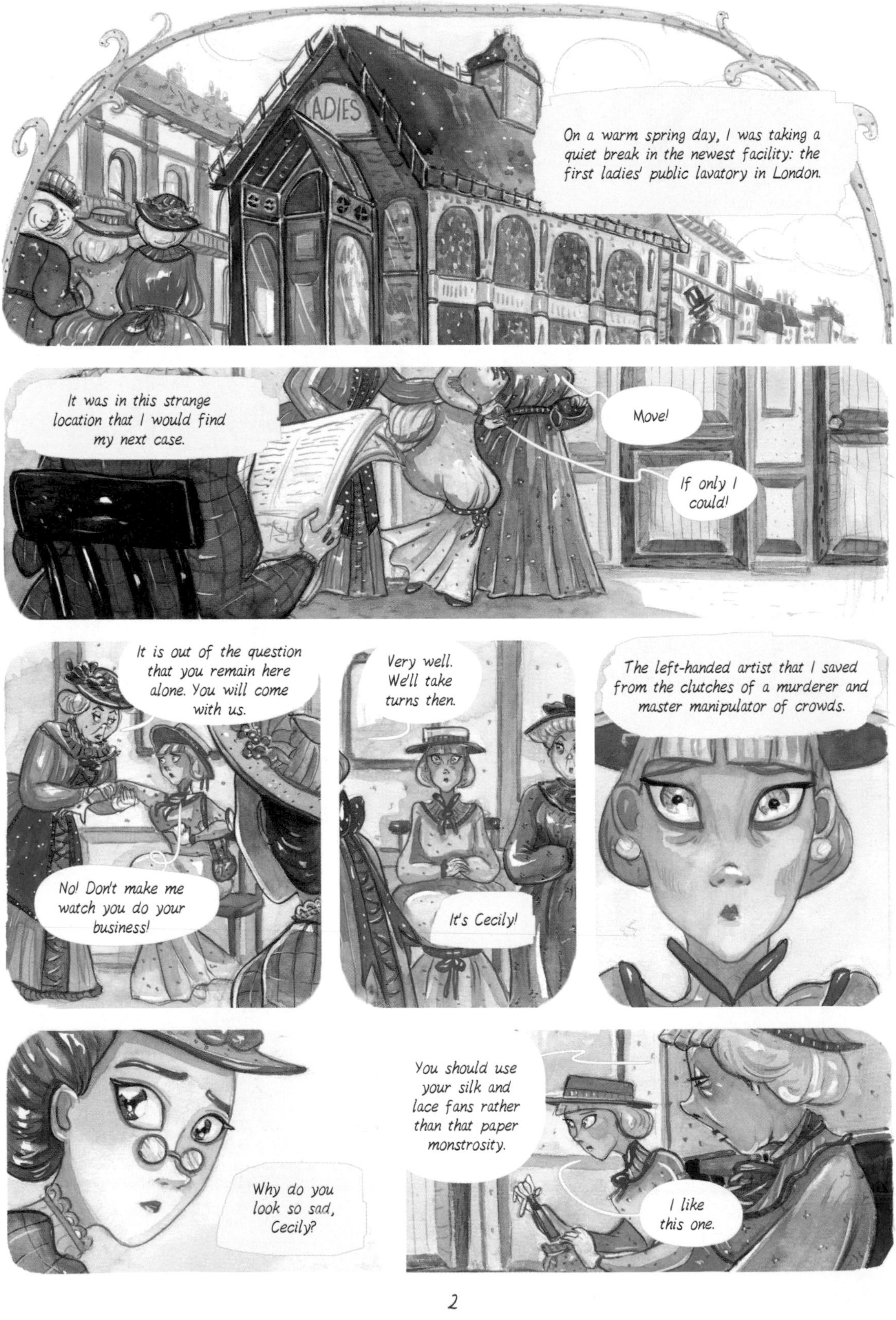
LADIES
On a warm spring day, I was taking a quiet break in the newest facility: the first ladies' public lavatory in London.
It was in this strange location that I would find my next case.
Move!
If only I could!
It is out of the question that you remain here alone. You will come with us.
No! Don't make me watch you do your business!
Very well. We'll take turns then.
It's Cecily!
The left-handed artist that I saved from the clutches of a murderer and master manipulator of crowds.
Why do you look so sad, Cecily?
You should use your silk and lace fans rather than that paper monstrosity.
I like this one.

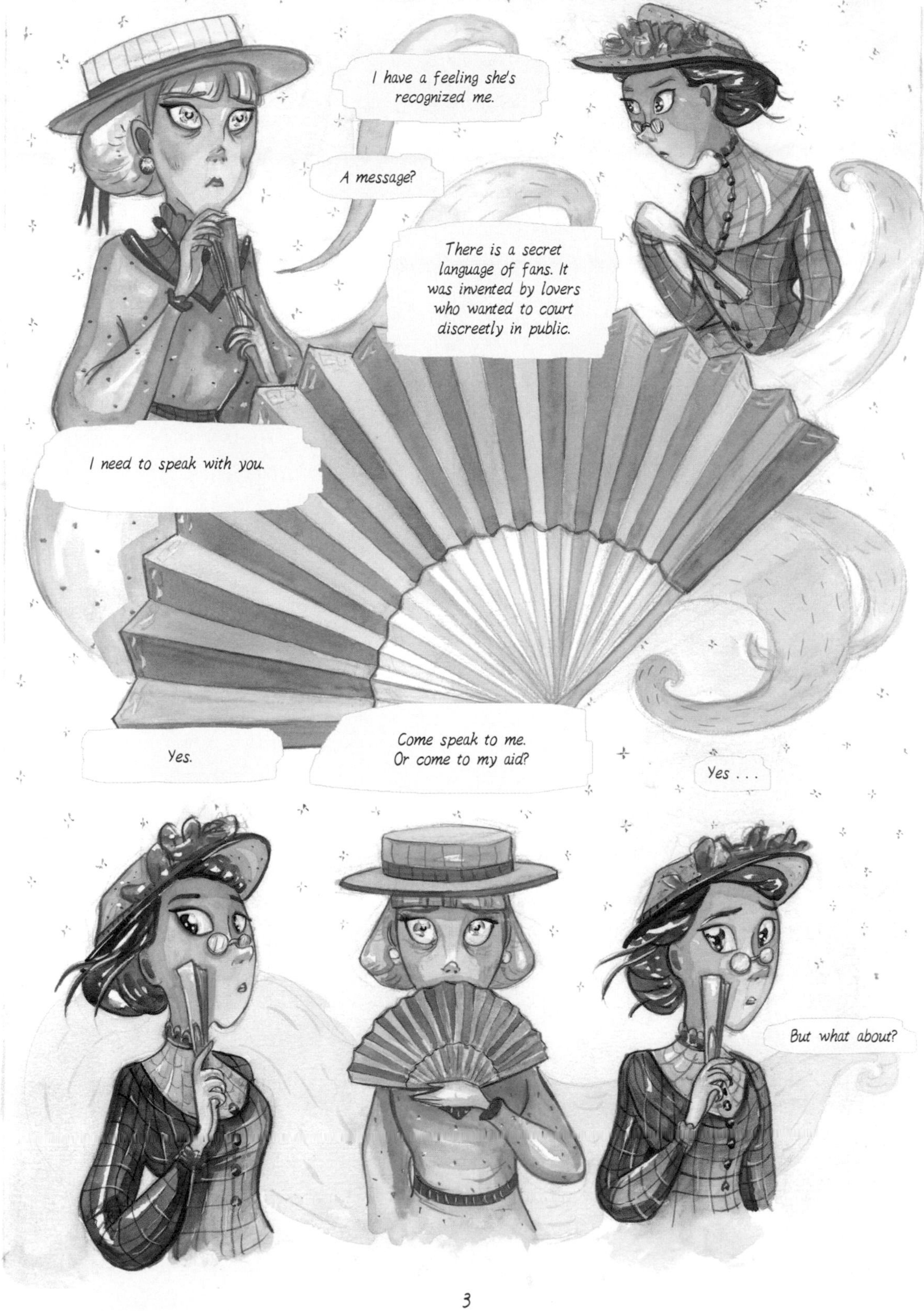
I have a feeling she's recognized me.
A message?
There is a secret language of fans. It was invented by lovers who wanted to court discreetly in public.
I need to speak with you.
Yes.
Come speak to me. Or come to my aid?
Yes . . .
But what about?

Your hand! Put that away.
No. I enjoy playing with it.
No?!
Fine. Resist if you must, as long as it's these insignificant things.
Tomorrow, we will take care of your trousseau.
You cannot make me!
We will see about that.
Let's go.

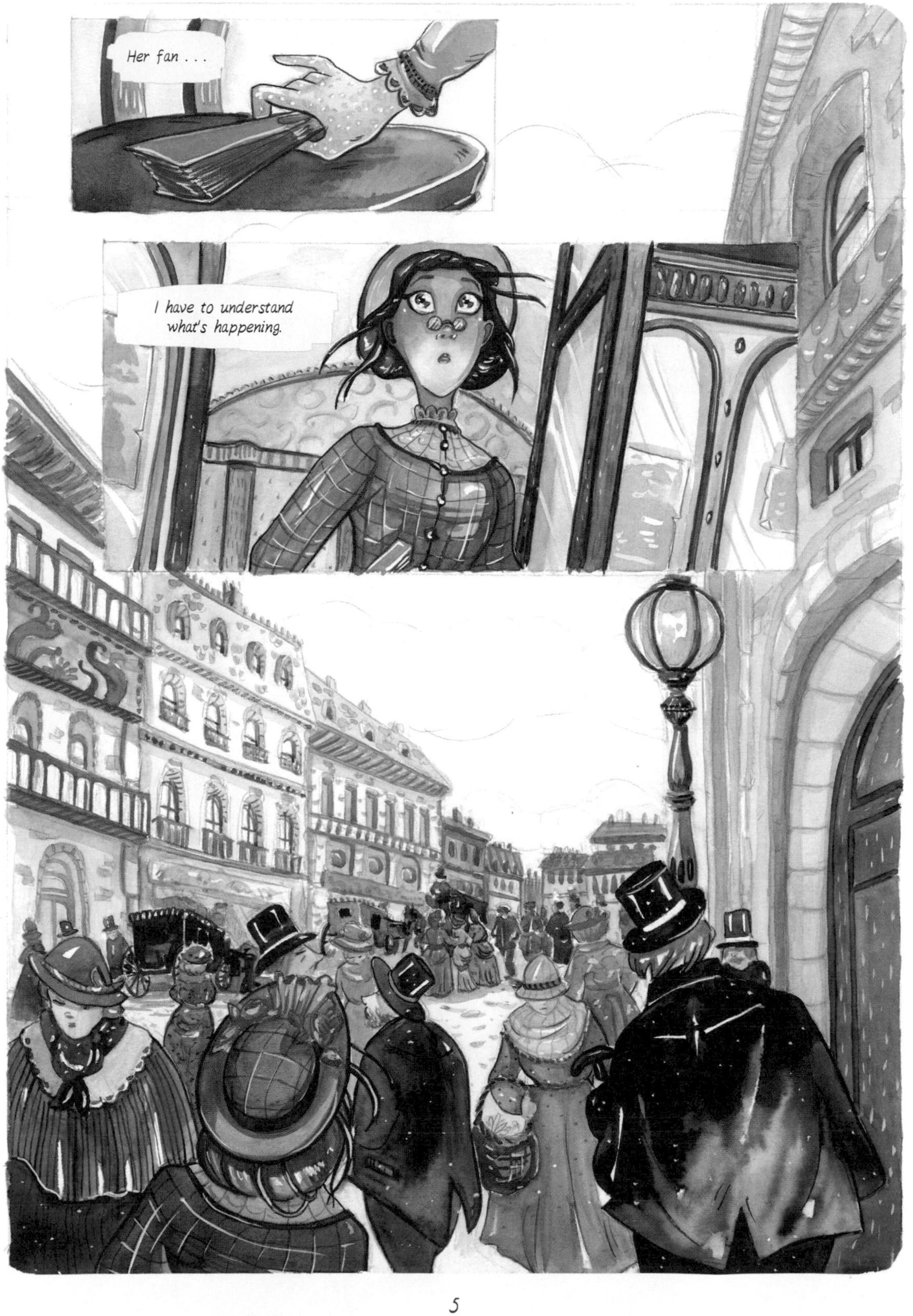
Her fan . . .
I have to understand what's happening.

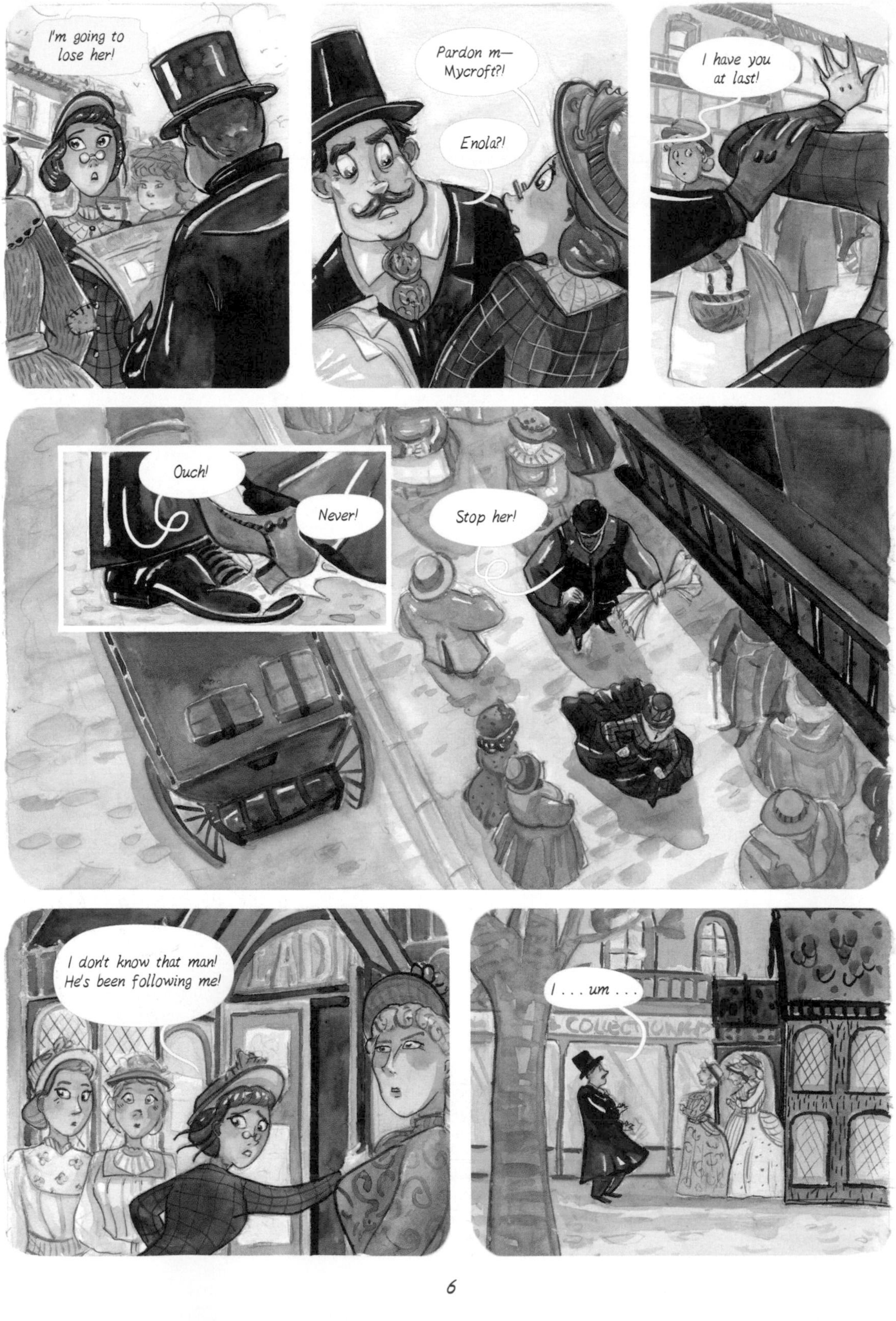
I'm going to lose her!
Pardon m— Mycroft?!
Enola?!
I have you at last!
Ouch!
Never!
Stop her!
I don't know that man! He's been following me!
I . . . um . . .

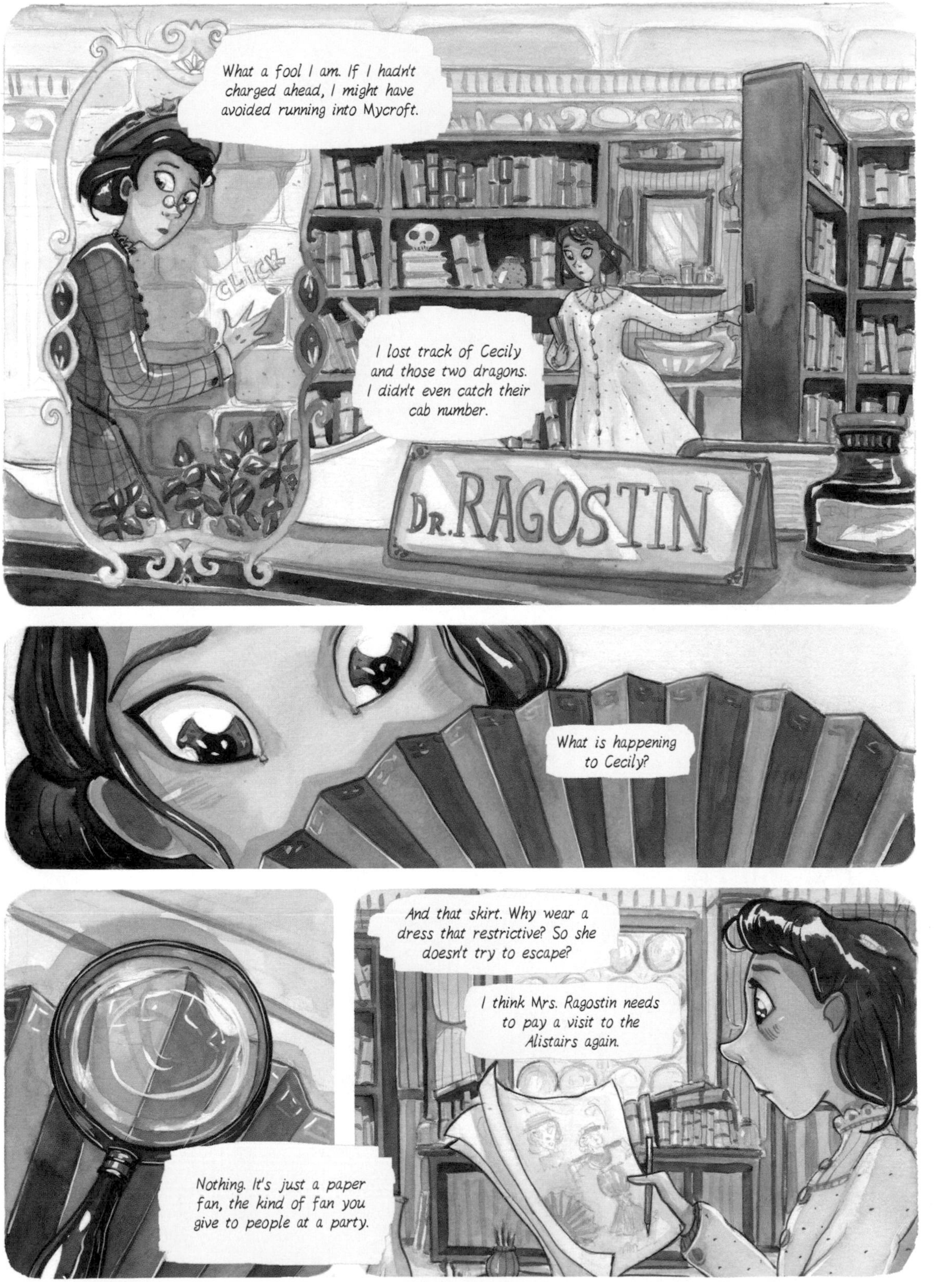
What a fool I am. If I hadn't charged ahead, I might have avoided running into Mycroft.
CLICK
I lost track of Cecily and those two dragons. I didn't even catch their cab number.
DR. RAGOSTIN
What is happening to Cecily?
Nothing. It's just a paper fan, the kind of fan you give to people at a party.
And that skirt. Why wear a dress that restrictive? So she doesn't try to escape?
I think Mrs. Ragostin needs to pay a visit to the Alistairs again.

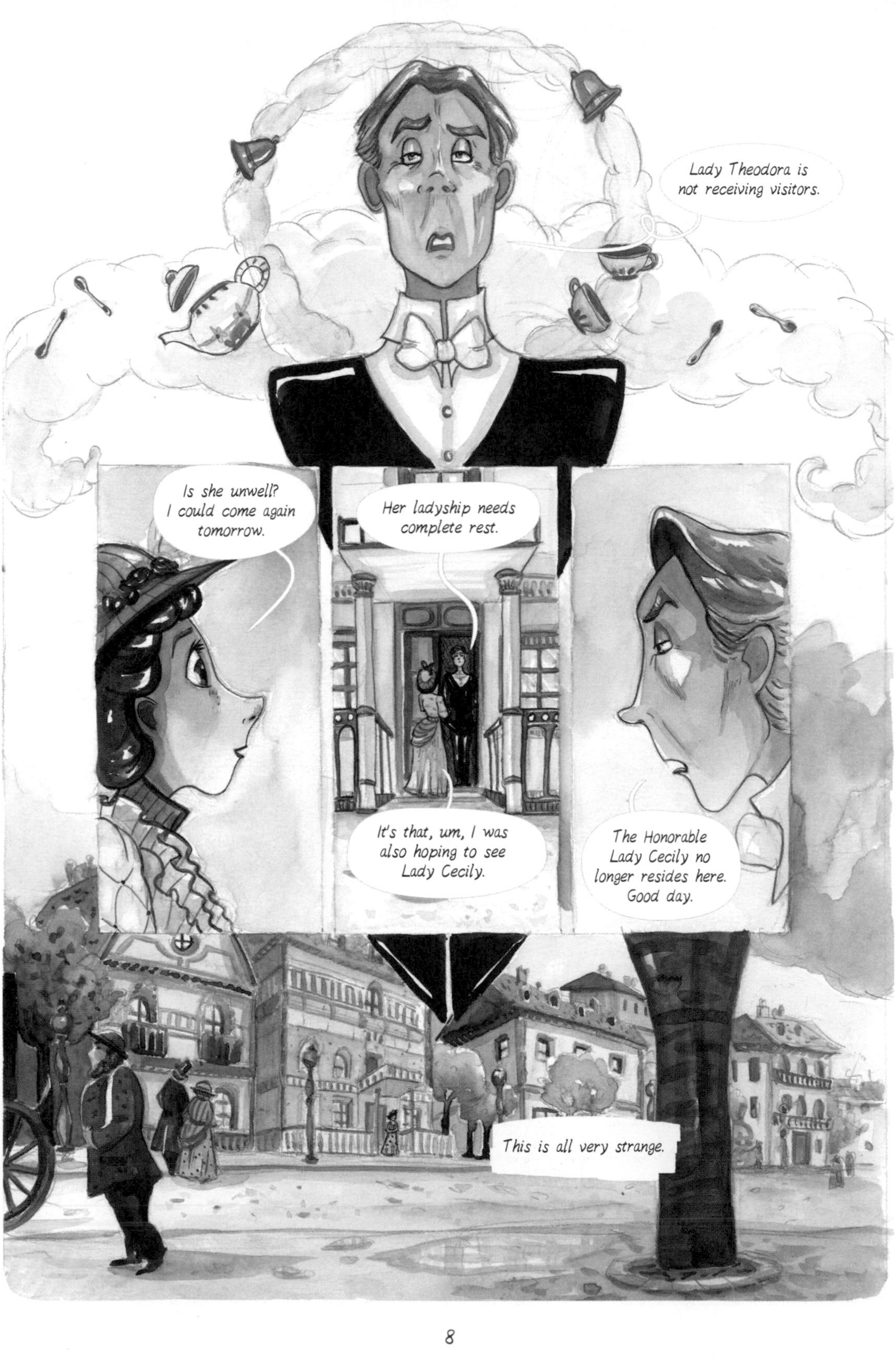
Lady Theodora is not receiving visitors.
Is she unwell? I could come again tomorrow.
Her ladyship needs complete rest.
It's that, um, I was also hoping to see Lady Cecily.
The Honorable Lady Cecily no longer resides here. Good day.
This is all very strange.

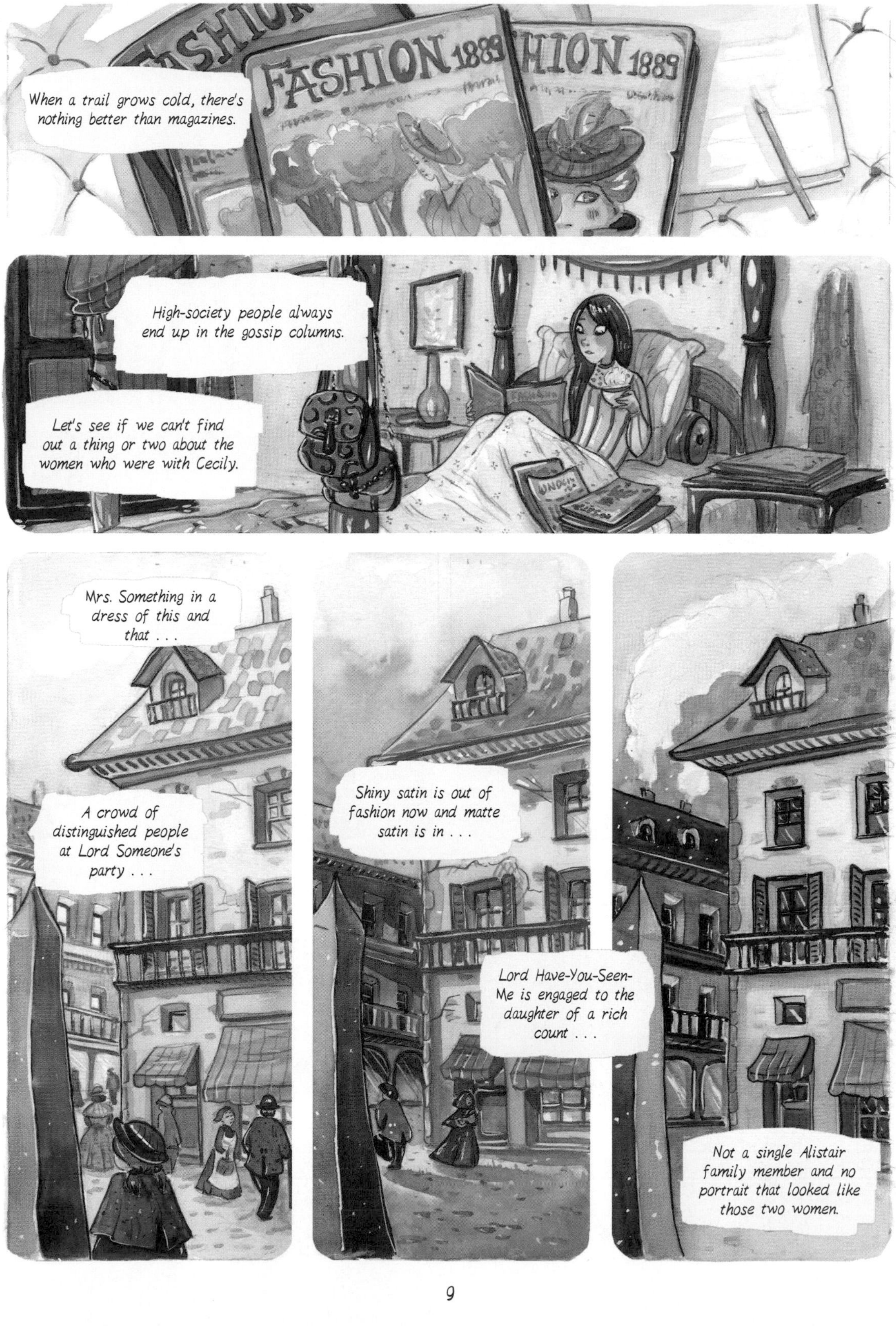
FASHION
FASHION 1889
HION 1889
When a trail grows cold, there's nothing better than magazines.
High-society people always end up in the gossip columns.
Let's see if we can't find out a thing or two about the women who were with Cecily.
Mrs. Something in a dress of this and that . . .
A crowd of distinguished people at Lord Someone's party . . .
Shiny satin is out of fashion now and matte satin is in . . .
Lord Have-You-Seen-Me is engaged to the daughter of a rich count . . .
Not a single Alistair family member and no portrait that looked like those two women.

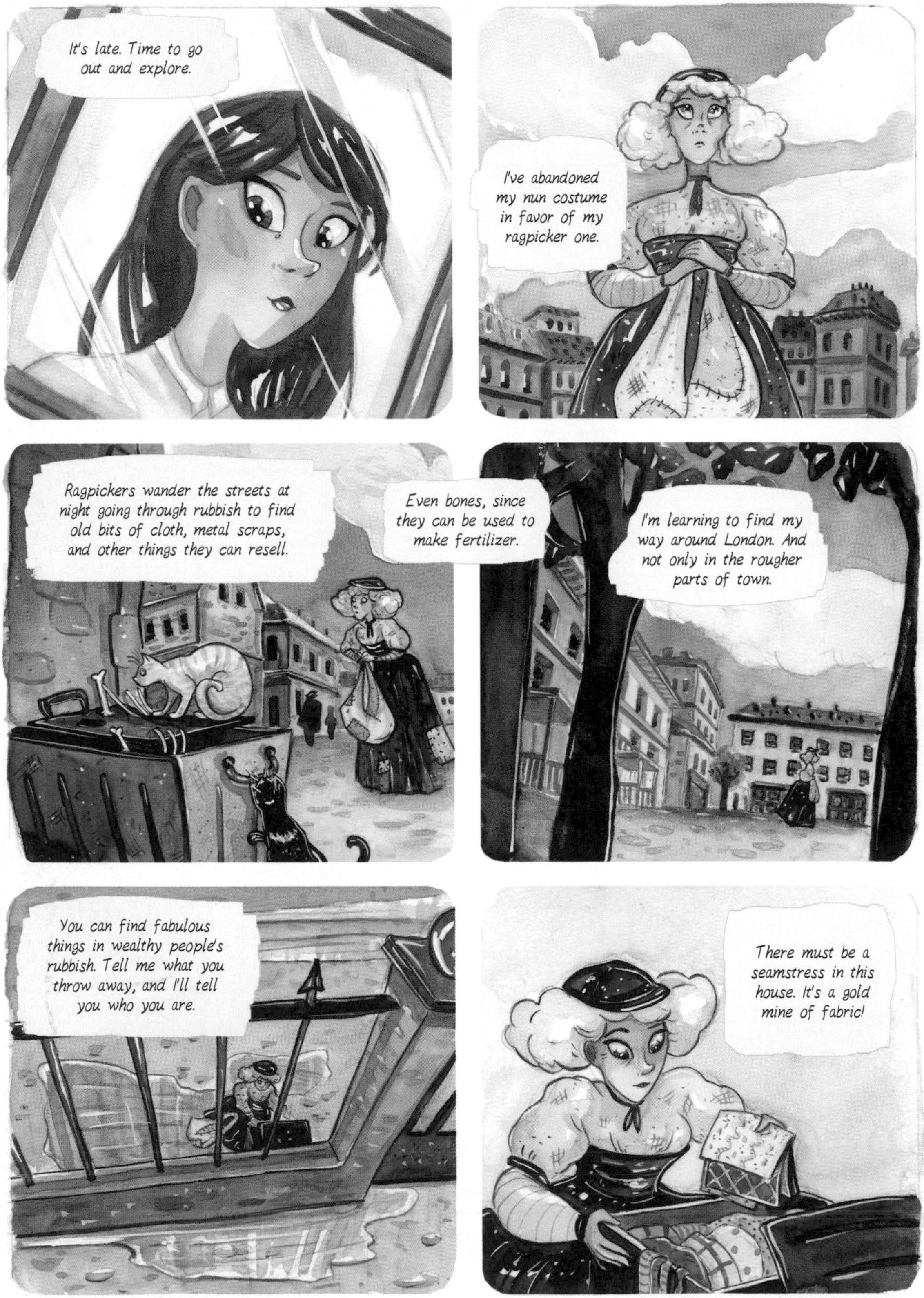
It's late. Time to go out and explore.
I've abandoned my nun costume in favor of my ragpicker one.
Ragpickers wander the streets at night going through rubbish to find old bits of cloth, metal scraps, and other things they can resell.
Even bones, since they can be used to make fertilizer.
I'm learning to find my way around London. And not only in the rougher parts of town.
You can find fabulous things in wealthy people's rubbish. Tell me what you throw away, and I'll tell you who you are.
There must be a seamstress in this house. It's a gold mine of fabric!

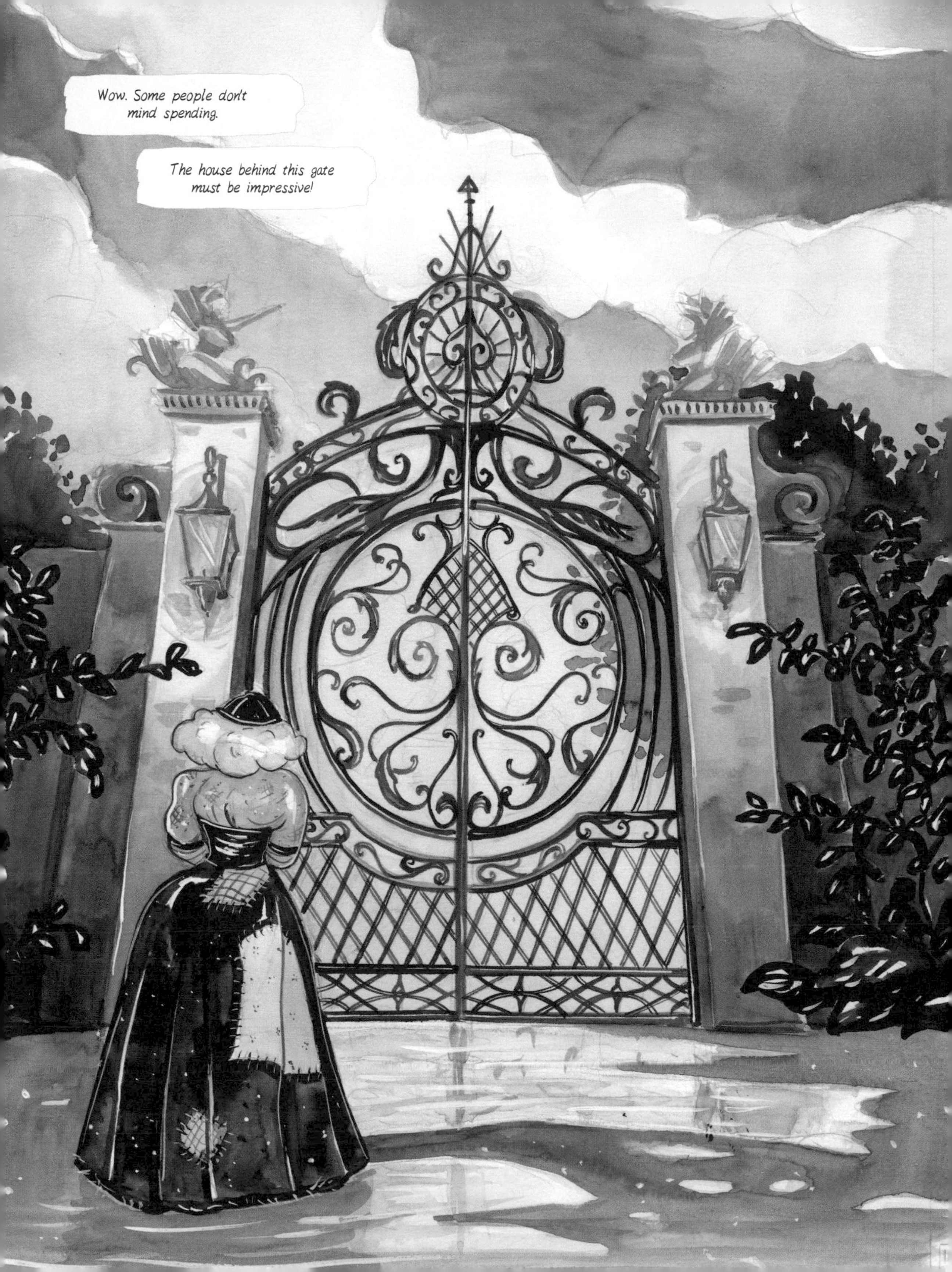
Wow. Some people don't mind spending.
The house behind this gate must be impressive!

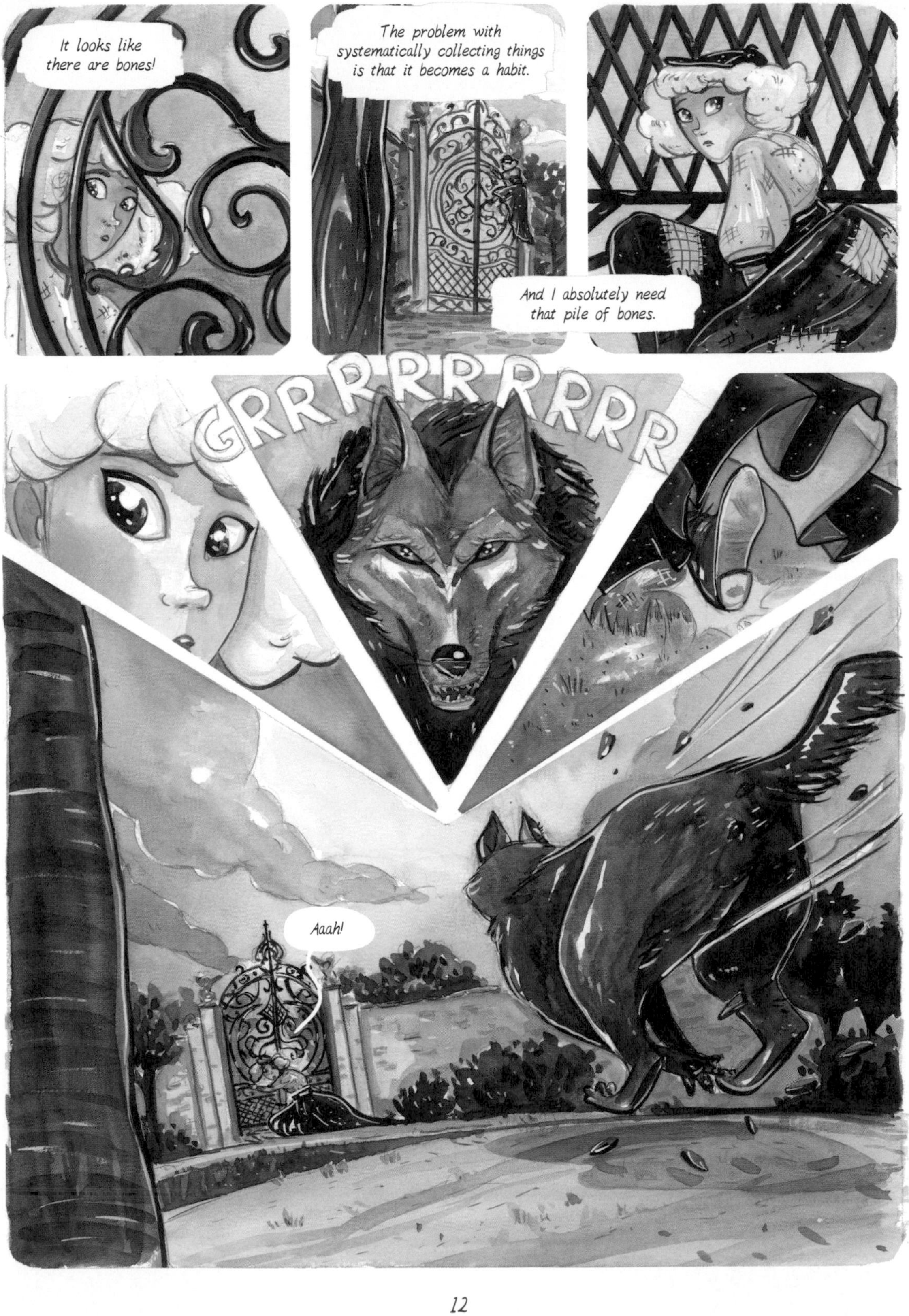
It looks like there are bones!
The problem with systematically collecting things is that it becomes a habit.
And I absolutely need that pile of bones.
GRRRRRRRRR
Aaah!

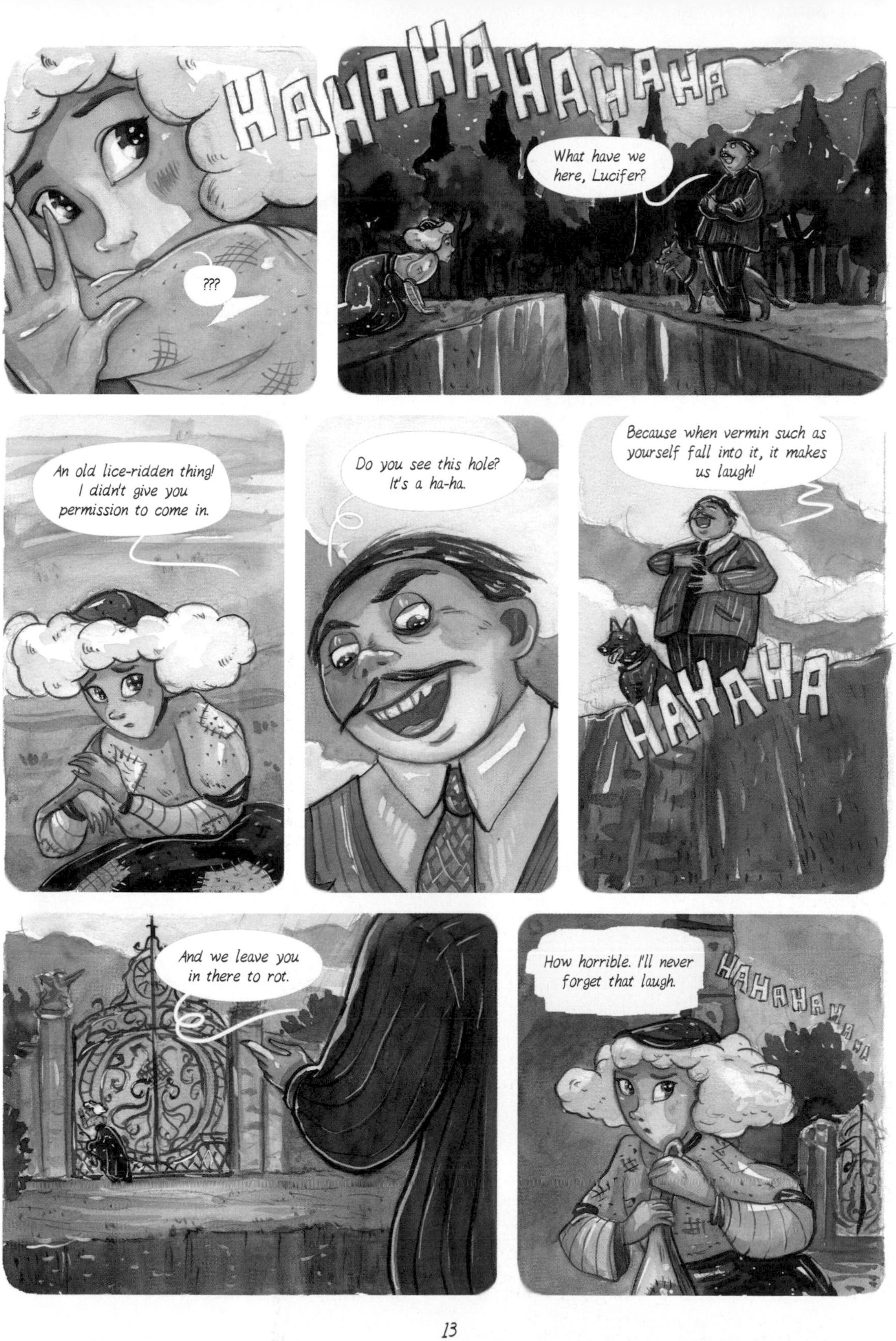
???
HAHAHAHAHAHAHAHA
What have we here, Lucifer?
An old lice-ridden thing! I didn't give you permission to come in.
Do you see this hole? It's a ha-ha.
Because when vermin such as yourself fall into it, it makes us laugh!
HAHAHA
And we leave you in there to rot.
How horrible. I'll never forget that laugh.
HAHAHAHAHA

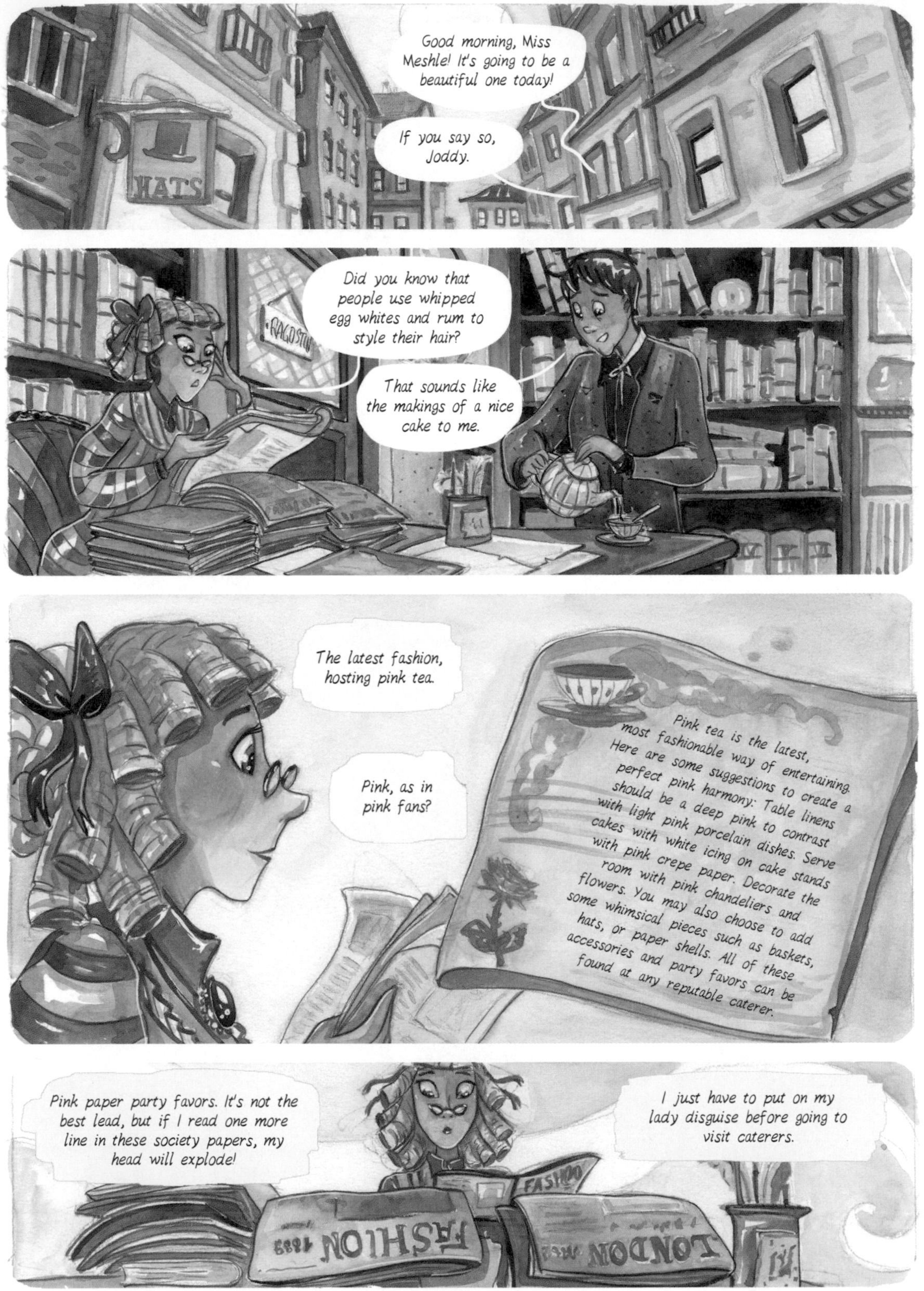
Good morning, Miss Meshle! It's going to be a beautiful one today!
If you say so, Joddy.
HATS
Did you know that people use whipped egg whites and rum to style their hair?
That sounds like the makings of a nice cake to me.
The latest fashion, hosting pink tea.
Pink, as in pink fans?
Pink tea is the latest, most fashionable way of entertaining. Here are some suggestions to create a perfect pink harmony: Table linens should be a deep pink to contrast with light pink porcelain dishes. Serve cakes with white icing on cake stands with pink crepe paper. Decorate the room with pink chandeliers and flowers. You may also choose to add some whimsical pieces such as baskets, hats, or paper shells. All of these accessories and party favors can be found at any reputable caterer.
Pink paper party favors. It's not the best lead, but if I read one more line in these society papers, my head will explode!
I just have to put on my lady disguise before going to visit caterers.

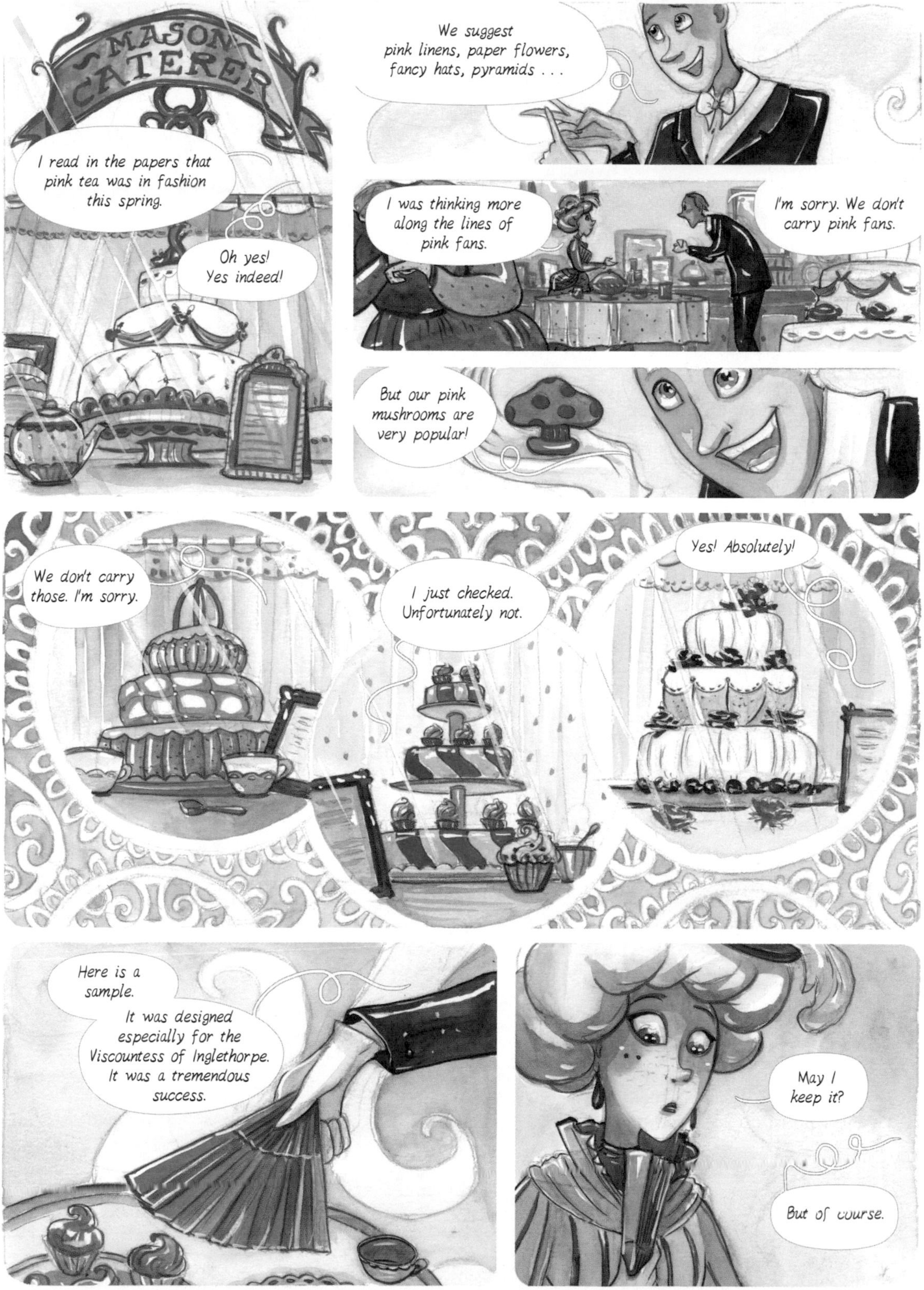
MASON CATERER
I read in the papers that pink tea was in fashion this spring.
Oh yes! Yes indeed!
We suggest pink linens, paper flowers, fancy hats, pyramids . . .
I was thinking more along the lines of pink fans.
I'm sorry. We don't carry pink fans.
But our pink mushrooms are very popular!
We don't carry those. I'm sorry.
I just checked. Unfortunately not.
Yes! Absolutely!
Here is a sample.
It was designed especially for the Viscountess of Inglethorpe. It was a tremendous success.
May I keep it?
But of course.

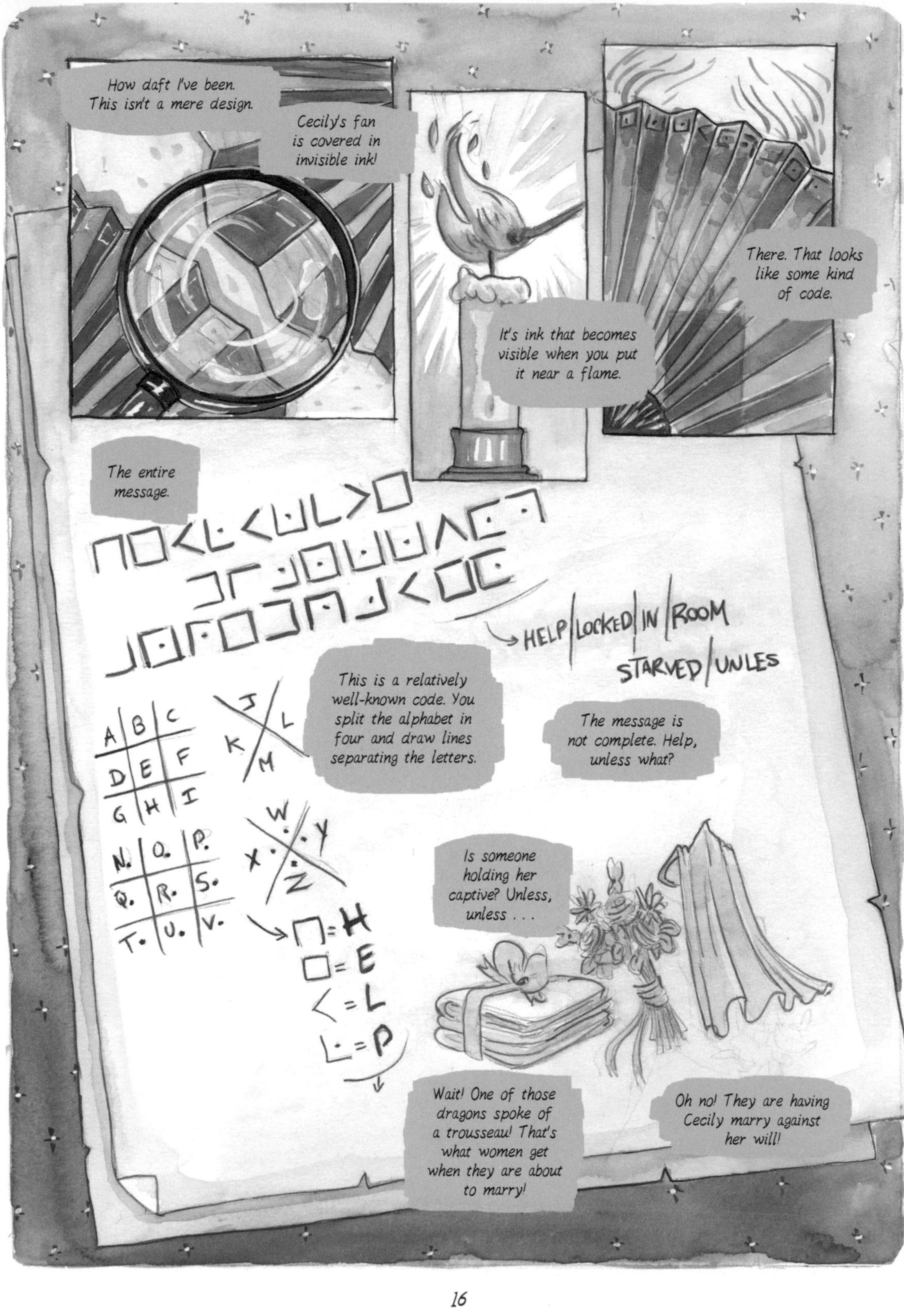
How daft I've been. This isn't a mere design.
Cecily's fan is covered in invisible ink!
It's ink that becomes visible when you put it near a flame.
There. That looks like some kind of code.
The entire message.
HELP LOCKED IN ROOM
STARVED UNLES
This is a relatively well-known code. You split the alphabet in four and draw lines separating the letters.
A B C D E F G H I
J K L M
N O P Q R S T U V
W X Y Z
= H
= E
= L
= P
The message is not complete. Help, unless what?
Is someone holding her captive? Unless, unless . . .
Wait! One of those dragons spoke of a trousseau! That's what women get when they are about to marry!
Oh no! They are having Cecily marry against her will!

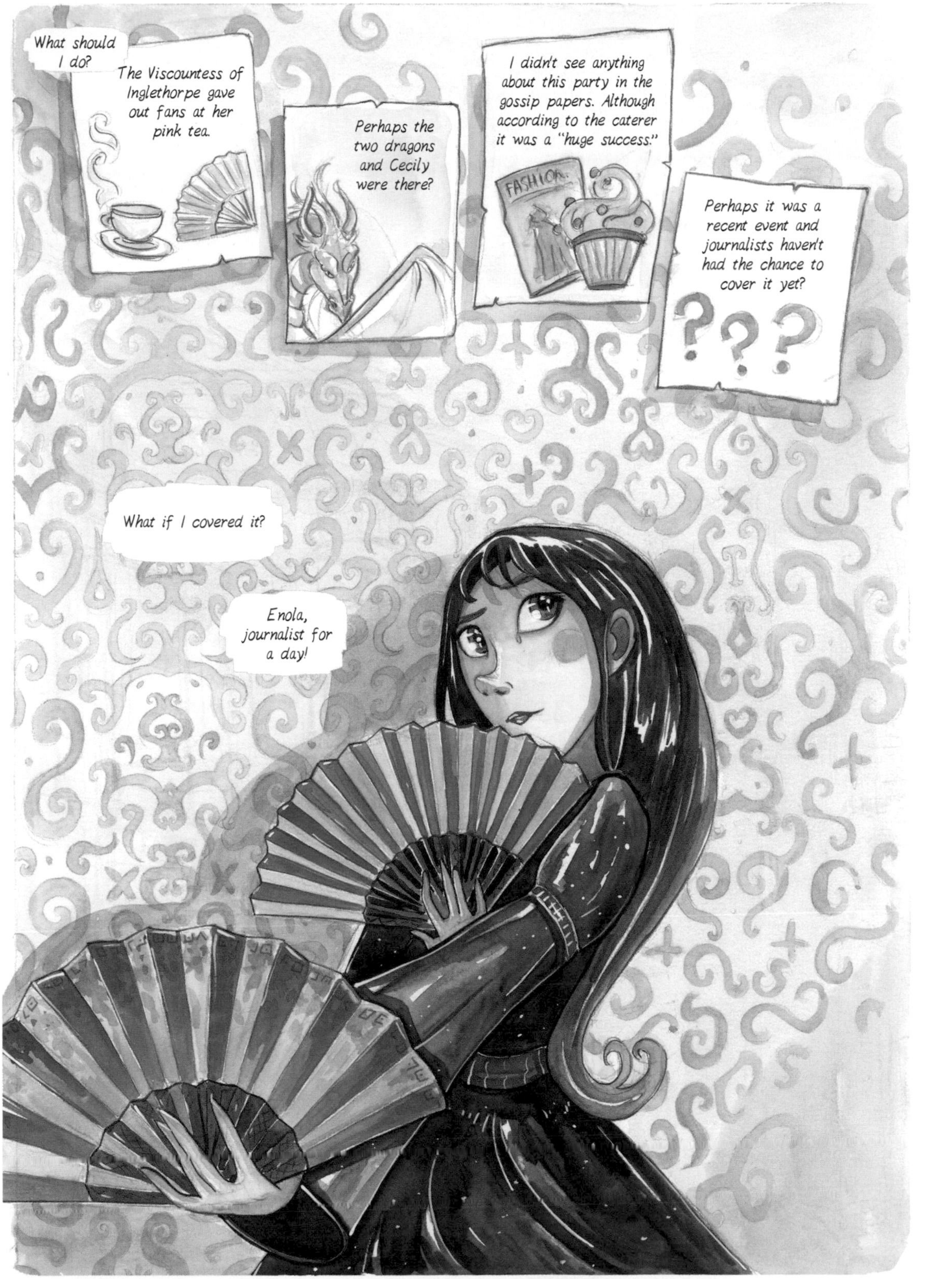
What should I do?
The Viscountess of Inglethorpe gave out fans at her pink tea.
Perhaps the two dragons and Cecily were there?
I didn't see anything about this party in the gossip papers. Although according to the caterer it was a "huge success."
FASHION
Perhaps it was a recent event and journalists haven't had the chance to cover it yet?
???
What if I covered it?
Enola, journalist for a day!

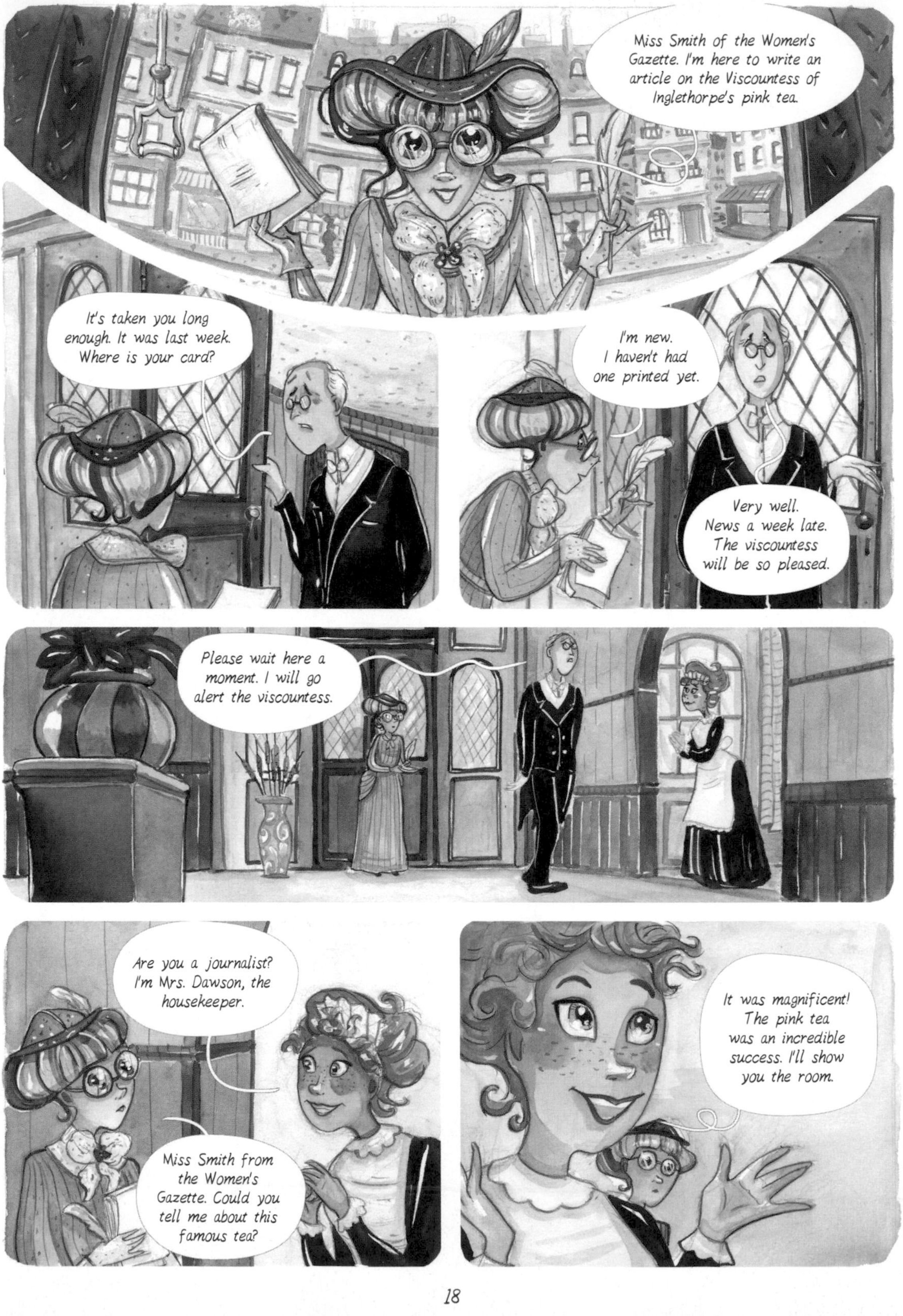
Miss Smith of the Women's Gazette. I'm here to write an article on the Viscountess of Inglethorpe's pink tea.
It's taken you long enough. It was last week. Where is your card?
I'm new. I haven't had one printed yet.
Very well. News a week late. The viscountess will be so pleased.
Please wait here a moment. I will go alert the viscountess.
Are you a journalist? I'm Mrs. Dawson, the housekeeper.
Miss Smith from the Women's Gazette. Could you tell me about this famous tea?
It was magnificent! The pink tea was an incredible success. I'll show you the room.

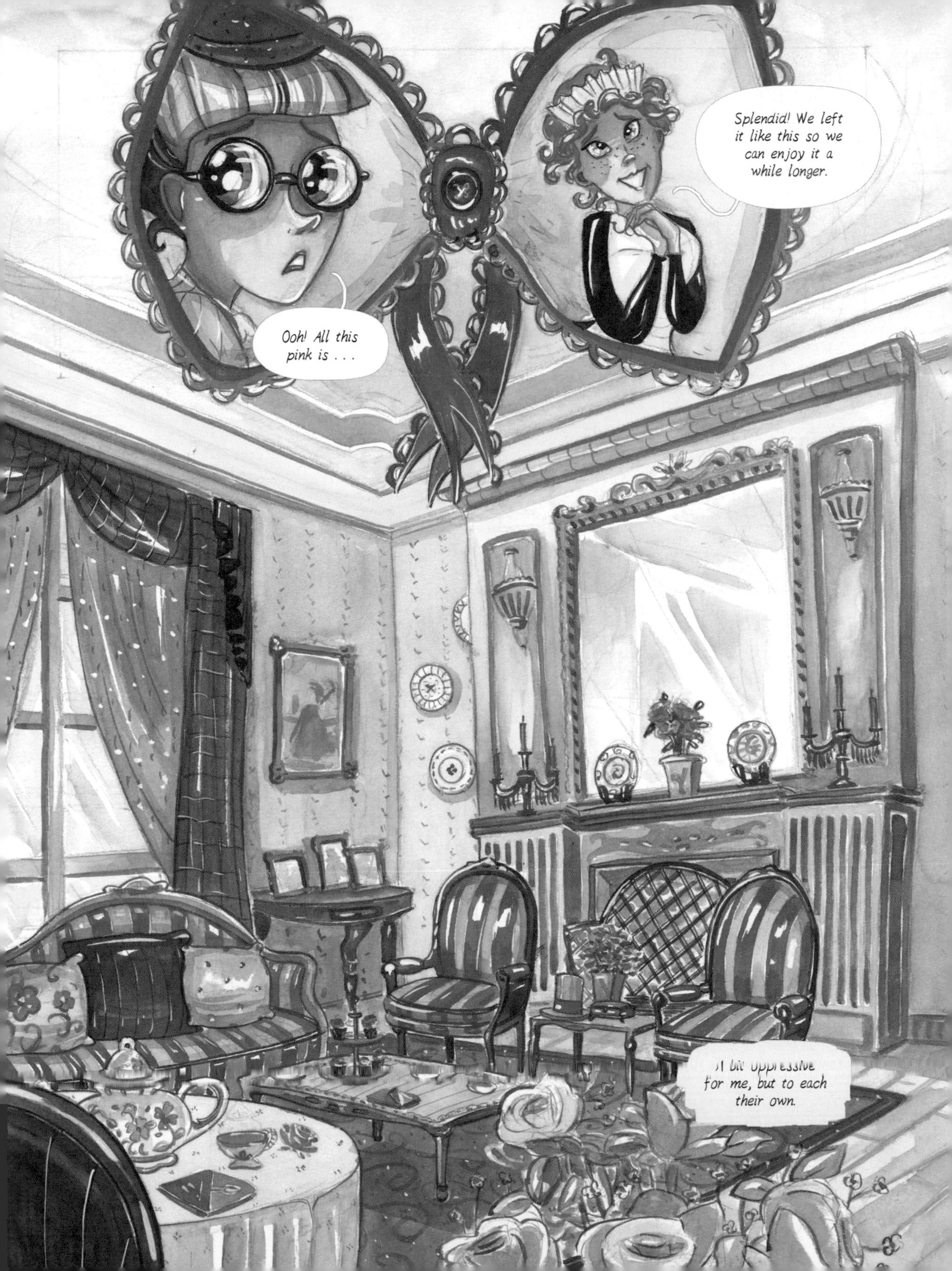
Splendid! We left it like this so we can enjoy it a while longer.
Ooh! All this pink is . . .
for me, but to each their own.

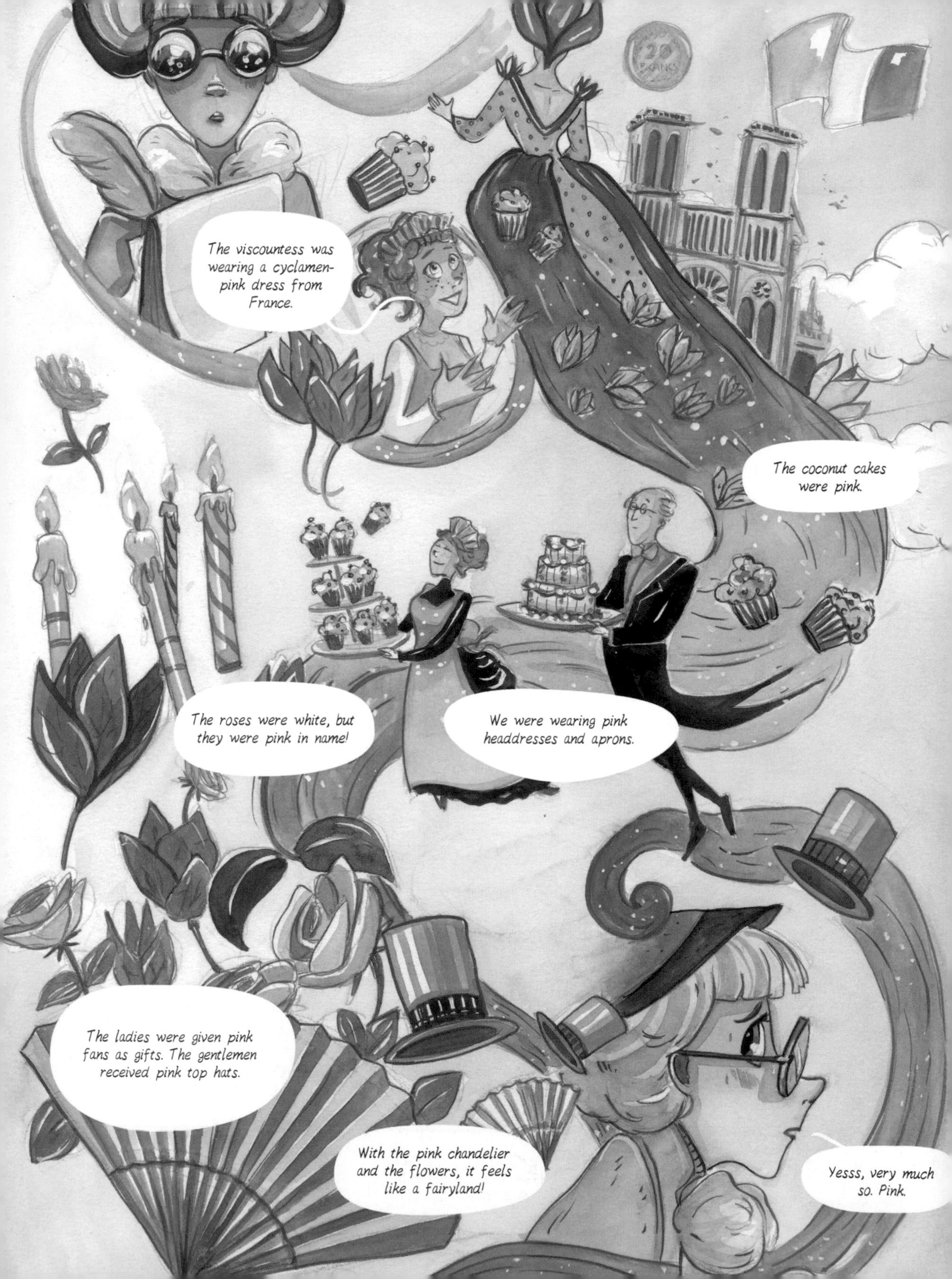
The viscountess was wearing a cyclamen-pink dress from France.
The coconut cakes were pink.
The roses were white, but they were pink in name!
We were wearing pink headdresses and aprons.
The ladies were given pink fans as gifts. The gentlemen received pink top hats.
With the pink chandelier and the flowers, it feels like a fairyland!
Yesss, very much so. Pink.

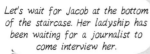

Let's wait for Jacob at the bottom of the staircase. Her ladyship has been waiting for a journalist to come interview her.

Oh! Who is that?

That's one of them! Cecily's dragons!

The Viscountess of Inglethorpe! Splendid, isn't it?

Yes . . . impressive.

Lady Otelia Thoroughfinch, Viscountess of Inglethorpe, will receive you in her private sitting room.

HAHAHAHA

???

That laugh! How is it possible?

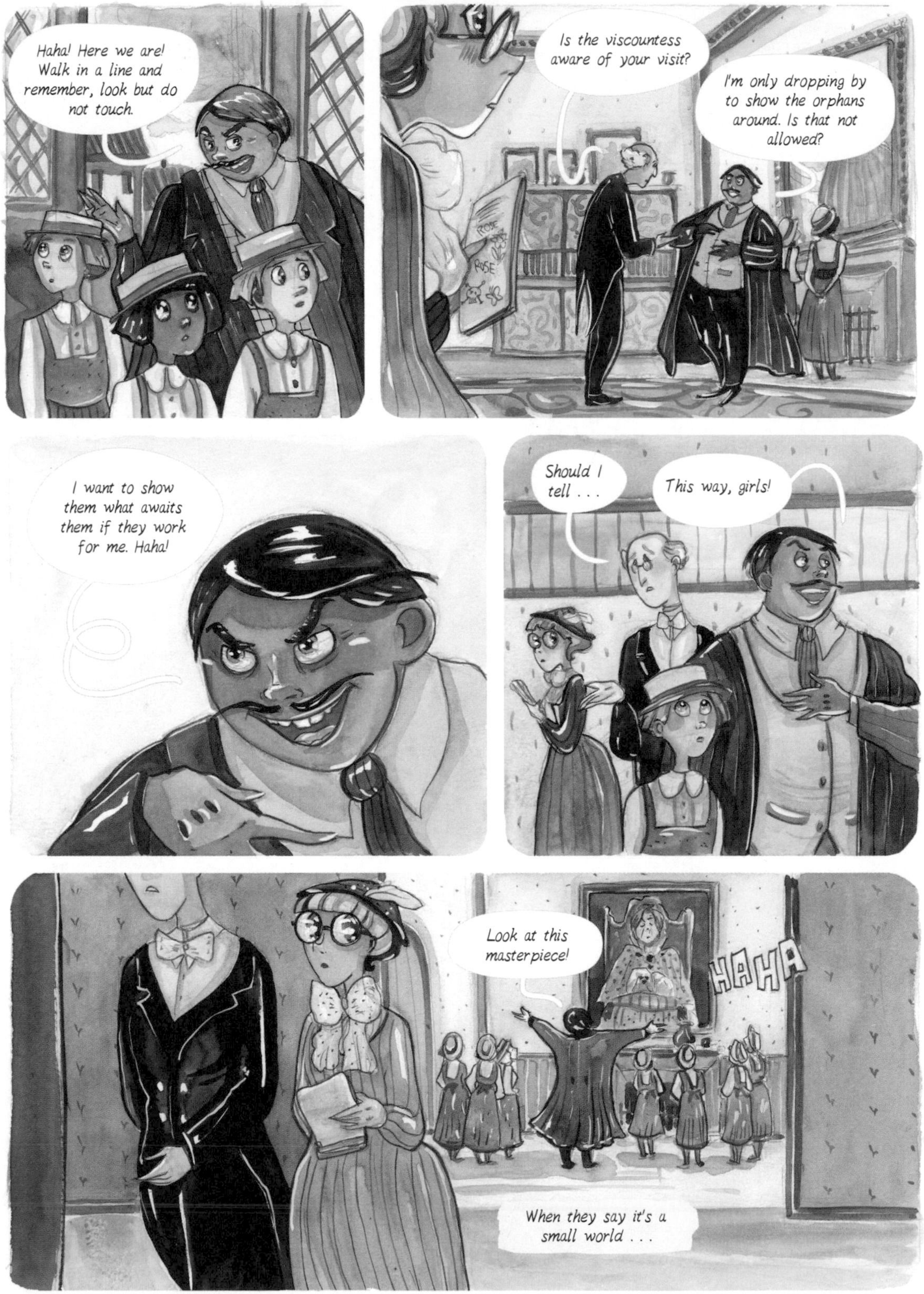
Haha! Here we are! Walk in a line and remember, look but do not touch.
Is the viscountess aware of your visit?
I'm only dropping by to show the orphans around. Is that not allowed?
ROSE
ROSE
I want to show them what awaits them if they work for me. Haha!
Should I tell . . .
This way, girls!
Look at this masterpiece!
HAHA
When they say it's a small world . . .

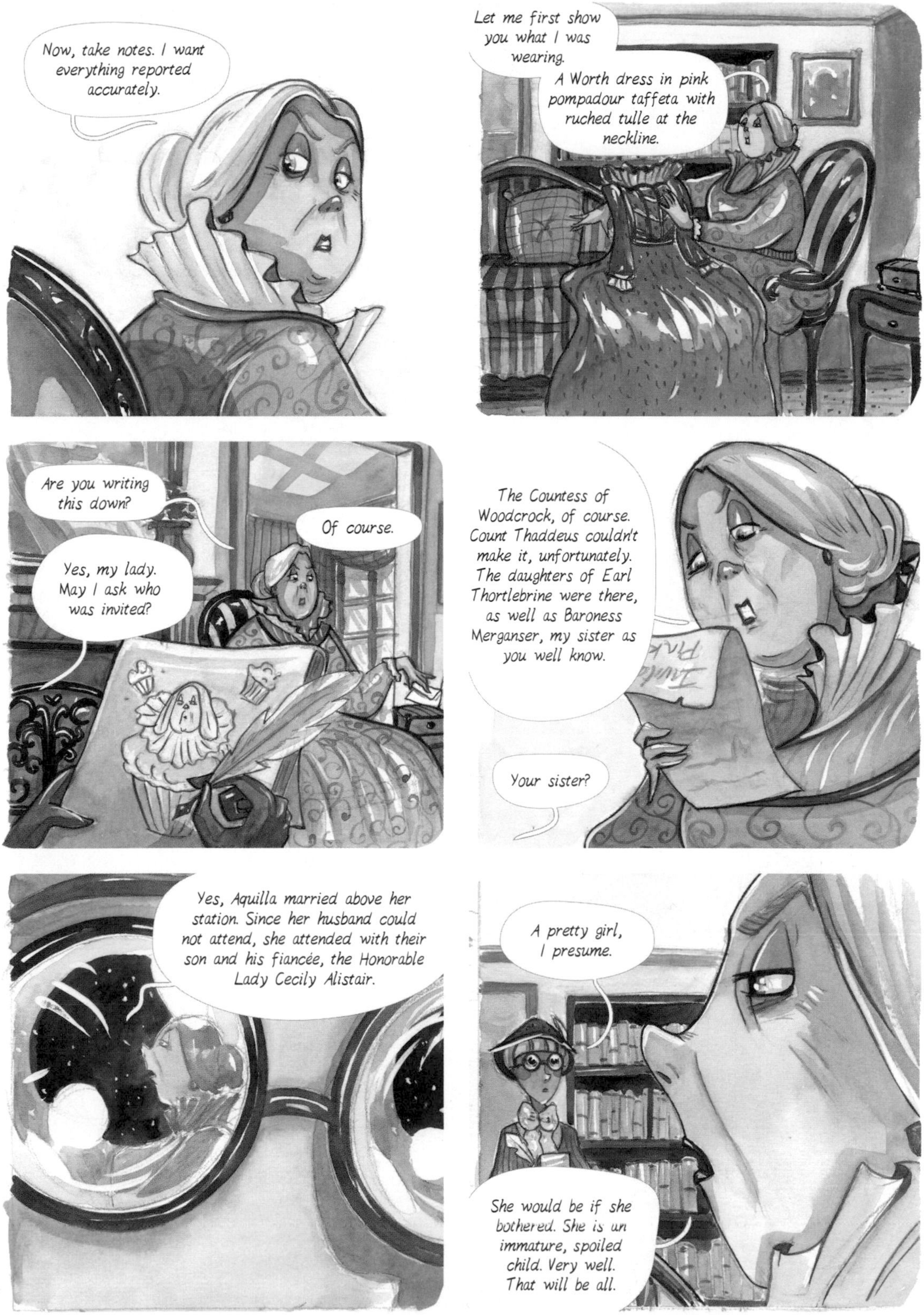
Now, take notes. I want everything reported accurately.
Let me first show you what I was wearing.
A Worth dress in pink pompadour taffeta with ruched tulle at the neckline.
Are you writing this down?
Of course.
Yes, my lady. May I ask who was invited?
The Countess of Woodcrock, of course. Count Thaddeus couldn't make it, unfortunately. The daughters of Earl Thortlebrine were there, as well as Baroness Merganser, my sister as you well know.
Your sister?
Yes, Aquilla married above her station. Since her husband could not attend, she attended with their son and his fiancée, the Honorable Lady Cecily Alistair.
A pretty girl, I presume.
She would be if she bothered. She is an immature, spoiled child. Very well. That will be all.

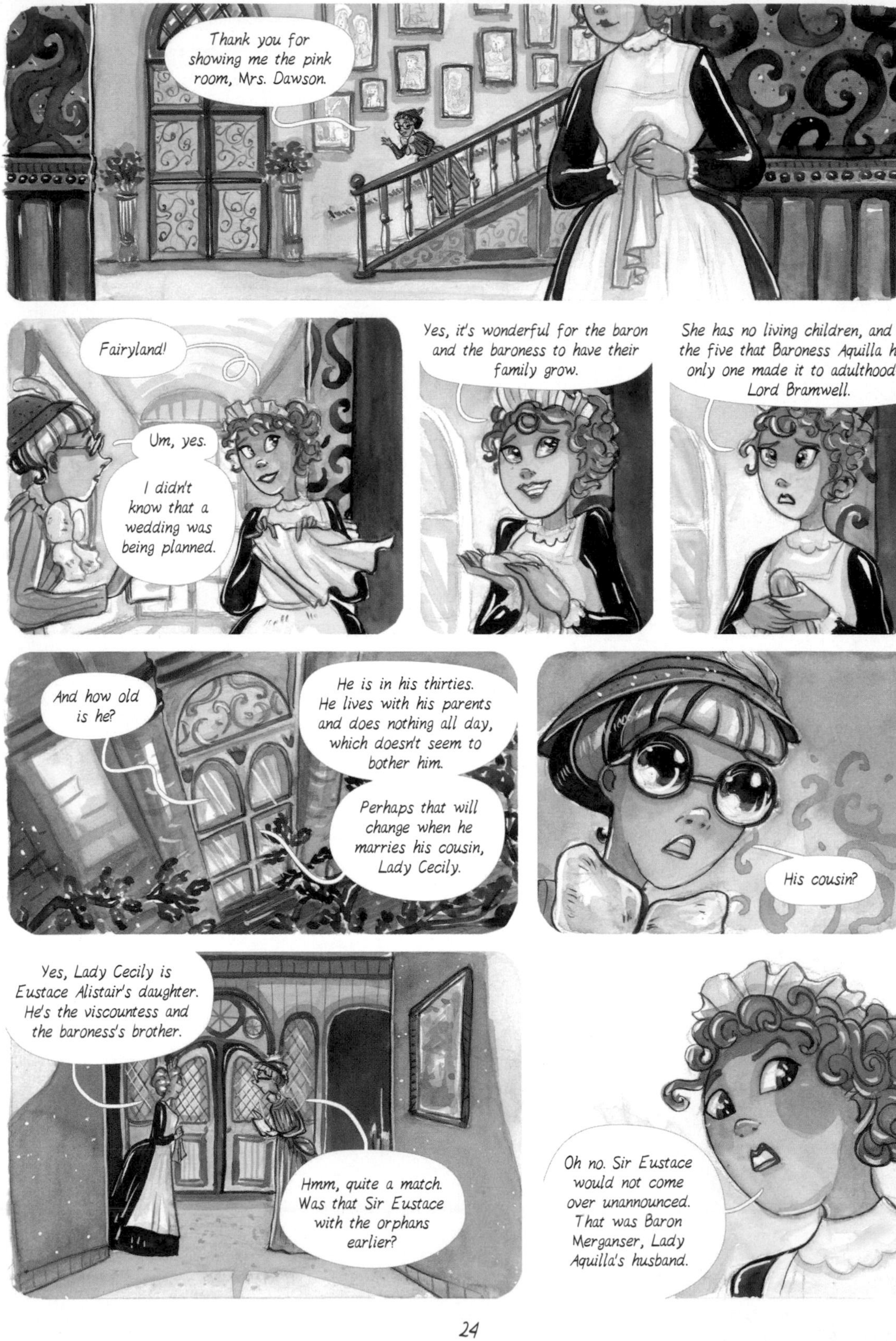
Thank you for showing me the pink room, Mrs. Dawson.
Fairyland!
Um, yes.
I didn't know that a wedding was being planned.
Yes, it's wonderful for the baron and the baroness to have their family grow.
She has no living children, and of the five that Baroness Aquilla had, only one made it to adulthood—Lord Bramwell.
And how old is he?
He is in his thirties. He lives with his parents and does nothing all day, which doesn't seem to bother him.
Perhaps that will change when he marries his cousin, Lady Cecily.
His cousin?
Yes, Lady Cecily is Eustace Alistair's daughter. He's the viscountess and the baroness's brother.
Hmm, quite a match. Was that Sir Eustace with the orphans earlier?
Oh no. Sir Eustace would not come over unannounced. That was Baron Merganser, Lady Aquilla's husband.

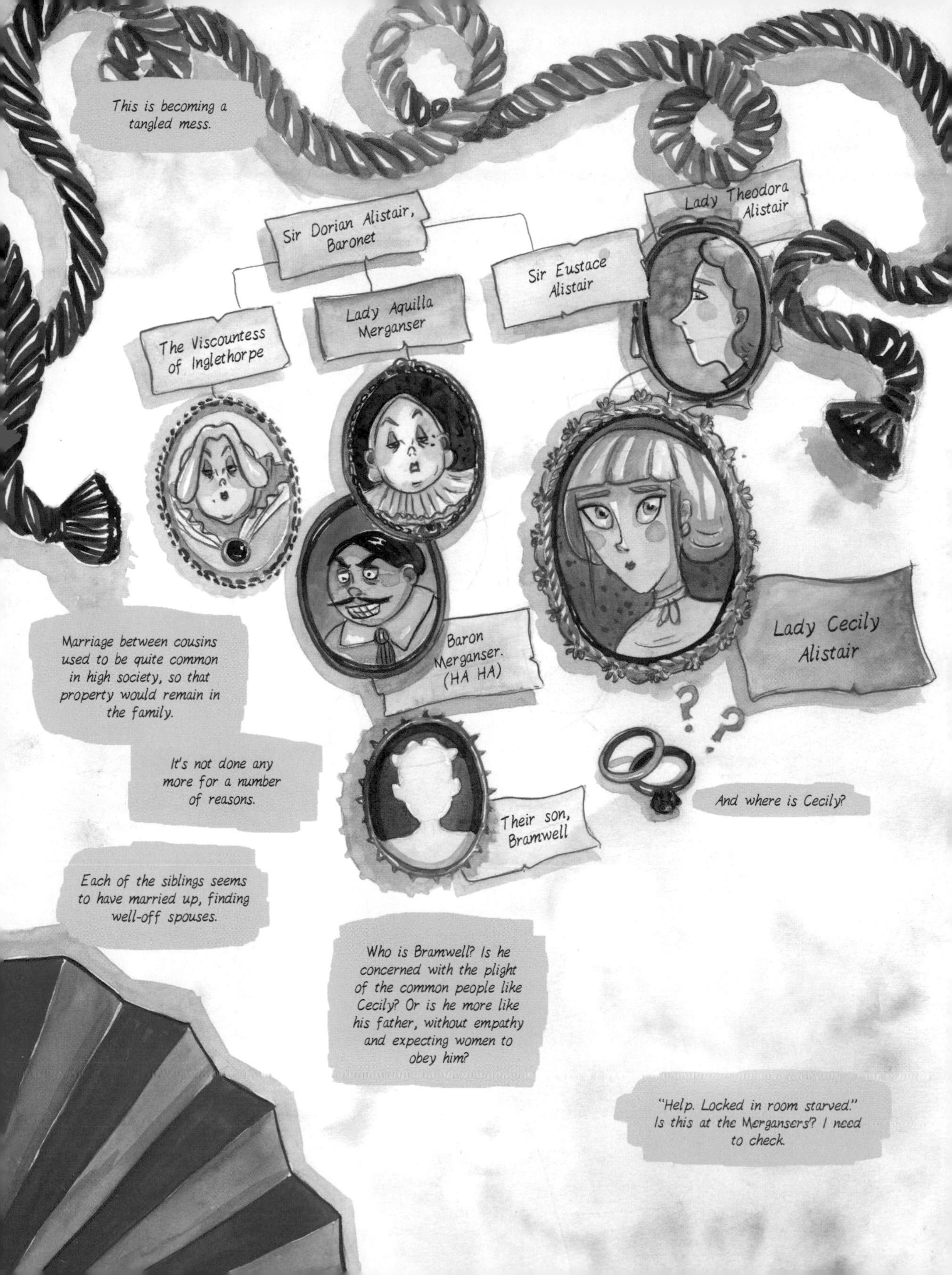
This is becoming a tangled mess.
Sir Dorian Alistair, Baronet
Lady Theodora Alistair
Sir Eustace Alistair
Lady Aquilla Merganser
The Viscountess of Inglethorpe
Marriage between cousins used to be quite common in high society, so that property would remain in the family.
Baron Merganser. (HA HA)
Lady Cecily Alistair
It's not done any more for a number of reasons.
And where is Cecily?
Their son, Bramwell
Each of the siblings seems to have married up, finding well-off spouses.
Who is Bramwell? Is he concerned with the plight of the common people like Cecily? Or is he more like his father, without empathy and expecting women to obey him?
"Help. Locked in room starved." Is this at the Mergansers'? I need to check.

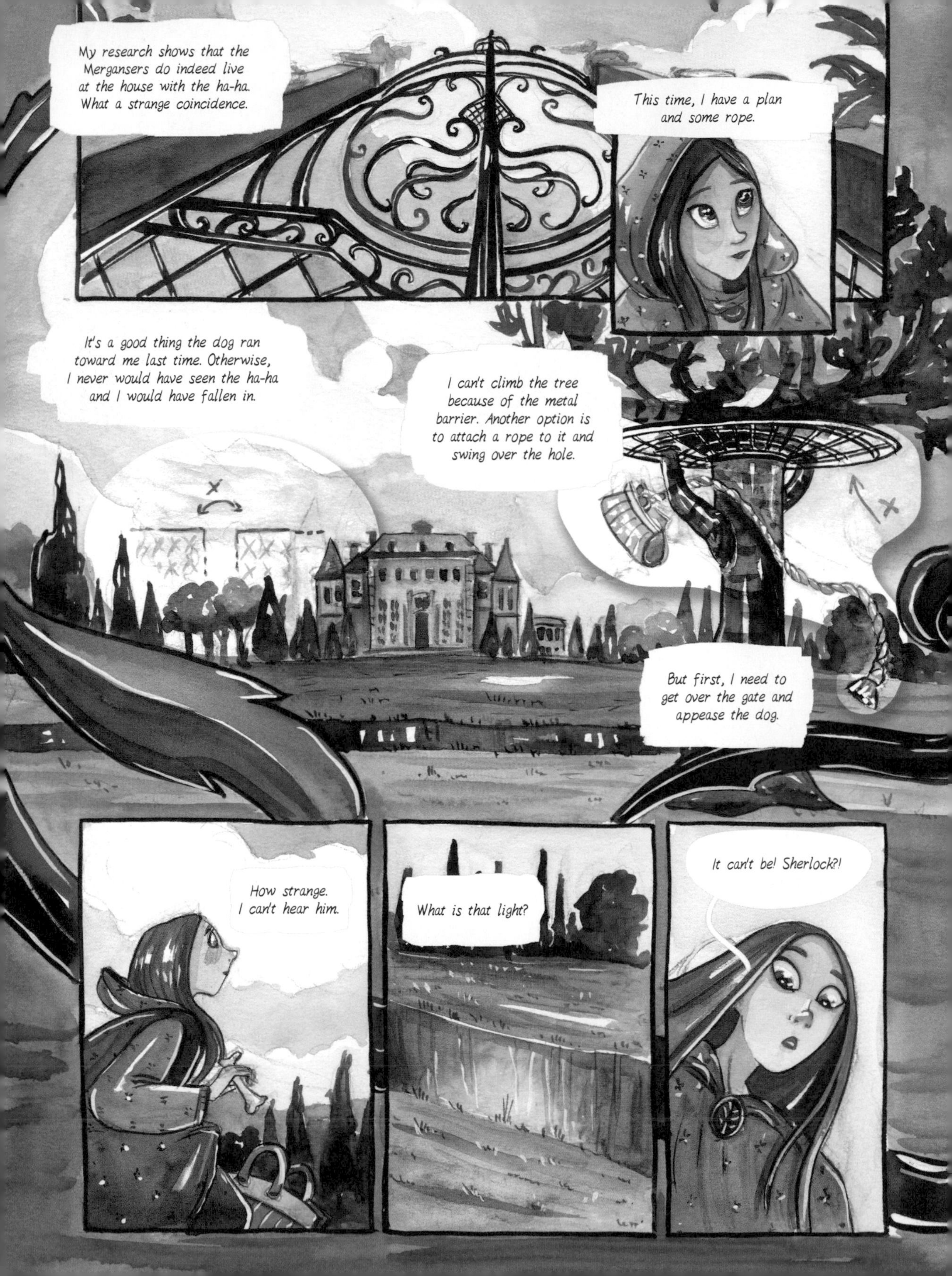
My research shows that the Mergansers do indeed live at the house with the ha-ha. What a strange coincidence.
This time, I have a plan and some rope.
It's a good thing the dog ran toward me last time. Otherwise, I never would have seen the ha-ha and I would have fallen in.
I can't climb the tree because of the metal barrier. Another option is to attach a rope to it and swing over the hole.
But first, I need to get over the gate and appease the dog.
How strange. I can't hear him.
What is that light?
It can't be! Sherlock?!

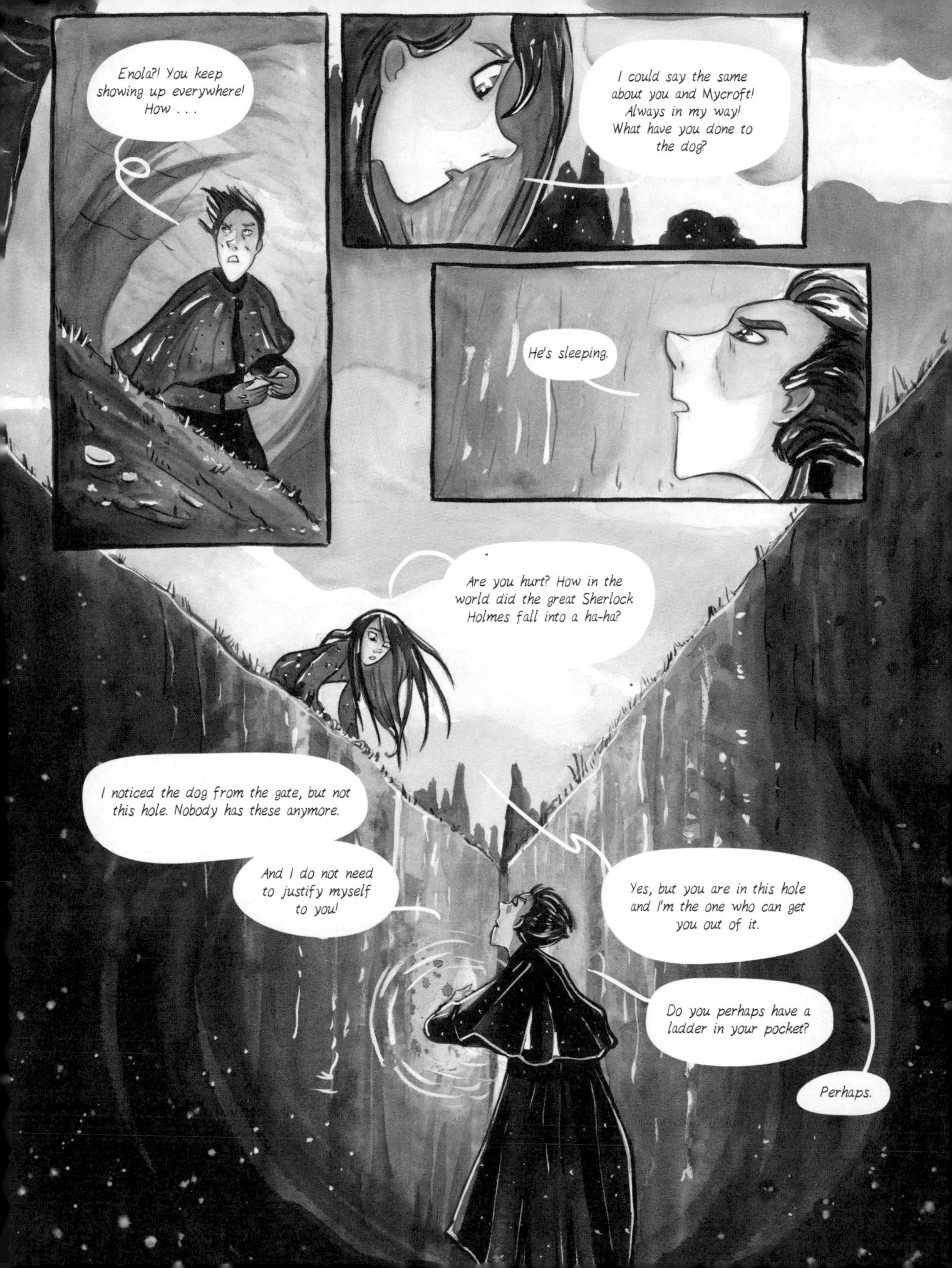

Enola?! You keep showing up everywhere! How . . .
I could say the same about you and Mycroft! Always in my way! What have you done to the dog?
He's sleeping.
Are you hurt? How in the world did the great Sherlock Holmes fall into a ha-ha?
I noticed the dog from the gate, but not this hole. Nobody has these anymore.
And I do not need to justify myself to you!
Yes, but you are in this hole and I'm the one who can get you out of it.
Do you perhaps have a ladder in your pocket?
Perhaps.

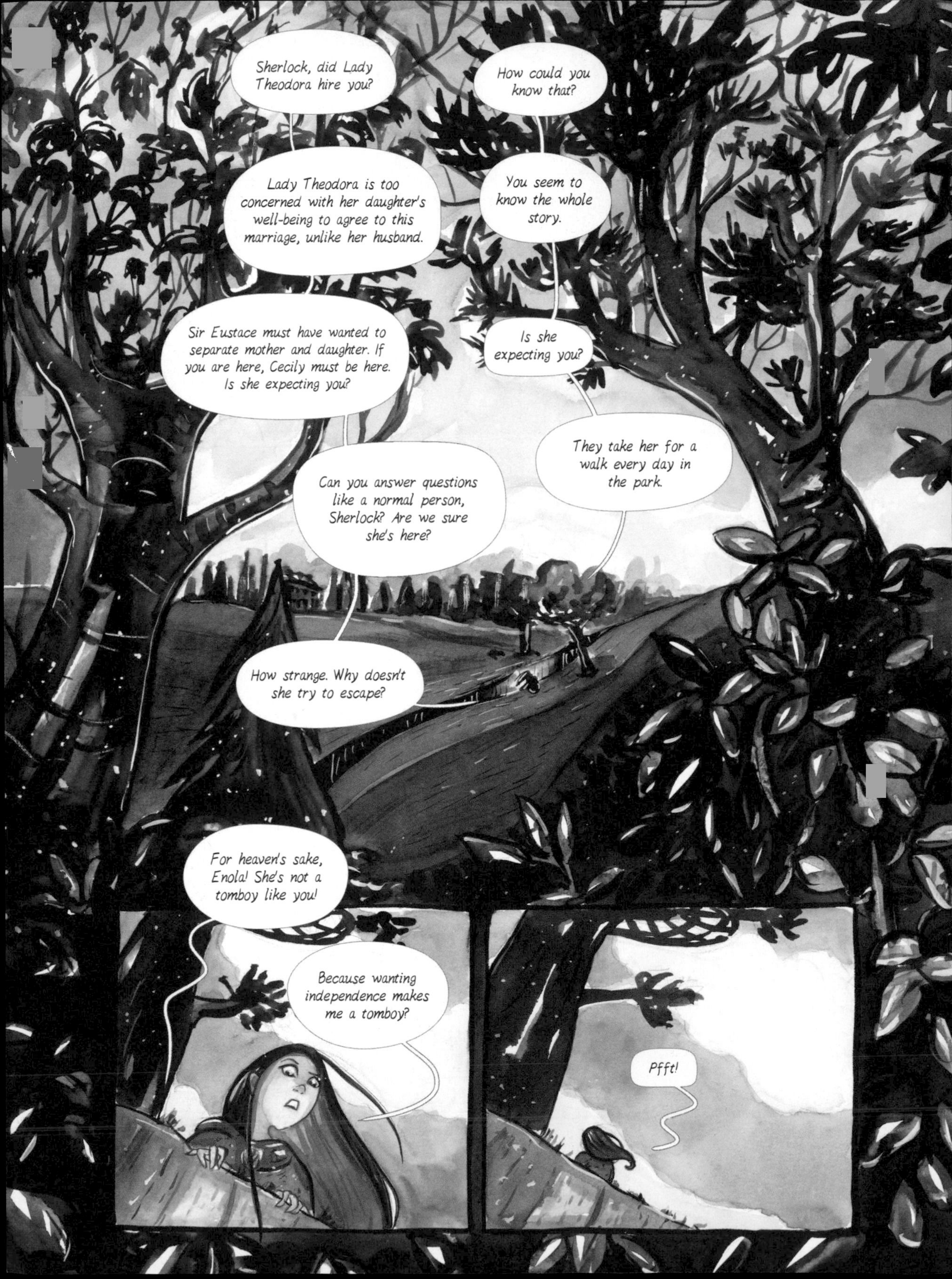
Sherlock, did Lady Theodora hire you?
How could you know that?
Lady Theodora is too concerned with her daughter's well-being to agree to this marriage, unlike her husband.
You seem to know the whole story.
Sir Eustace must have wanted to separate mother and daughter. If you are here, Cecily must be here. Is she expecting you?
Is she expecting you?
Can you answer questions like a normal person, Sherlock? Are we sure she's here?
They take her for a walk every day in the park.
How strange. Why doesn't she try to escape?
For heaven's sake, Enola! She's not a tomboy like you!
Because wanting independence makes me a tomboy?
Pfft!

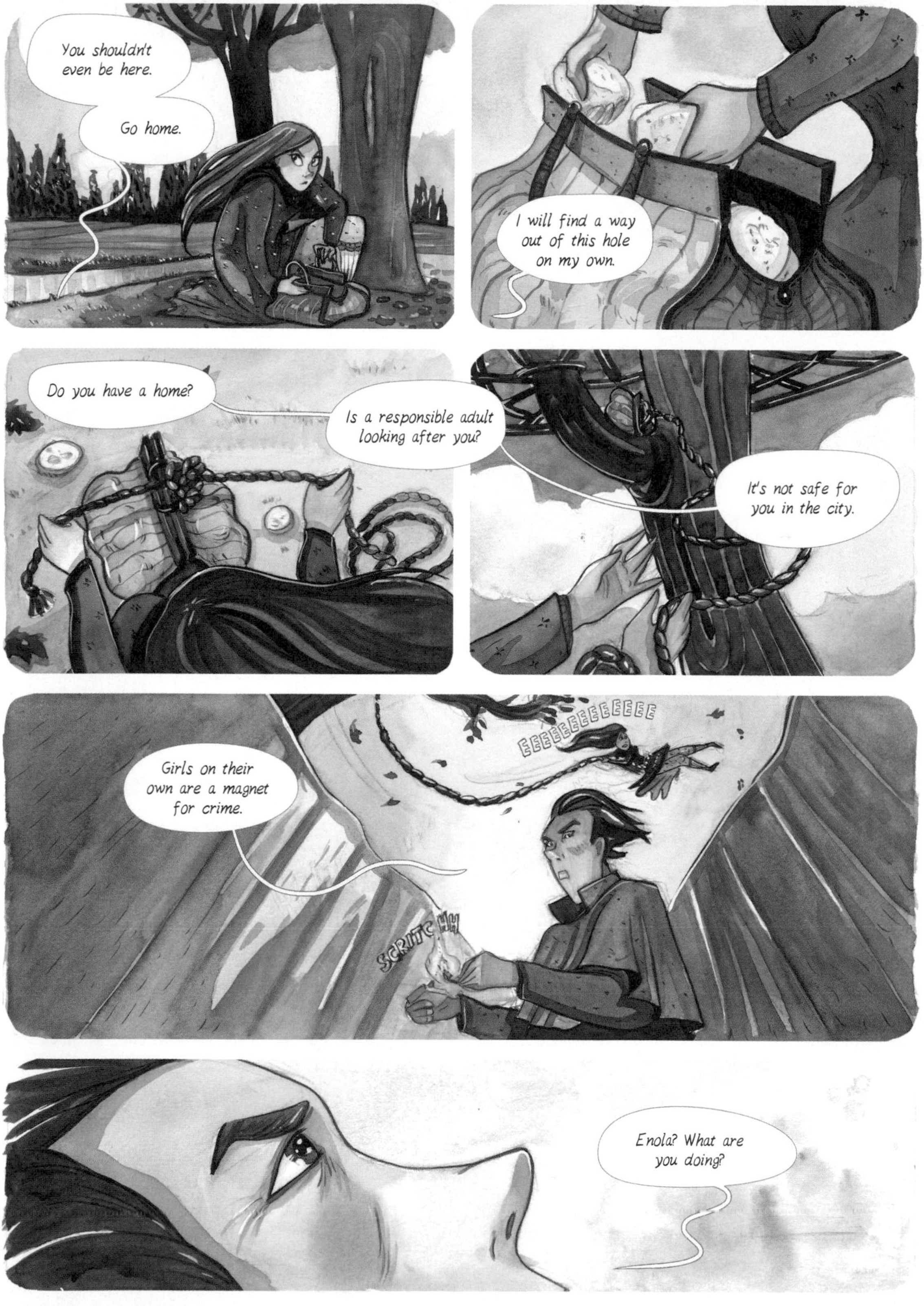

You shouldn't even be here.
Go home.
I will find a way out of this hole on my own.
Do you have a home?
Is a responsible adult looking after you?
It's not safe for you in the city.
EEEEEEEEEEEEE
Girls on their own are a magnet for crime.
SCRITCHH
Enola? What are you doing?

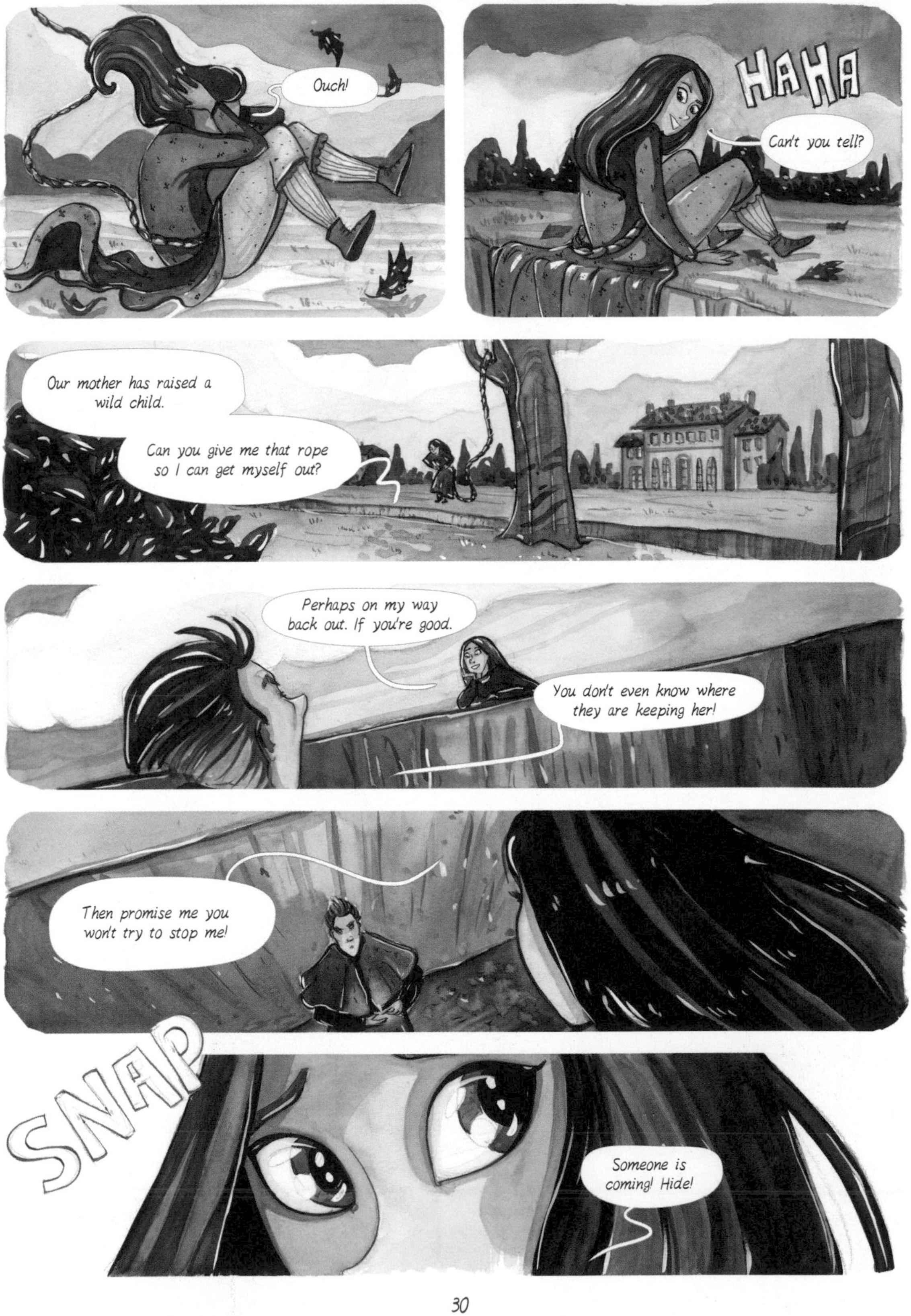
Ouch!
HAHA
Can't you tell?
Our mother has raised a wild child.
Can you give me that rope so I can get myself out?
Perhaps on my way back out. If you're good.
You don't even know where they are keeping her!
Then promise me you won't try to stop me!
SNAP
Someone is coming! Hide!

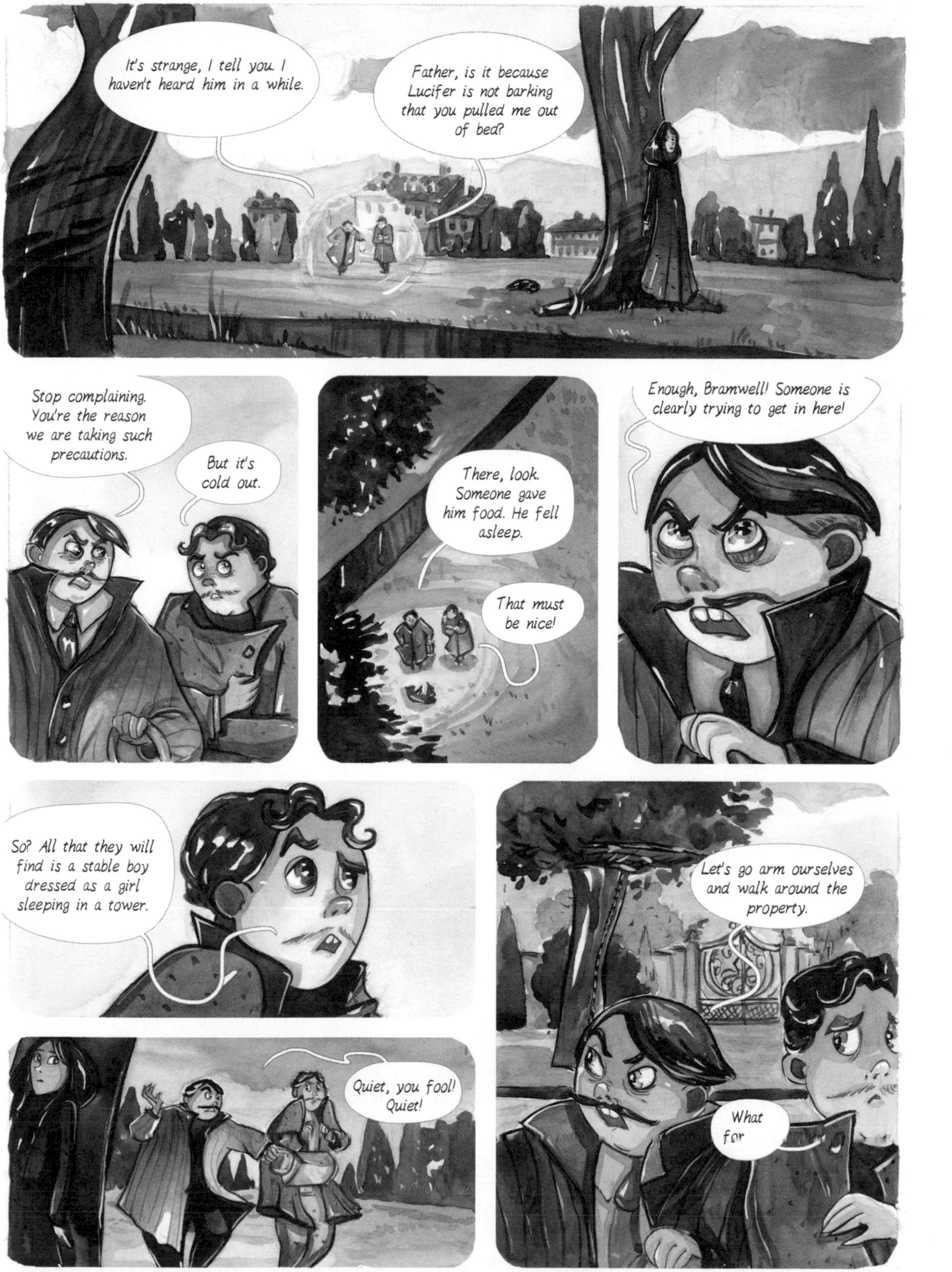

It's strange, I tell you. I haven't heard him in a while.
Father, is it because Lucifer is not barking that you pulled me out of bed?
Stop complaining. You're the reason we are taking such precautions.
But it's cold out.
There, look. Someone gave him food. He fell asleep.
That must be nice!
Enough, Bramwell! Someone is clearly trying to get in here!
So? All that they will find is a stable boy dressed as a girl sleeping in a tower.
Let's go arm ourselves and walk around the property.
What for
Quiet, you fool! Quiet!

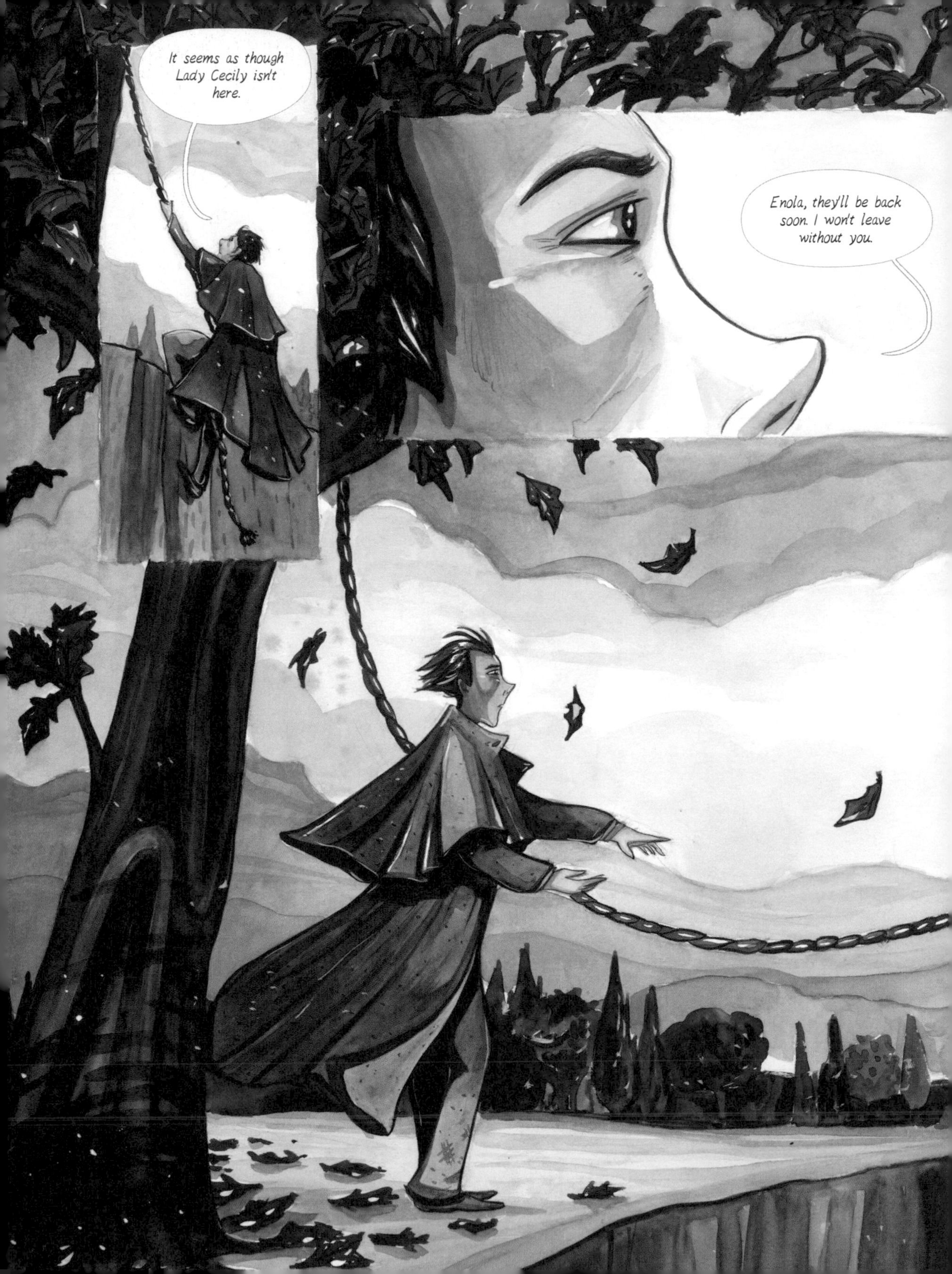
It seems as though Lady Cecily isn't here.
Enola, they'll be back soon. I won't leave without you.

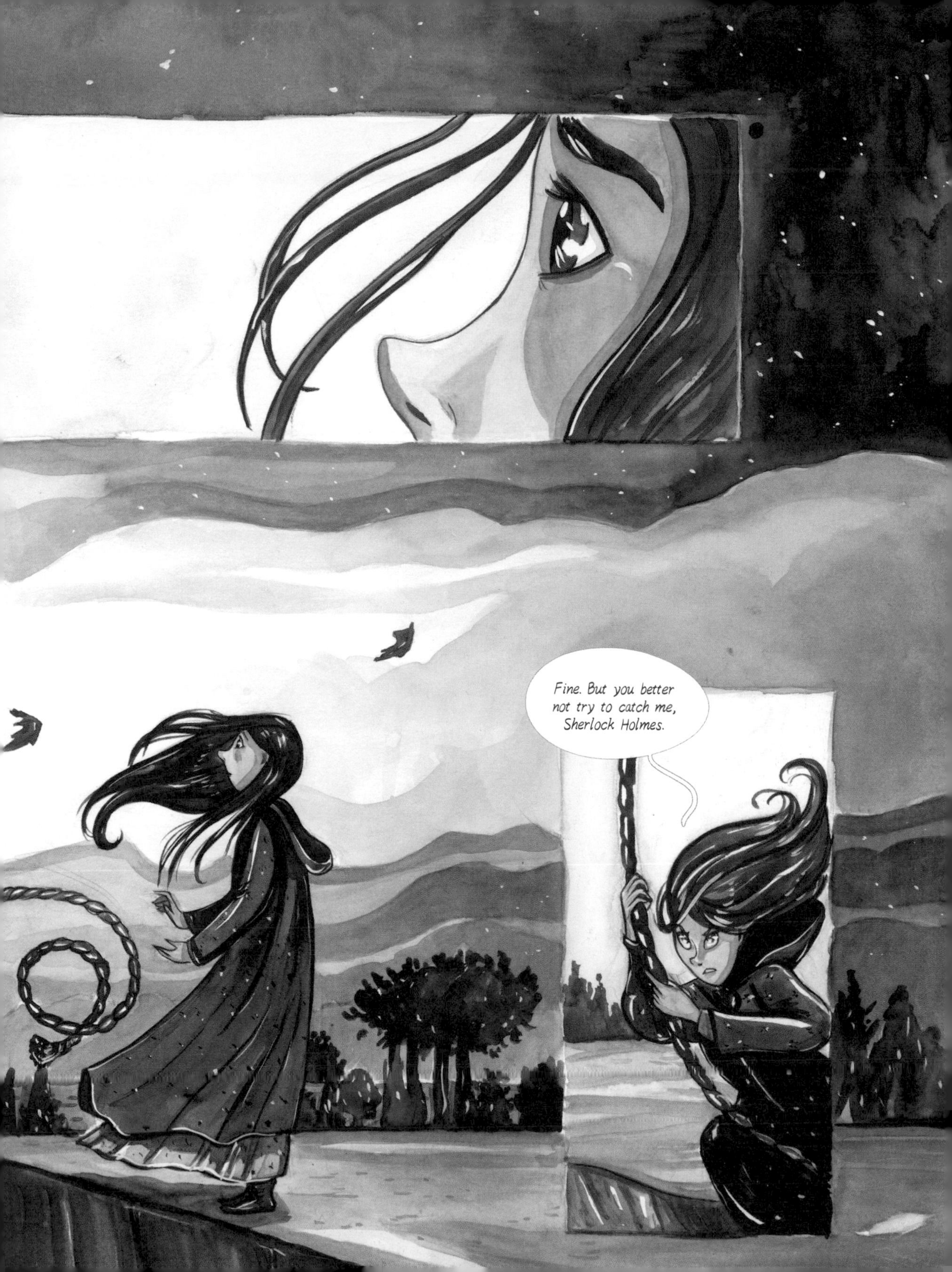
Fine. But you better not try to catch me, Sherlock Holmes.

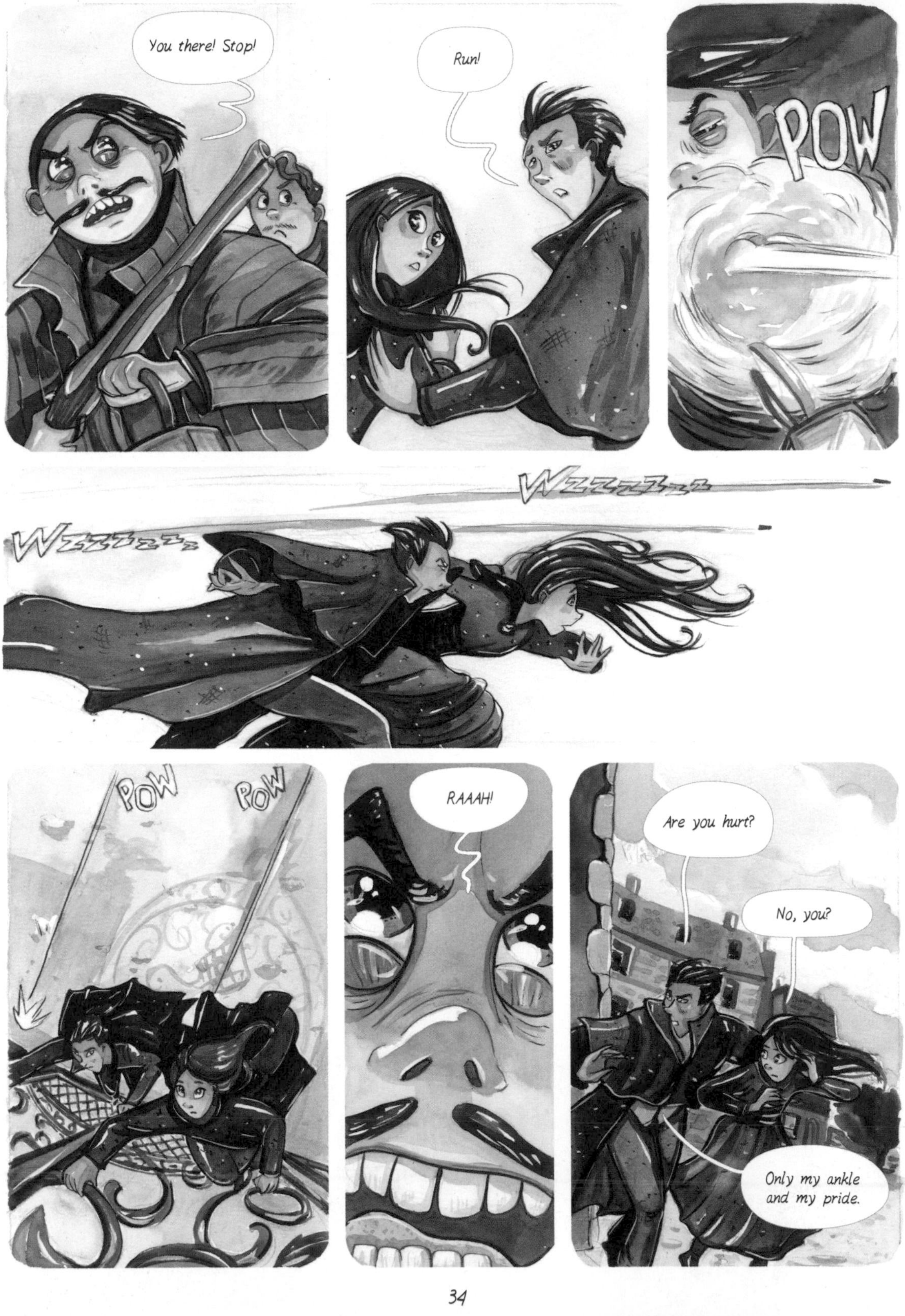
You there! Stop!
Run!
POW
WZZZZZZZ
WZZZZZZZ
POW
POW
RAAAH!
Are you hurt?
No, you?
Only my ankle and my pride.

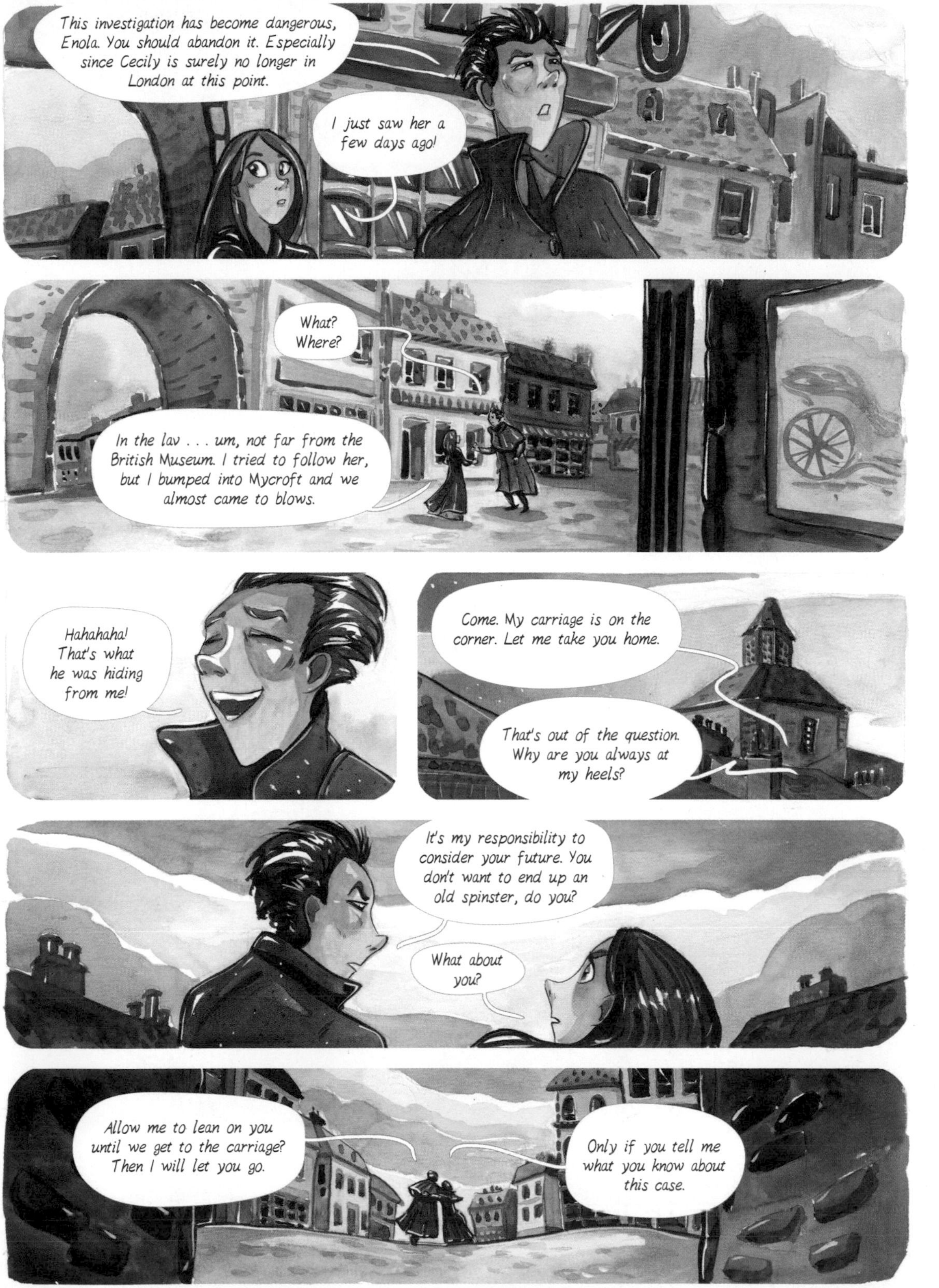
This investigation has become dangerous, Enola. You should abandon it. Especially since Cecily is surely no longer in London at this point.
I just saw her a few days ago!
What? Where?
In the lav . . . um, not far from the British Museum. I tried to follow her, but I bumped into Mycroft and we almost came to blows.
Hahahaha! That's what he was hiding from me!
Come. My carriage is on the corner. Let me take you home.
That's out of the question. Why are you always at my heels?
It's my responsibility to consider your future. You don't want to end up an old spinster, do you?
What about you?
Allow me to lean on you until we get to the carriage? Then I will let you go.
Only if you tell me what you know about this case.

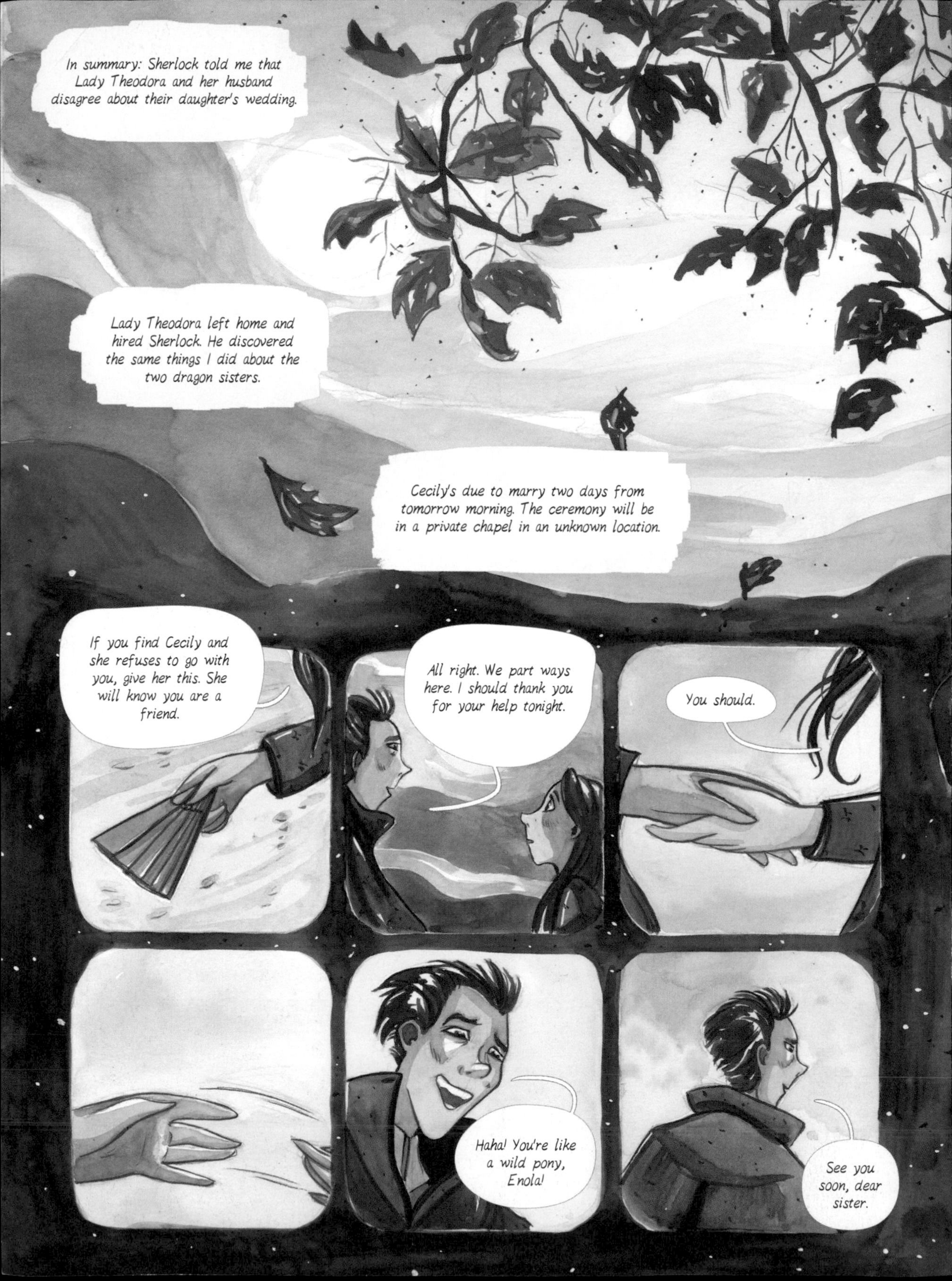
In summary: Sherlock told me that Lady Theodora and her husband disagree about their daughter's wedding.
Lady Theodora left home and hired Sherlock. He discovered the same things I did about the two dragon sisters.
Cecily's due to marry two days from tomorrow morning. The ceremony will be in a private chapel in an unknown location.
If you find Cecily and she refuses to go with you, give her this. She will know you are a friend.
All right. We part ways here. I should thank you for your help tonight.
You should.
Haha! You're like a wild pony, Enola!
See you soon, dear sister.

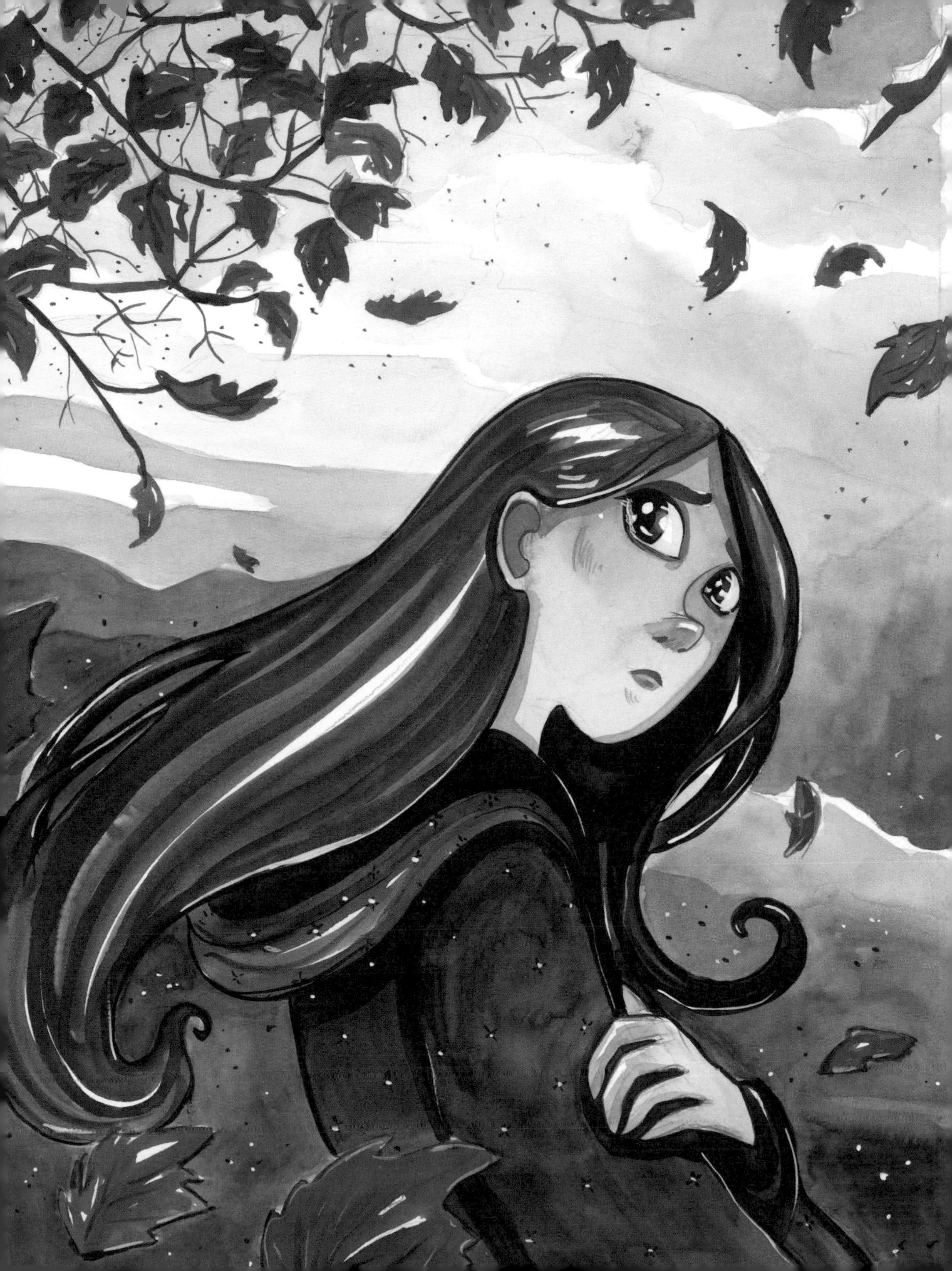

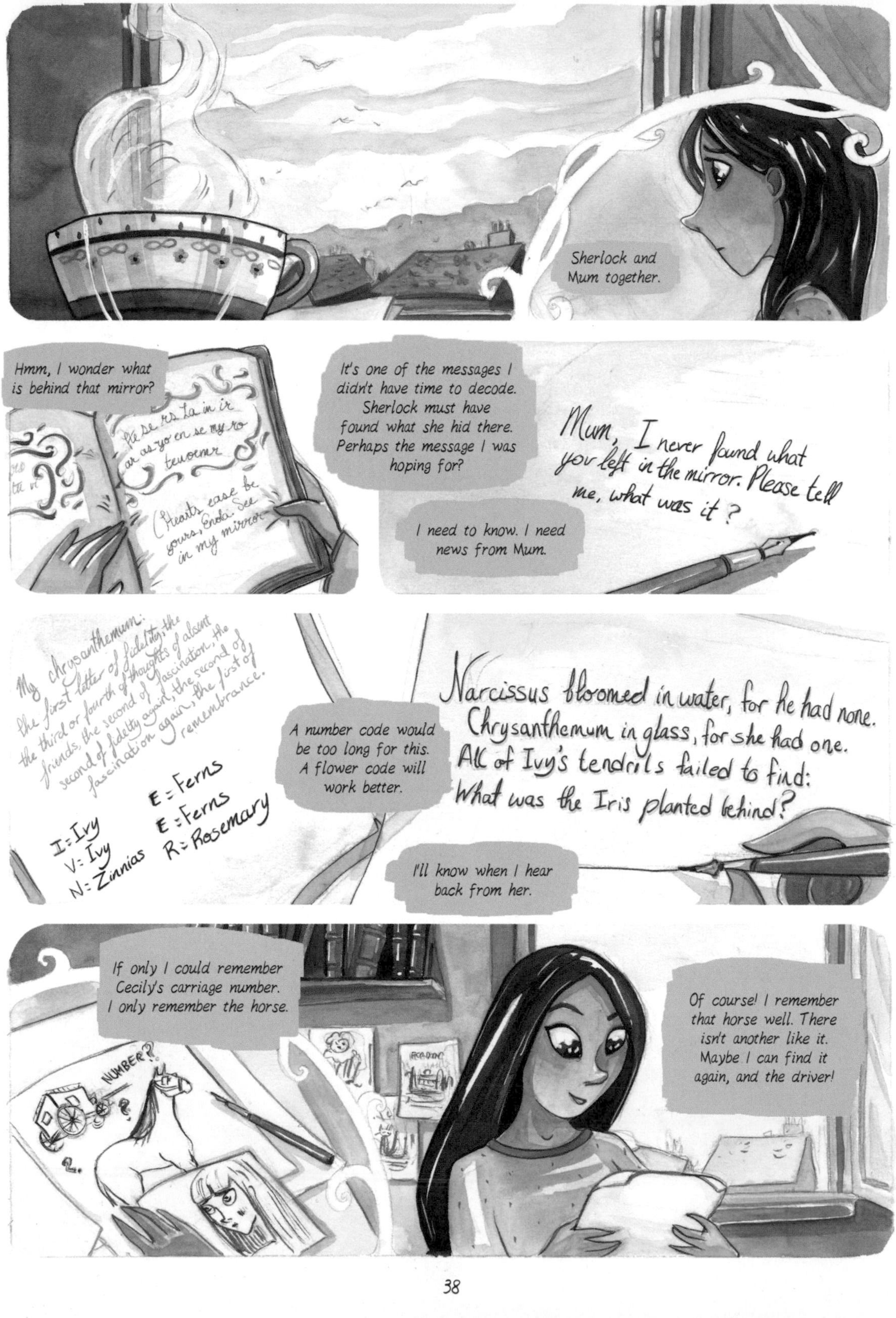

Sherlock and Mum together.
Hmm, I wonder what is behind that mirror?
Ple se rs La in ir
ar as yo en se my ro
tenoemr
(Hearts ease be yours, Enola. See in my mirror
It's one of the messages I didn't have time to decode. Sherlock must have found what she hid there. Perhaps the message I was hoping for?
Mum, I never found what you left in the mirror. Please tell me, what was it ?
I need to know. I need news from Mum.
My chrysanthemum: the first letter of fidelity, the the third or fourth of thoughts of absent friends, the second of fascination, the second of fidelity again, the second of fascination again, the first of remembrance.
I = Ivy
V = Ivy
N = Zinnias
E = Ferns
E = Ferns
R = Rosemary
A number code would be too long for this. A flower code will work better.
Narcissus bloomed in water, for he had none.
Chrysanthemum in glass, for she had one.
All of Ivy's tendrils failed to find:
What was the Iris planted behind?
I'll know when I hear back from her.
If only I could remember Cecily's carriage number. I only remember the horse.
NUMBER??
Of course! I remember that horse well. There isn't another like it. Maybe I can find it again, and the driver!

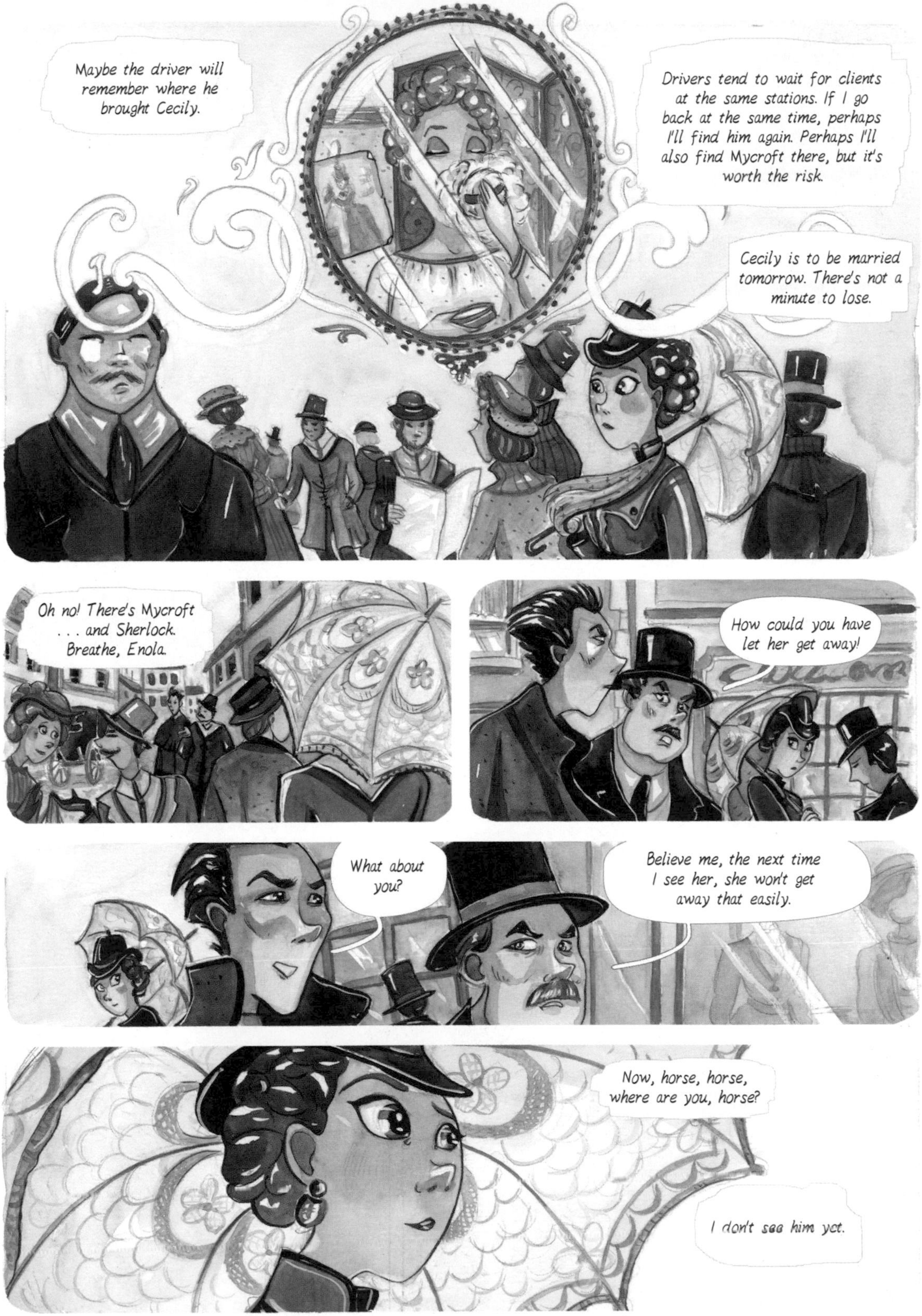
Maybe the driver will remember where he brought Cecily.
Drivers tend to wait for clients at the same stations. If I go back at the same time, perhaps I'll find him again. Perhaps I'll also find Mycroft there, but it's worth the risk.
Cecily is to be married tomorrow. There's not a minute to lose.
Oh no! There's Mycroft . . . and Sherlock. Breathe, Enola.
How could you have let her get away!
What about you?
Believe me, the next time I see her, she won't get away that easily.
Now, horse, horse, where are you, horse?
I don't see him yet.

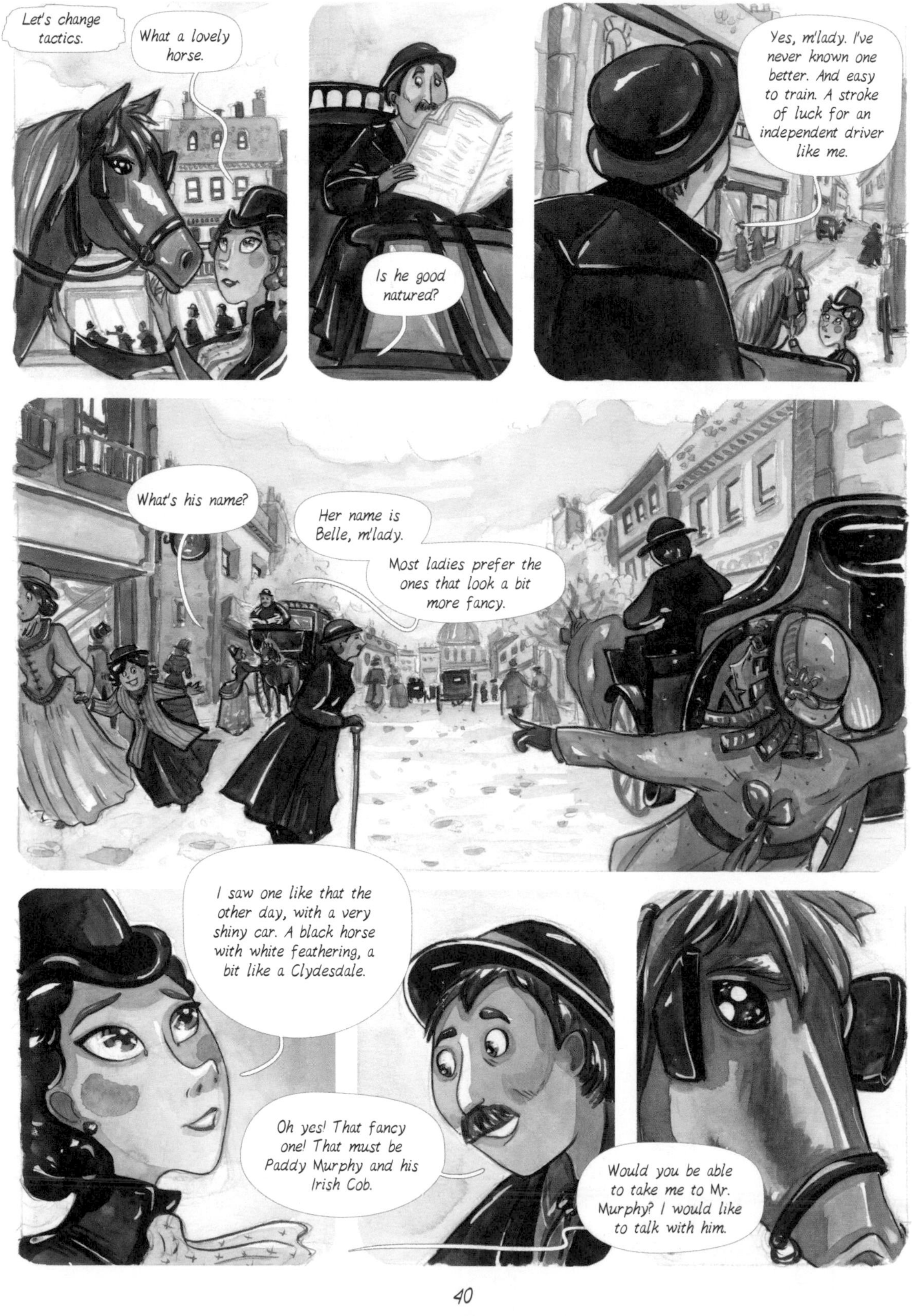
Let's change tactics.
What a lovely horse.
Is he good natured?
Yes, m'lady. I've never known one better. And easy to train. A stroke of luck for an independent driver like me.
What's his name?
Her name is Belle, m'lady.
Most ladies prefer the ones that look a bit more fancy.
I saw one like that the other day, with a very shiny car. A black horse with white feathering, a bit like a Clydesdale.
Oh yes! That fancy one! That must be Paddy Murphy and his Irish Cob.
Would you be able to take me to Mr. Murphy? I would like to talk with him.

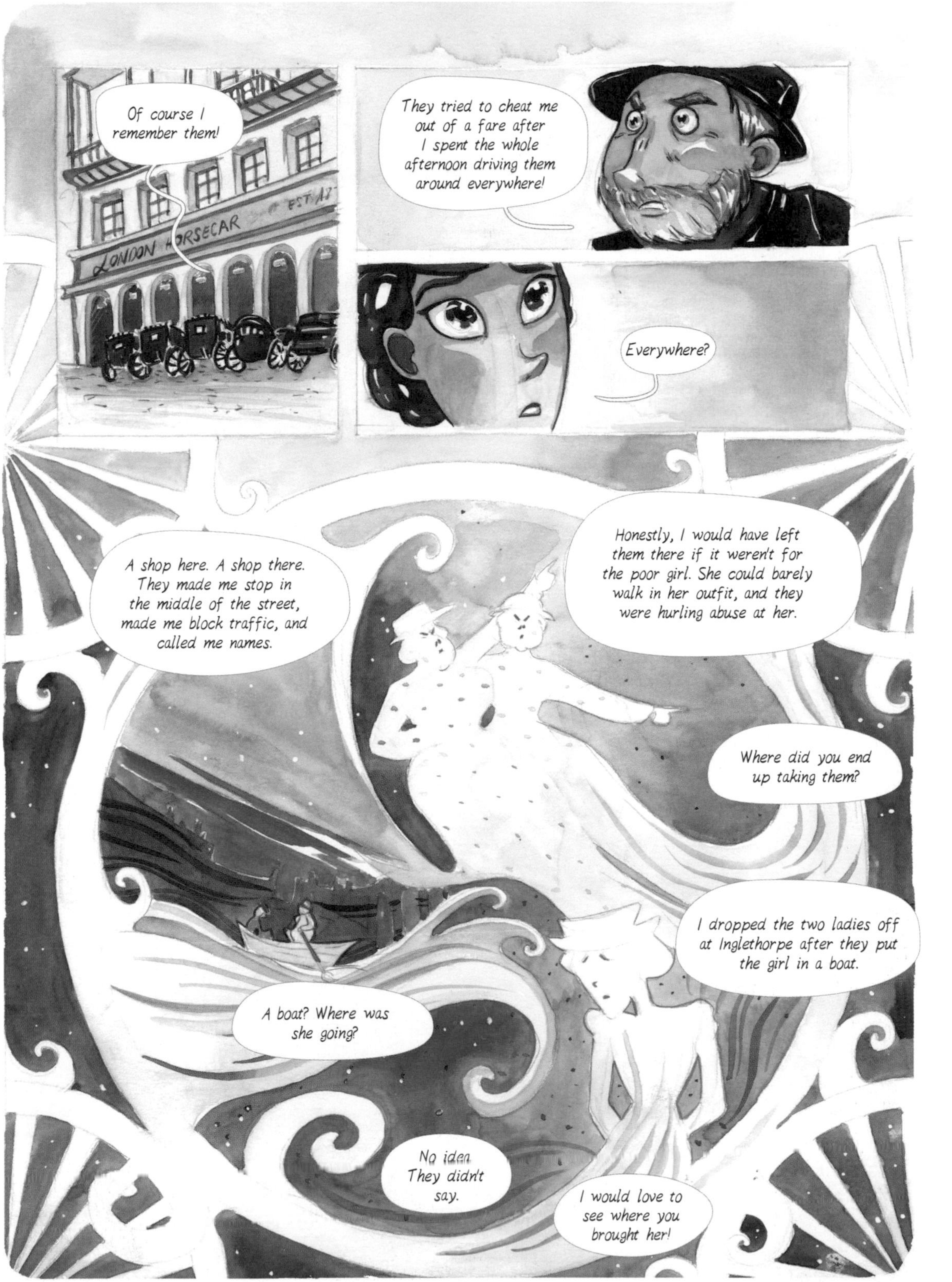

Of course I remember them!
LONDON HORSECAR
They tried to cheat me out of a fare after I spent the whole afternoon driving them around everywhere!
Everywhere?
A shop here. A shop there. They made me stop in the middle of the street, made me block traffic, and called me names.
Honestly, I would have left them there if it weren't for the poor girl. She could barely walk in her outfit, and they were hurling abuse at her.
Where did you end up taking them?
I dropped the two ladies off at Inglethorpe after they put the girl in a boat.
A boat? Where was she going?
No idea. They didn't say.
I would love to see where you brought her!

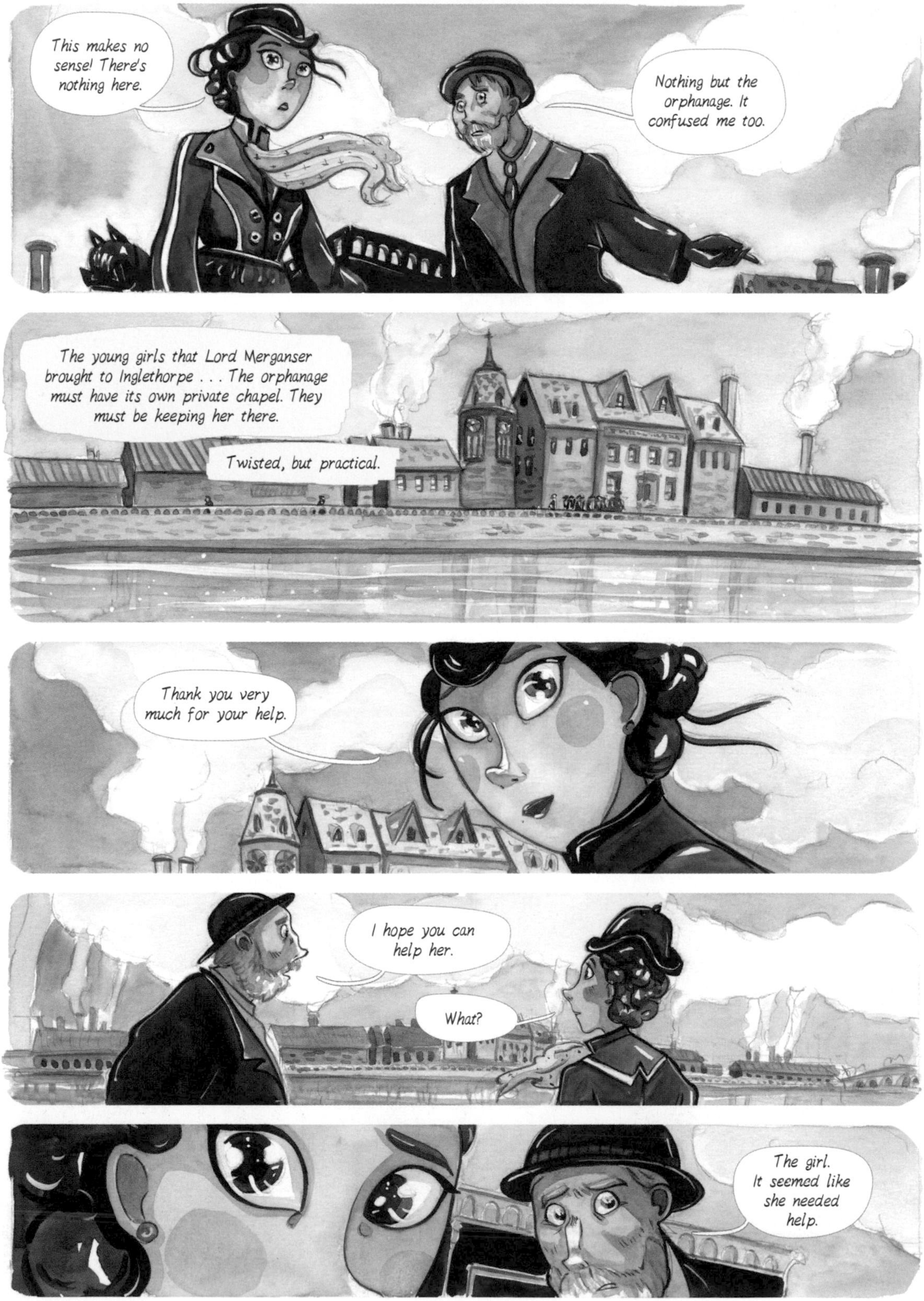
This makes no sense! There's nothing here.
Nothing but the orphanage. It confused me too.
The young girls that Lord Merganser brought to Inglethorpe . . . The orphanage must have its own private chapel. They must be keeping her there.
Twisted, but practical.
Thank you very much for your help.
I hope you can help her.
What?
The girl. It seemed like she needed help.

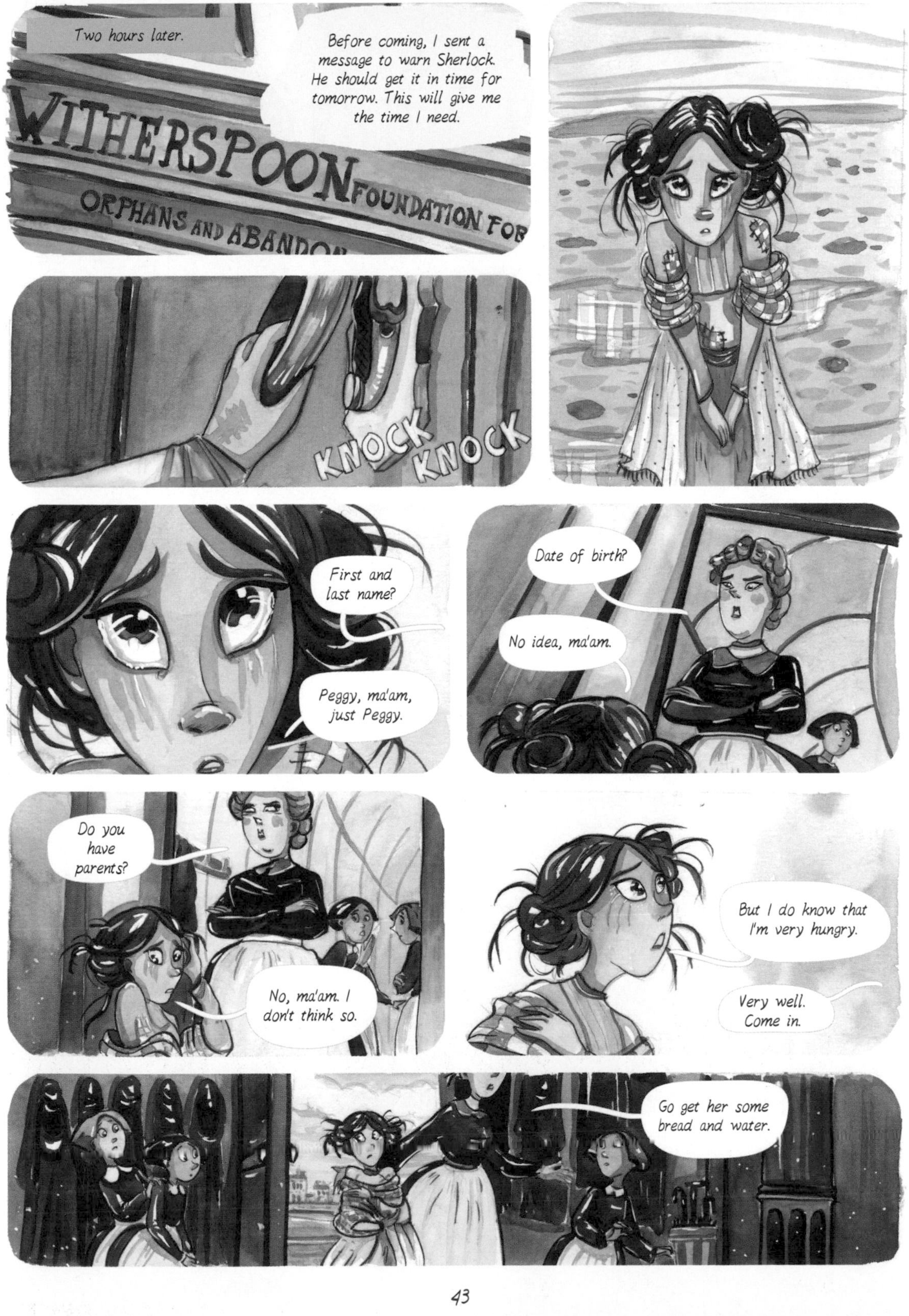
Two hours later.
Before coming, I sent a message to warn Sherlock. He should get it in time for tomorrow. This will give me the time I need.
WITHERSPOON FOUNDATION FOR
ORPHANS AND ABANDON
KNOCK KNOCK
First and last name?
Peggy, ma'am, just Peggy.
Date of birth?
No idea, ma'am.
Do you have parents?
No, ma'am. I don't think so.
But I do know that I'm very hungry.
Very well. Come in.
Go get her some bread and water.

Have you ever been to prison?

No, ma'am.

Have you ever had fits?

No idea.

Incontinence?

Incontiwhat?

Do you wet the bed?

Oh, no, ma'am!

All right. Let's get you in the bath.

Then I'll take you to have your hair cut.

My hair? I don't want to cut my hair!

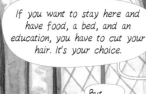

If you want to stay here and have food, a bed, and an education, you have to cut your hair. It's your choice.

But . . .

You'll also get inoculated against smallpox. You get the haircut or you leave.

This is such a hard choice, ma'am. Can I say a prayer first? Do you have a chapel here?

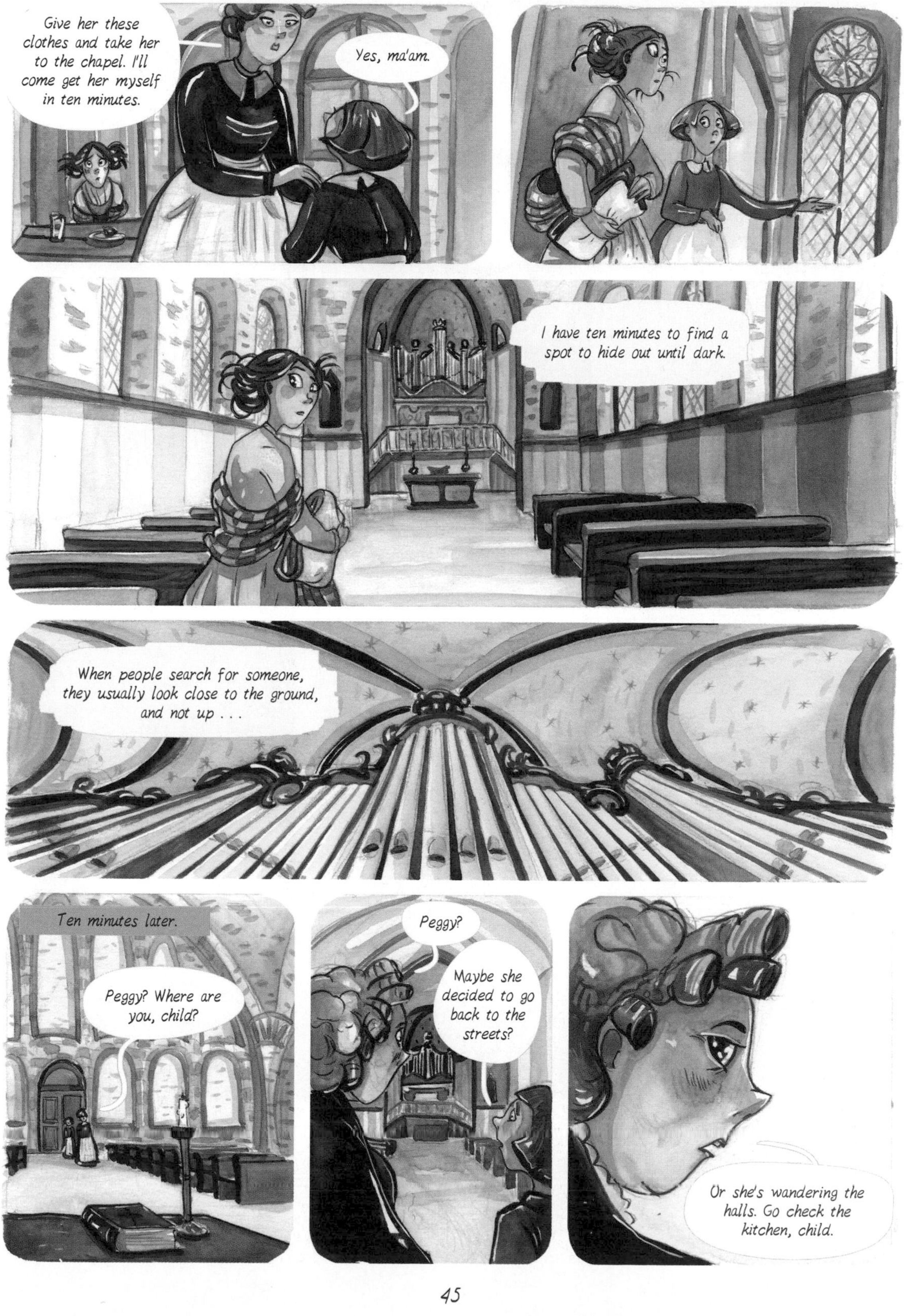
Give her these clothes and take her to the chapel. I'll come get her myself in ten minutes.
Yes, ma'am.
I have ten minutes to find a spot to hide out until dark.
When people search for someone, they usually look close to the ground, and not up . . .
Ten minutes later.
Peggy? Where are you, child?
Peggy?
Maybe she decided to go back to the streets?
Or she's wandering the halls. Go check the kitchen, child.

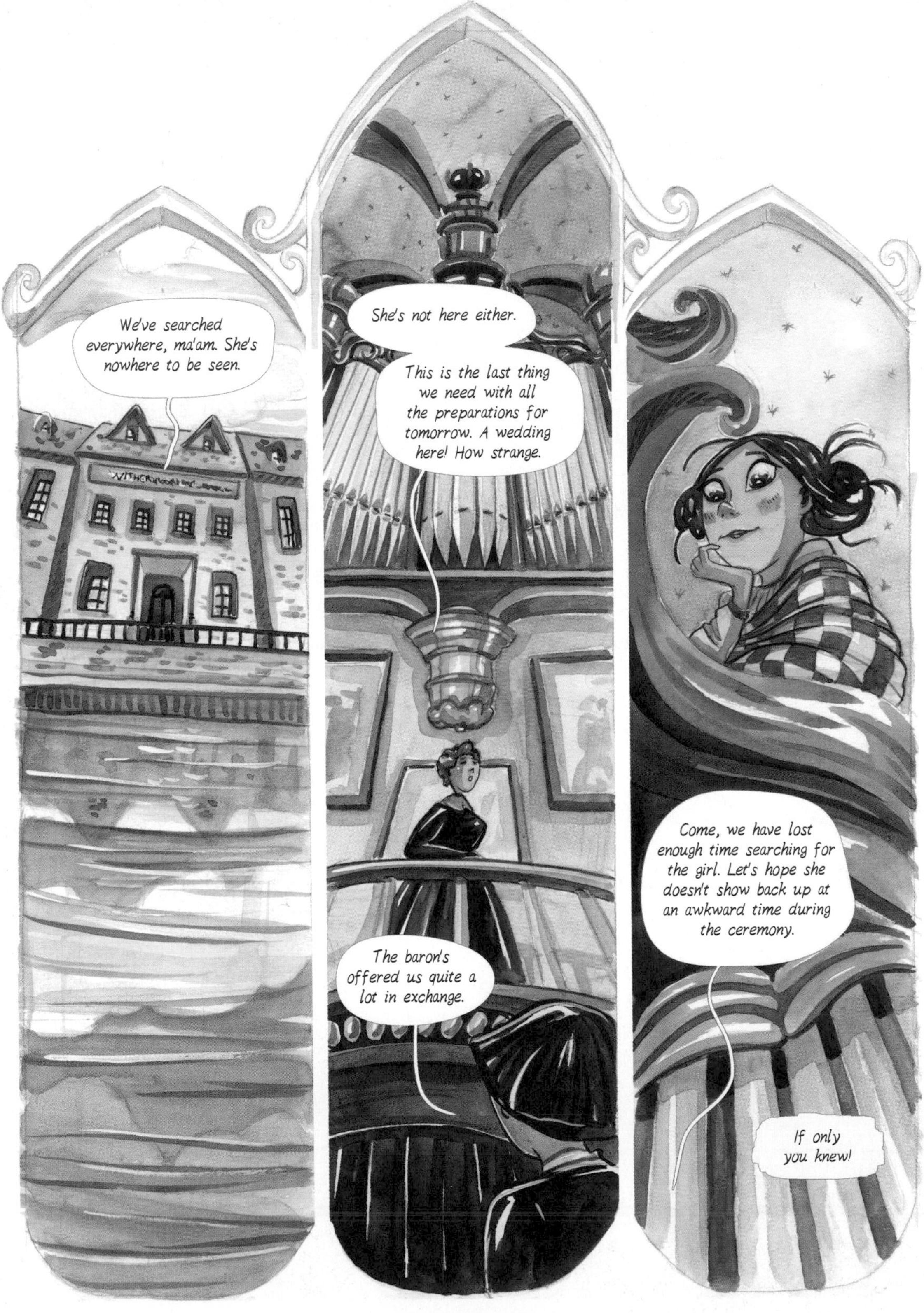
We've searched everywhere, ma'am. She's nowhere to be seen.
She's not here either.
This is the last thing we need with all the preparations for tomorrow. A wedding here! How strange.
The baron's offered us quite a lot in exchange.
Come, we have lost enough time searching for the girl. Let's hope she doesn't show back up at an awkward time during the ceremony.
If only you knew!

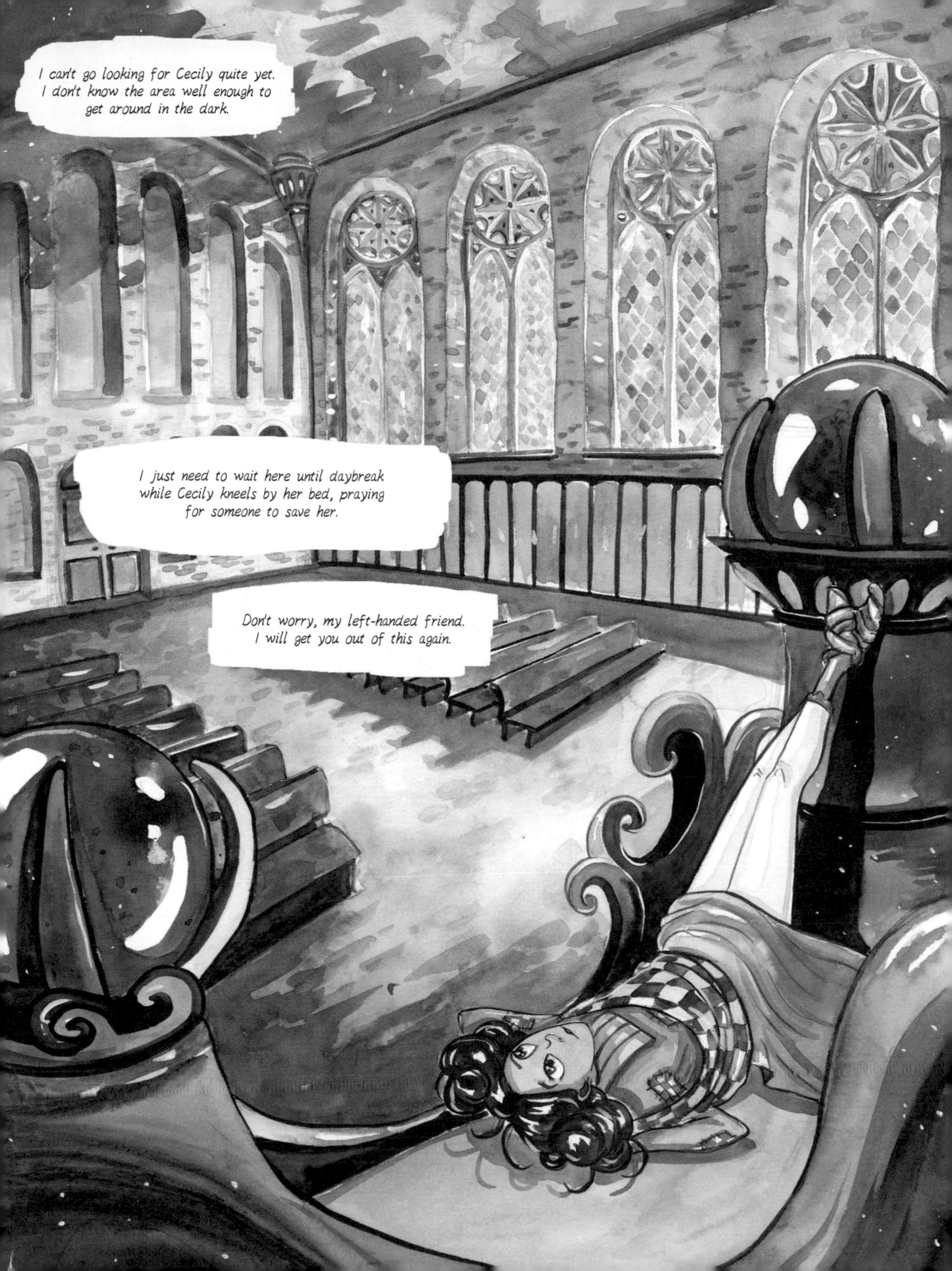
I can't go looking for Cecily quite yet. I don't know the area well enough to get around in the dark.
I just need to wait here until daybreak while Cecily kneels by her bed, praying for someone to save her.
Don't worry, my left-handed friend. I will get you out of this again.

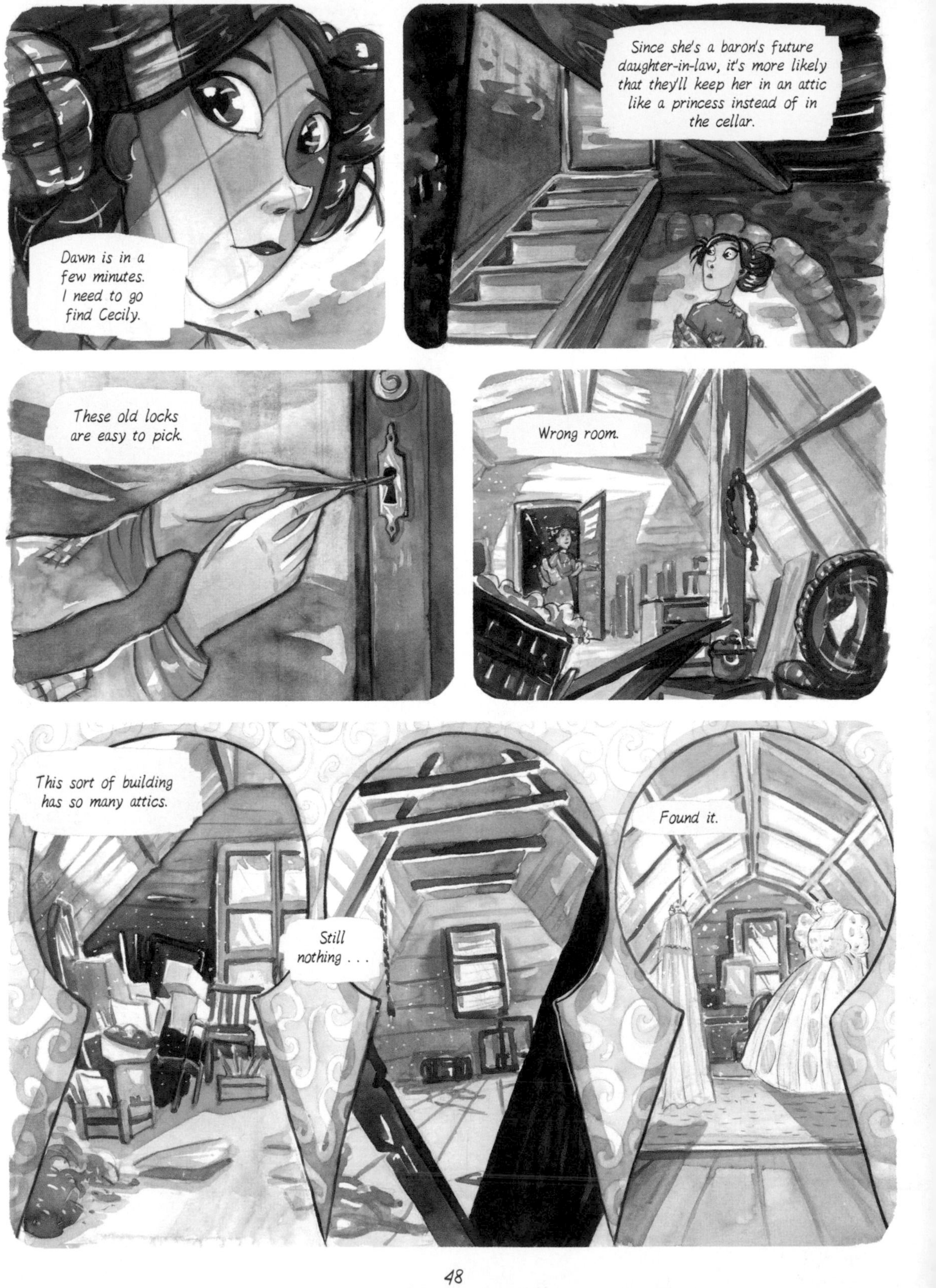
Dawn is in a few minutes. I need to go find Cecily.
Since she's a baron's future daughter-in-law, it's more likely that they'll keep her in an attic like a princess instead of in the cellar.
These old locks are easy to pick.
Wrong room.
This sort of building has so many attics.
Still nothing . . .
Found it.

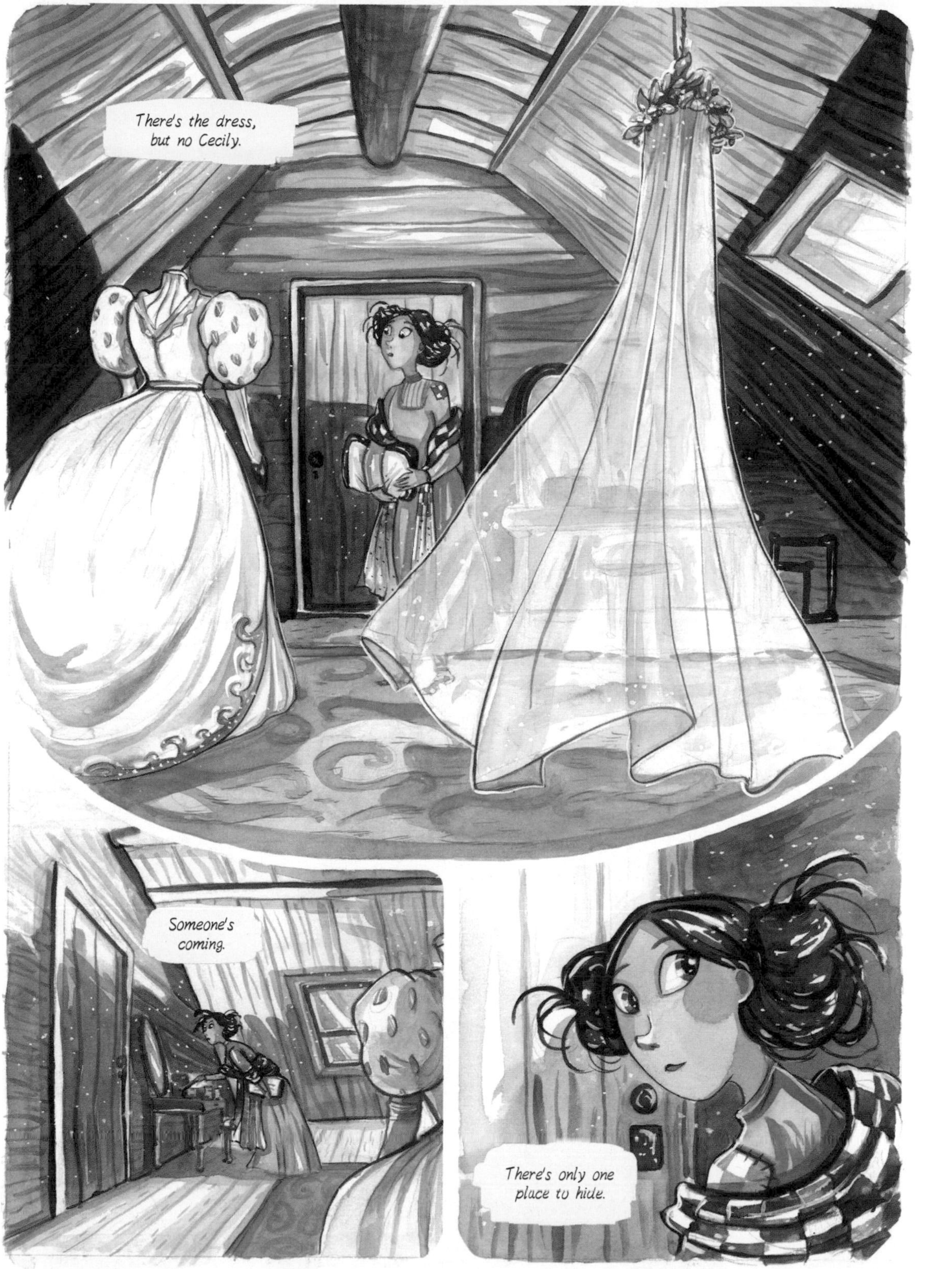
There's the dress,
but no Cecily.
Someone's
coming.
There's only one
place to hide.

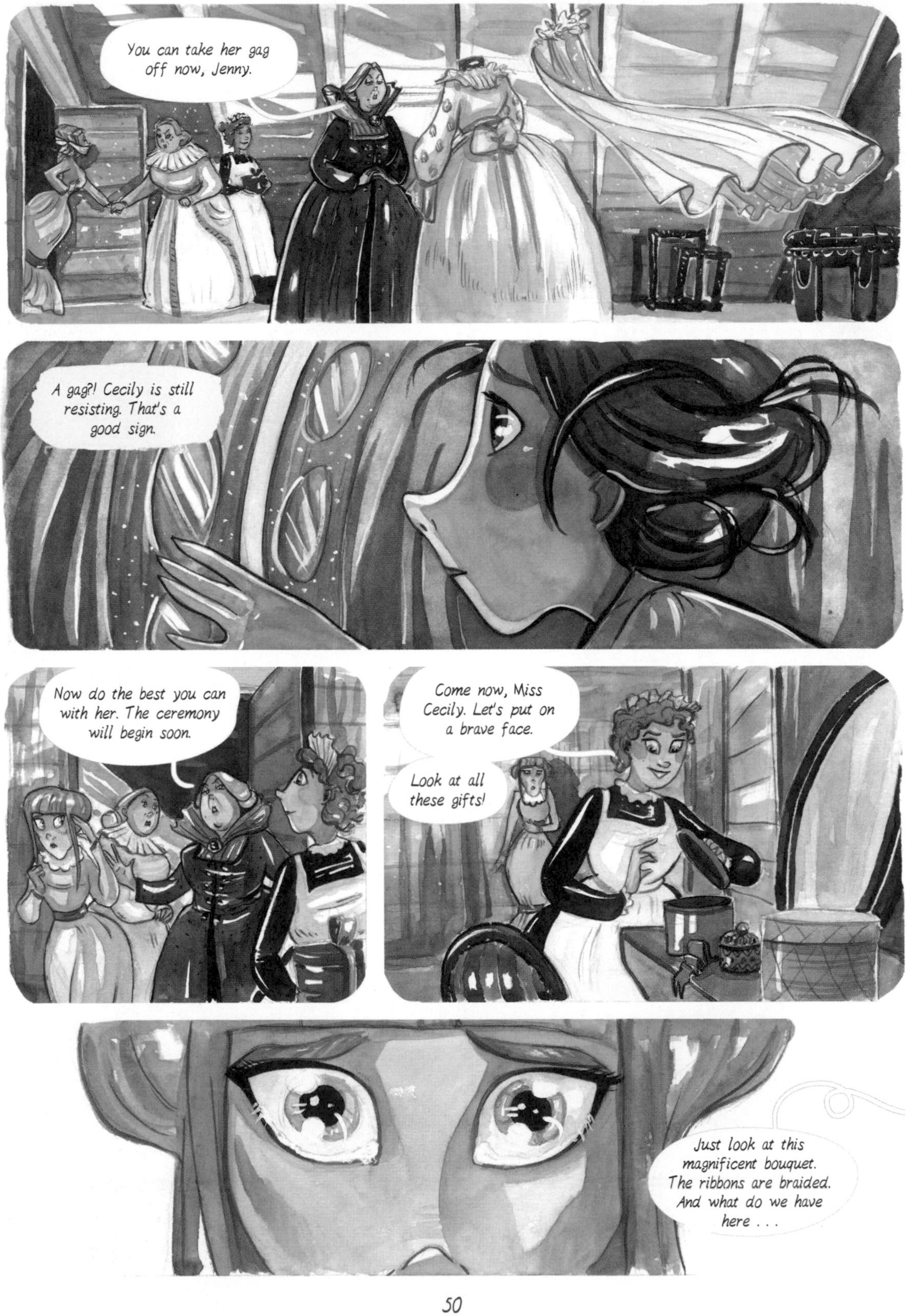
You can take her gag off now, Jenny.
A gag?! Cecily is still resisting. That's a good sign.
Now do the best you can with her. The ceremony will begin soon.
Come now, Miss Cecily. Let's put on a brave face.
Look at all these gifts!
Just look at this magnificent bouquet. The ribbons are braided. And what do we have here . . .

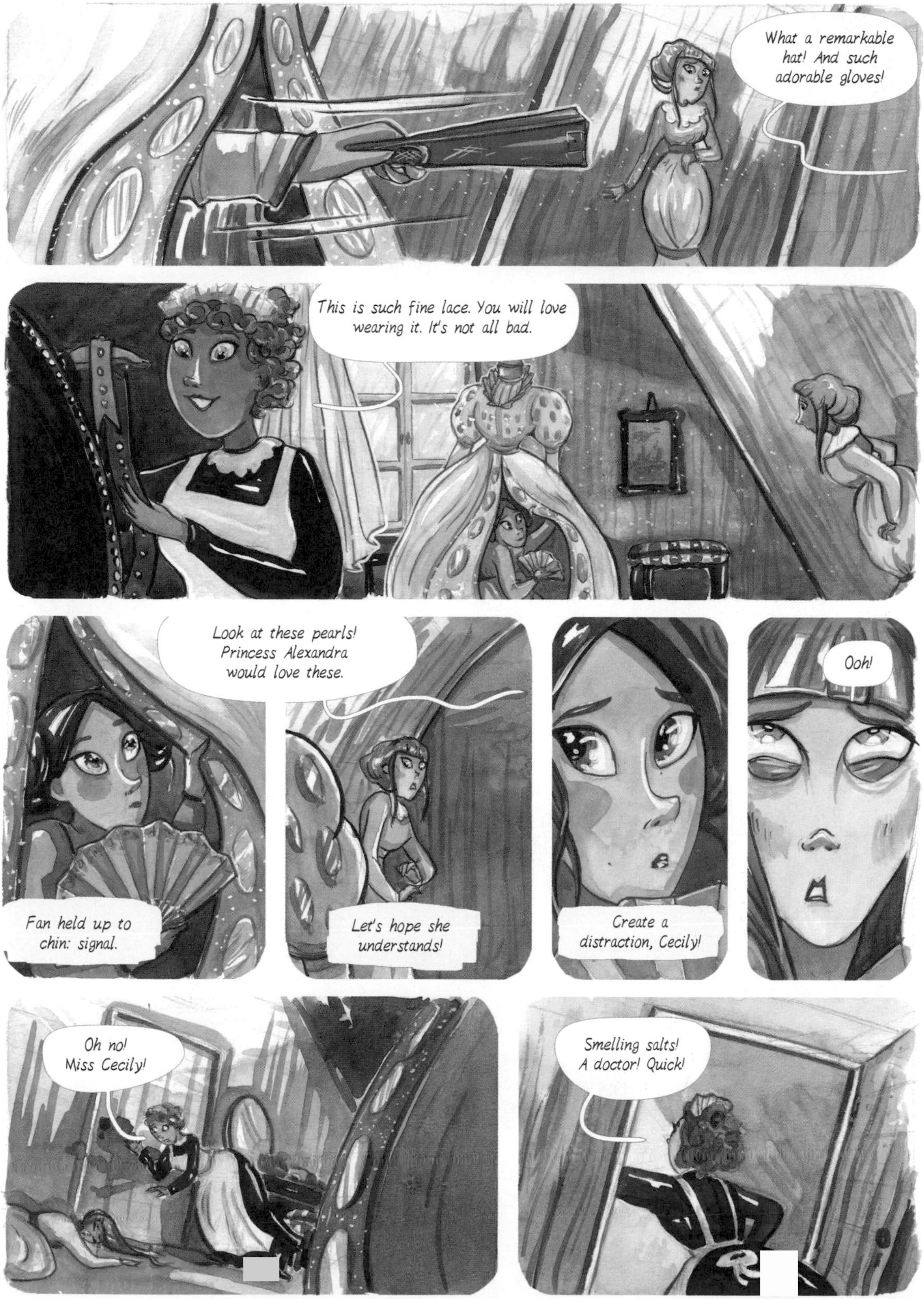
What a remarkable hat! And such adorable gloves!
This is such fine lace. You will love wearing it. It's not all bad.
Look at these pearls! Princess Alexandra would love these.
Fan held up to chin: signal.
Let's hope she understands!
Create a distraction, Cecily!
Ooh!
Oh no! Miss Cecily!
Smelling salts! A doctor! Quick!

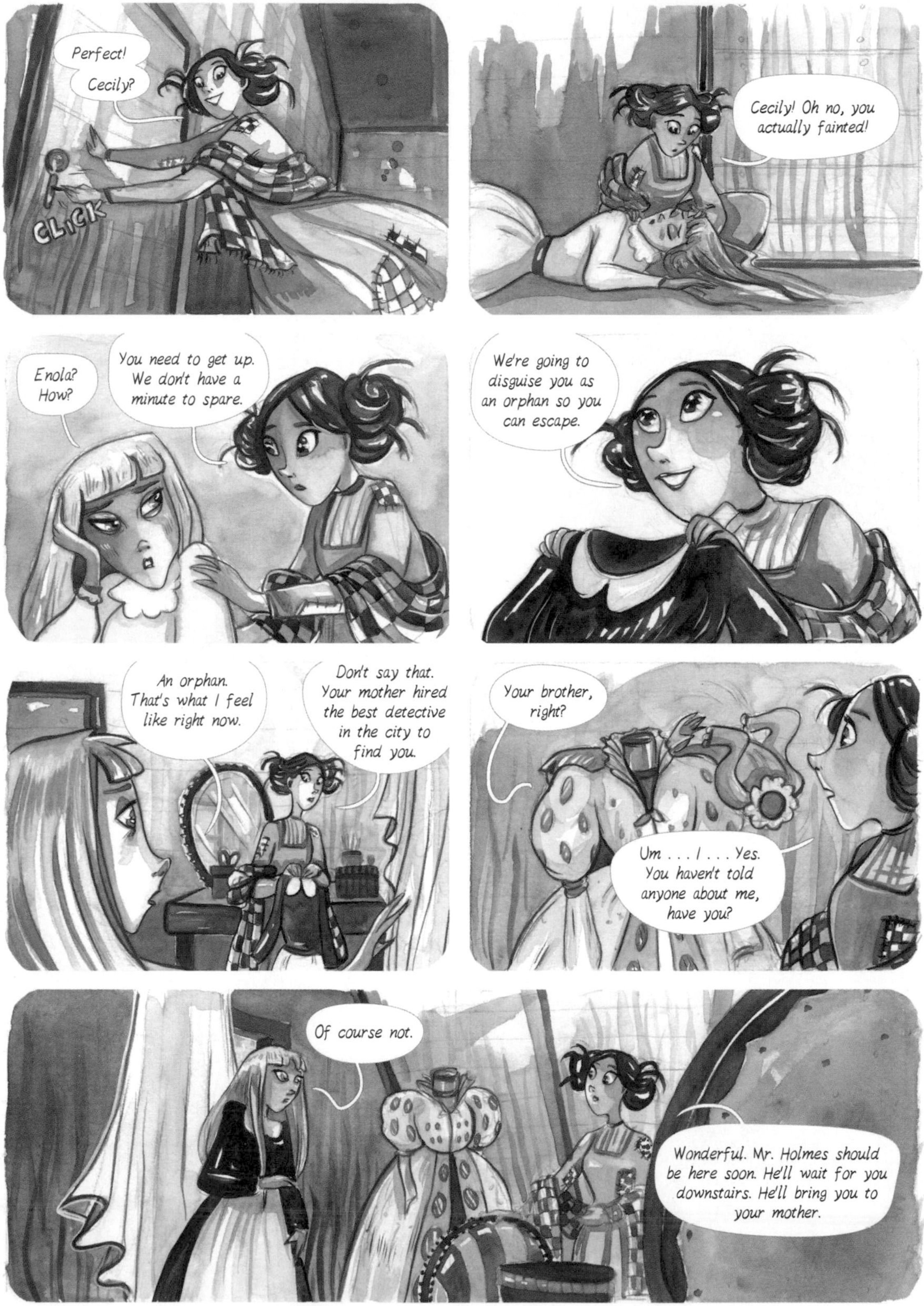
Perfect!
Cecily?
CLICK
Cecily! Oh no, you actually fainted!
Enola? How?
You need to get up. We don't have a minute to spare.
We're going to disguise you as an orphan so you can escape.
An orphan. That's what I feel like right now.
Don't say that. Your mother hired the best detective in the city to find you.
Your brother, right?
Um . . . I . . . Yes. You haven't told anyone about me, have you?
Of course not.
Wonderful. Mr. Holmes should be here soon. He'll wait for you downstairs. He'll bring you to your mother.

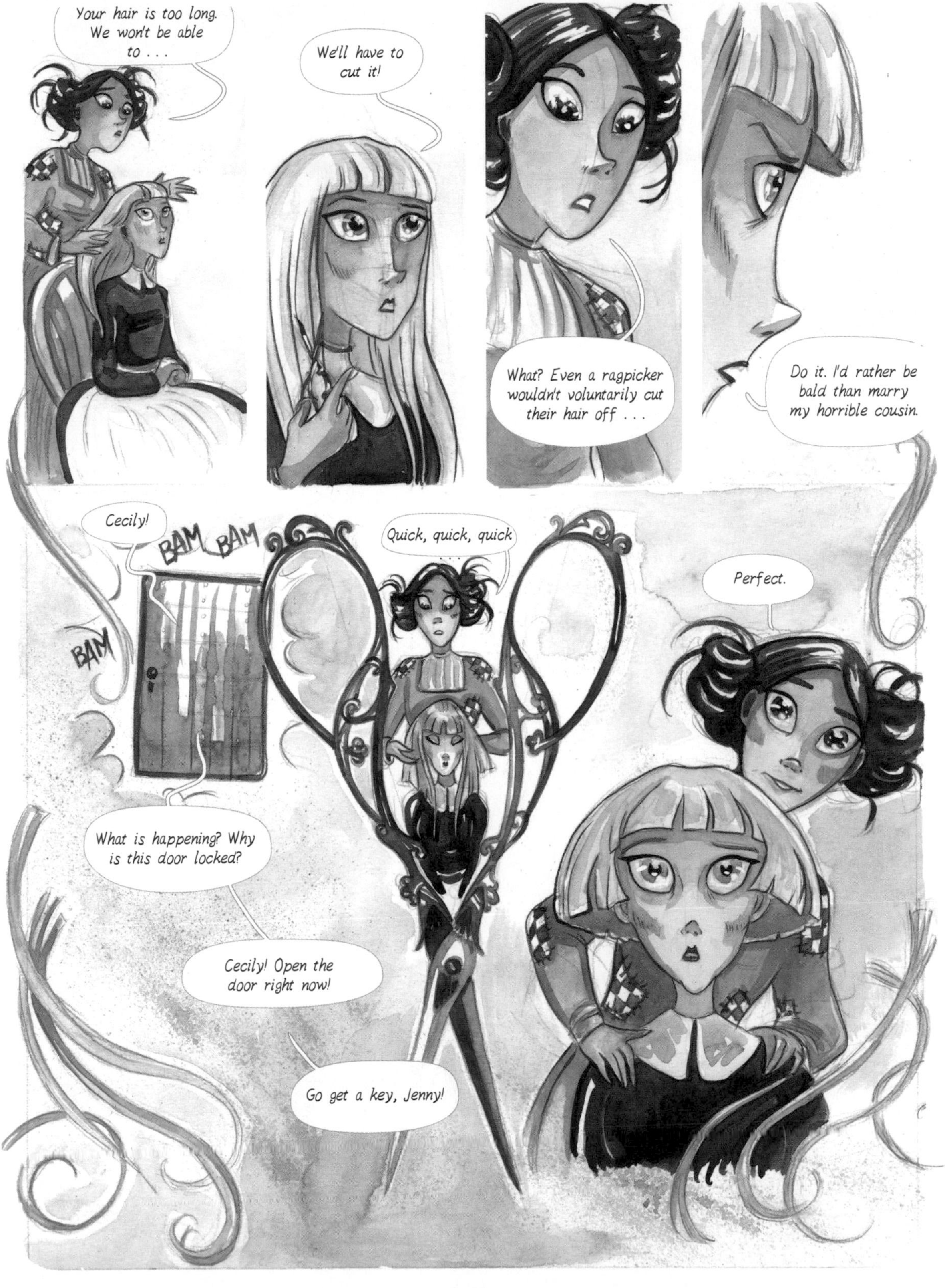
Your hair is too long. We won't be able to . . .
We'll have to cut it!
What? Even a ragpicker wouldn't voluntarily cut their hair off . . .
Do it. I'd rather be bald than marry my horrible cousin.
Cecily!
BAM BAM
BAM
Quick, quick, quick . . .
What is happening? Why is this door locked?
Cecily! Open the door right now!
Go get a key, Jenny!
Perfect.

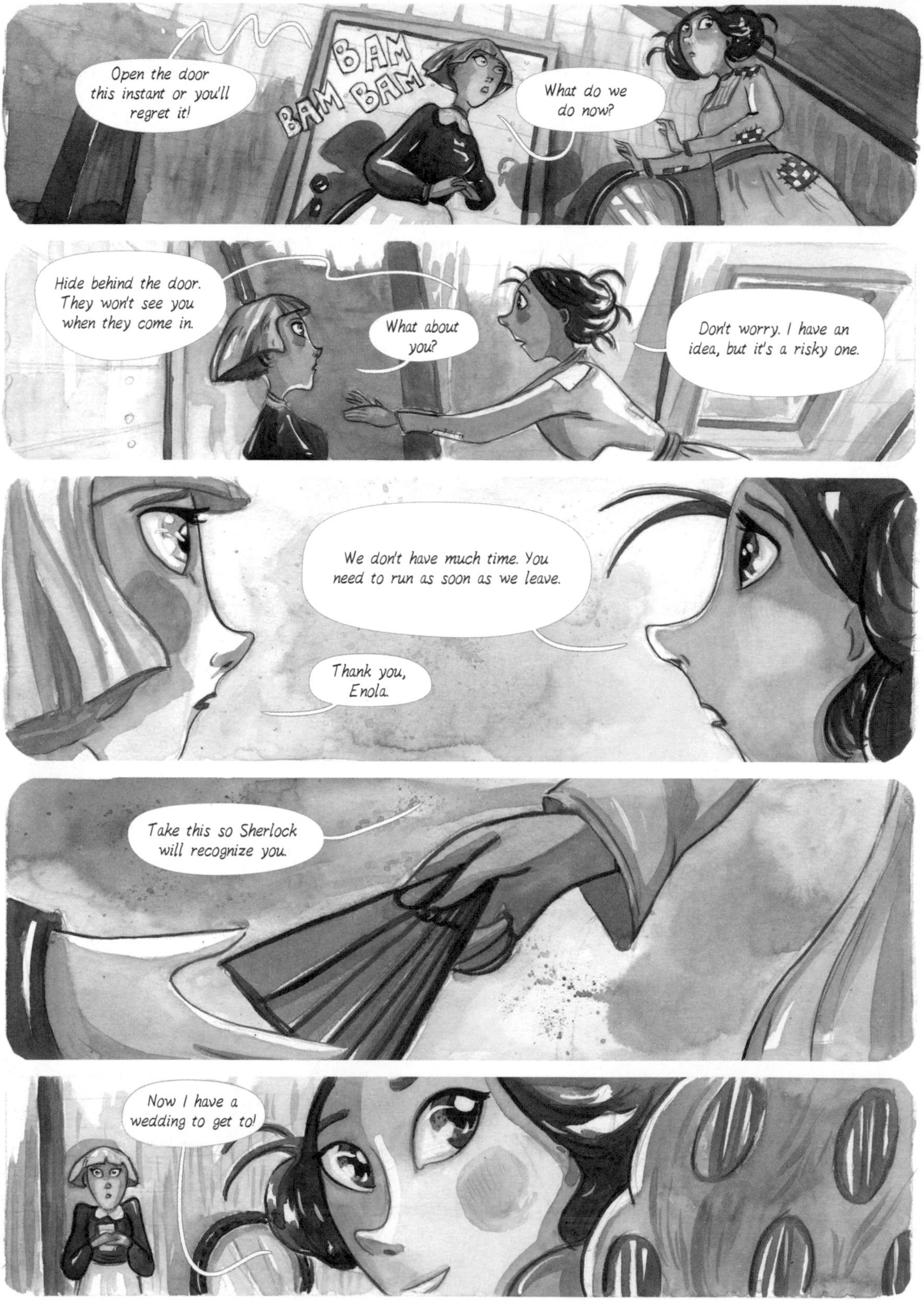
Open the door this instant or you'll regret it!
BAM BAM BAM
What do we do now?
Hide behind the door. They won't see you when they come in.
What about you?
Don't worry. I have an idea, but it's a risky one.
We don't have much time. You need to run as soon as we leave.
Thank you, Enola.
Take this so Sherlock will recognize you.
Now I have a wedding to get to!

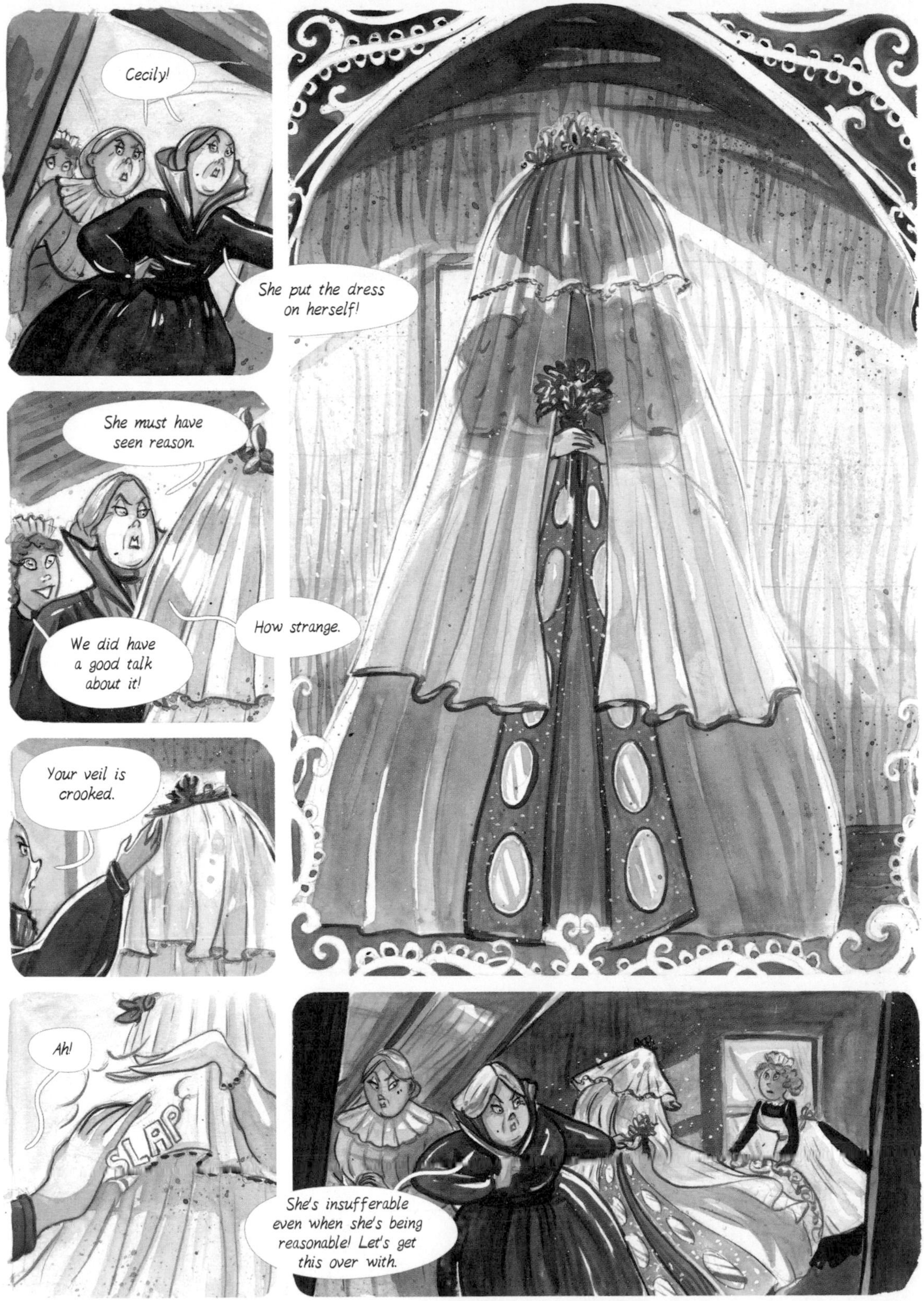
Cecily!
She put the dress on herself!
She must have seen reason.
How strange.
We did have a good talk about it!
Your veil is crooked.
Ah!
SLAP
She's insufferable even when she's being reasonable! Let's get this over with.

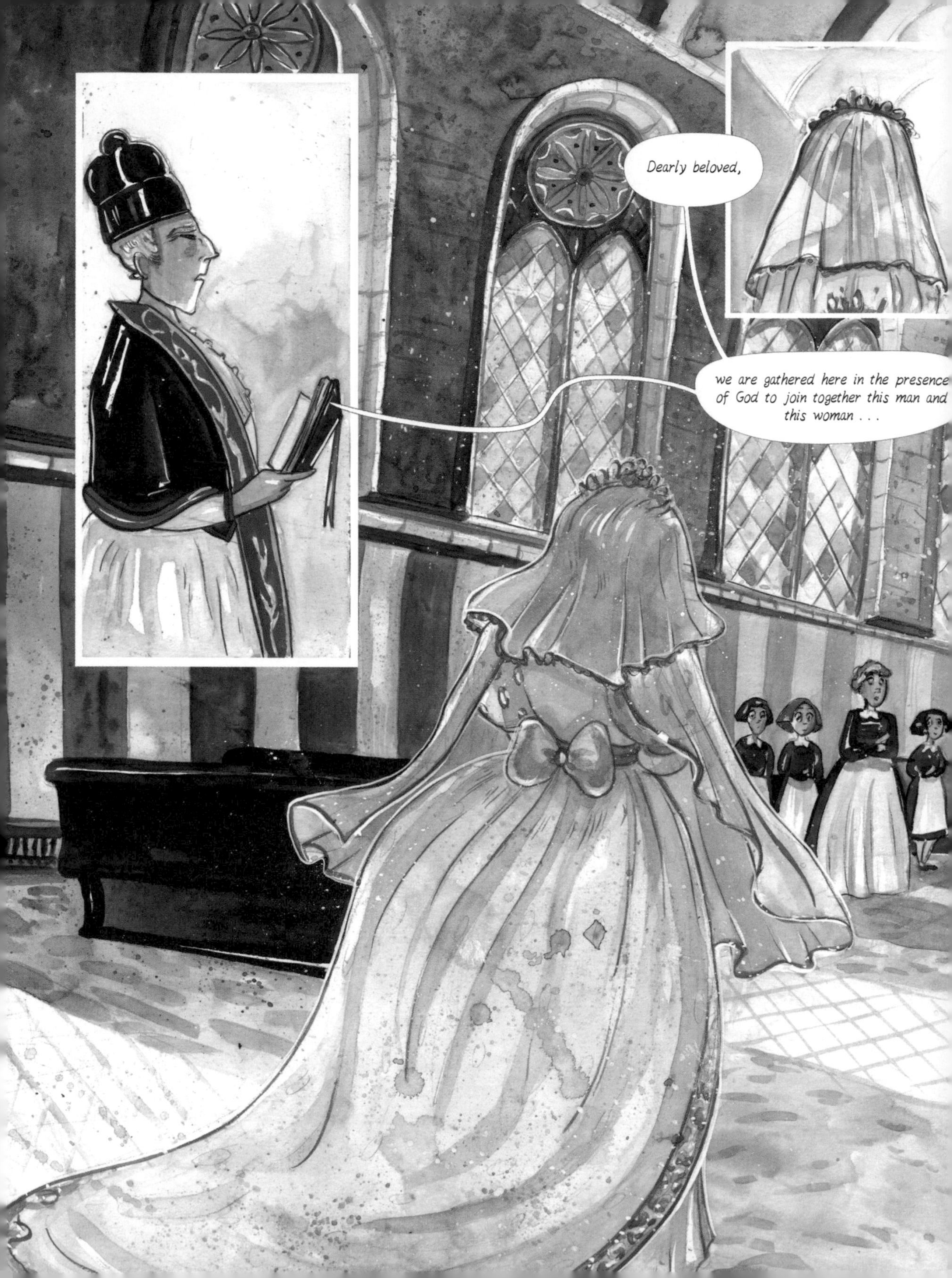

Dearly beloved,
we are gathered here in the presence of God to join together this man and this woman . . .

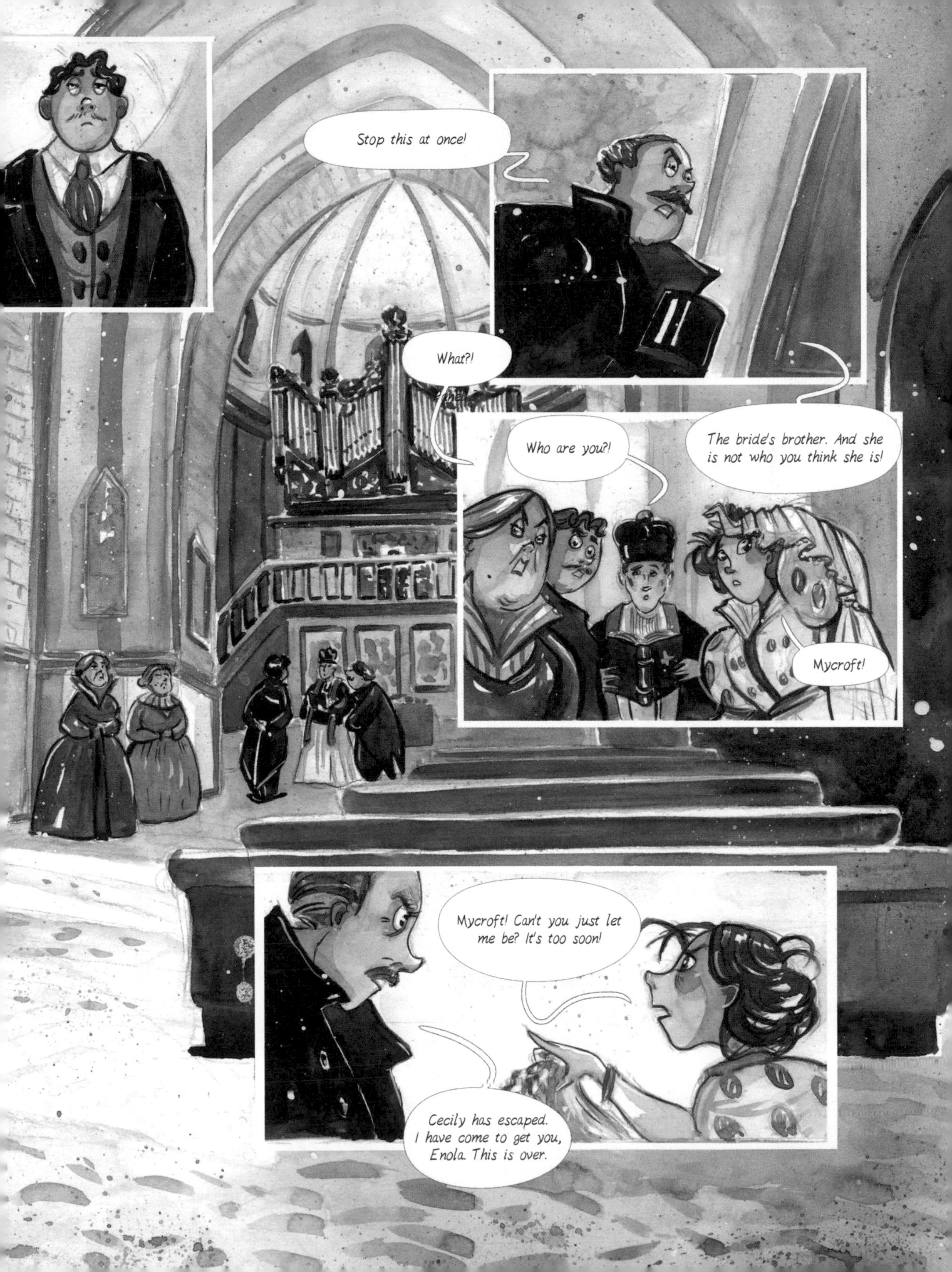

Stop this at once!
What?!
Who are you?!
The bride's brother. And she is not who you think she is!
Mycroft!
Mycroft! Can't you just let me be? It's too soon!
Cecily has escaped. I have come to get you, Enola. This is over.

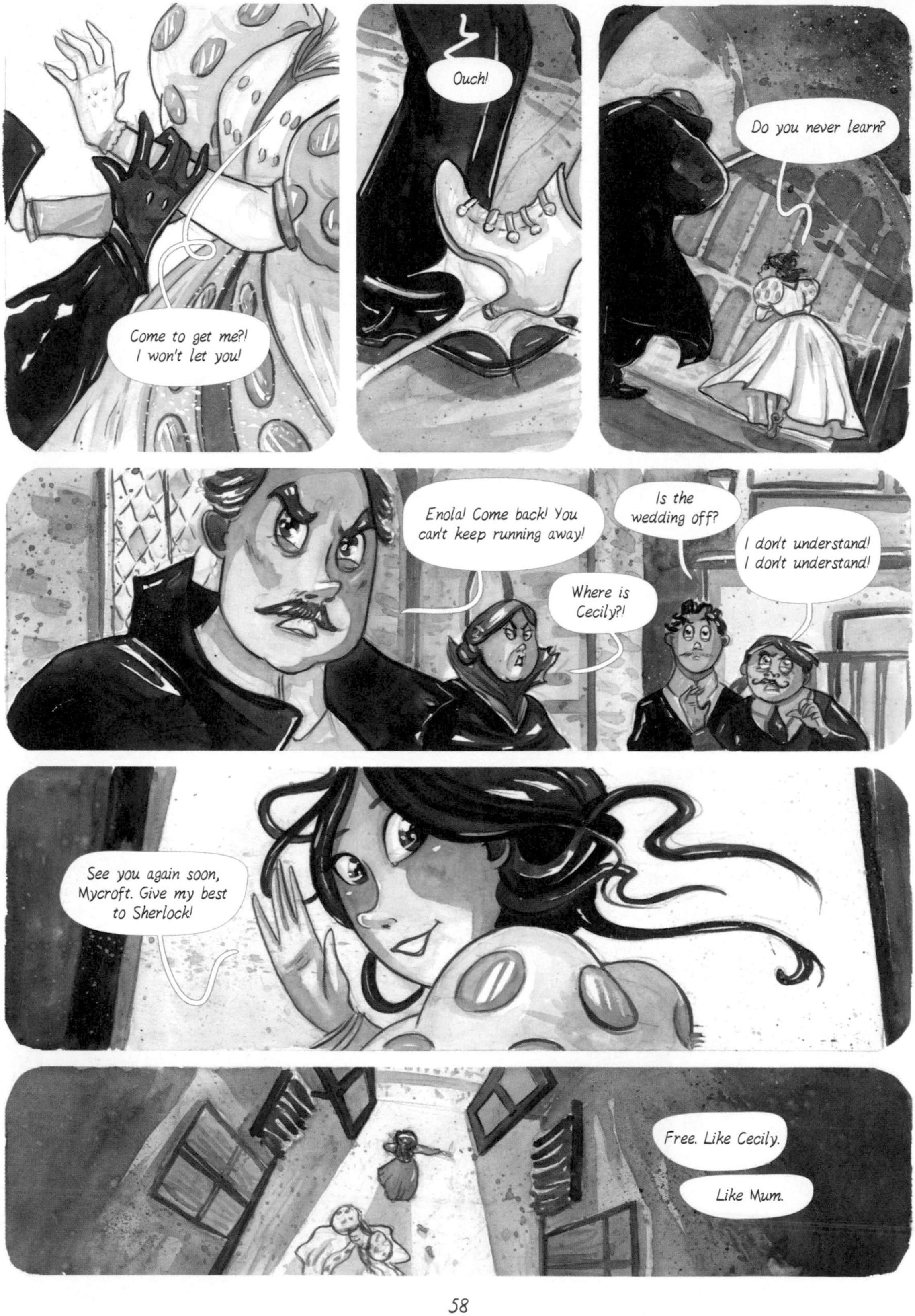
Come to get me?! I won't let you!
Ouch!
Do you never learn?
Enola! Come back! You can't keep running away!
Where is Cecily?!
Is the wedding off?
I don't understand! I don't understand!
See you again soon, Mycroft. Give my best to Sherlock!
Free. Like Cecily.
Like Mum.

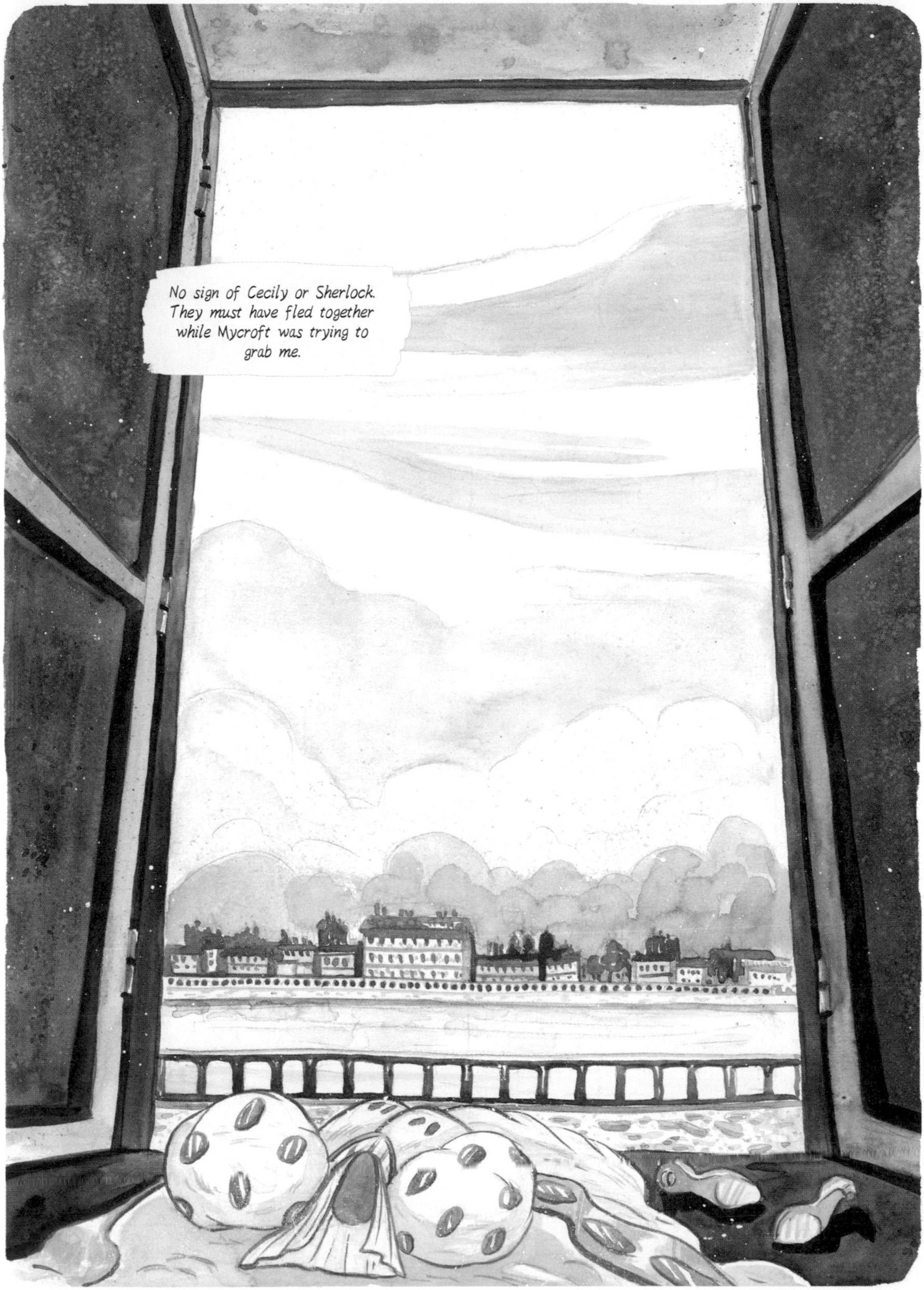
No sign of Cecily or Sherlock. They must have fled together while Mycroft was trying to grab me.

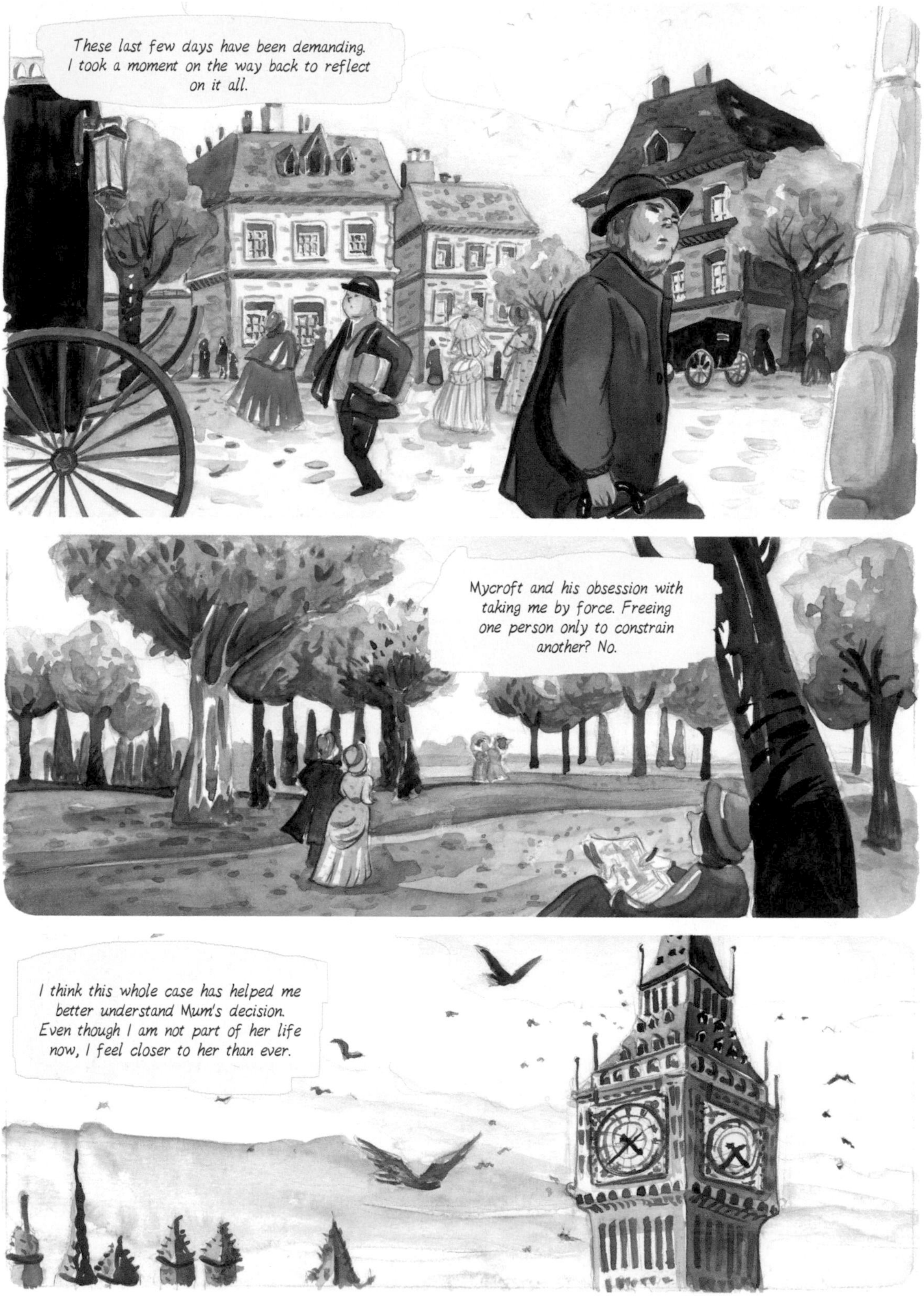
These last few days have been demanding. I took a moment on the way back to reflect on it all.
Mycroft and his obsession with taking me by force. Freeing one person only to constrain another? No.
I think this whole case has helped me better understand Mum's decision. Even though I am not part of her life now, I feel closer to her than ever.

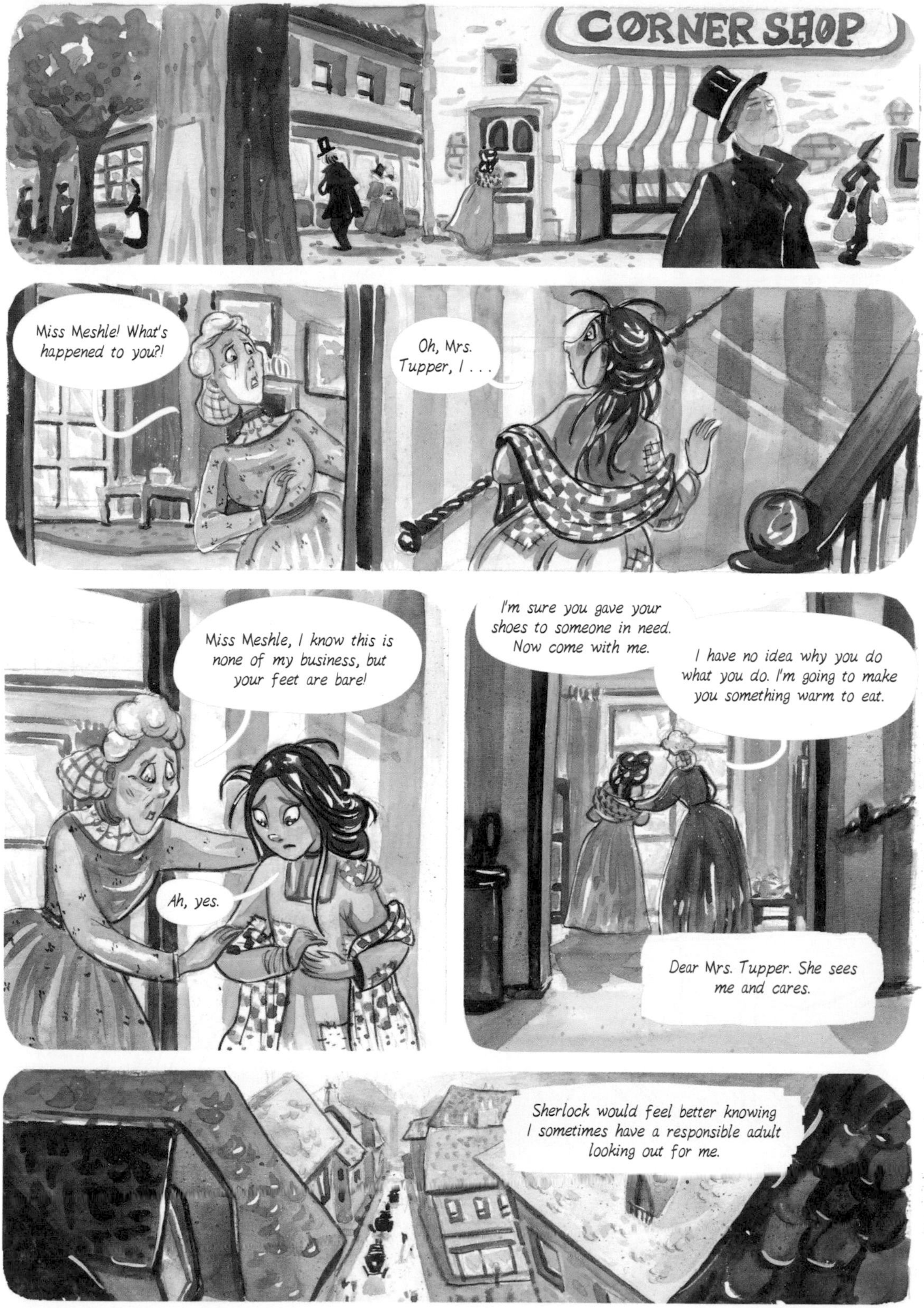
CORNER SHOP
Miss Meshle! What's happened to you?!
Oh, Mrs. Tupper, I . . .
Miss Meshle, I know this is none of my business, but your feet are bare!
Ah, yes.
I'm sure you gave your shoes to someone in need. Now come with me.
I have no idea why you do what you do. I'm going to make you something warm to eat.
Dear Mrs. Tupper. She sees me and cares.
Sherlock would feel better knowing I sometimes have a responsible adult looking out for me.

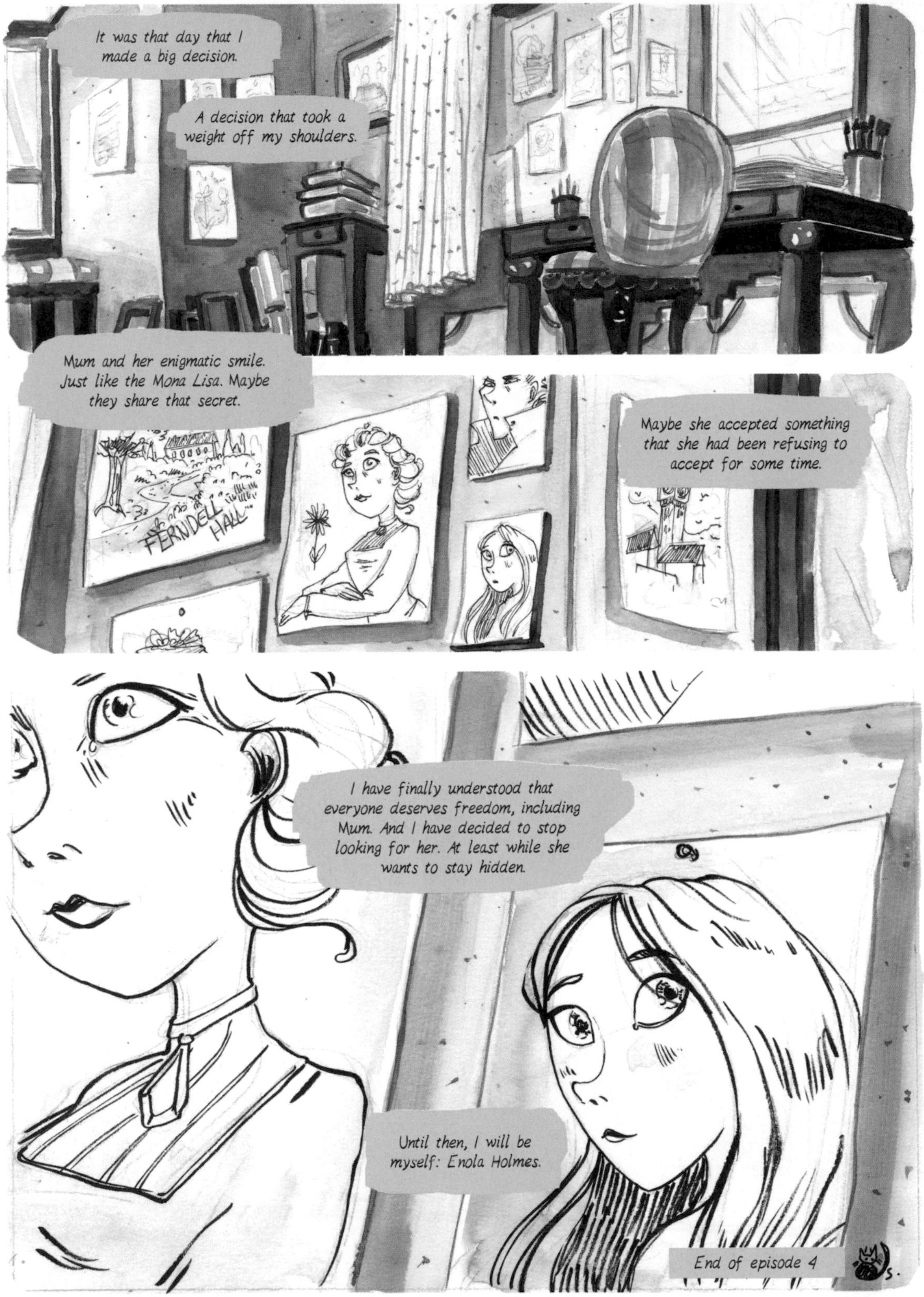
It was that day that I made a big decision.
A decision that took a weight off my shoulders.
Mum and her enigmatic smile. Just like the Mona Lisa. Maybe they share that secret.
FERNDELL HALL
Maybe she accepted something that she had been refusing to accept for some time.
I have finally understood that everyone deserves freedom, including Mum. And I have decided to stop looking for her. At least while she wants to stay hidden.
Until then, I will be myself: Enola Holmes.
End of episode 4

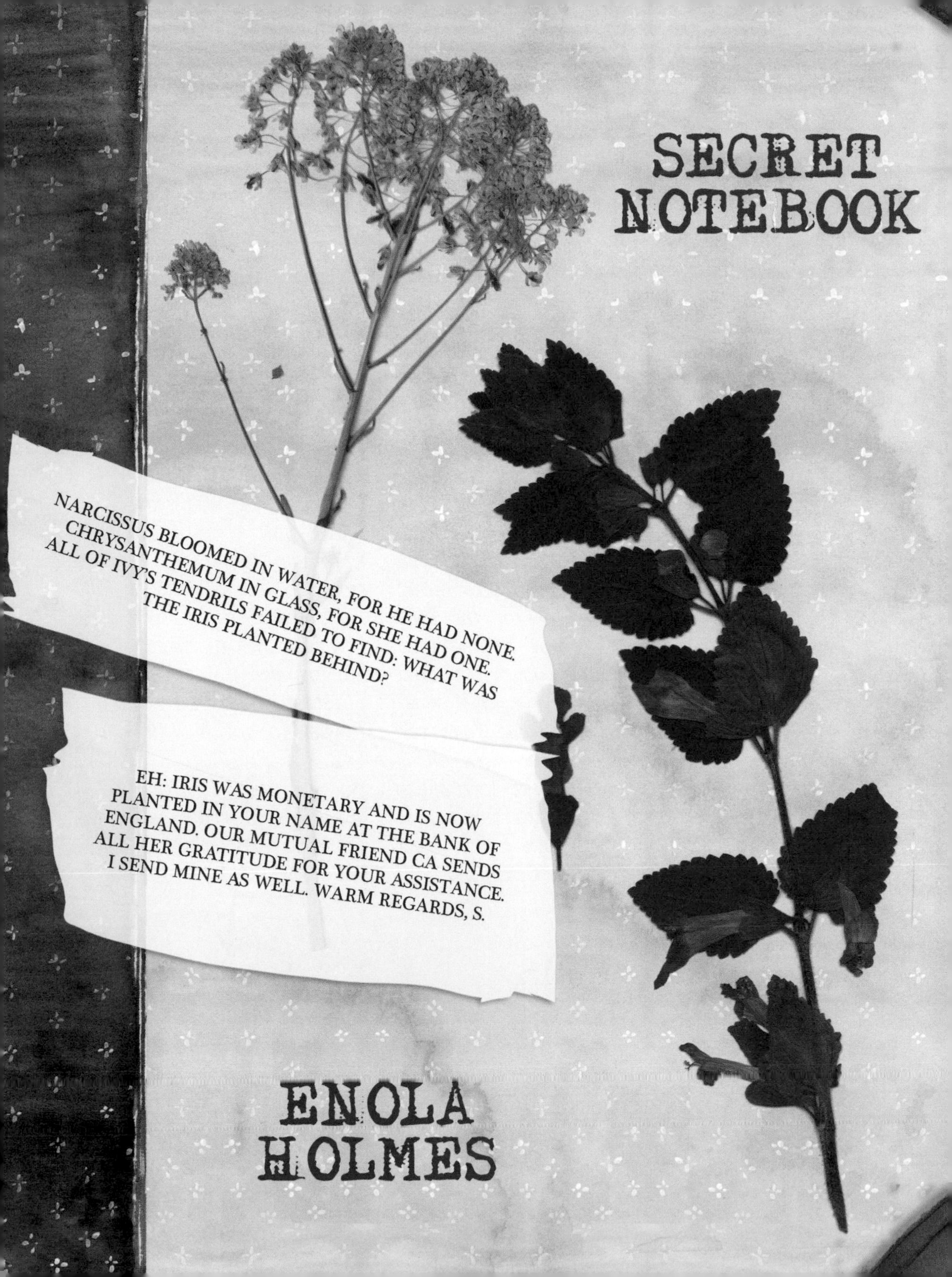
SECRET NOTEBOOK
NARCISSUS BLOOMED IN WATER, FOR HE HAD NONE. CHRYSANTHEMUM IN GLASS, FOR SHE HAD ONE. ALL OF IVY'S TENDRILS FAILED TO FIND: WHAT WAS THE IRIS PLANTED BEHIND?
EH: IRIS WAS MONETARY AND IS NOW PLANTED IN YOUR NAME AT THE BANK OF ENGLAND. OUR MUTUAL FRIEND CA SENDS ALL HER GRATITUDE FOR YOUR ASSISTANCE. I SEND MINE AS WELL. WARM REGARDS, S.
ENOLA HOLMES

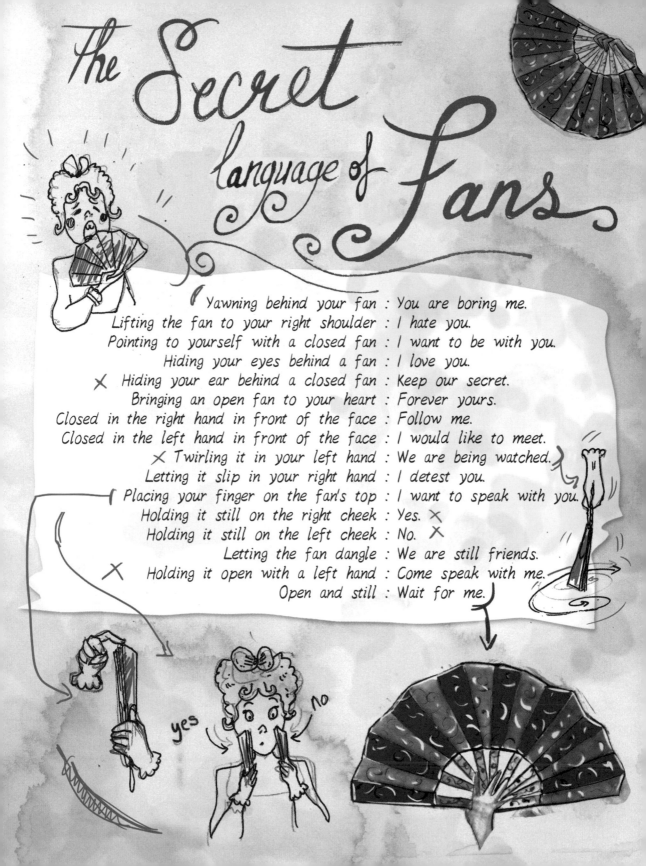

The Secret language of Fans

Yawning behind your fan : You are boring me.
Lifting the fan to your right shoulder : I hate you.
Pointing to yourself with a closed fan : I want to be with you.
Hiding your eyes behind a fan : I love you.
Hiding your ear behind a closed fan : Keep our secret.
Bringing an open fan to your heart : Forever yours.
Closed in the right hand in front of the face : Follow me.
Closed in the left hand in front of the face : I would like to meet.
Twirling it in your left hand : We are being watched.
Letting it slip in your right hand : I detest you.
Placing your finger on the fan's top : I want to speak with you.
Holding it still on the right cheek : Yes.
Holding it still on the left cheek : No.
Letting the fan dangle : We are still friends.
Holding it open with a left hand : Come speak with me.
Open and still : Wait for me.

yes   no

The Alistair Mystery

The two dragon sisters are rather intimidating. And not in a good way.

Eustace, brother dragon, Cecily's father.

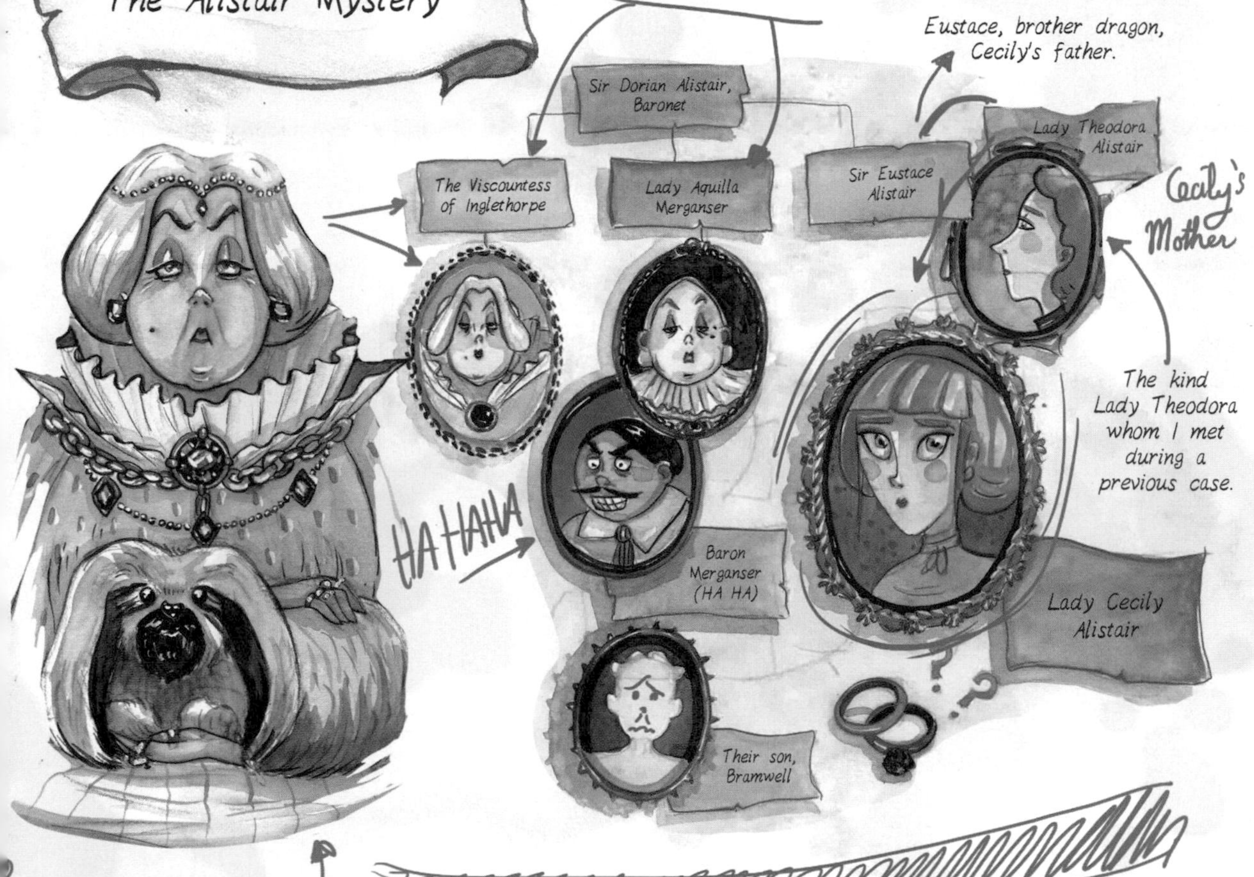

Sir Dorian Alistair, Baronet
The Viscountess of Inglethorpe
Lady Aquilla Merganser
Sir Eustace Alistair
Lady Theodora Alistair
Cecily's Mother
HA HAHA
Baron Merganser (HA HA)
Lady Cecily Alistair
Their son, Bramwell

The kind Lady Theodora whom I met during a previous case.

The Viscountess of Inglethorpe's pink tea

That room might have scarred me for life! If you like pink, it's perfect; if you don't . . .

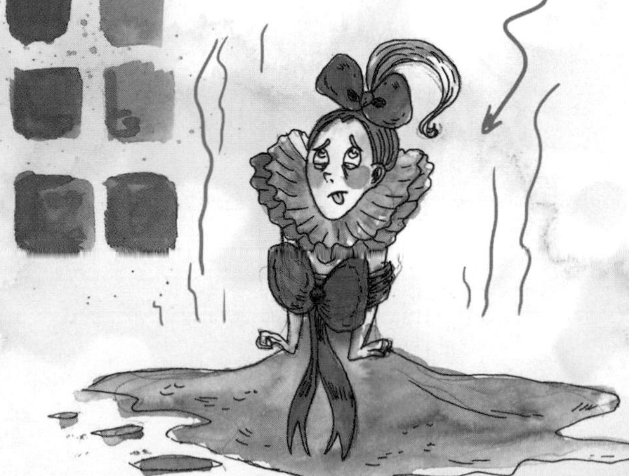

The ha-ha is a ditch you can't see from a distance. If you're not paying attention, you fall in and can only get back out if the homeowner wants to let you.

Sherlock fell in and I didn't!

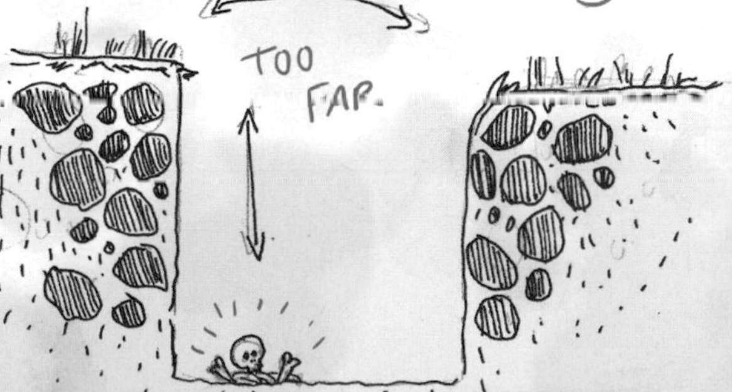

TOO FAR.

New Code

A B C D E F G H I
J K L M
N. O. P. Q. R. S. T. U. V.
W X Y Z

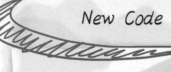

You reproduce the lines and dots where the letter is.

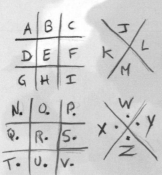

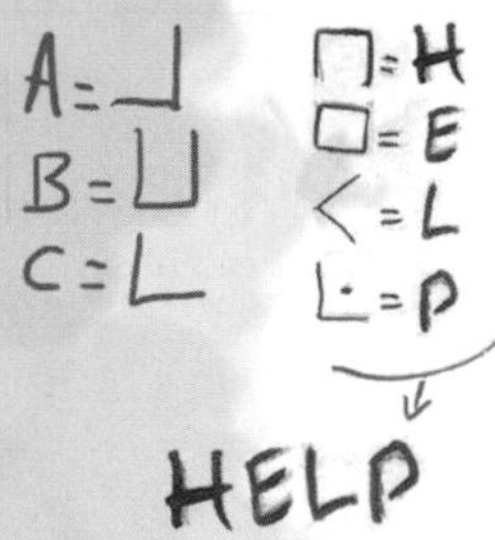

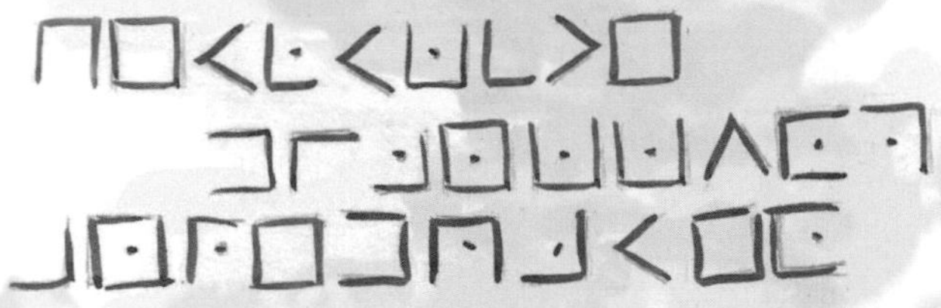

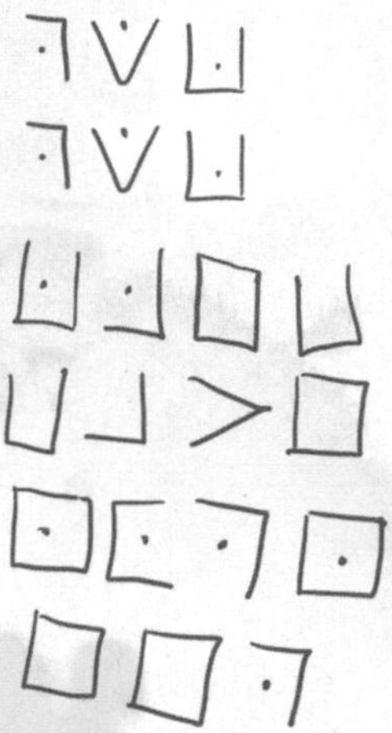

A=
B=
C=
=H
=E
=L
=P
HELP

HELP | LOCKED | IN | ROOM
STARVED | UNLES

Writing a message in invisible ink:

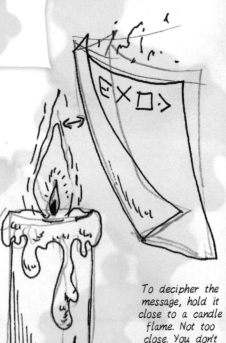

You need a lemon, a little bowl for the lemon juice, a paint brush, and a piece of blank paper.

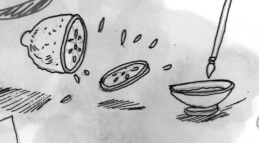

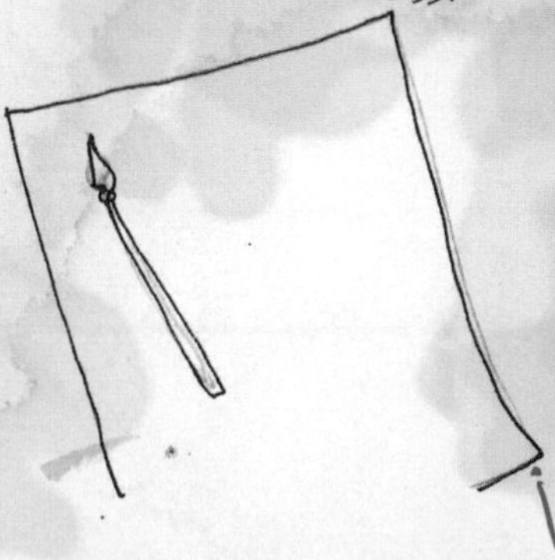

Write the message on the paper using the brush dipped in lemon juice, then let the paper dry. Consider what you want to write ahead of time because it's like writing with water.

INVISIBLE

To decipher the message, hold it close to a candle flame. Not too close. You don't want to burn the paper.

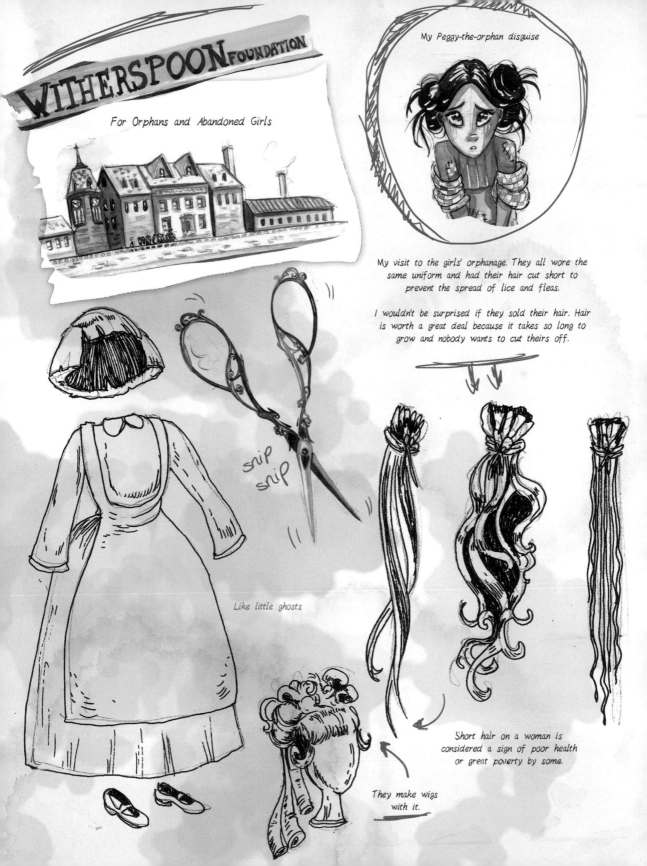

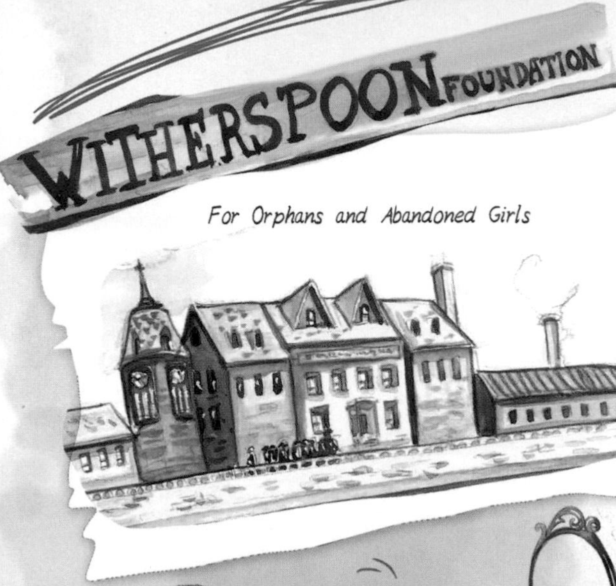
WITHERSPOON FOUNDATION
For Orphans and Abandoned Girls

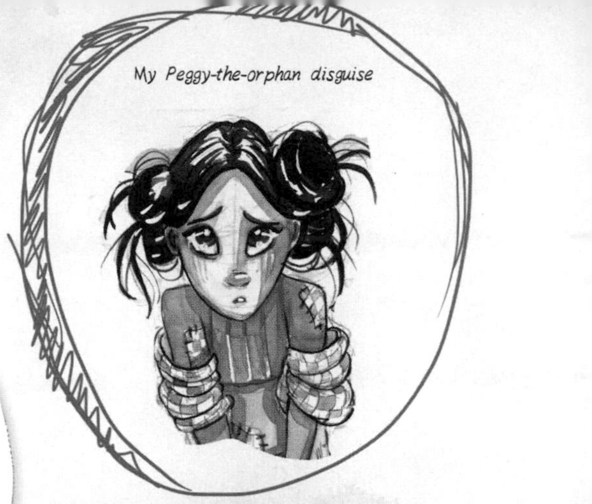

My Peggy-the-orphan disguise

My visit to the girls' orphanage. They all wore the same uniform and had their hair cut short to prevent the spread of lice and fleas.

I wouldn't be surprised if they sold their hair. Hair is worth a great deal because it takes so long to grow and nobody wants to cut theirs off.

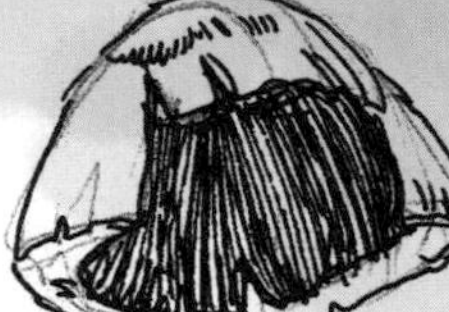

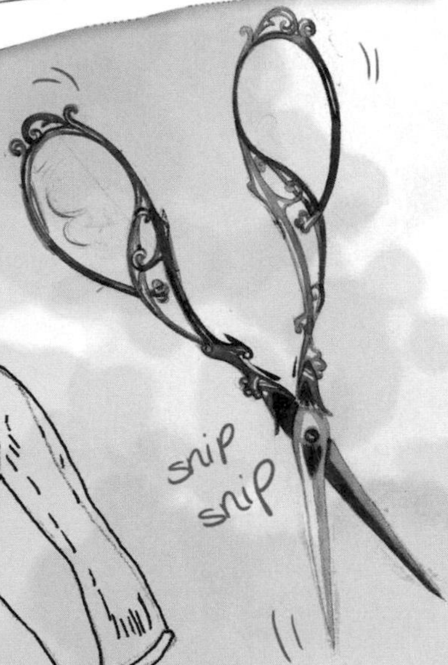
snip
snip

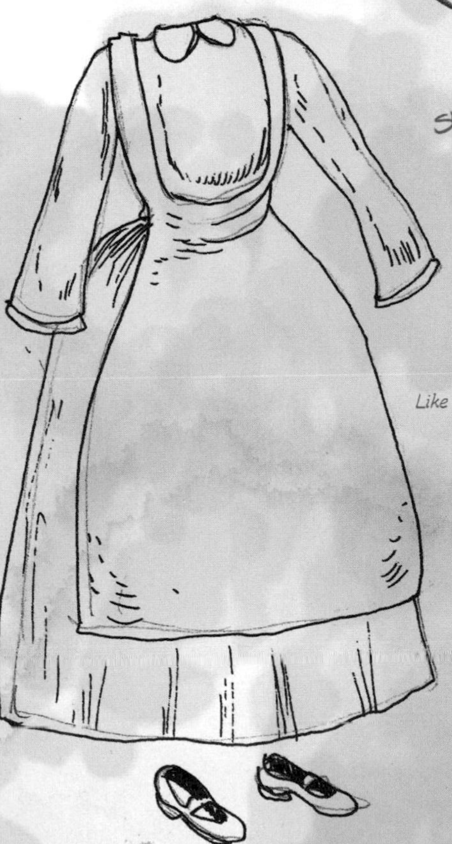

Like little ghosts

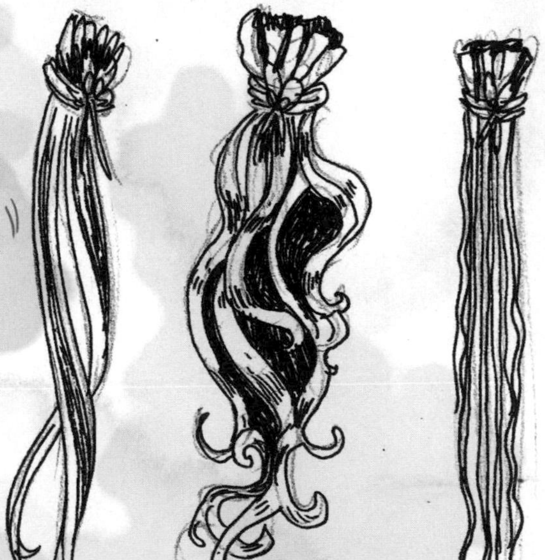

Short hair on a woman is considered a sign of poor health or great poverty by some.

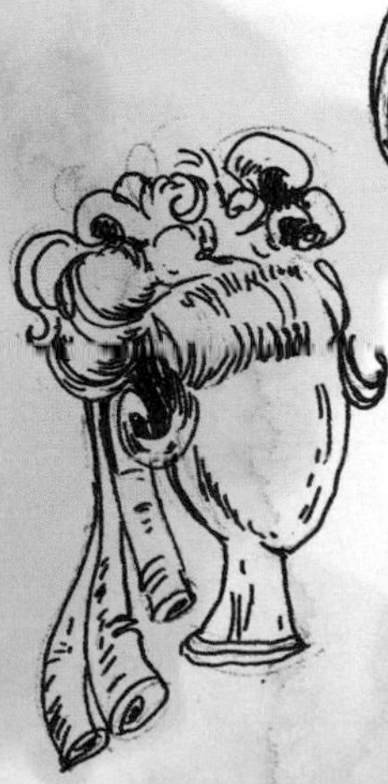

They make wigs with it.

Sherlock,
Tomorrow morning, shortly before the wedding is due to begin, CA will try to escape from the Witherspoon orphanage, 472 Huxtable Lane, with a pink fan in hand. I am counting on you to help her from there.
E.H

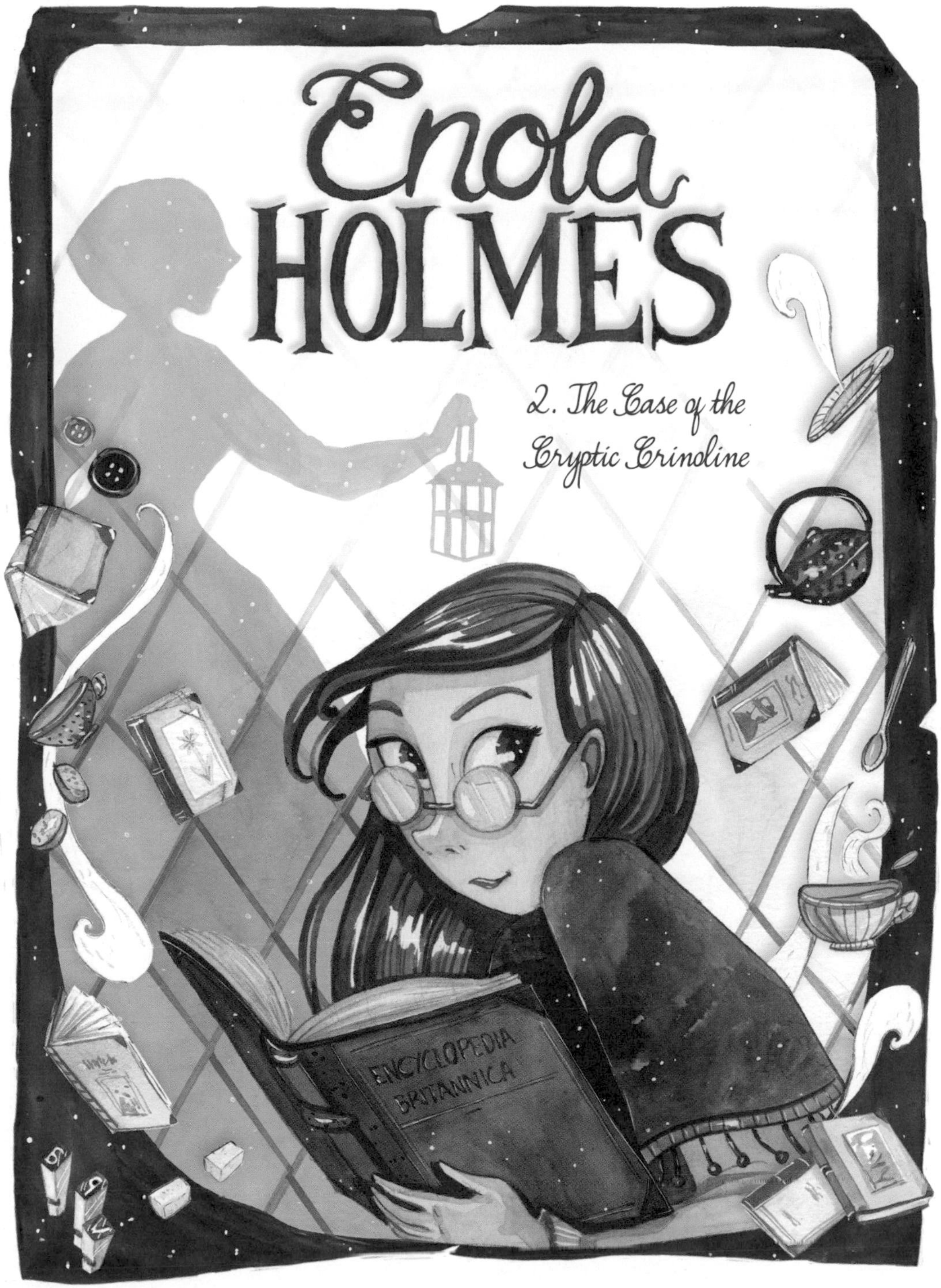
Enola
HOLMES
2. The Case of the
Cryptic Crinoline
ENCYCLOPEDIA
BRITANNICA

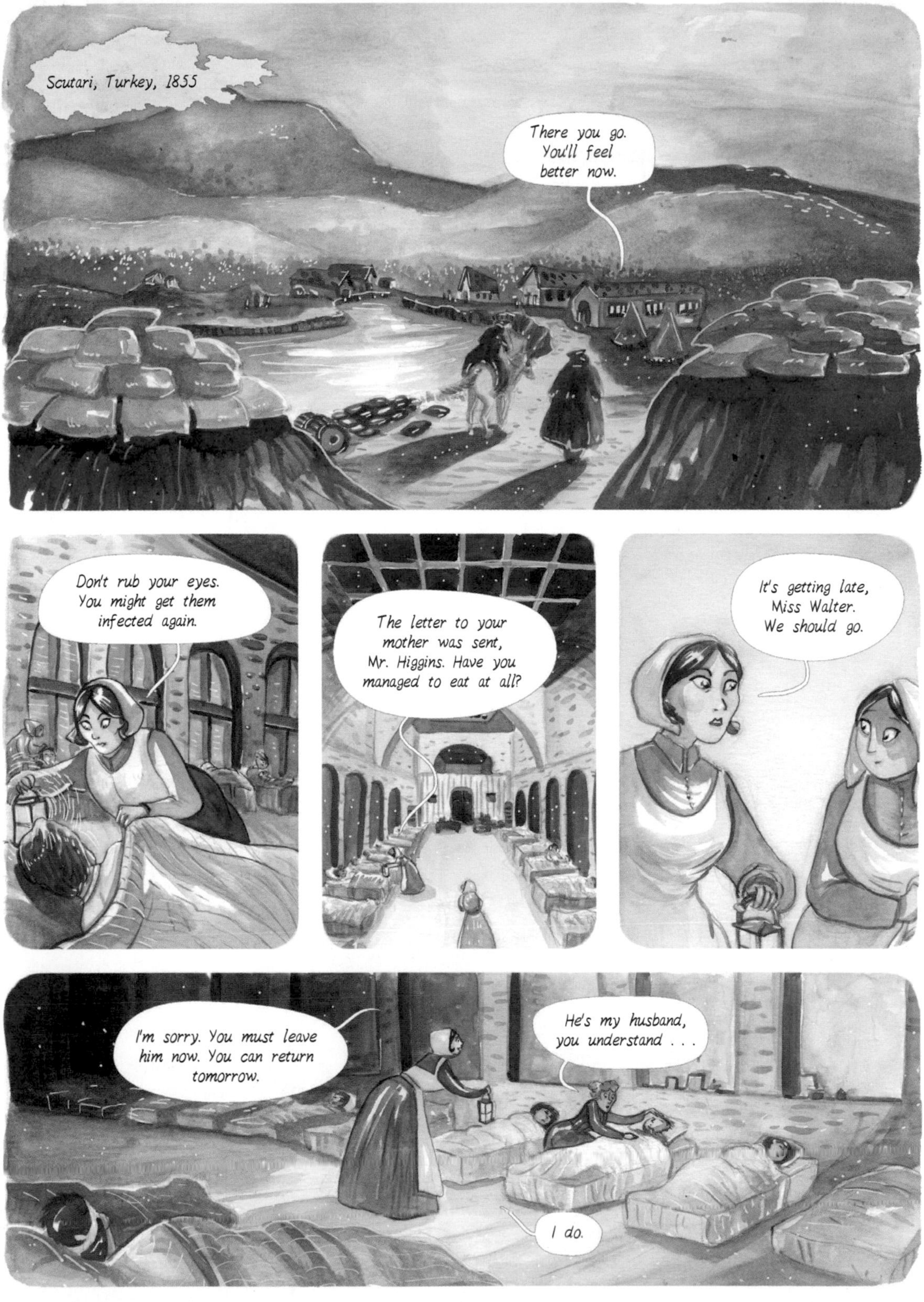
Scutari, Turkey, 1855
There you go. You'll feel better now.
Don't rub your eyes. You might get them infected again.
The letter to your mother was sent, Mr. Higgins. Have you managed to eat at all?
It's getting late, Miss Walter. We should go.
I'm sorry. You must leave him now. You can return tomorrow.
He's my husband, you understand . . .
I do.

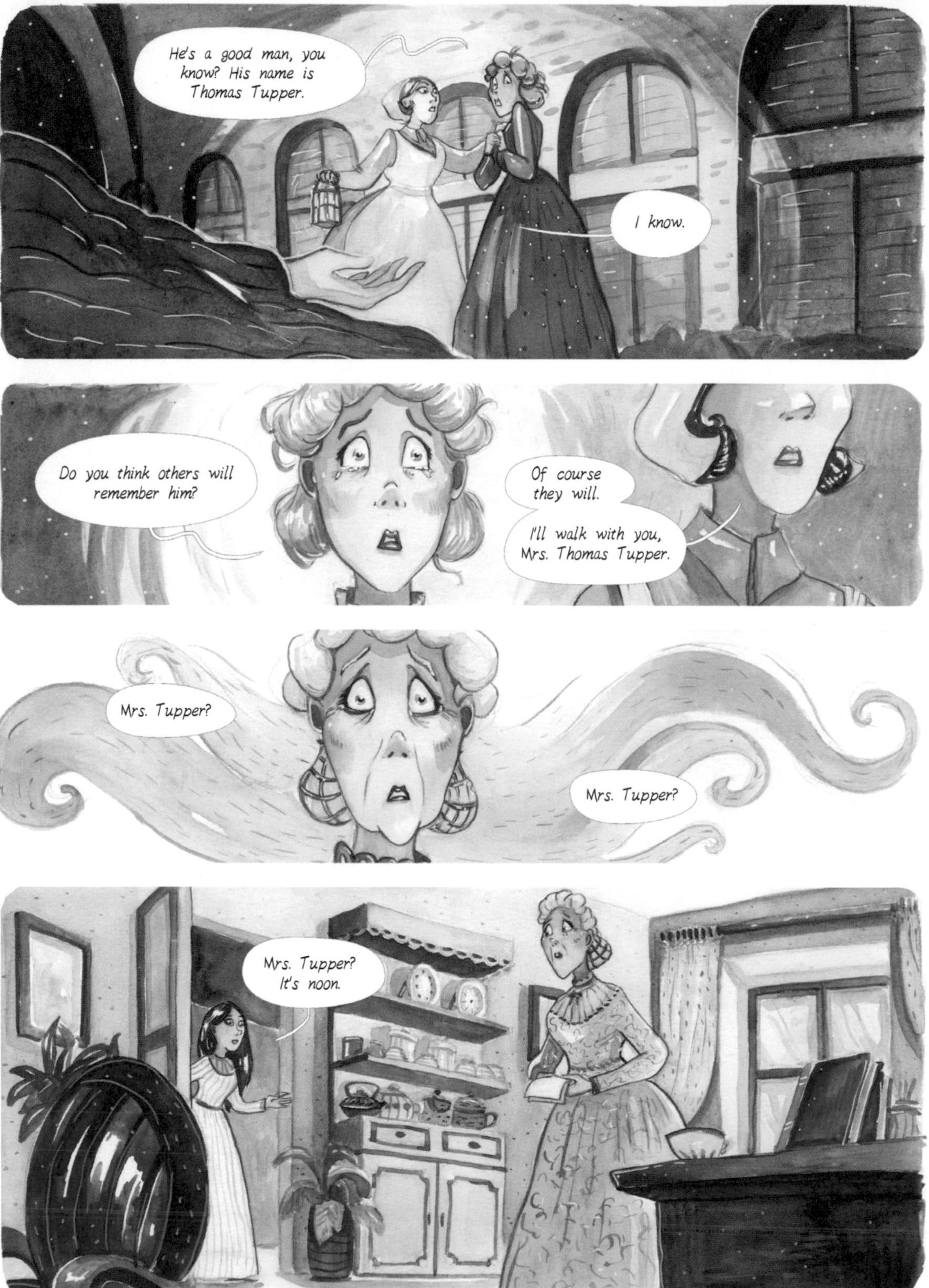
He's a good man, you know? His name is Thomas Tupper.
I know.
Do you think others will remember him?
Of course they will.
I'll walk with you, Mrs. Thomas Tupper.
Mrs. Tupper?
Mrs. Tupper?
Mrs. Tupper? It's noon.

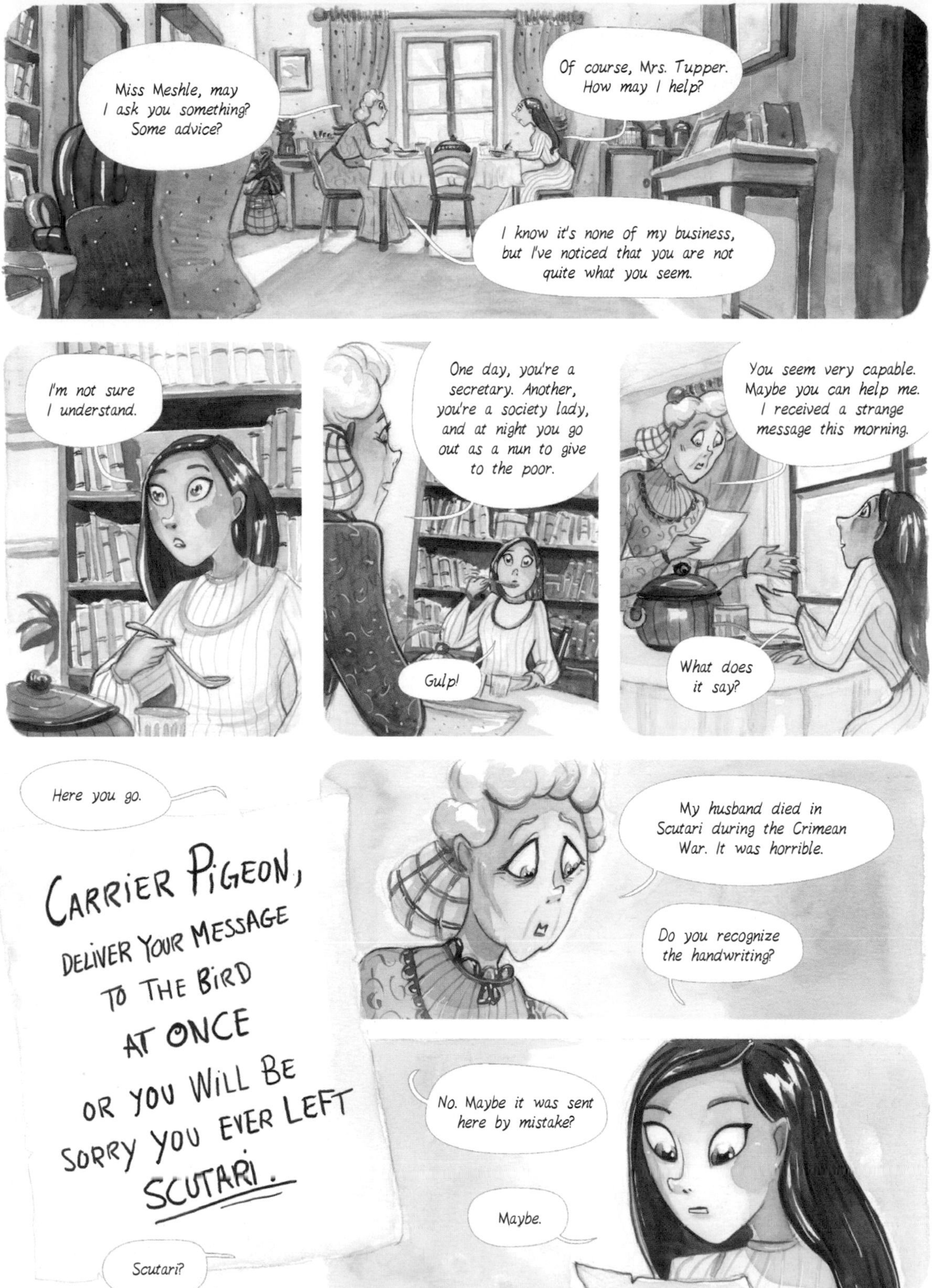

Miss Meshle, may I ask you something? Some advice?
Of course, Mrs. Tupper. How may I help?
I know it's none of my business, but I've noticed that you are not quite what you seem.
I'm not sure I understand.
One day, you're a secretary. Another, you're a society lady, and at night you go out as a nun to give to the poor.
Gulp!
You seem very capable. Maybe you can help me. I received a strange message this morning.
What does it say?
Here you go.
CARRIER PIGEON, DELIVER YOUR MESSAGE TO THE BIRD AT ONCE OR YOU WILL BE SORRY YOU EVER LEFT SCUTARI.
Scutari?
My husband died in Scutari during the Crimean War. It was horrible.
Do you recognize the handwriting?
No. Maybe it was sent here by mistake?
Maybe.

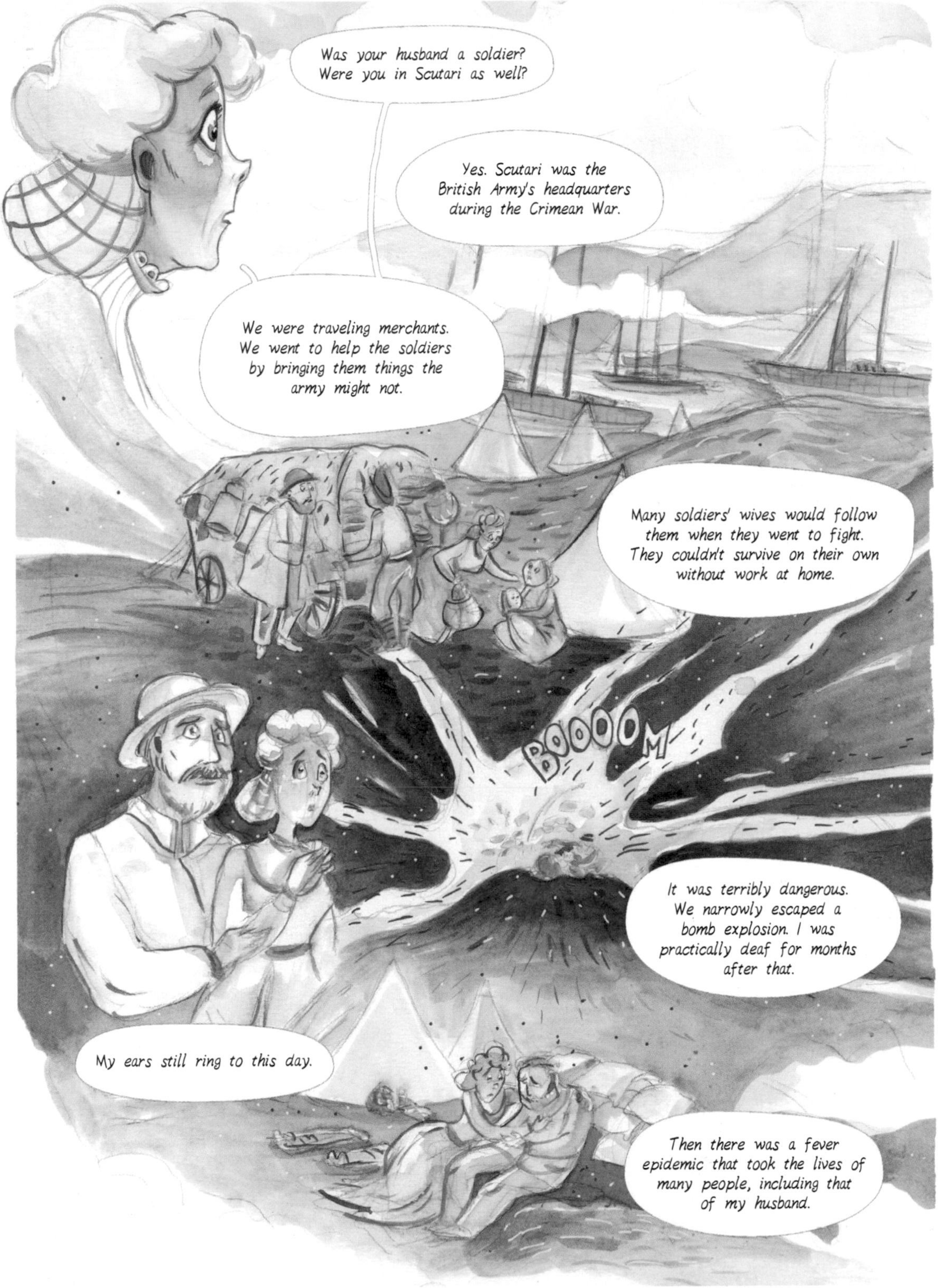
Was your husband a soldier? Were you in Scutari as well?
Yes. Scutari was the British Army's headquarters during the Crimean War.
We were traveling merchants. We went to help the soldiers by bringing them things the army might not.
Many soldiers' wives would follow them when they went to fight. They couldn't survive on their own without work at home.
BOOOOM
It was terribly dangerous. We narrowly escaped a bomb explosion. I was practically deaf for months after that.
My ears still ring to this day.
Then there was a fever epidemic that took the lives of many people, including that of my husband.

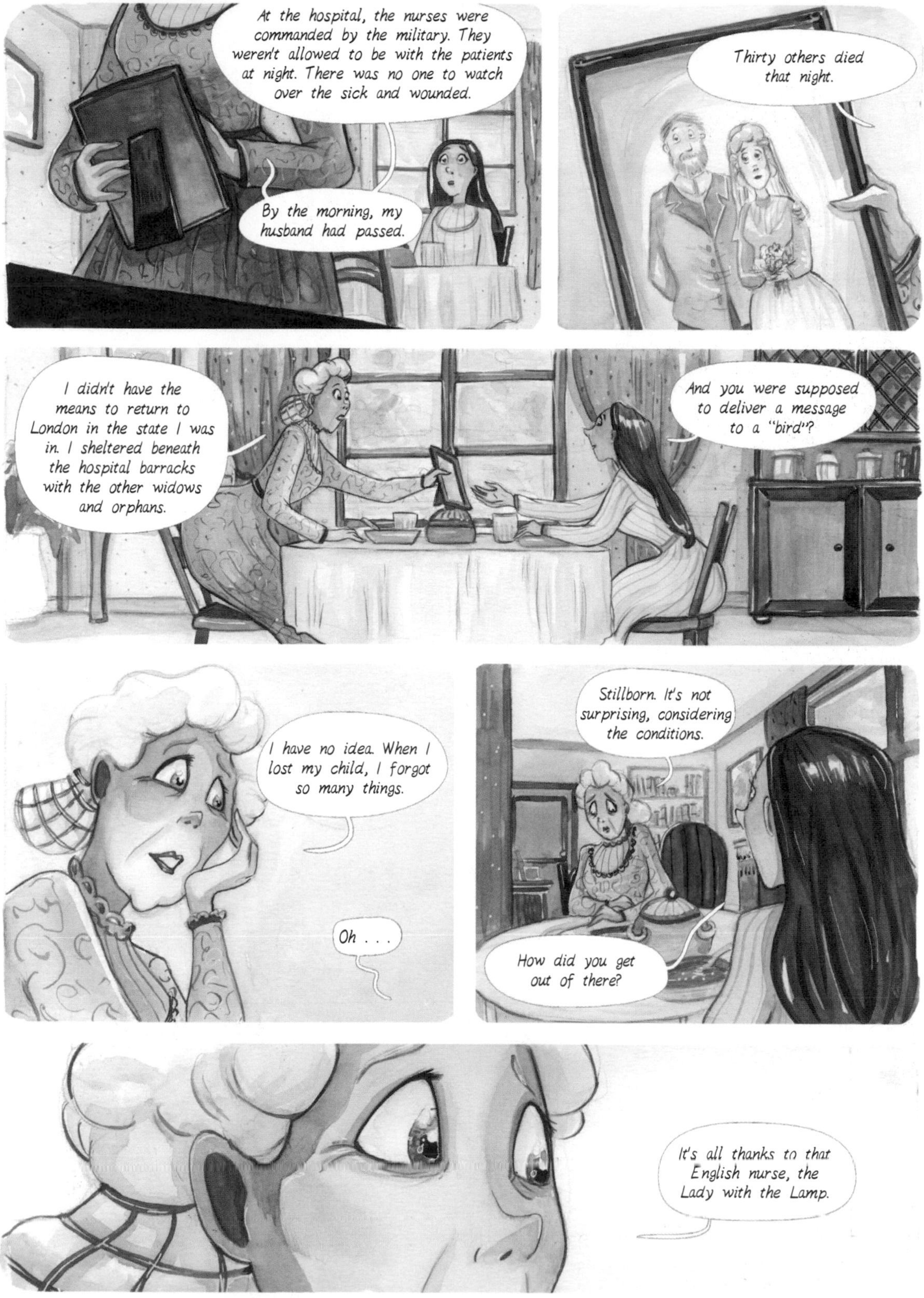
At the hospital, the nurses were commanded by the military. They weren't allowed to be with the patients at night. There was no one to watch over the sick and wounded.
By the morning, my husband had passed.
Thirty others died that night.
I didn't have the means to return to London in the state I was in. I sheltered beneath the hospital barracks with the other widows and orphans.
And you were supposed to deliver a message to a "bird"?
I have no idea. When I lost my child, I forgot so many things.
Oh . . .
Stillborn. It's not surprising, considering the conditions.
How did you get out of there?
It's all thanks to that English nurse, the Lady with the Lamp.

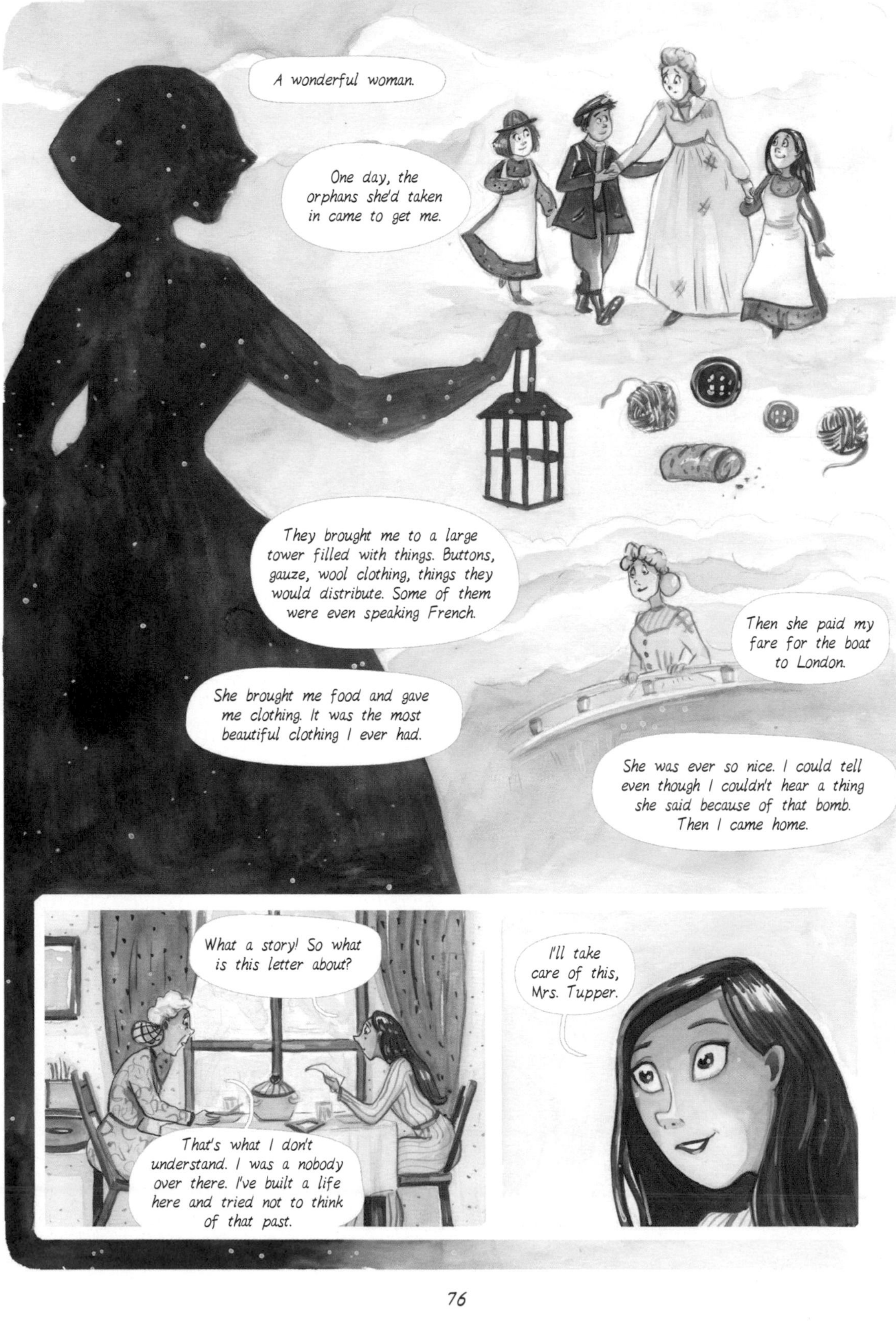
A wonderful woman.
One day, the orphans she'd taken in came to get me.
They brought me to a large tower filled with things. Buttons, gauze, wool clothing, things they would distribute. Some of them were even speaking French.
She brought me food and gave me clothing. It was the most beautiful clothing I ever had.
Then she paid my fare for the boat to London.
She was ever so nice. I could tell even though I couldn't hear a thing she said because of that bomb. Then I came home.
What a story! So what is this letter about?
That's what I don't understand. I was a nobody over there. I've built a life here and tried not to think of that past.
I'll take care of this, Mrs. Tupper.

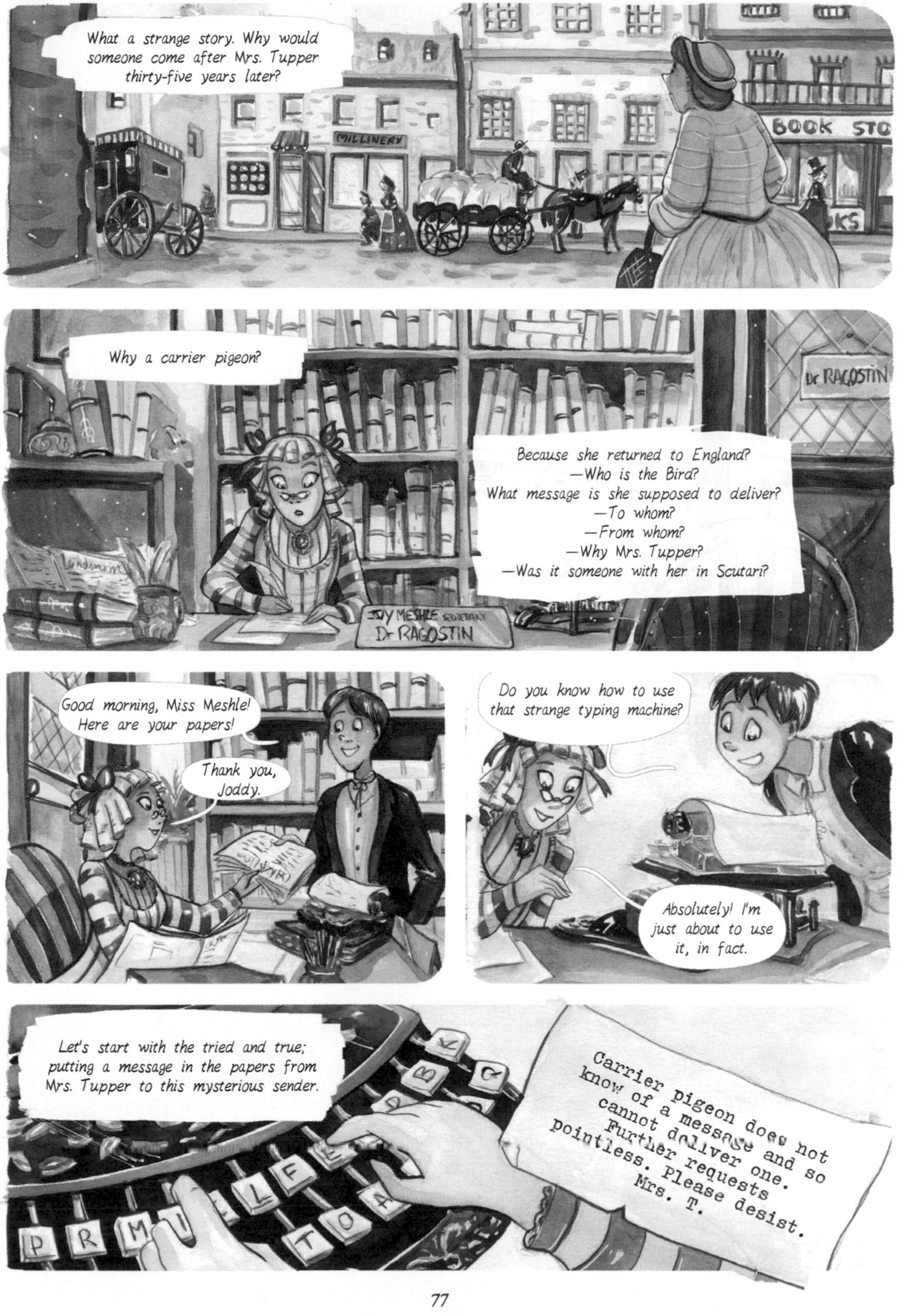
What a strange story. Why would someone come after Mrs. Tupper thirty-five years later?
MILLINERY
BOOK STO
Why a carrier pigeon?
Dr RAGOSTIN
Because she returned to England? —Who is the Bird? What message is she supposed to deliver? —To whom? —From whom? —Why Mrs. Tupper? —Was it someone with her in Scutari?
JOY MESHLE SECRETARY
Dr RAGOSTIN
Good morning, Miss Meshle! Here are your papers!
Thank you, Joddy.
Do you know how to use that strange typing machine?
Absolutely! I'm just about to use it, in fact.
Let's start with the tried and true; putting a message in the papers from Mrs. Tupper to this mysterious sender.
Carrier pigeon does not know of a message and so cannot deliver one. Further requests pointless. Please desist. Mrs. T.

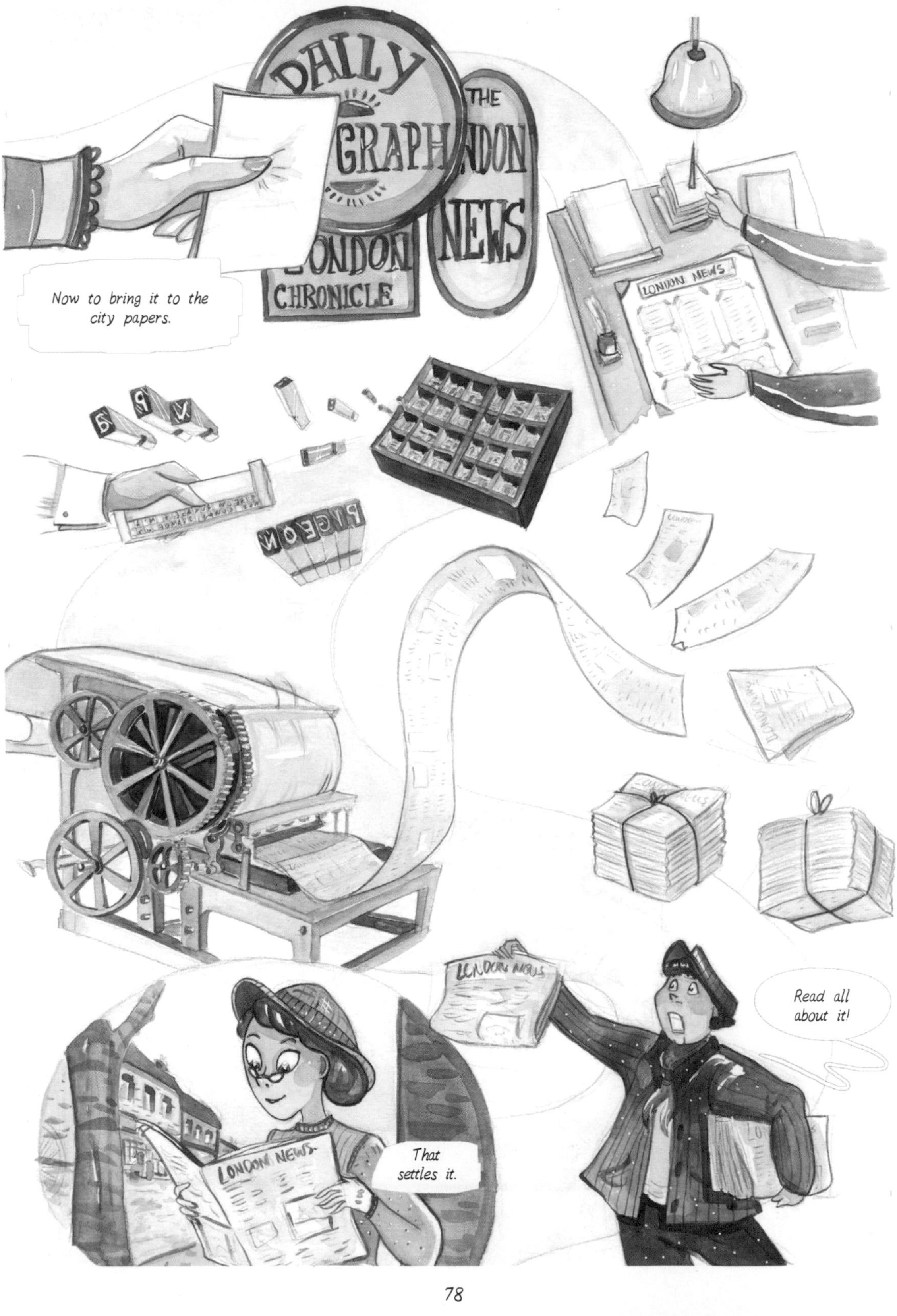

DAILY
GRAPH
LONDON
CHRONICLE
THE
LONDON
NEWS
Now to bring it to the city papers.
LONDON NEWS
PIGEON
LONDON NEWS
Read all about it!
LONDON NEWS
That settles it.

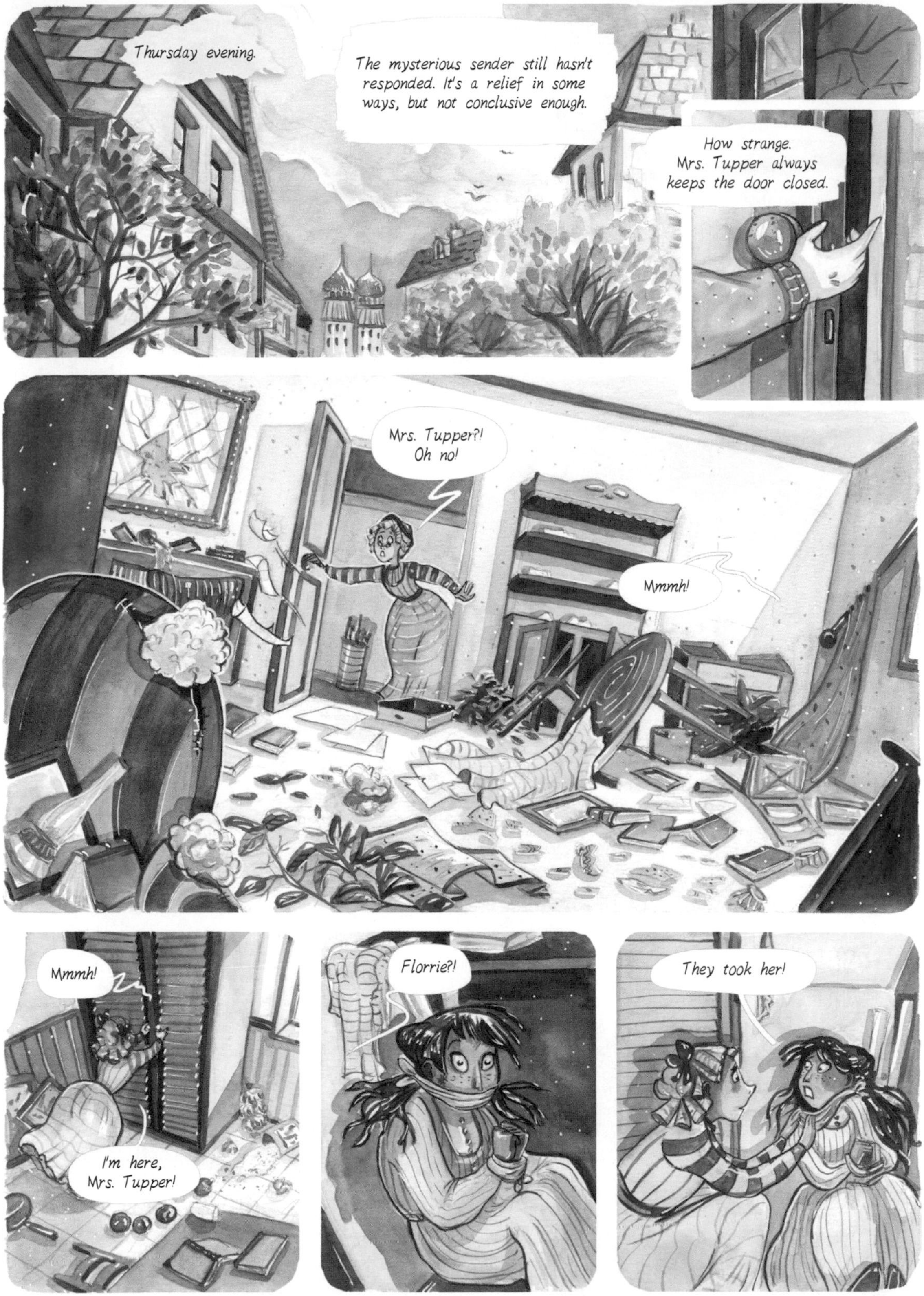
Thursday evening.
The mysterious sender still hasn't responded. It's a relief in some ways, but not conclusive enough.
How strange. Mrs. Tupper always keeps the door closed.
Mrs. Tupper?! Oh no!
Mmmh!
Mmmh!
I'm here, Mrs. Tupper!
Florrie?!
They took her!

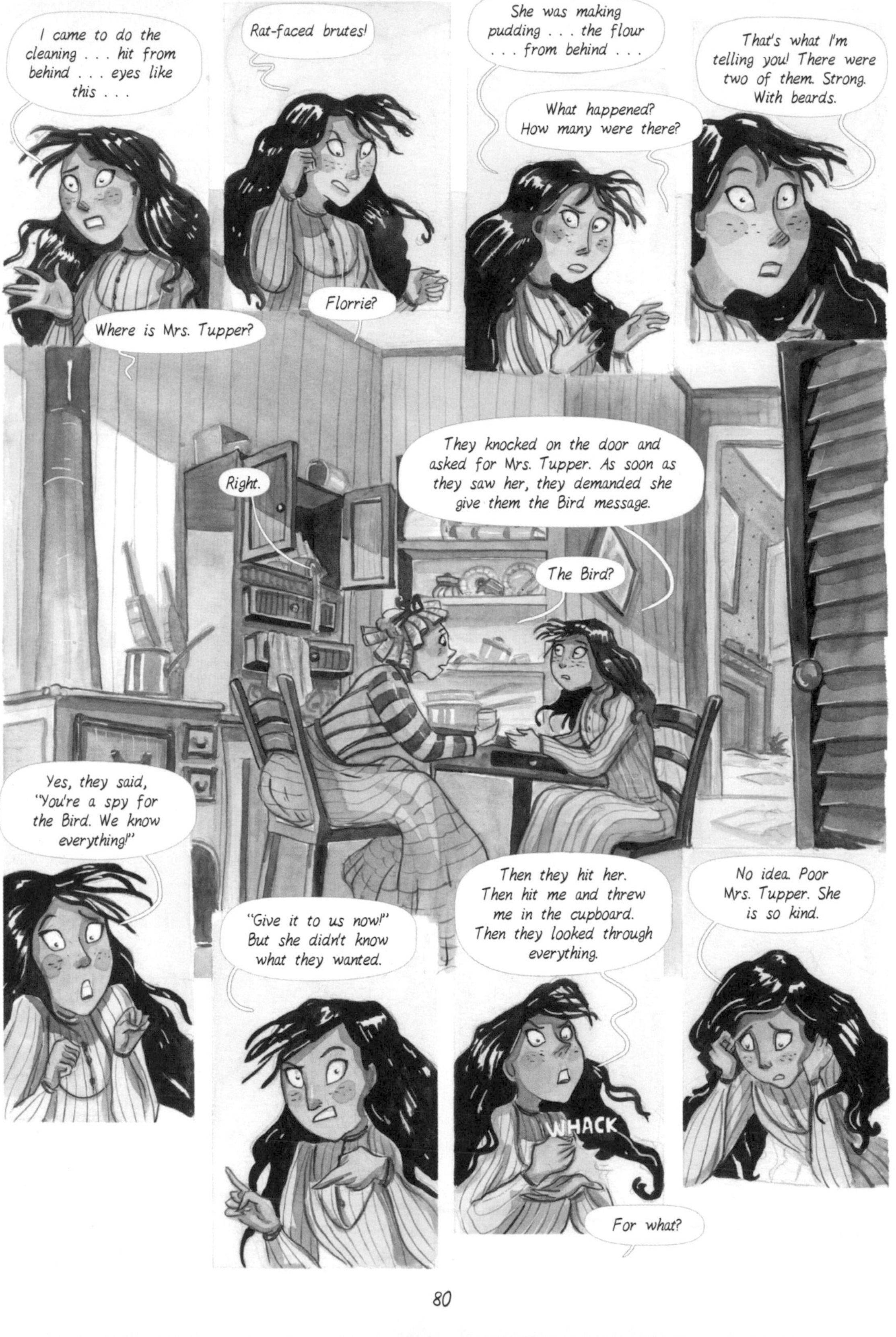
I came to do the cleaning . . . hit from behind . . . eyes like this . . .
Rat-faced brutes!
She was making pudding . . . the flour . . . from behind . . .
What happened? How many were there?
That's what I'm telling you! There were two of them. Strong. With beards.
Where is Mrs. Tupper?
Florrie?
Right.
They knocked on the door and asked for Mrs. Tupper. As soon as they saw her, they demanded she give them the Bird message.
The Bird?
Yes, they said, "You're a spy for the Bird. We know everything!"
"Give it to us now!" But she didn't know what they wanted.
Then they hit her. Then hit me and threw me in the cupboard. Then they looked through everything.
WHACK
For what?
No idea. Poor Mrs. Tupper. She is so kind.

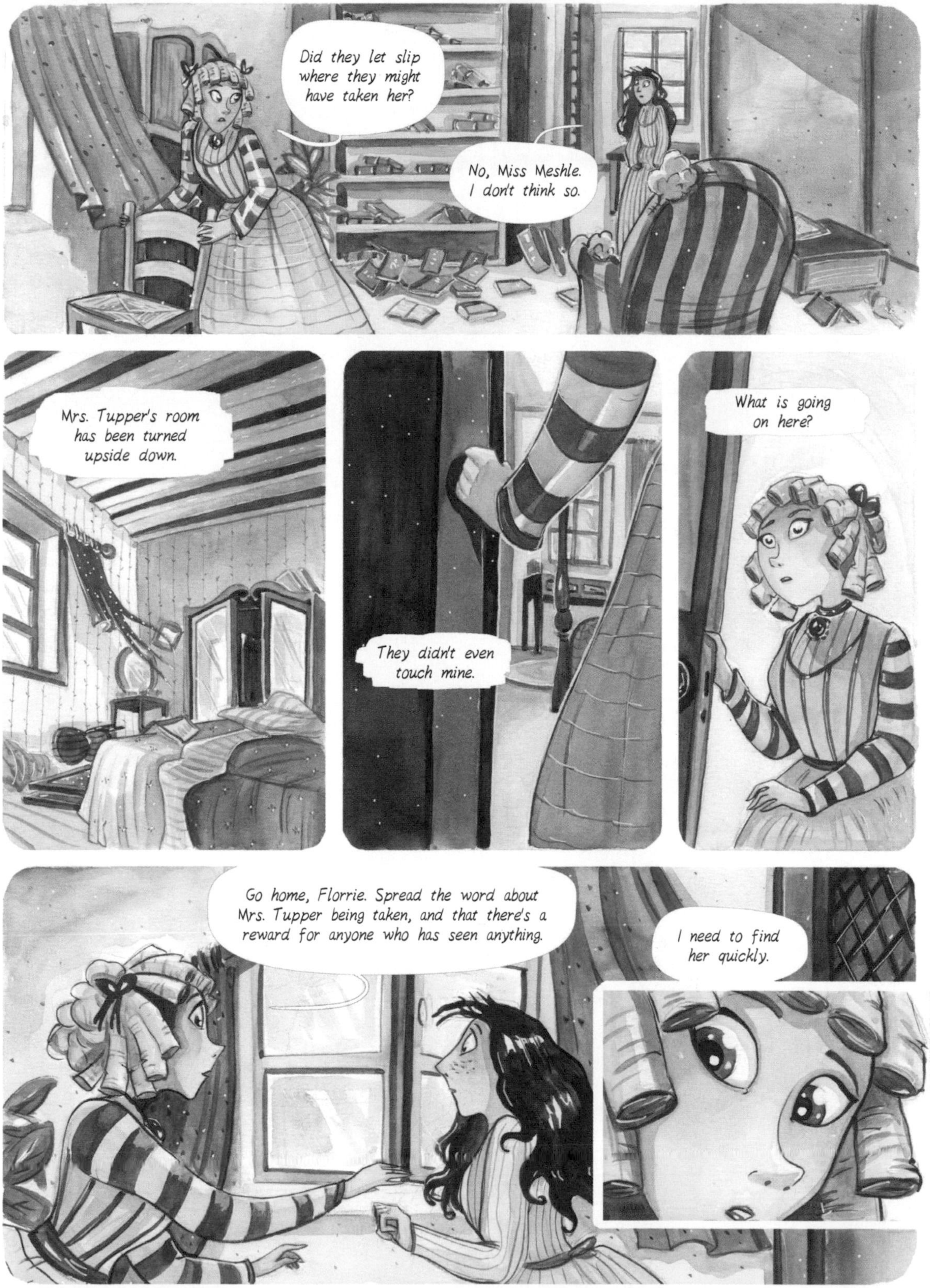
Did they let slip where they might have taken her?
No, Miss Meshle. I don't think so.
Mrs. Tupper's room has been turned upside down.
They didn't even touch mine.
What is going on here?
Go home, Florrie. Spread the word about Mrs. Tupper being taken, and that there's a reward for anyone who has seen anything.
I need to find her quickly.

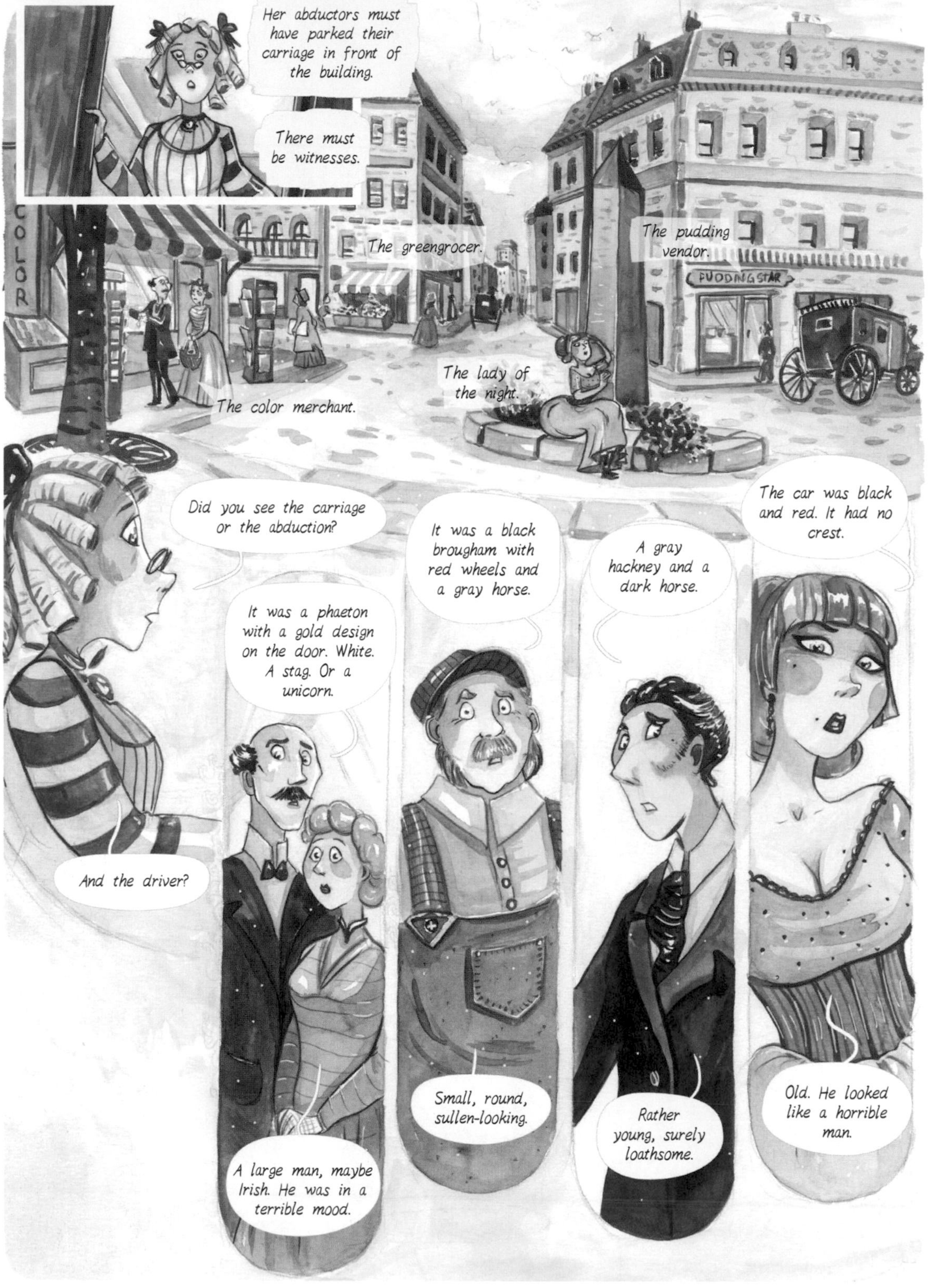
Her abductors must have parked their carriage in front of the building.
There must be witnesses.
COLOR
The greengrocer.
The pudding vendor.
PUDDING STAR
The color merchant.
The lady of the night.
Did you see the carriage or the abduction?
It was a phaeton with a gold design on the door. White. A stag. Or a unicorn.
It was a black brougham with red wheels and a gray horse.
A gray hackney and a dark horse.
The car was black and red. It had no crest.
And the driver?
A large man, maybe Irish. He was in a terrible mood.
Small, round, sullen-looking.
Rather young, surely loathsome.
Old. He looked like a horrible man.

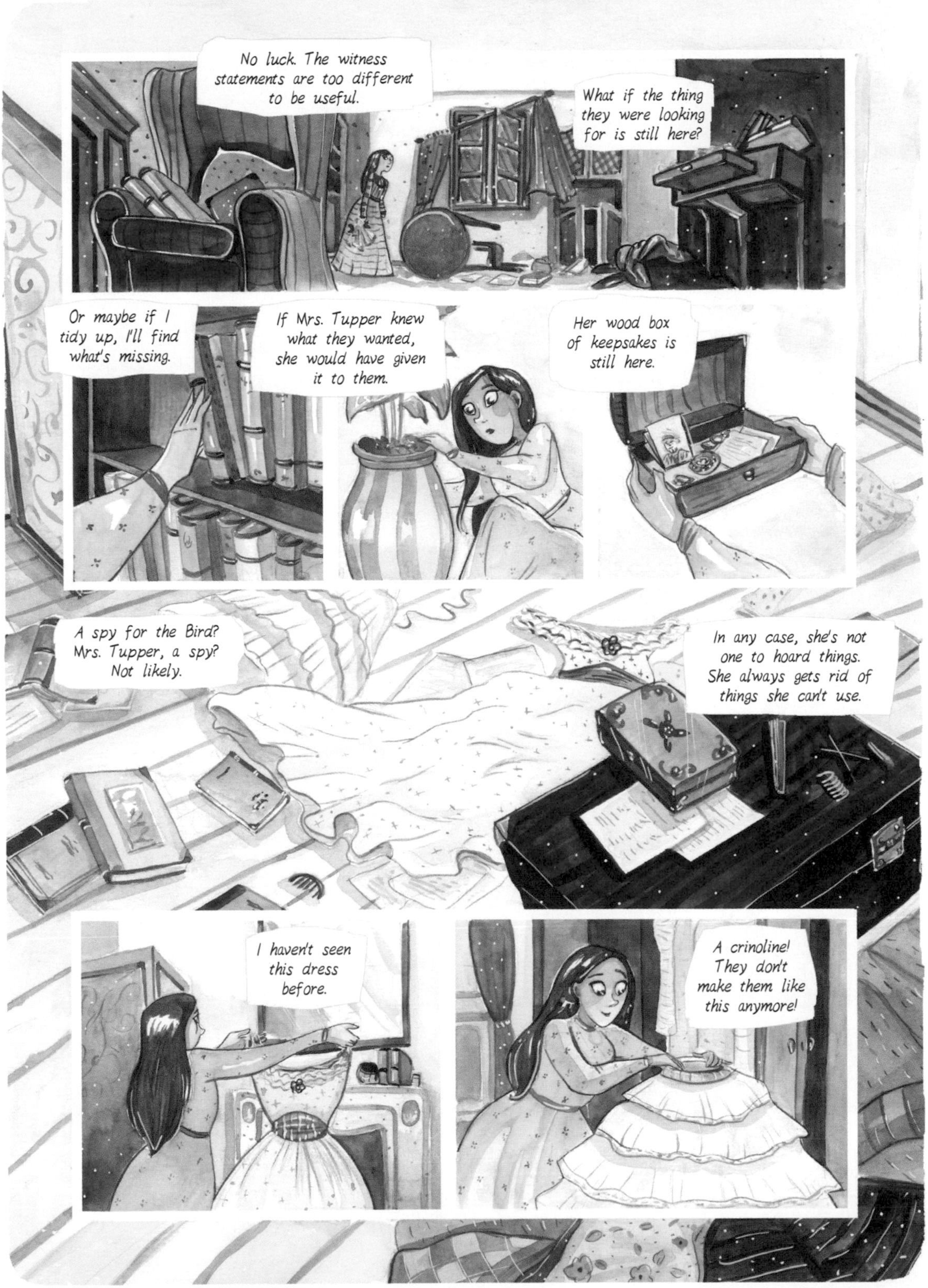
No luck. The witness statements are too different to be useful.
What if the thing they were looking for is still here?
Or maybe if I tidy up, I'll find what's missing.
If Mrs. Tupper knew what they wanted, she would have given it to them.
Her wood box of keepsakes is still here.
A spy for the Bird? Mrs. Tupper, a spy? Not likely.
In any case, she's not one to hoard things. She always gets rid of things she can't use.
I haven't seen this dress before.
A crinoline! They don't make them like this anymore!

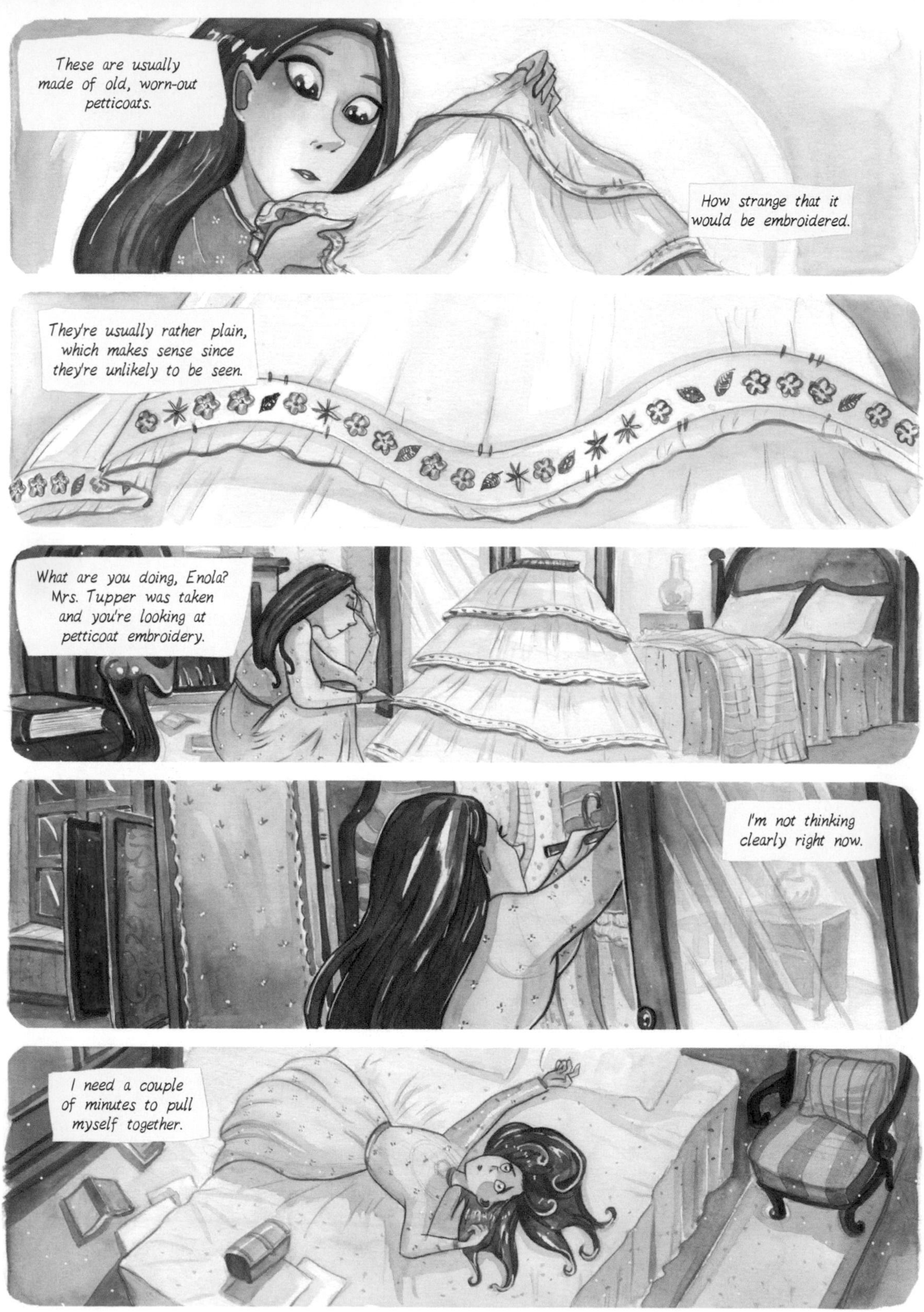
These are usually made of old, worn-out petticoats.
How strange that it would be embroidered.
They're usually rather plain, which makes sense since they're unlikely to be seen.
What are you doing, Enola? Mrs. Tupper was taken and you're looking at petticoat embroidery.
I'm not thinking clearly right now.
I need a couple of minutes to pull myself together.

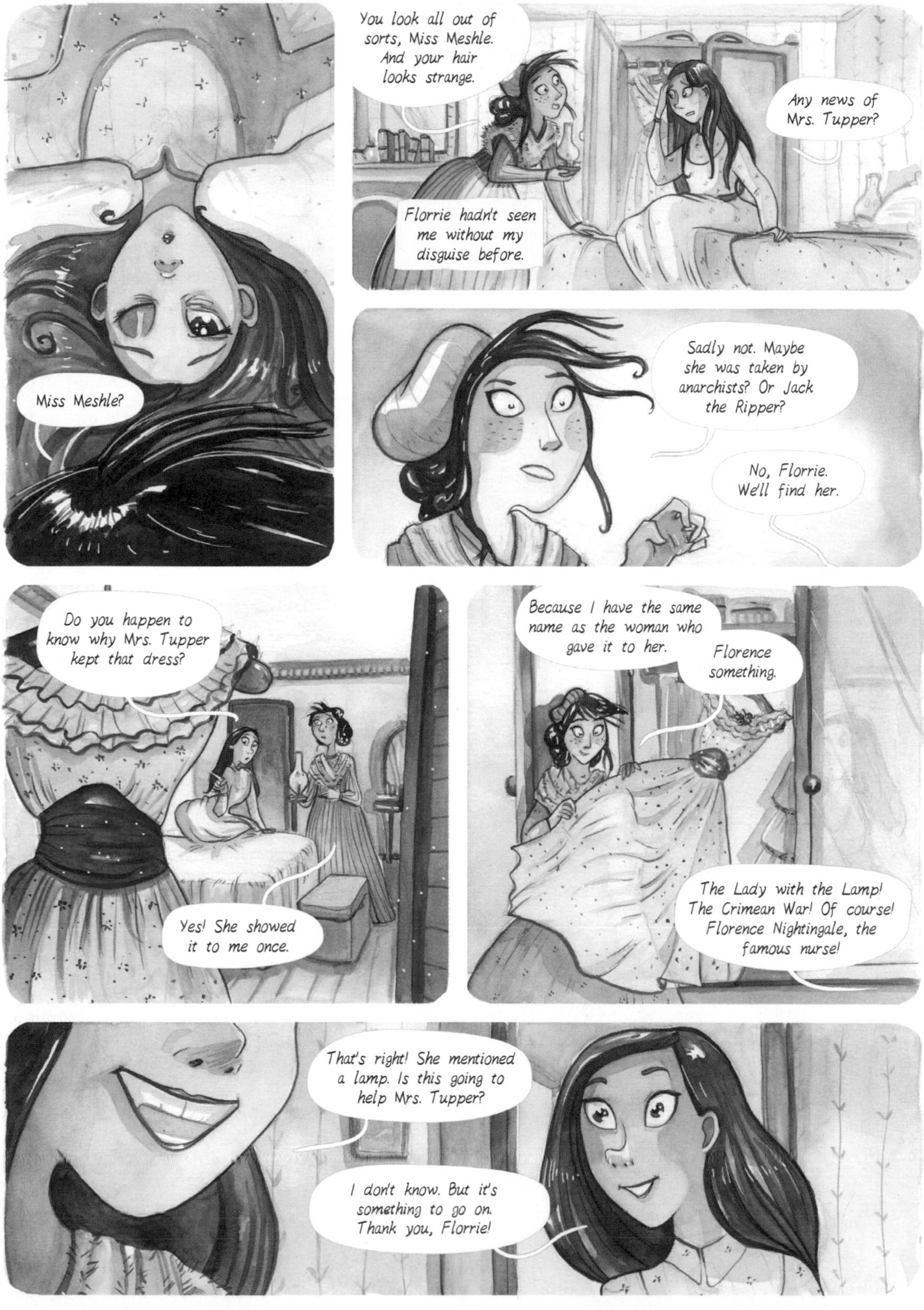
Miss Meshle?
You look all out of sorts, Miss Meshle. And your hair looks strange.
Florrie hadn't seen me without my disguise before.
Any news of Mrs. Tupper?
Sadly not. Maybe she was taken by anarchists? Or Jack the Ripper?
No, Florrie. We'll find her.
Do you happen to know why Mrs. Tupper kept that dress?
Yes! She showed it to me once.
Because I have the same name as the woman who gave it to her.
Florence something.
The Lady with the Lamp! The Crimean War! Of course! Florence Nightingale, the famous nurse!
That's right! She mentioned a lamp. Is this going to help Mrs. Tupper?
I don't know. But it's something to go on. Thank you, Florrie!

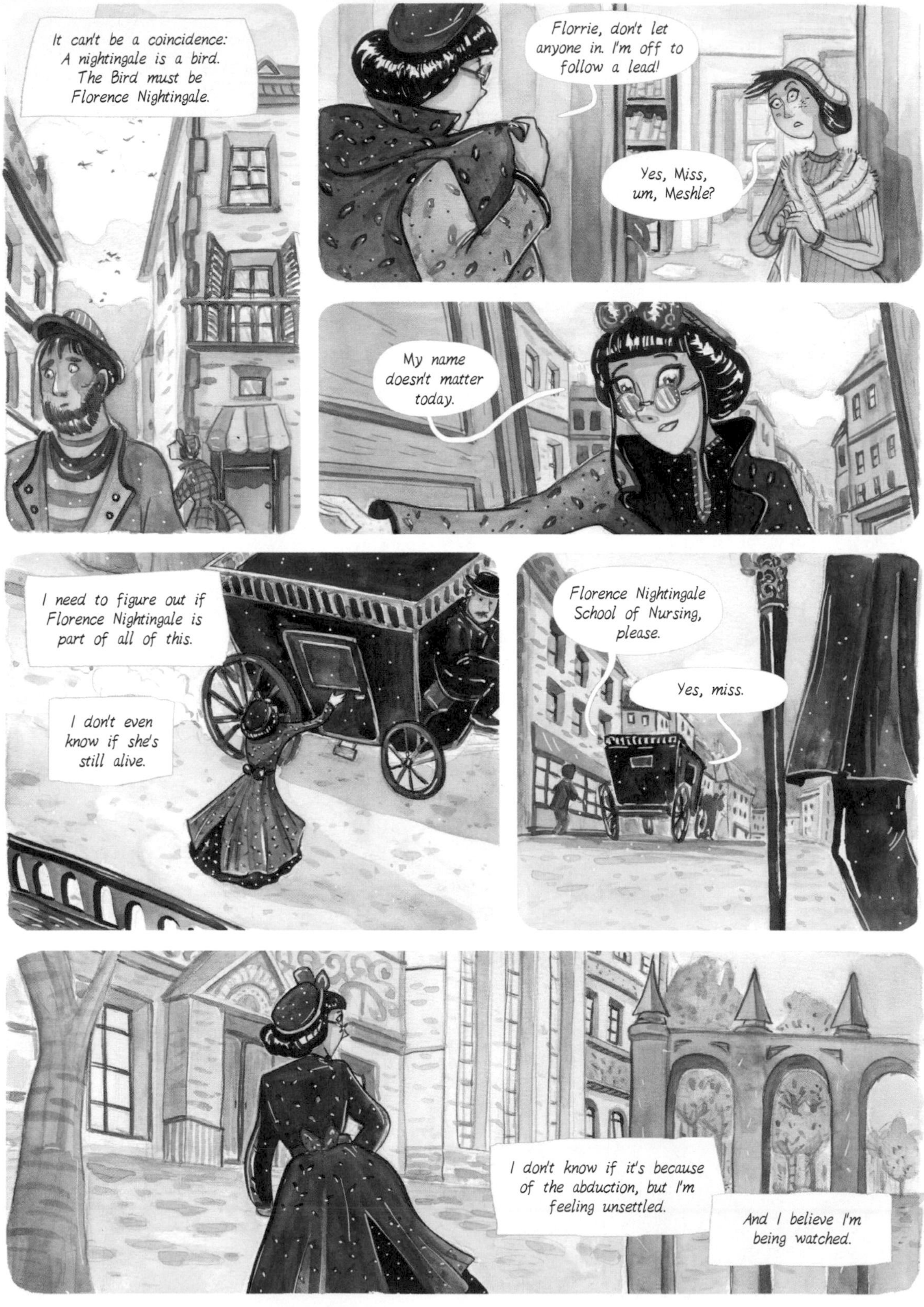

It can't be a coincidence: A nightingale is a bird. The Bird must be Florence Nightingale.
Florrie, don't let anyone in. I'm off to follow a lead!
Yes, Miss, um, Meshle?
My name doesn't matter today.
I need to figure out if Florence Nightingale is part of all of this.
I don't even know if she's still alive.
Florence Nightingale School of Nursing, please.
Yes, miss.
I don't know if it's because of the abduction, but I'm feeling unsettled.
And I believe I'm being watched.

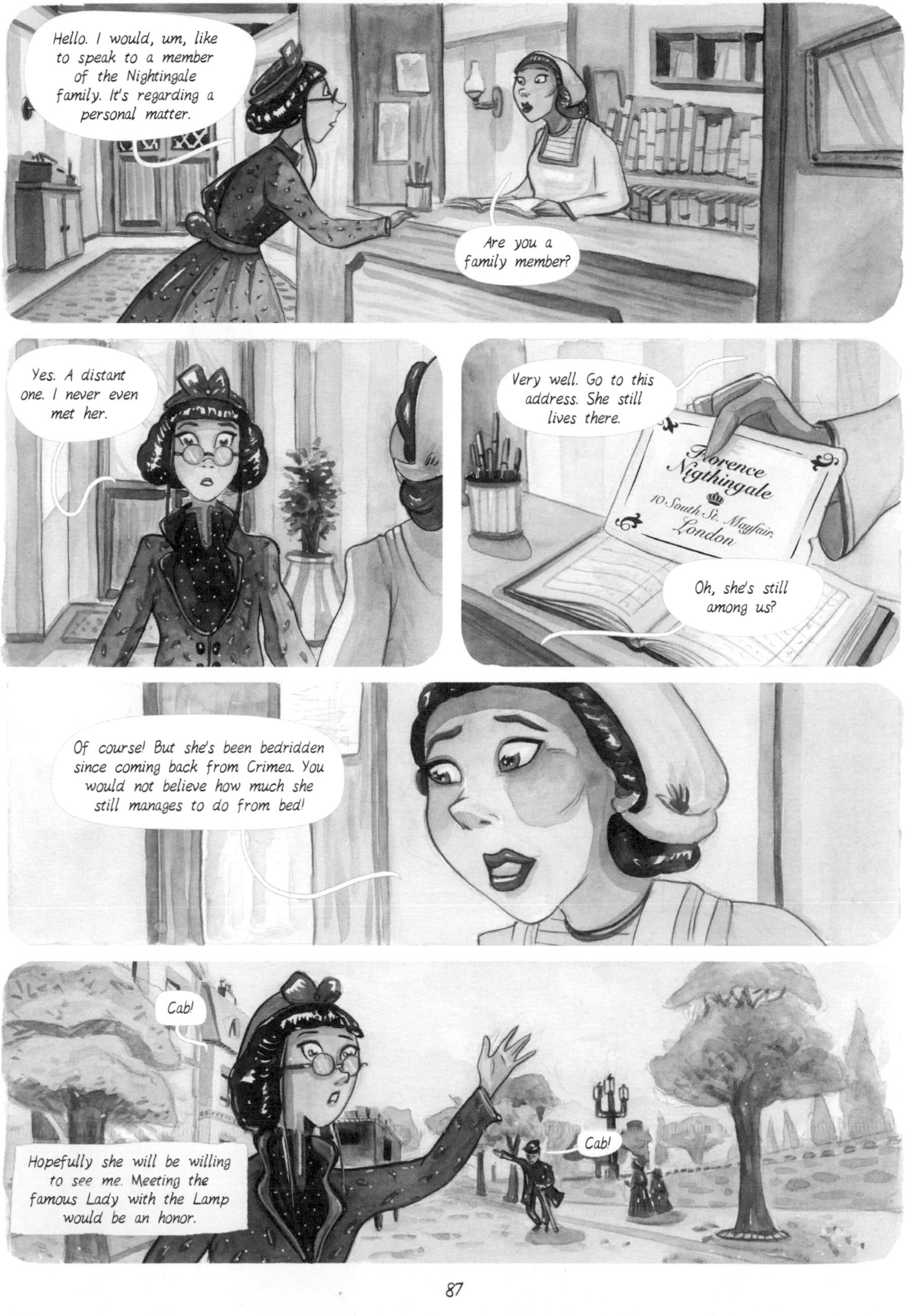
Hello. I would, um, like to speak to a member of the Nightingale family. It's regarding a personal matter.
Are you a family member?
Yes. A distant one. I never even met her.
Very well. Go to this address. She still lives there.
Florence Nigthingale
10 South St. Mayfair, London
Oh, she's still among us?
Of course! But she's been bedridden since coming back from Crimea. You would not believe how much she still manages to do from bed!
Cab!
Cab!
Hopefully she will be willing to see me. Meeting the famous Lady with the Lamp would be an honor.

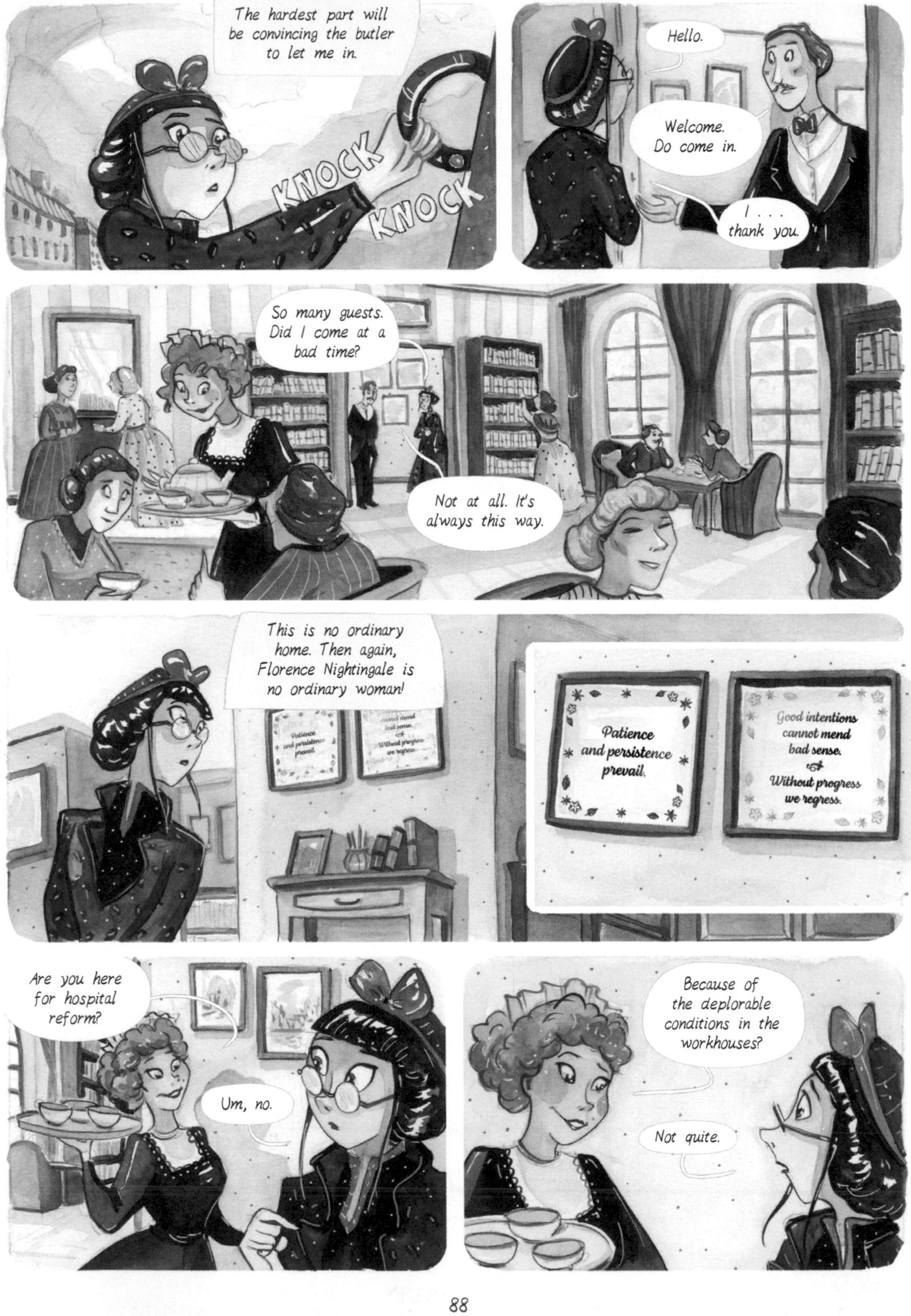
The hardest part will be convincing the butler to let me in.
KNOCK KNOCK
Hello.
Welcome. Do come in.
I . . . thank you.
So many guests. Did I come at a bad time?
Not at all. It's always this way.
This is no ordinary home. Then again, Florence Nightingale is no ordinary woman!
Patience and persistence prevail.
Good intentions cannot mend bad sense.
Without progress we regress.
Are you here for hospital reform?
Um, no.
Because of the deplorable conditions in the workhouses?
Not quite.

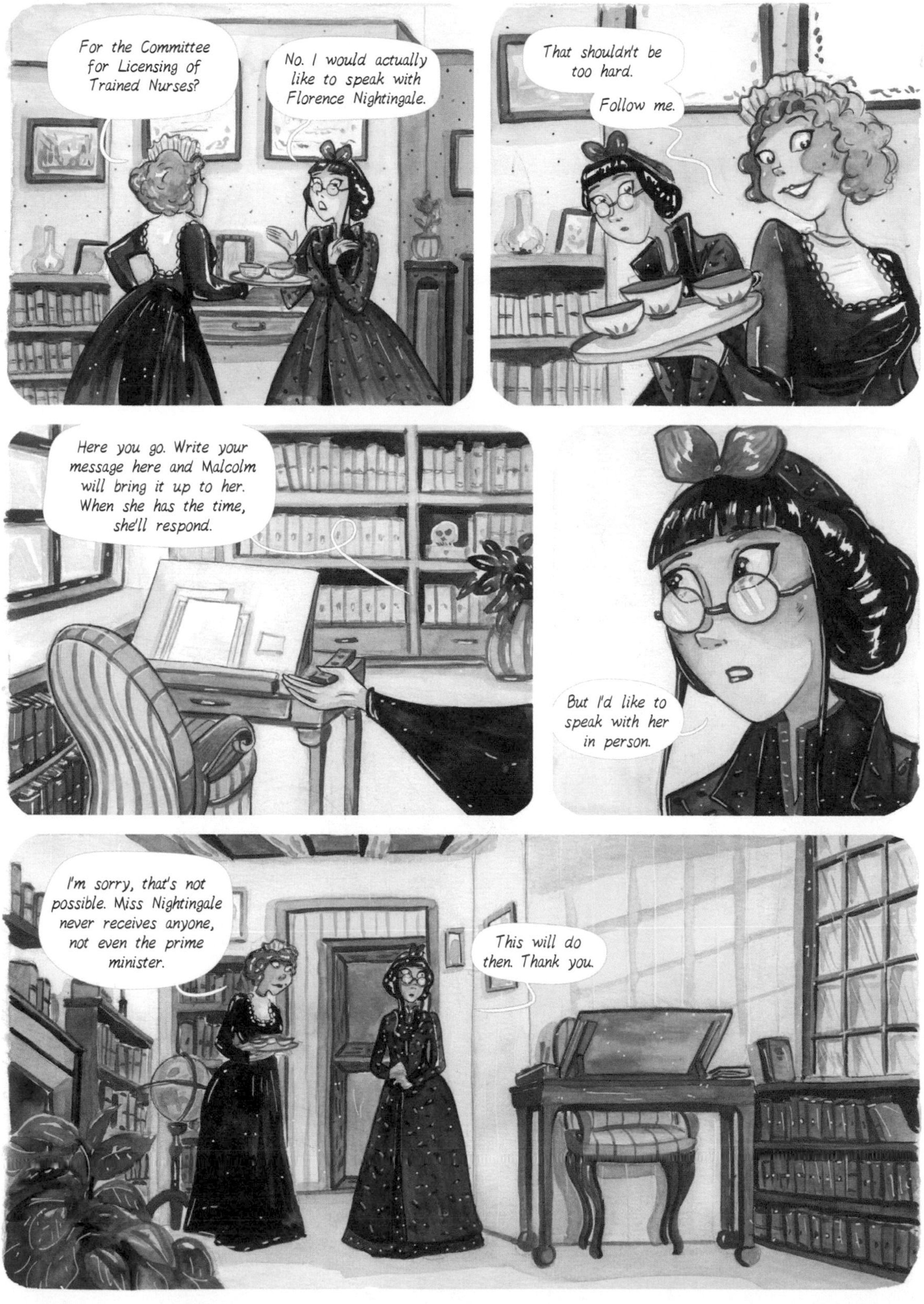
For the Committee for Licensing of Trained Nurses?
No. I would actually like to speak with Florence Nightingale.
That shouldn't be too hard.
Follow me.
Here you go. Write your message here and Malcolm will bring it up to her. When she has the time, she'll respond.
But I'd like to speak with her in person.
I'm sorry, that's not possible. Miss Nightingale never receives anyone, not even the prime minister.
This will do then. Thank you.

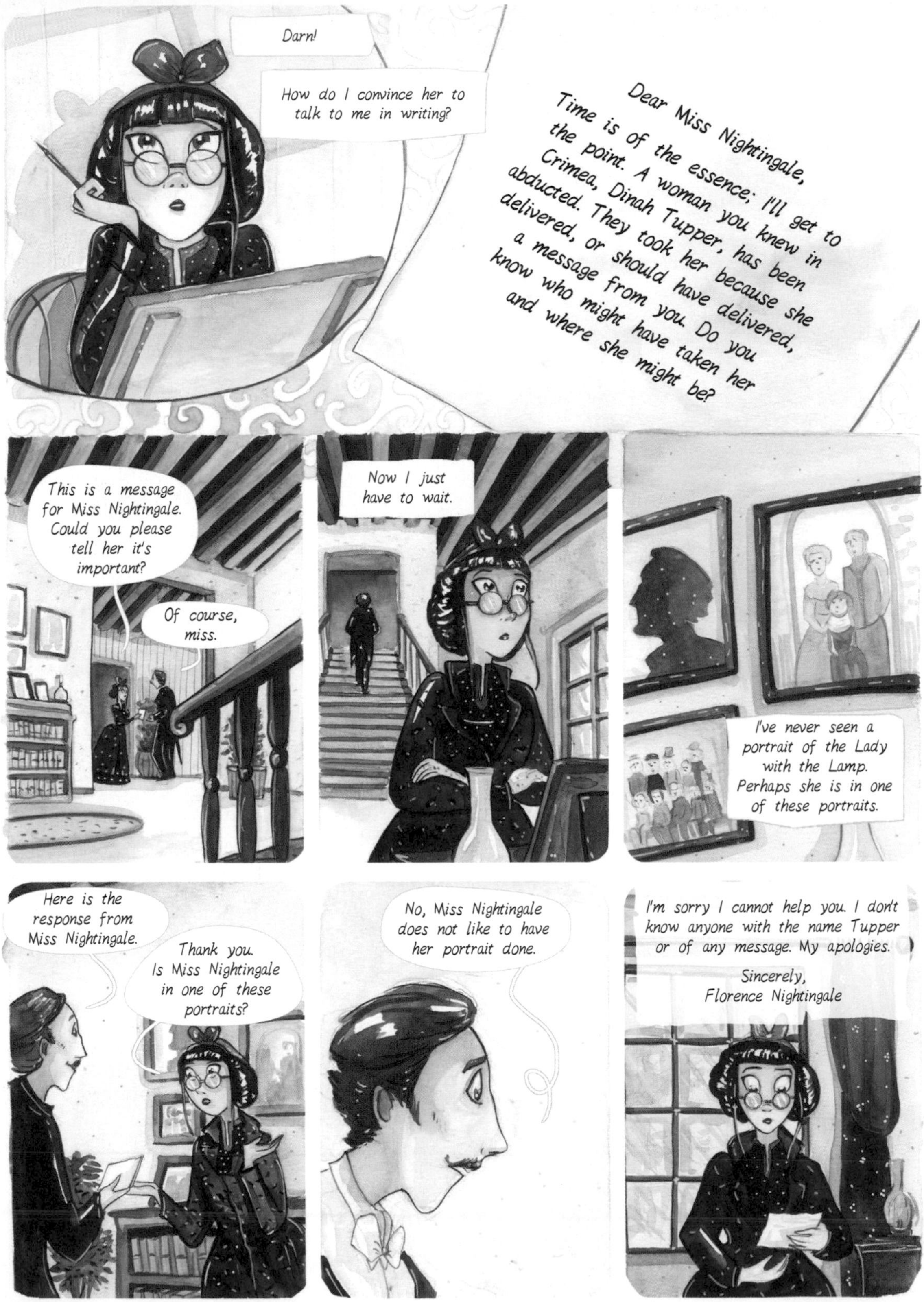

Darn!
How do I convince her to talk to me in writing?
Dear Miss Nightingale,
Time is of the essence; I'll get to the point. A woman you knew in Crimea, Dinah Tupper, has been abducted. They took her because she delivered, or should have delivered, a message from you. Do you know who might have taken her and where she might be?
This is a message for Miss Nightingale. Could you please tell her it's important?
Of course, miss.
Now I just have to wait.
I've never seen a portrait of the Lady with the Lamp. Perhaps she is in one of these portraits.
Here is the response from Miss Nightingale.
Thank you. Is Miss Nightingale in one of these portraits?
No, Miss Nightingale does not like to have her portrait done.
I'm sorry I cannot help you. I don't know anyone with the name Tupper or of any message. My apologies.
Sincerely,
Florence Nightingale

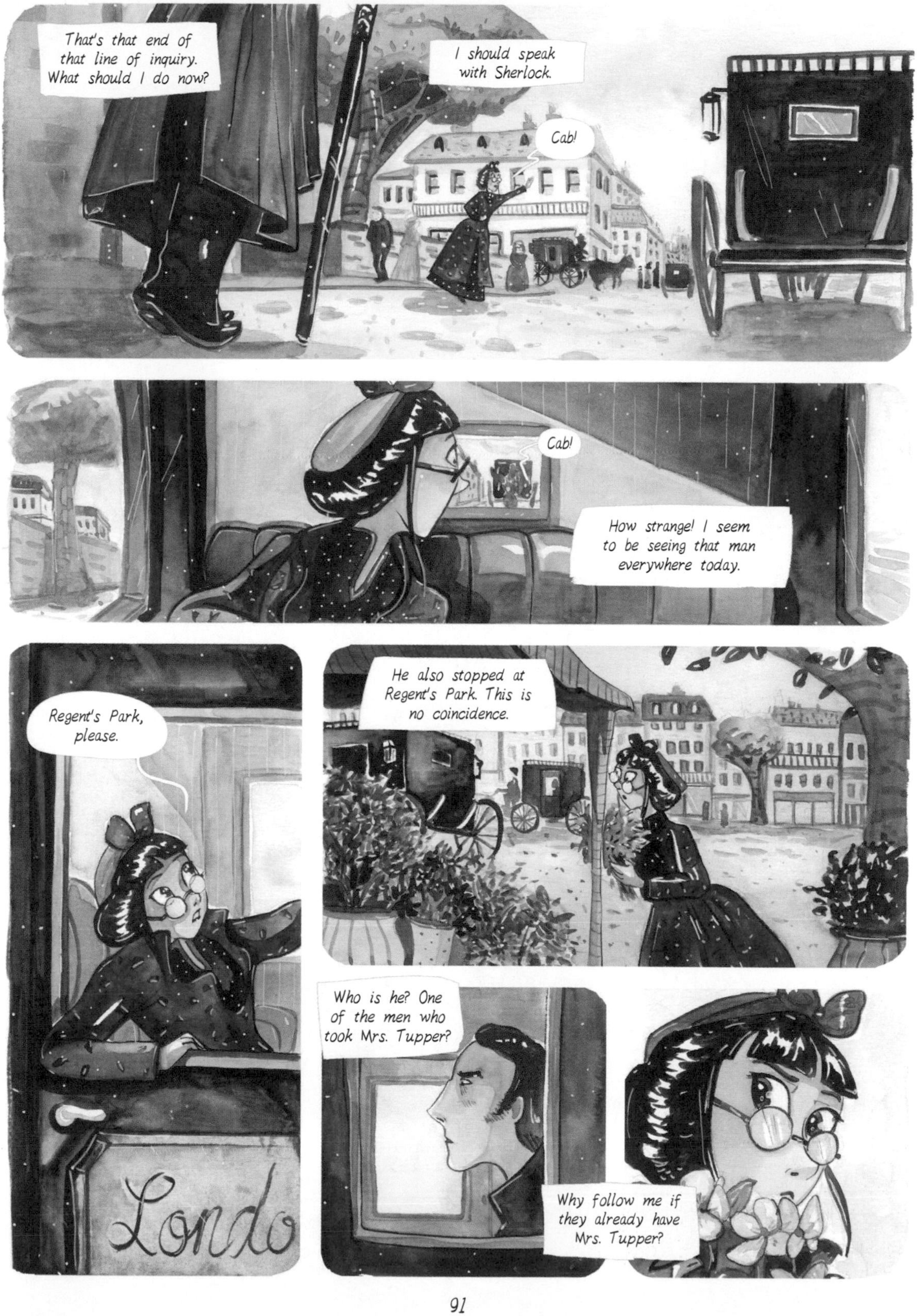
That's that end of that line of inquiry. What should I do now?
I should speak with Sherlock.
Cab!
Cab!
How strange! I seem to be seeing that man everywhere today.
Regent's Park, please.
Londo
He also stopped at Regent's Park. This is no coincidence.
Who is he? One of the men who took Mrs. Tupper?
Why follow me if they already have Mrs. Tupper?

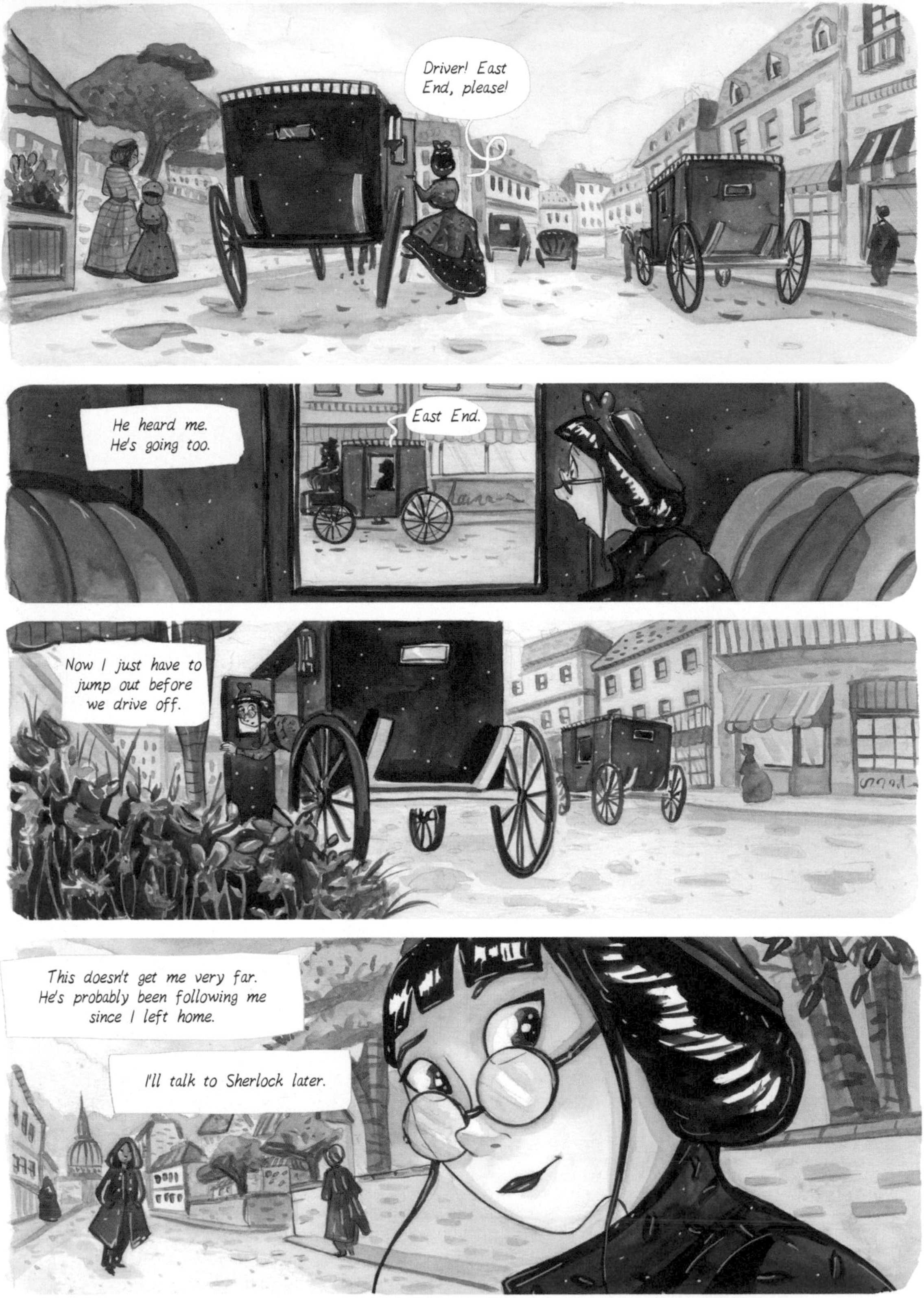
Driver! East End, please!
He heard me. He's going too.
East End.
Now I just have to jump out before we drive off.
This doesn't get me very far. He's probably been following me since I left home.
I'll talk to Sherlock later.

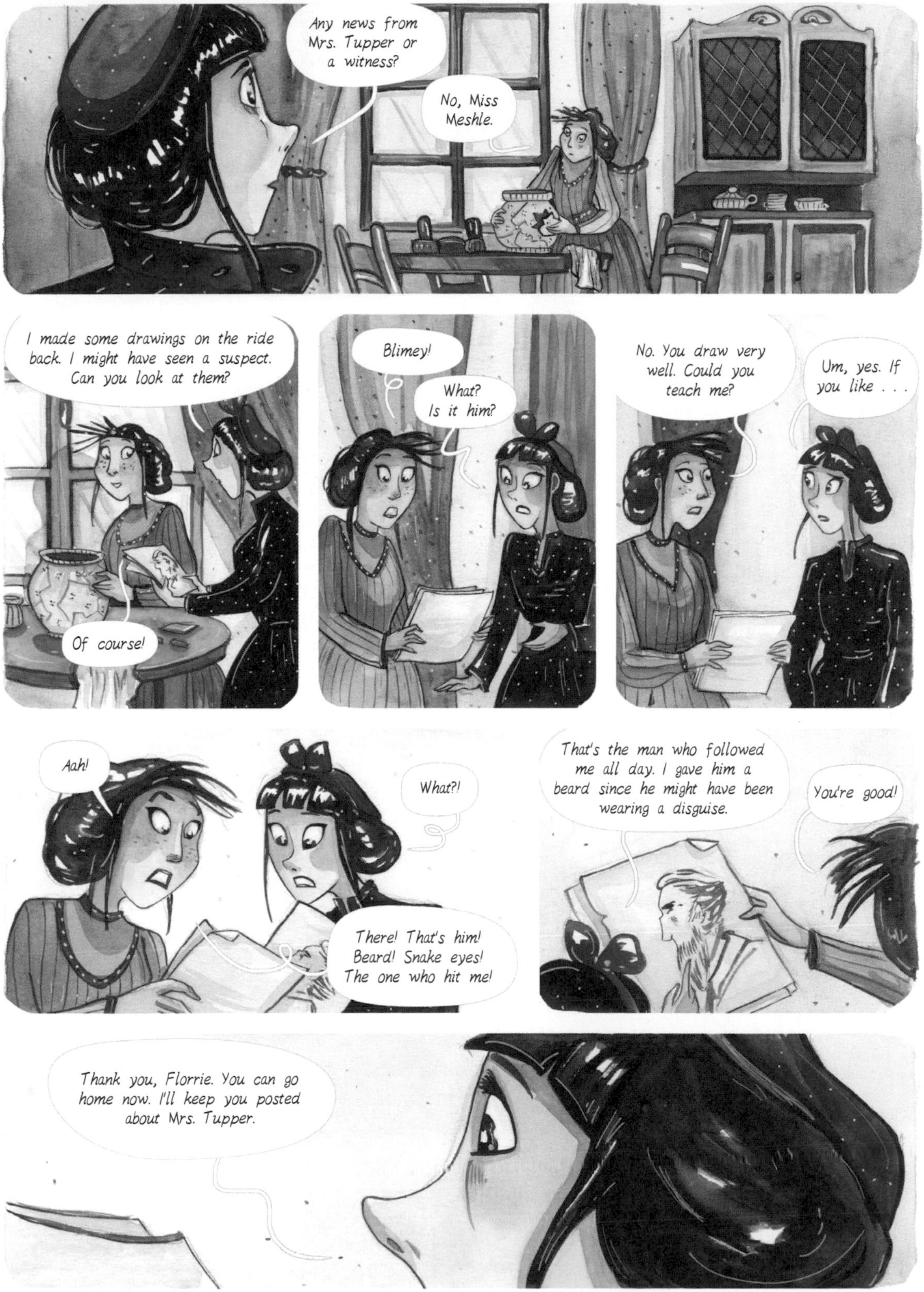
Any news from Mrs. Tupper or a witness?
No, Miss Meshle.
I made some drawings on the ride back. I might have seen a suspect. Can you look at them?
Of course!
Blimey!
What? Is it him?
No. You draw very well. Could you teach me?
Um, yes. If you like . . .
Aah!
What?!
There! That's him! Beard! Snake eyes! The one who hit me!
That's the man who followed me all day. I gave him a beard since he might have been wearing a disguise.
You're good!
Thank you, Florrie. You can go home now. I'll keep you posted about Mrs. Tupper.

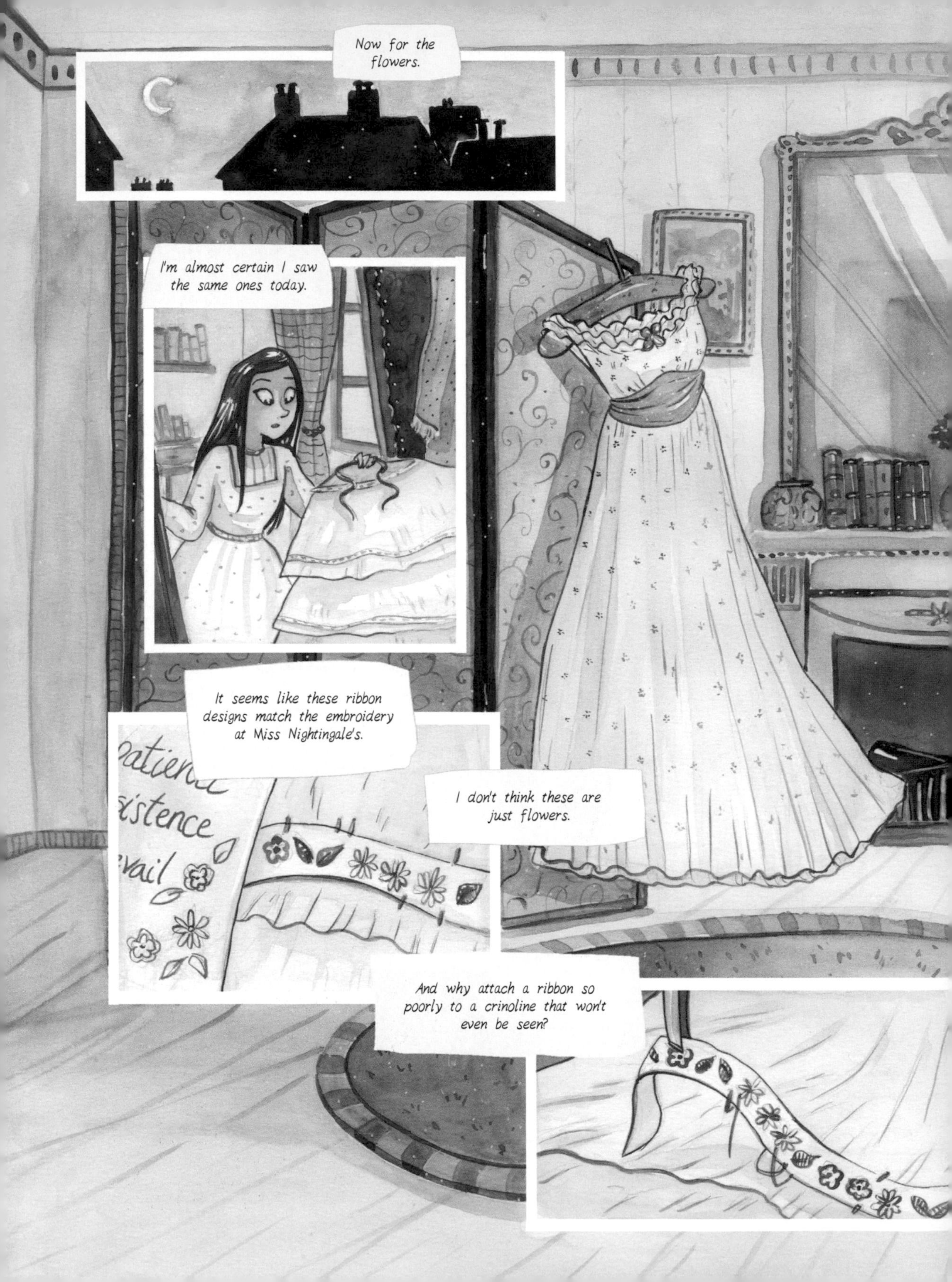

Now for the flowers.
I'm almost certain I saw the same ones today.
It seems like these ribbon designs match the embroidery at Miss Nightingale's.
I don't think these are just flowers.
And why attach a ribbon so poorly to a crinoline that won't even be seen?

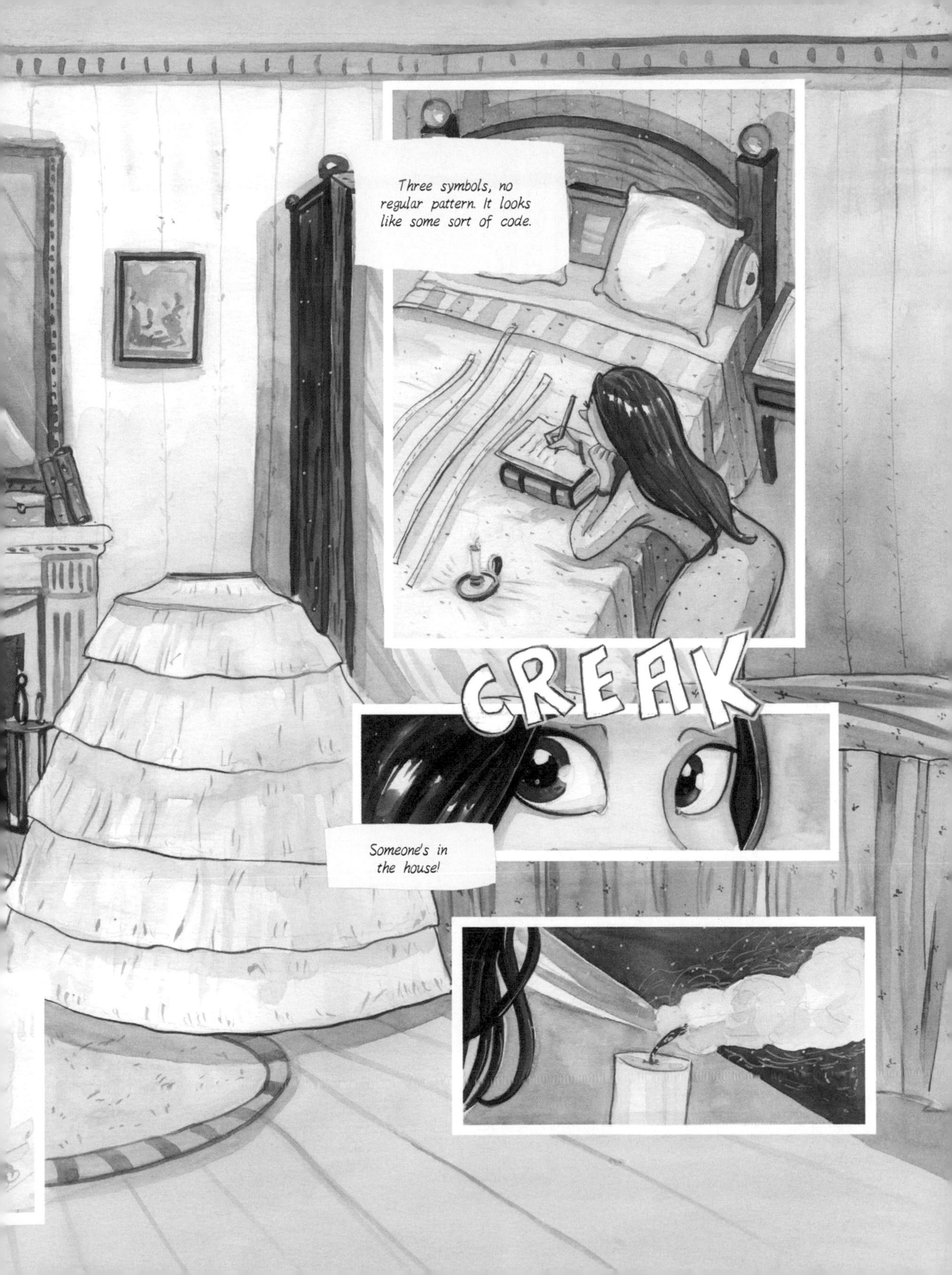
Three symbols, no regular pattern. It looks like some sort of code.
CREAK
Someone's in the house!

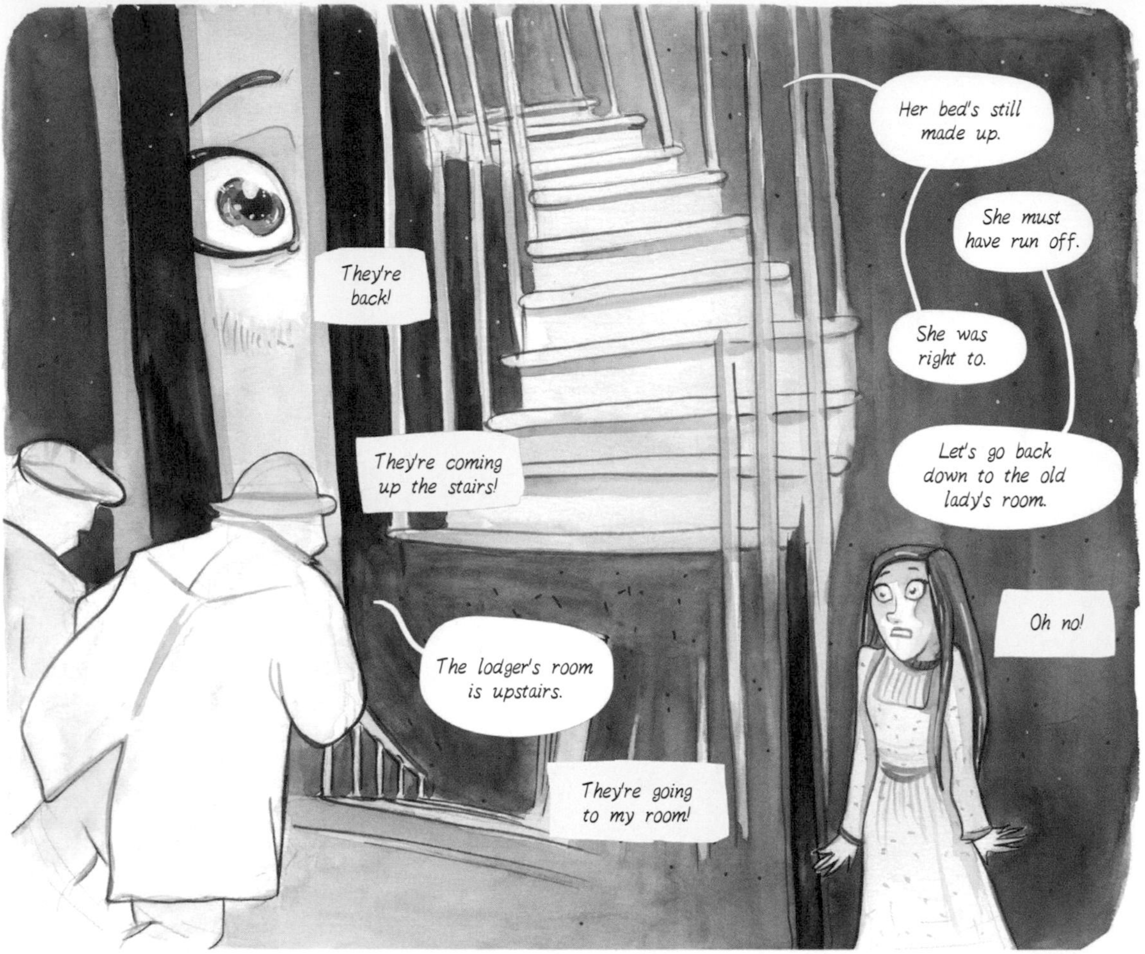
They're back!
They're coming up the stairs!
The lodger's room is upstairs.
They're going to my room!
Her bed's still made up.
She must have run off.
She was right to.
Let's go back down to the old lady's room.
Oh no!

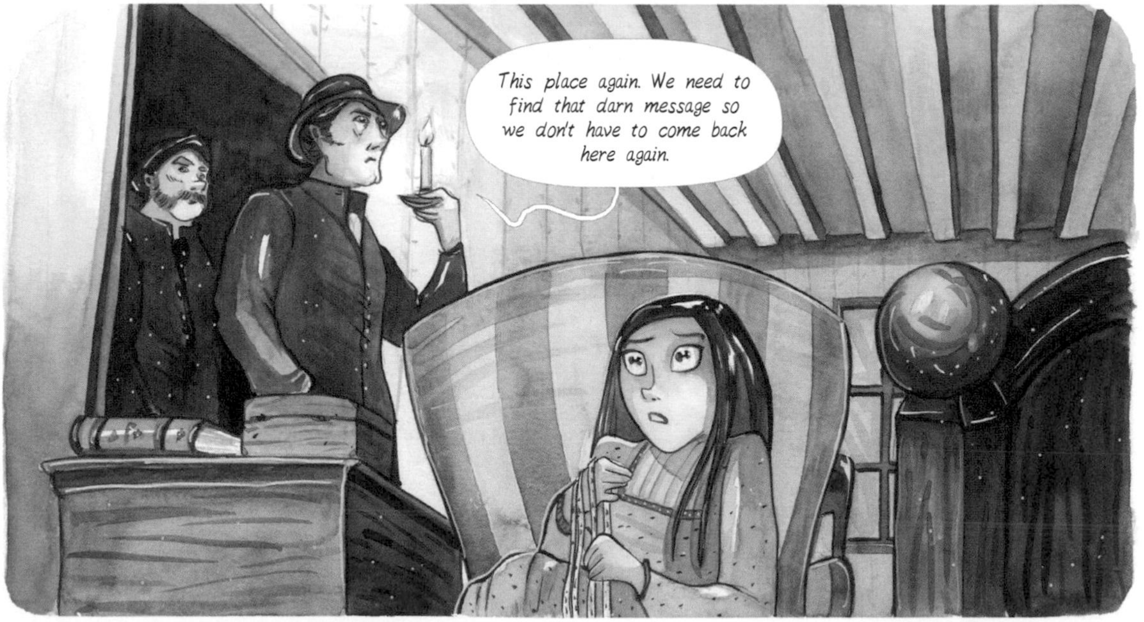
This place again. We need to find that darn message so we don't have to come back here again.

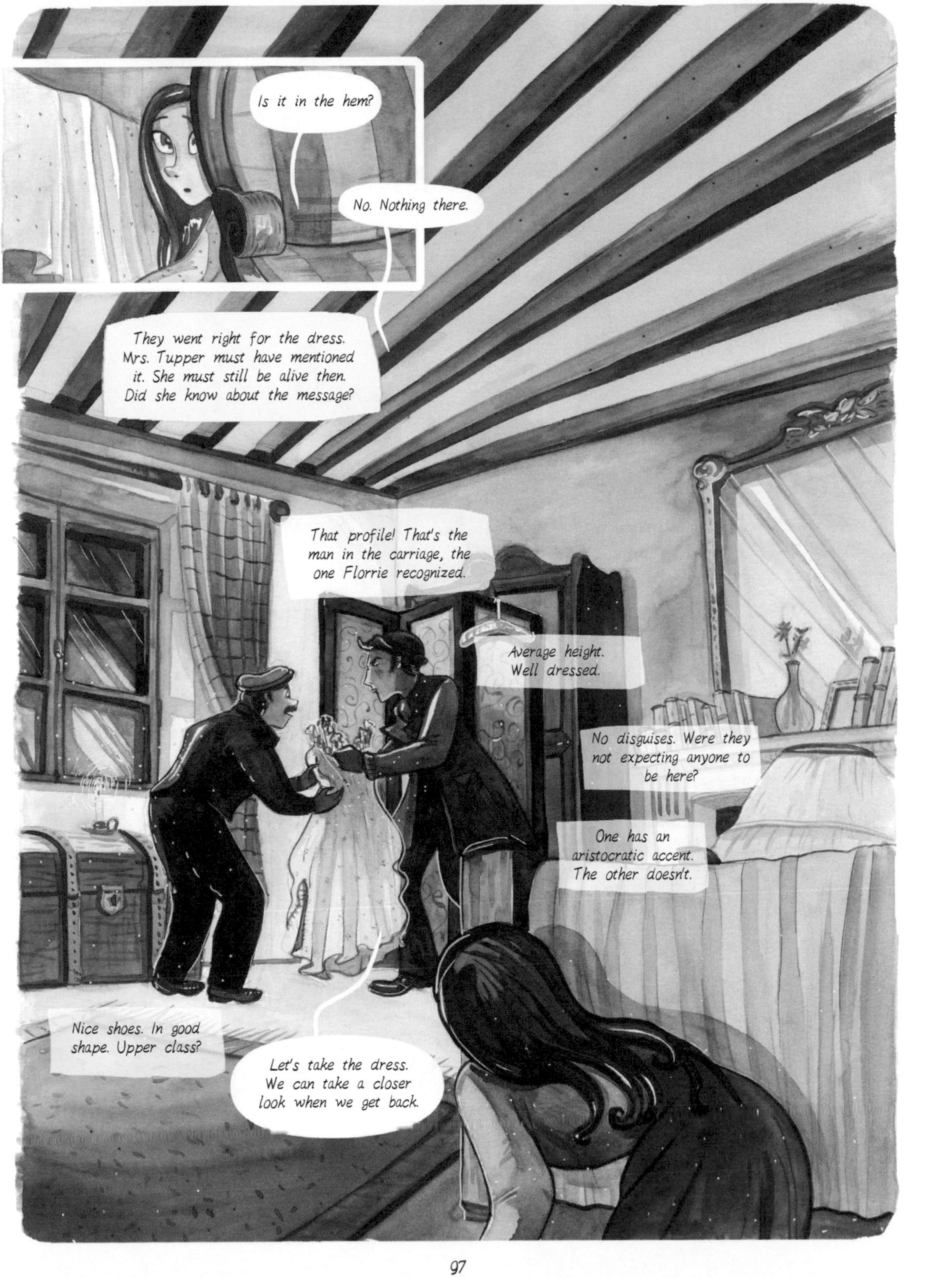

Is it in the hem?
No. Nothing there.
They went right for the dress. Mrs. Tupper must have mentioned it. She must still be alive then. Did she know about the message?
That profile! That's the man in the carriage, the one Florrie recognized.
Average height. Well dressed.
No disguises. Were they not expecting anyone to be here?
One has an aristocratic accent. The other doesn't.
Nice shoes. In good shape. Upper class?
Let's take the dress. We can take a closer look when we get back.

I have to follow them!

They'll bring me right to Mrs. Tupper.

Darn. There are no cabs in sight.

Okay, Enola. Just like in adventure novels!

Almost there!

I'm slipping! I can't hold on!

I had to try . . .

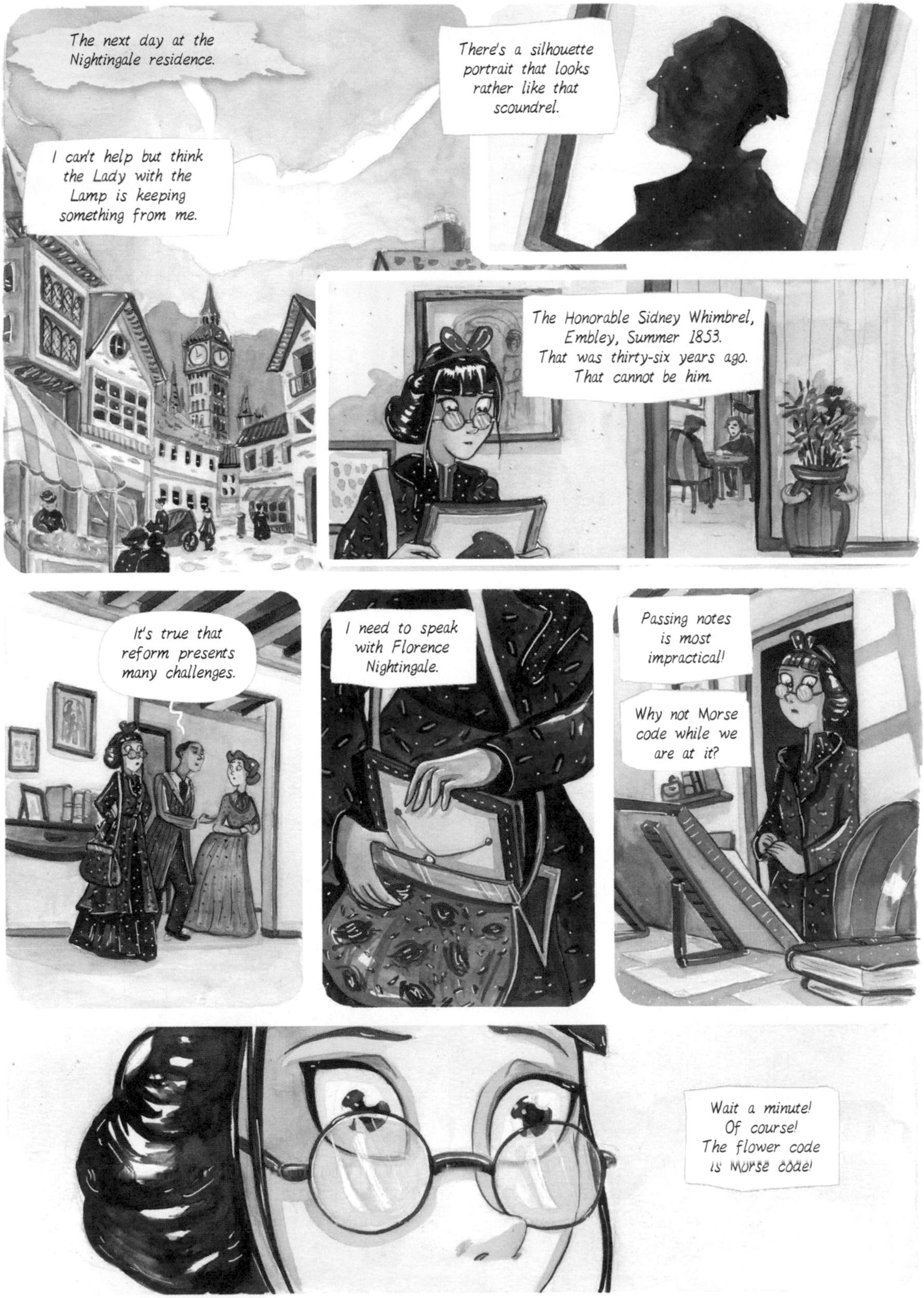
The next day at the Nightingale residence.
I can't help but think the Lady with the Lamp is keeping something from me.
There's a silhouette portrait that looks rather like that scoundrel.
The Honorable Sidney Whimbrel, Embley, Summer 1853. That was thirty-six years ago. That cannot be him.
It's true that reform presents many challenges.
I need to speak with Florence Nightingale.
Passing notes is most impractical!
Why not Morse code while we are at it?
Wait a minute! Of course! The flower code is Morse code!

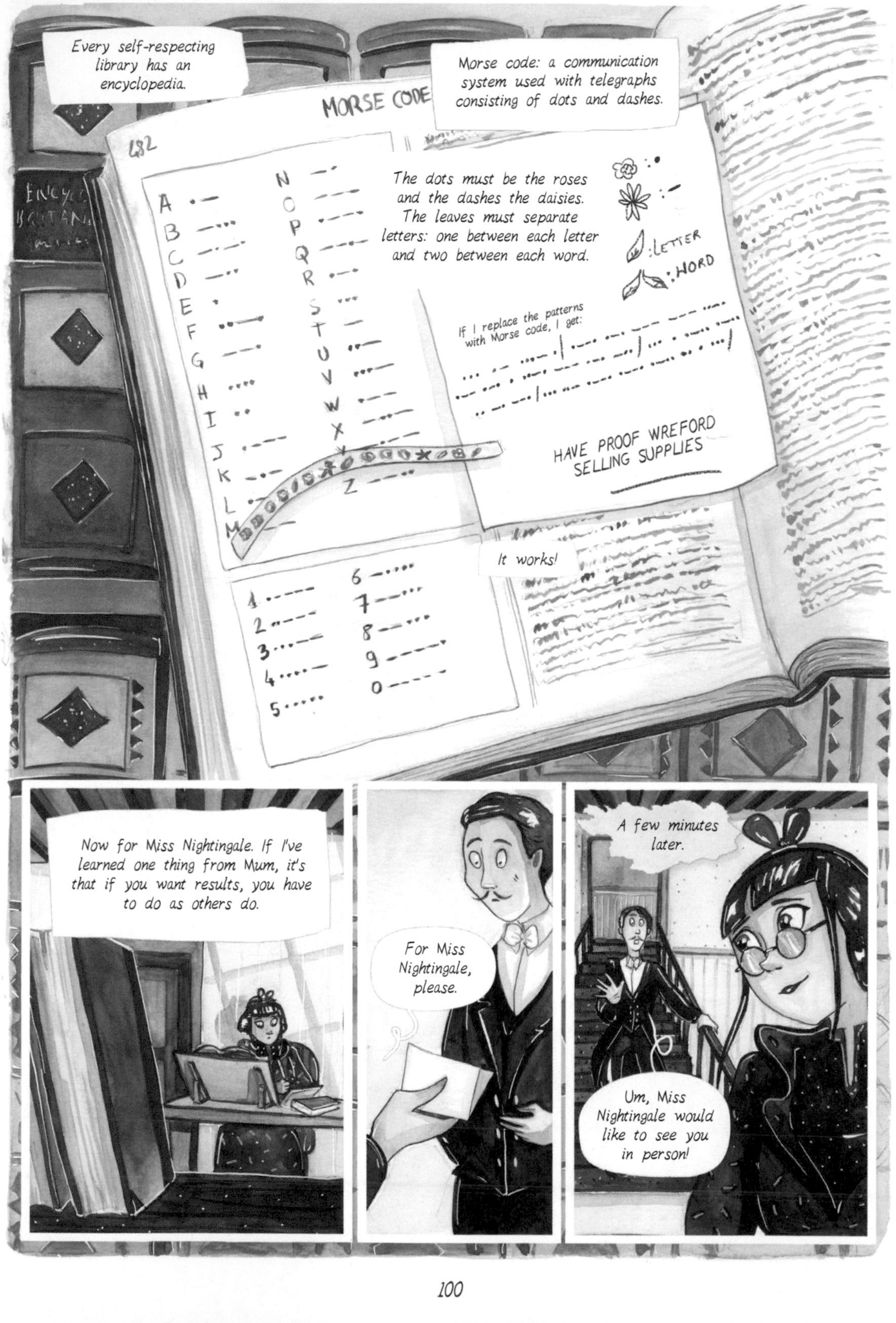
Every self-respecting library has an encyclopedia.
Morse code: a communication system used with telegraphs consisting of dots and dashes.
MORSE CODE
The dots must be the roses and the dashes the daisies. The leaves must separate letters: one between each letter and two between each word.
:LETTER
:WORD
If I replace the patterns with Morse code, I get:
HAVE PROOF WREFORD SELLING SUPPLIES
It works!
Now for Miss Nightingale. If I've learned one thing from Mum, it's that if you want results, you have to do as others do.
For Miss Nightingale, please.
A few minutes later.
Um, Miss Nightingale would like to see you in person!

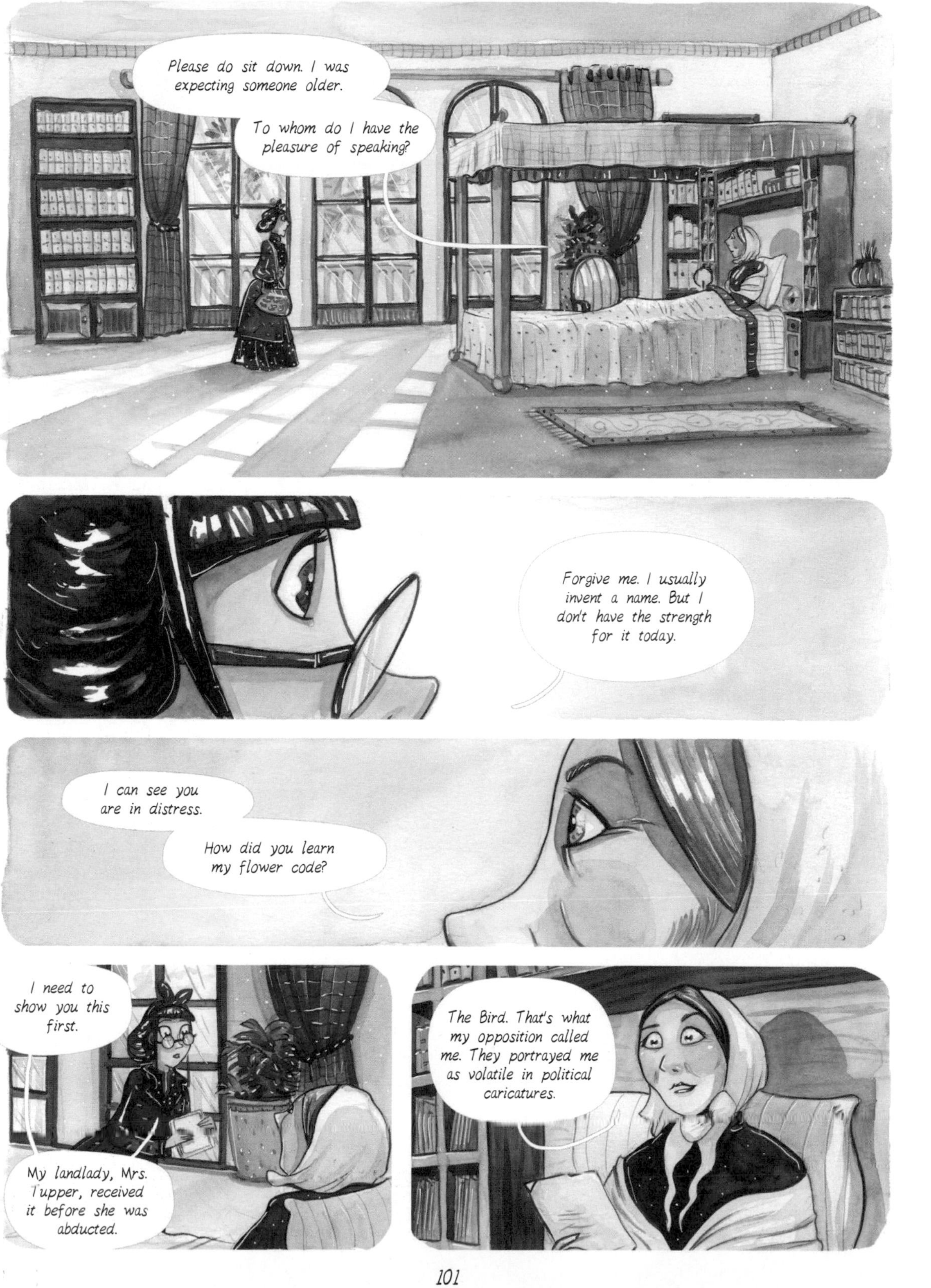
Please do sit down. I was expecting someone older.
To whom do I have the pleasure of speaking?
Forgive me. I usually invent a name. But I don't have the strength for it today.
I can see you are in distress.
How did you learn my flower code?
I need to show you this first.
My landlady, Mrs. Tupper, received it before she was abducted.
The Bird. That's what my opposition called me. They portrayed me as volatile in political caricatures.

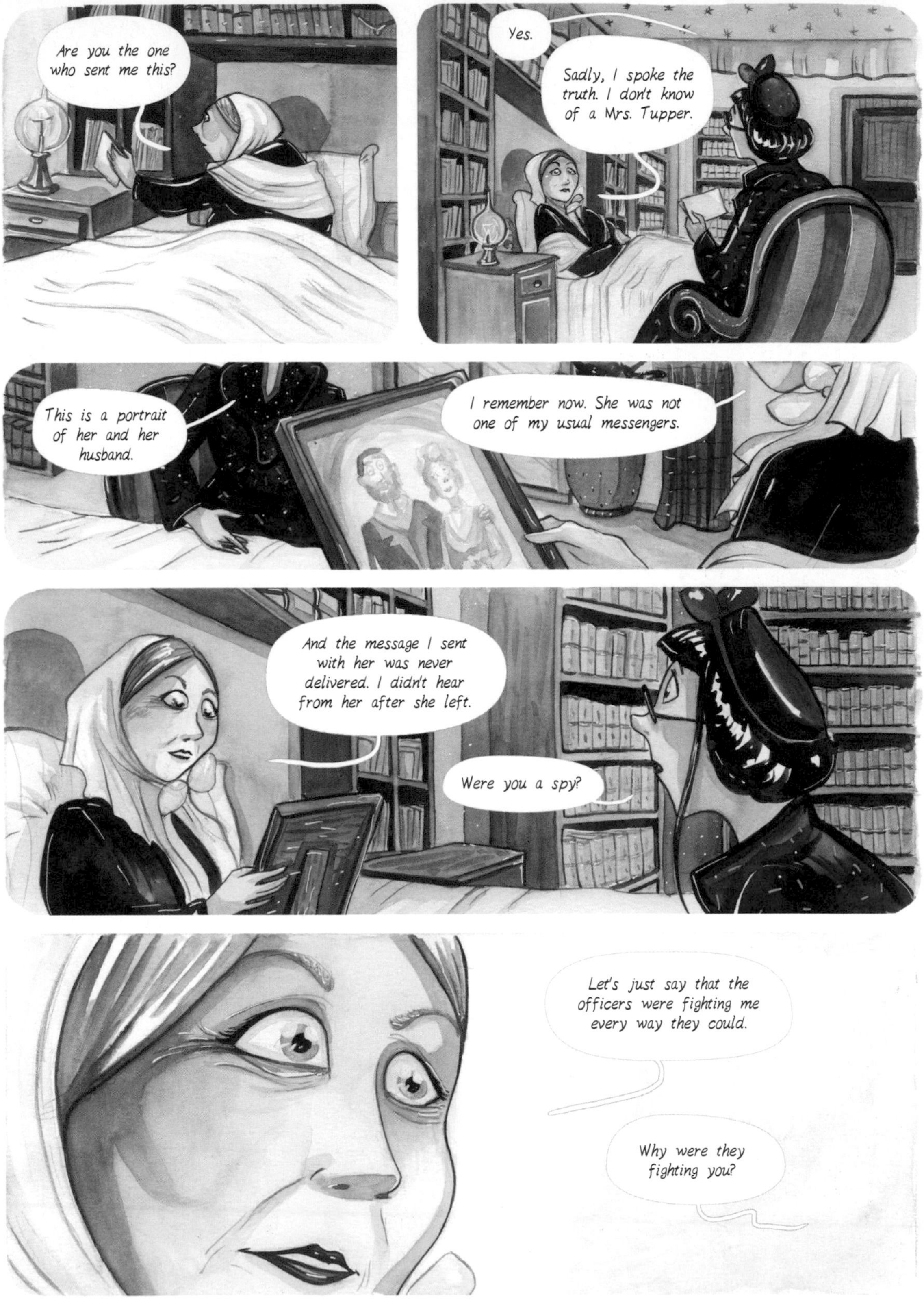
Are you the one who sent me this?
Yes.
Sadly, I spoke the truth. I don't know of a Mrs. Tupper.
This is a portrait of her and her husband.
I remember now. She was not one of my usual messengers.
And the message I sent with her was never delivered. I didn't hear from her after she left.
Were you a spy?
Let's just say that the officers were fighting me every way they could.
Why were they fighting you?

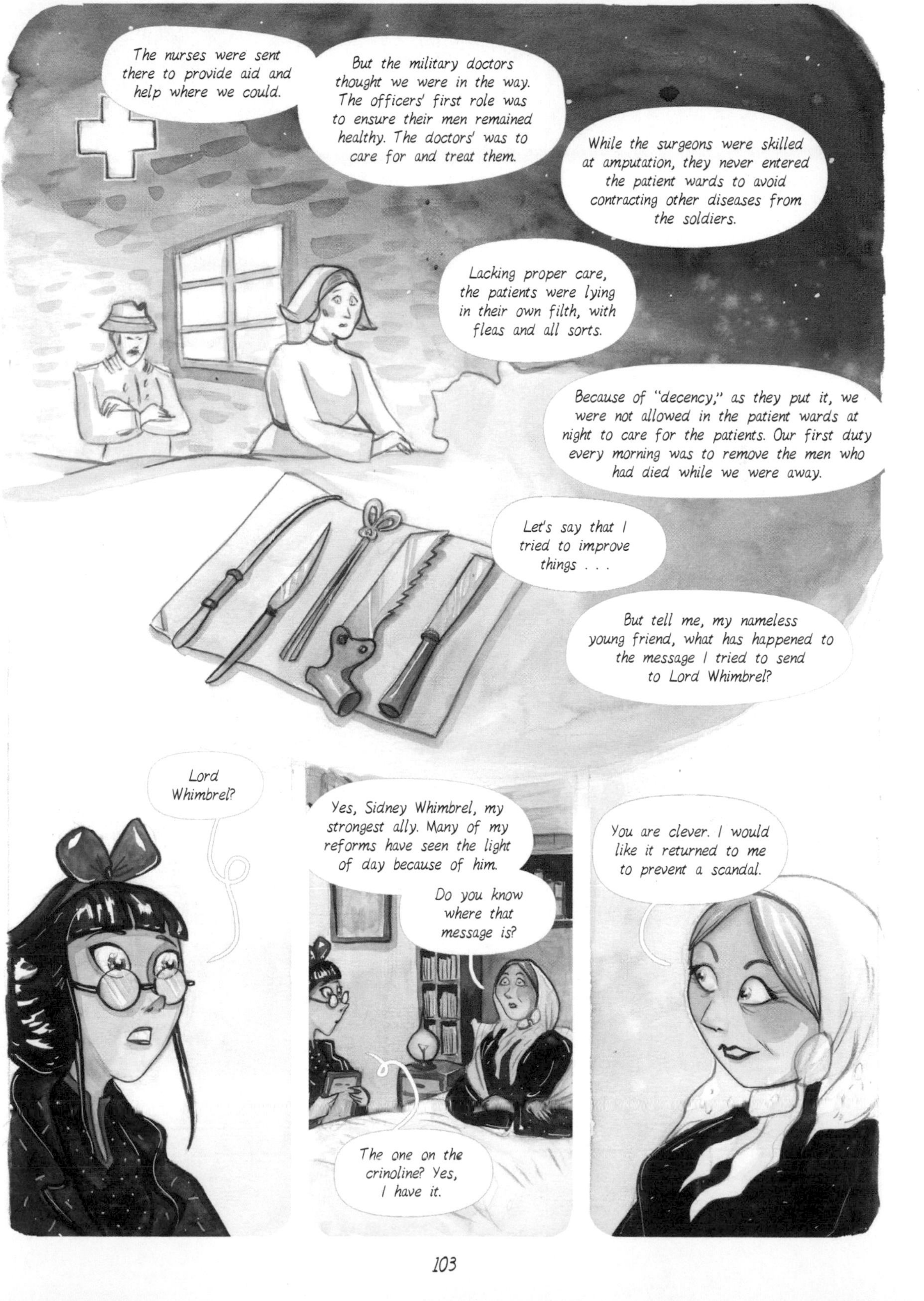
The nurses were sent there to provide aid and help where we could.
But the military doctors thought we were in the way. The officers' first role was to ensure their men remained healthy. The doctors' was to care for and treat them.
While the surgeons were skilled at amputation, they never entered the patient wards to avoid contracting other diseases from the soldiers.
Lacking proper care, the patients were lying in their own filth, with fleas and all sorts.
Because of "decency," as they put it, we were not allowed in the patient wards at night to care for the patients. Our first duty every morning was to remove the men who had died while we were away.
Let's say that I tried to improve things . . .
But tell me, my nameless young friend, what has happened to the message I tried to send to Lord Whimbrel?
Lord Whimbrel?
Yes, Sidney Whimbrel, my strongest ally. Many of my reforms have seen the light of day because of him.
Do you know where that message is?
The one on the crinoline? Yes, I have it.
You are clever. I would like it returned to me to prevent a scandal.

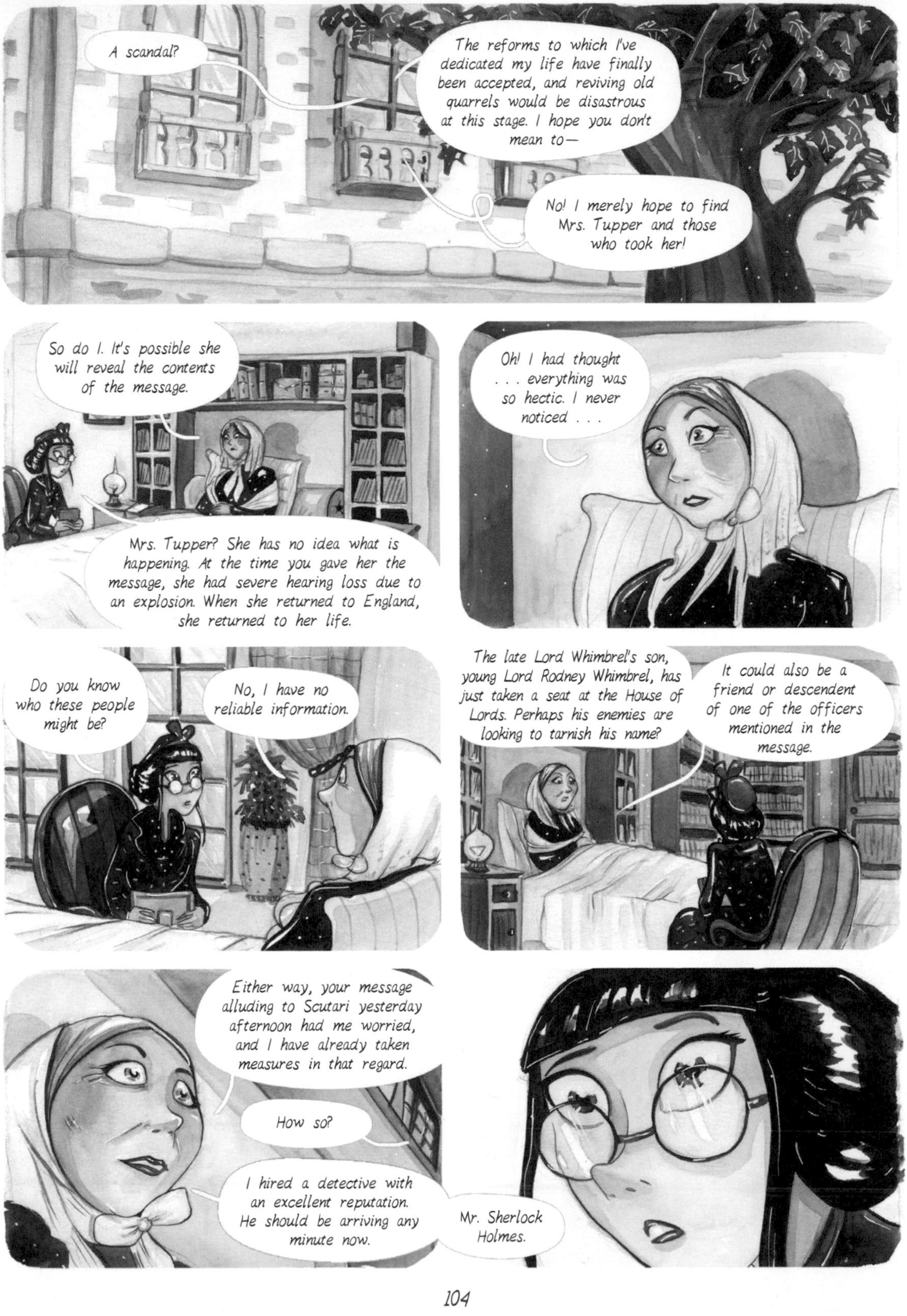
A scandal?
The reforms to which I've dedicated my life have finally been accepted, and reviving old quarrels would be disastrous at this stage. I hope you don't mean to—
No! I merely hope to find Mrs. Tupper and those who took her!
So do I. It's possible she will reveal the contents of the message.
Mrs. Tupper? She has no idea what is happening. At the time you gave her the message, she had severe hearing loss due to an explosion. When she returned to England, she returned to her life.
Oh! I had thought . . . everything was so hectic. I never noticed . . .
Do you know who these people might be?
No, I have no reliable information.
The late Lord Whimbrel's son, young Lord Rodney Whimbrel, has just taken a seat at the House of Lords. Perhaps his enemies are looking to tarnish his name?
It could also be a friend or descendent of one of the officers mentioned in the message.
Either way, your message alluding to Scutari yesterday afternoon had me worried, and I have already taken measures in that regard.
How so?
I hired a detective with an excellent reputation. He should be arriving any minute now.
Mr. Sherlock Holmes.

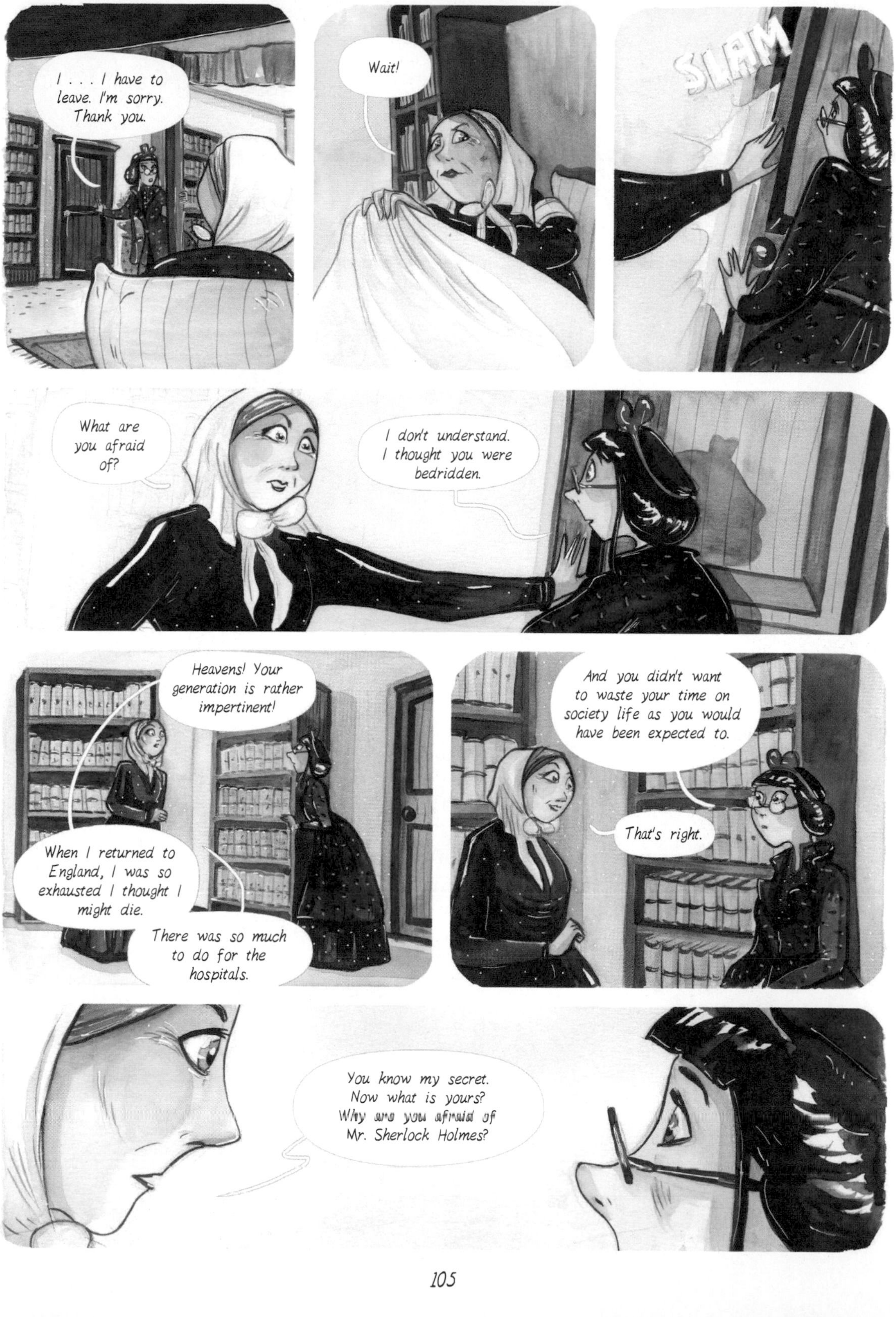
I . . . I have to leave. I'm sorry. Thank you.
Wait!
SLAM
What are you afraid of?
I don't understand. I thought you were bedridden.
Heavens! Your generation is rather impertinent!
When I returned to England, I was so exhausted I thought I might die.
There was so much to do for the hospitals.
And you didn't want to waste your time on society life as you would have been expected to.
That's right.
You know my secret. Now what is yours? Why are you afraid of Mr. Sherlock Holmes?

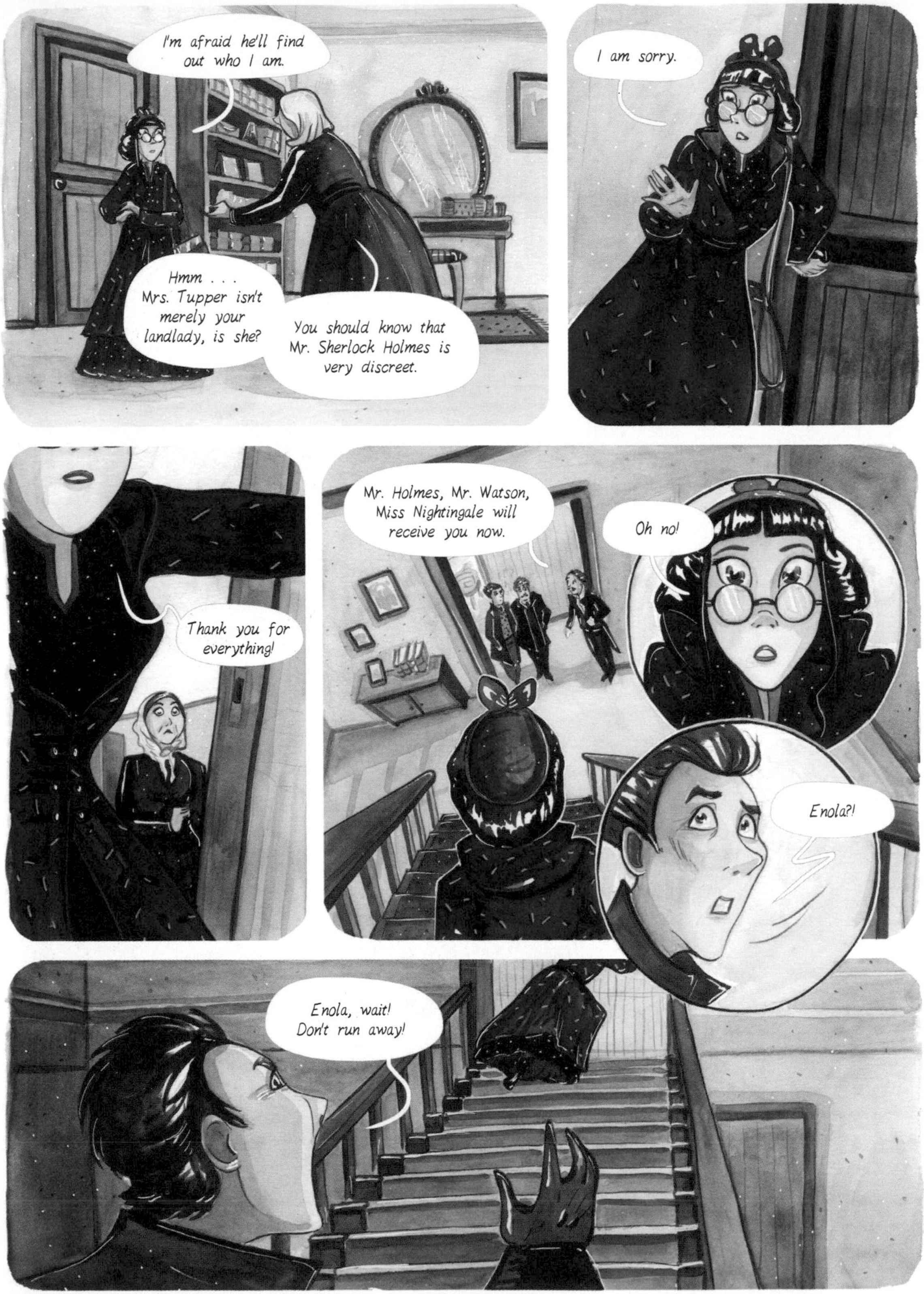
I'm afraid he'll find out who I am.
Hmm . . . Mrs. Tupper isn't merely your landlady, is she?
You should know that Mr. Sherlock Holmes is very discreet.
I am sorry.
Thank you for everything!
Mr. Holmes, Mr. Watson, Miss Nightingale will receive you now.
Oh no!
Enola?!
Enola, wait! Don't run away!

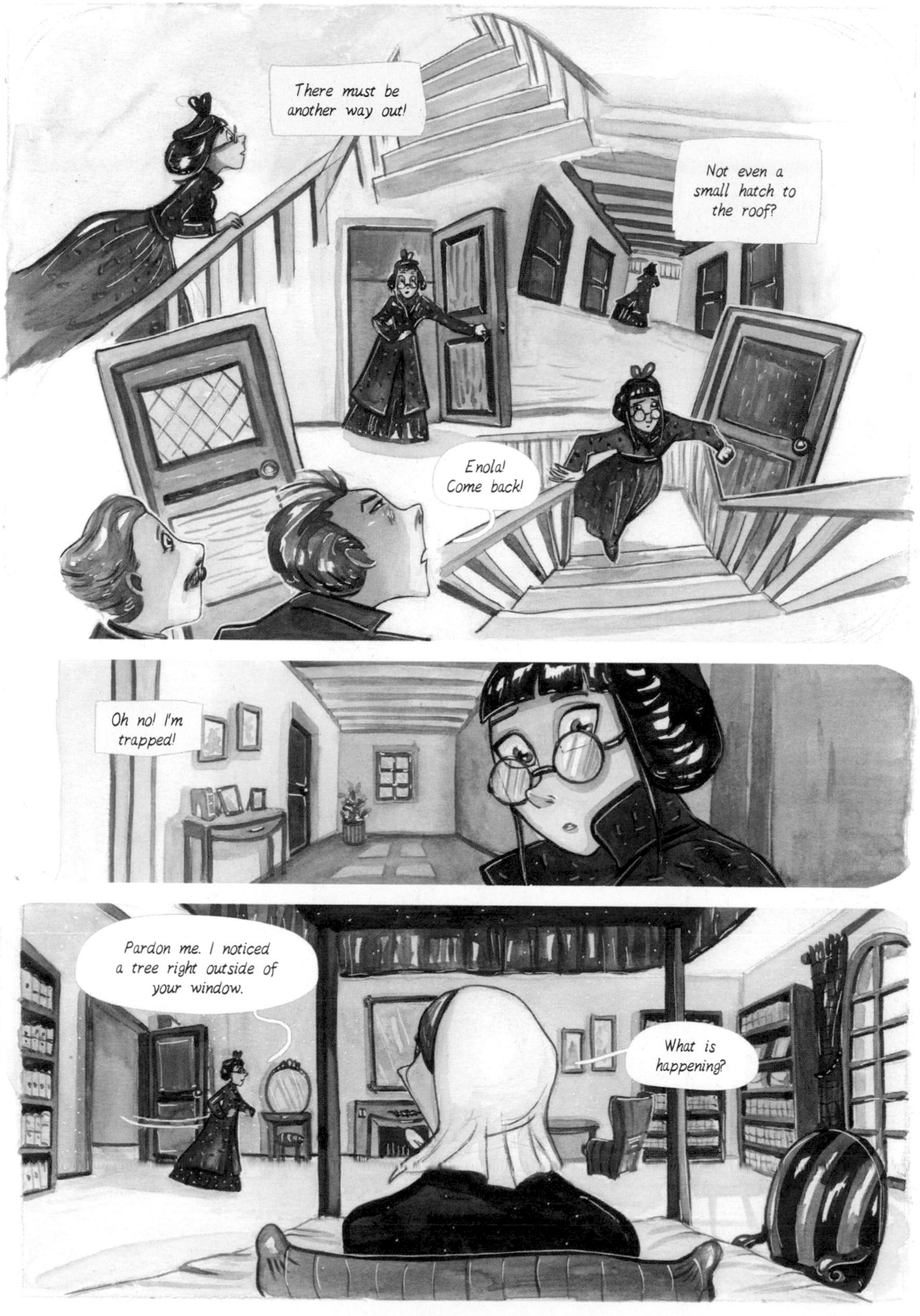
There must be another way out!
Not even a small hatch to the roof?
Enola! Come back!
Oh no! I'm trapped!
Pardon me. I noticed a tree right outside of your window.
What is happening?

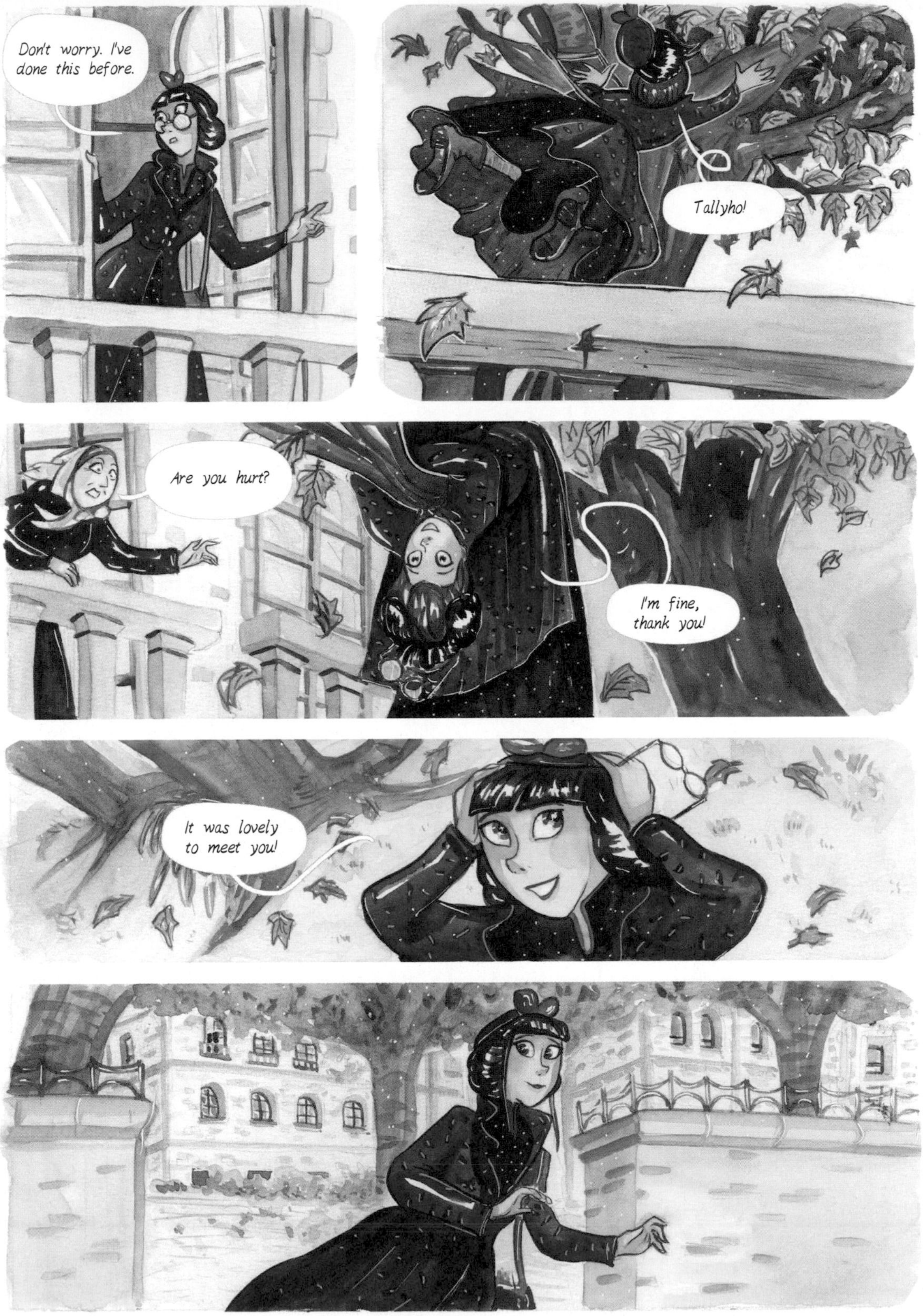
Don't worry. I've done this before.
Tallyho!
Are you hurt?
I'm fine, thank you!
It was lovely to meet you!

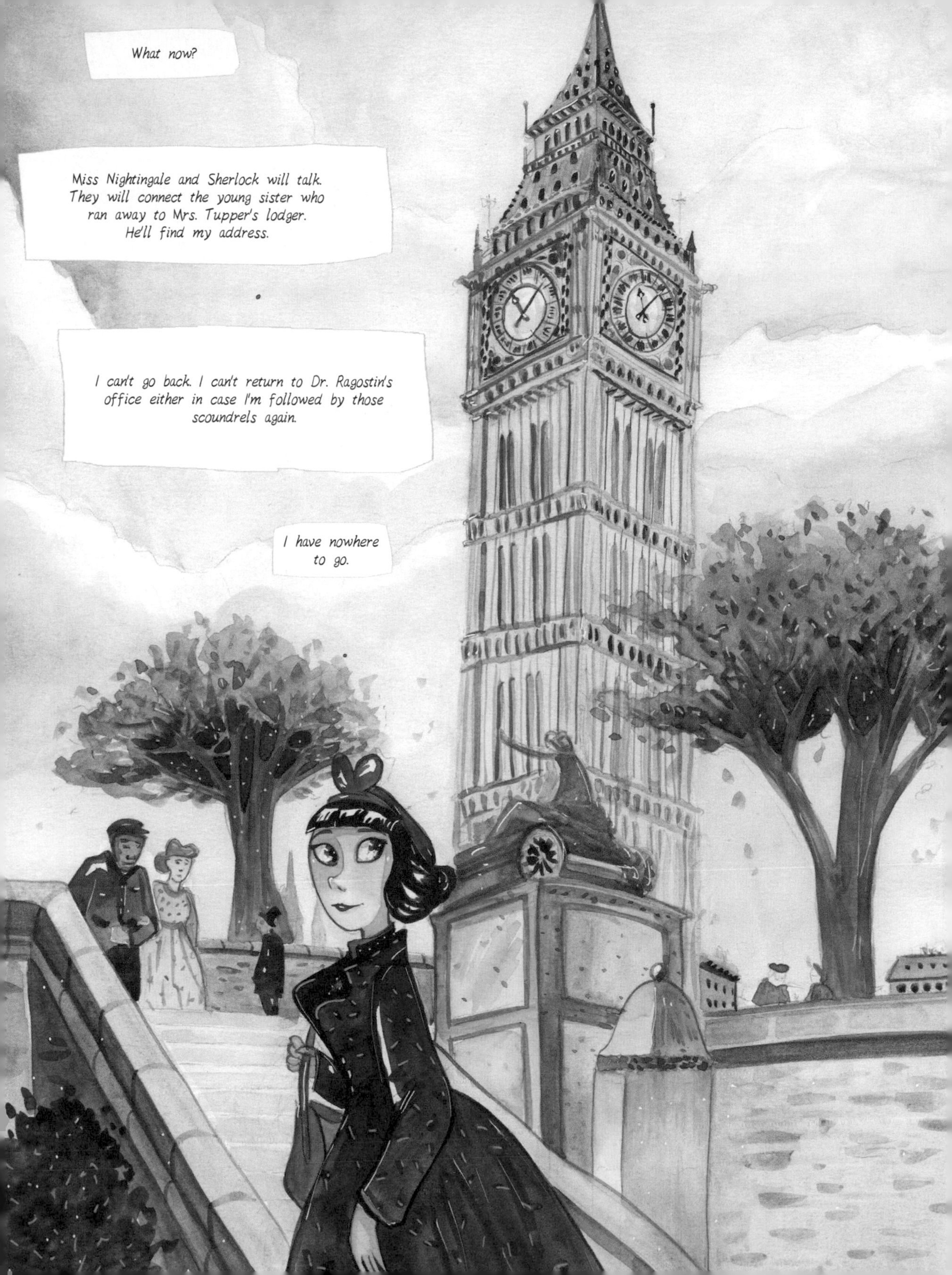
What now?
Miss Nightingale and Sherlock will talk. They will connect the young sister who ran away to Mrs. Tupper's lodger. He'll find my address.
I can't go back. I can't return to Dr. Ragostin's office either in case I'm followed by those scoundrels again.
I have nowhere to go.

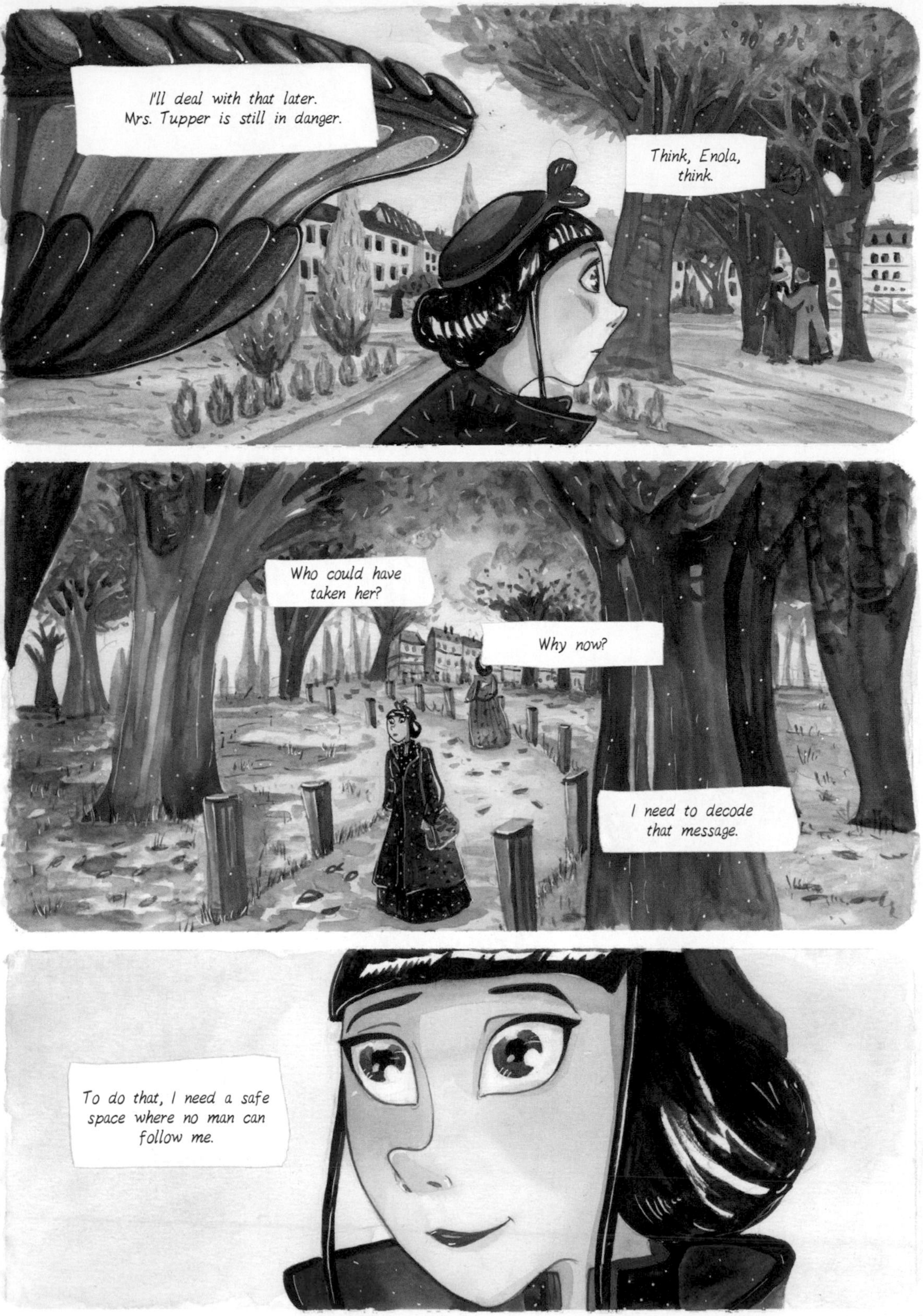
I'll deal with that later.
Mrs. Tupper is still in danger.
Think, Enola, think.
Who could have taken her?
Why now?
I need to decode that message.
To do that, I need a safe space where no man can follow me.

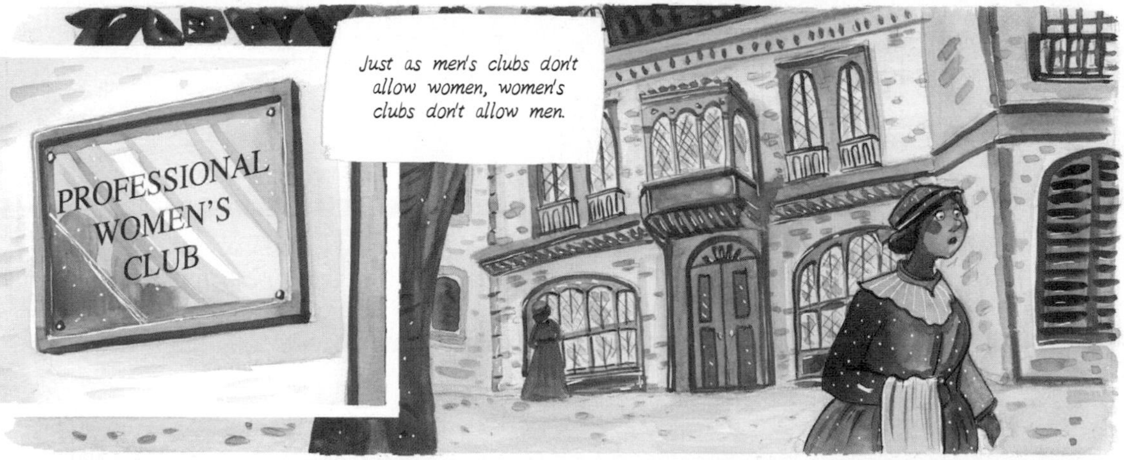
Just as men's clubs don't allow women, women's clubs don't allow men.
PROFESSIONAL WOMEN'S CLUB

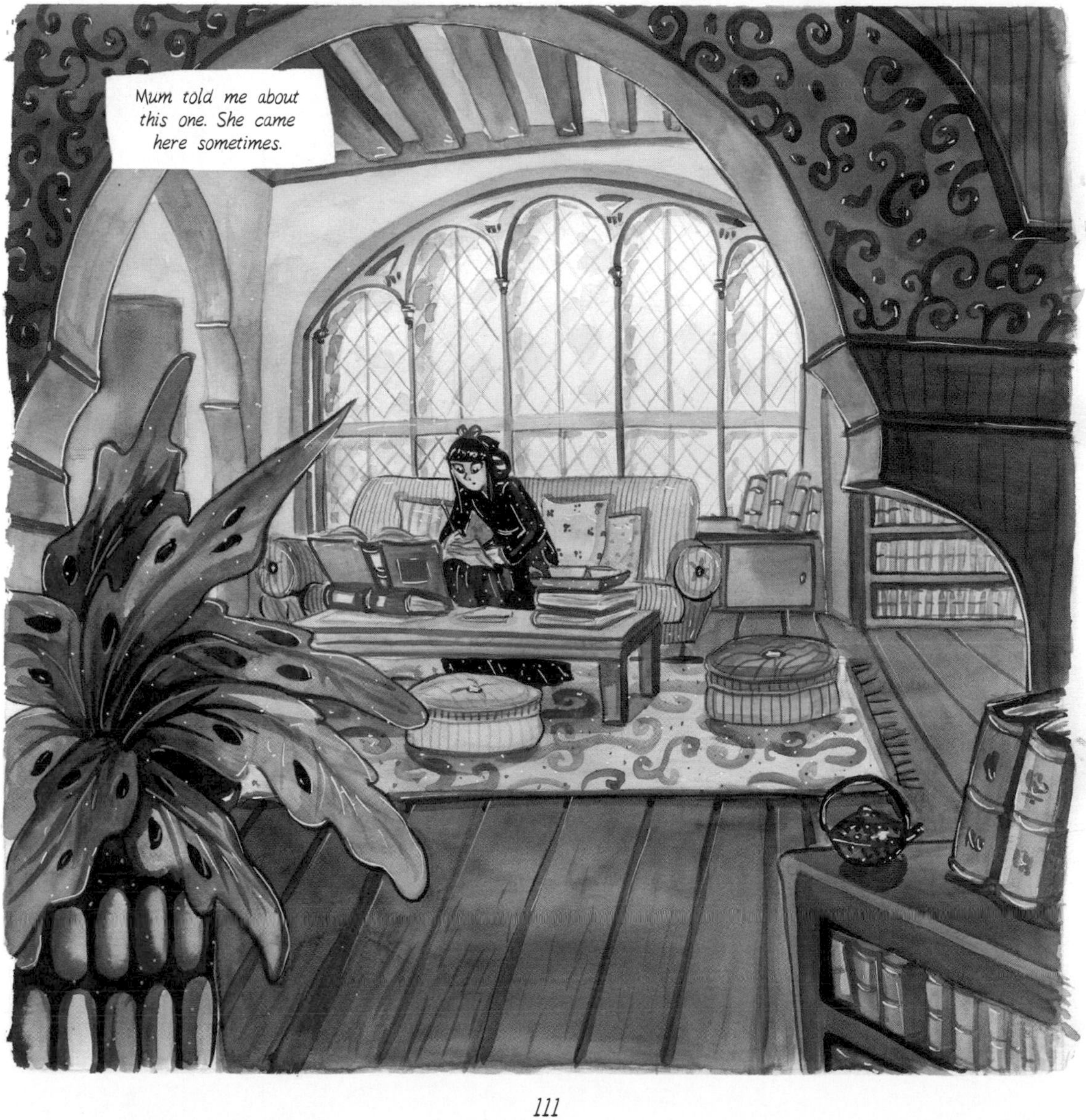
Mum told me about this one. She came here sometimes.

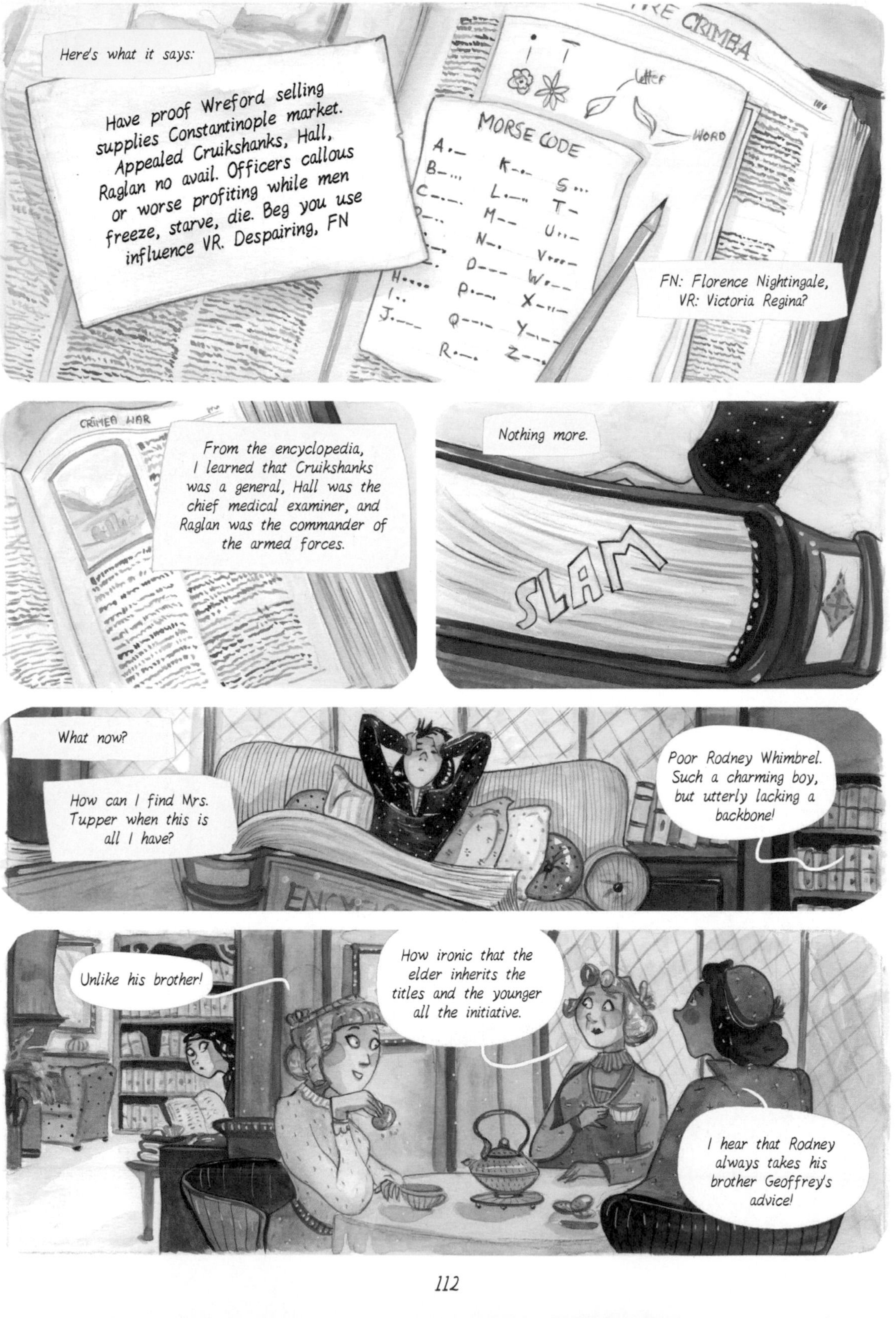
Here's what it says:
Have proof Wreford selling supplies Constantinople market. Appealed Cruikshanks, Hall, Raglan no avail. Officers callous or worse profiting while men freeze, starve, die. Beg you use influence VR. Despairing, FN
THE CRIMEA
LETTER
WORD
MORSE CODE
FN: Florence Nightingale, VR: Victoria Regina?
CRIMEA WAR
From the encyclopedia, I learned that Cruikshanks was a general, Hall was the chief medical examiner, and Raglan was the commander of the armed forces.
Nothing more.
SLAM
What now?
How can I find Mrs. Tupper when this is all I have?
Poor Rodney Whimbrel. Such a charming boy, but utterly lacking a backbone!
Unlike his brother!
How ironic that the elder inherits the titles and the younger all the initiative.
I hear that Rodney always takes his brother Geoffrey's advice!

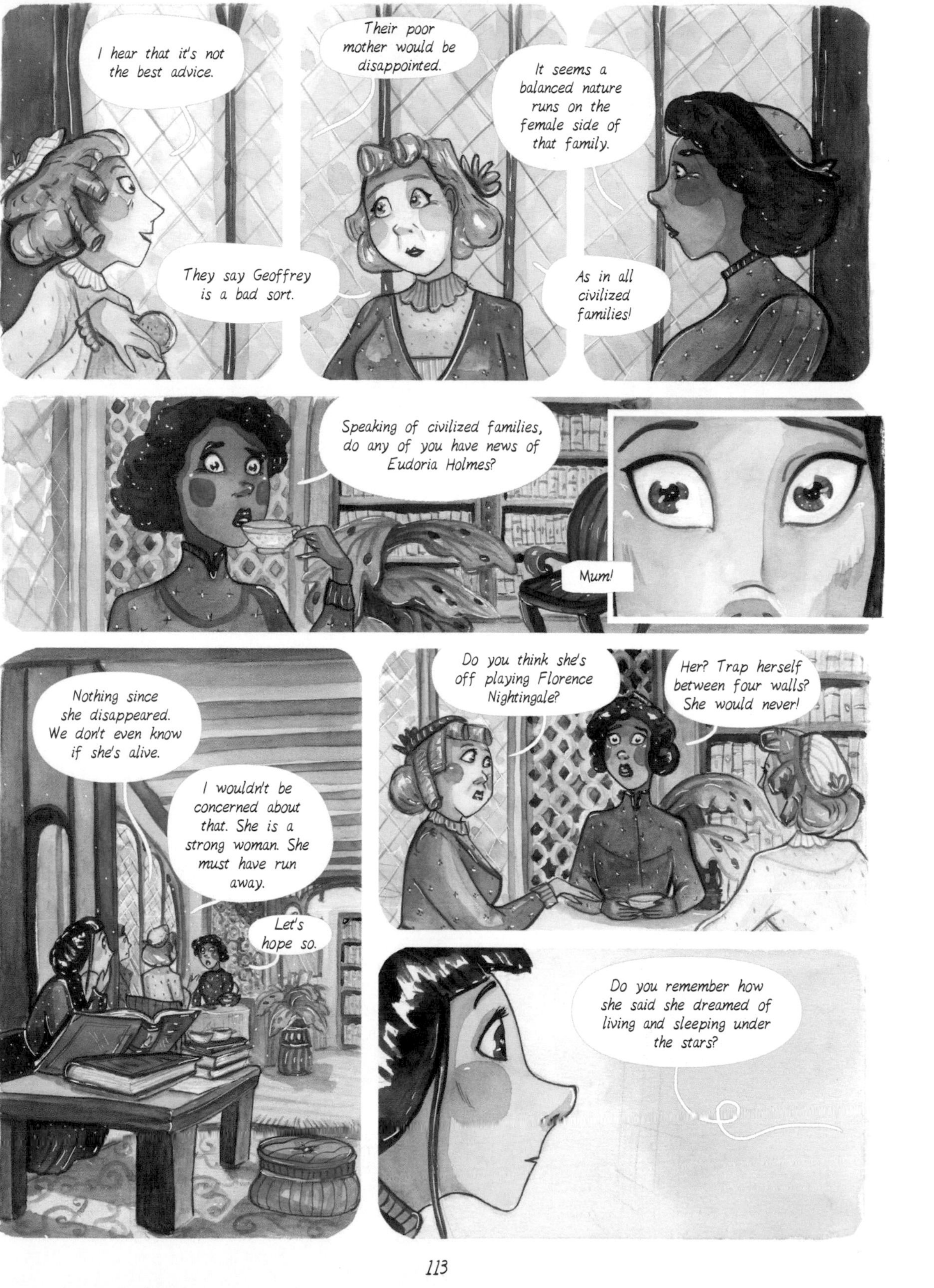
I hear that it's not the best advice.
They say Geoffrey is a bad sort.
Their poor mother would be disappointed.
It seems a balanced nature runs on the female side of that family.
As in all civilized families!
Speaking of civilized families, do any of you have news of Eudoria Holmes?
Mum!
Nothing since she disappeared. We don't even know if she's alive.
I wouldn't be concerned about that. She is a strong woman. She must have run away.
Let's hope so.
Do you think she's off playing Florence Nightingale?
Her? Trap herself between four walls? She would never!
Do you remember how she said she dreamed of living and sleeping under the stars?

Speaking of Nightingale, did you hear the reform news?

Right, they are changing topics.

Mum, under the stars . . .

Time is running out. I need to focus on Mrs. Tupper.

FLORENCE NIGHTINGALE

I can eliminate Florence Nightingale as a suspect. She wants the message back and wouldn't have hired Sherlock Holmes if she were involved in the abduction.

LORD WHIMBREL

SHERLOCK HOLMES

Miss Nightingale said the message was for Lord Whimbrel.

Lord Whimbrel is an ally, and he is no longer alive.

Unless his ghost . . .

RODNEY-GEOFFREY

Perhaps a descendent? Apparently the elder one, Rodney, has just taken a seat in the House of Lords. A scandal would not be welcome.

Could Rodney or Geoffrey be the scoundrels? Are they trying to nip a scandal in the bud?

114

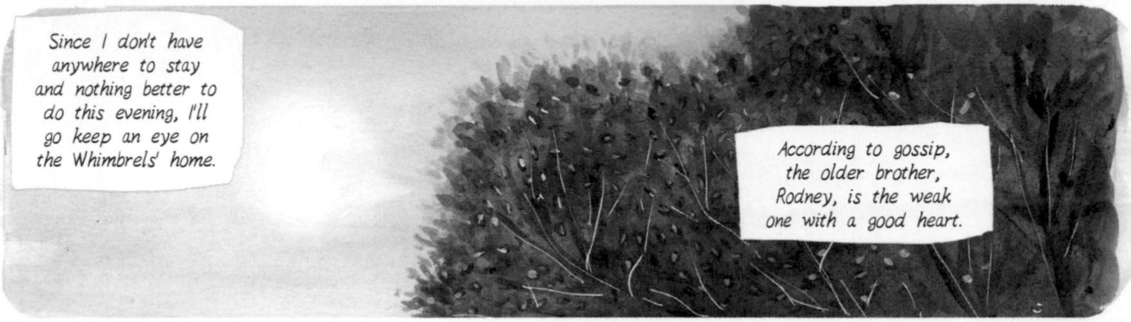
Since I don't have anywhere to stay and nothing better to do this evening, I'll go keep an eye on the Whimbrels' home.
According to gossip, the older brother, Rodney, is the weak one with a good heart.

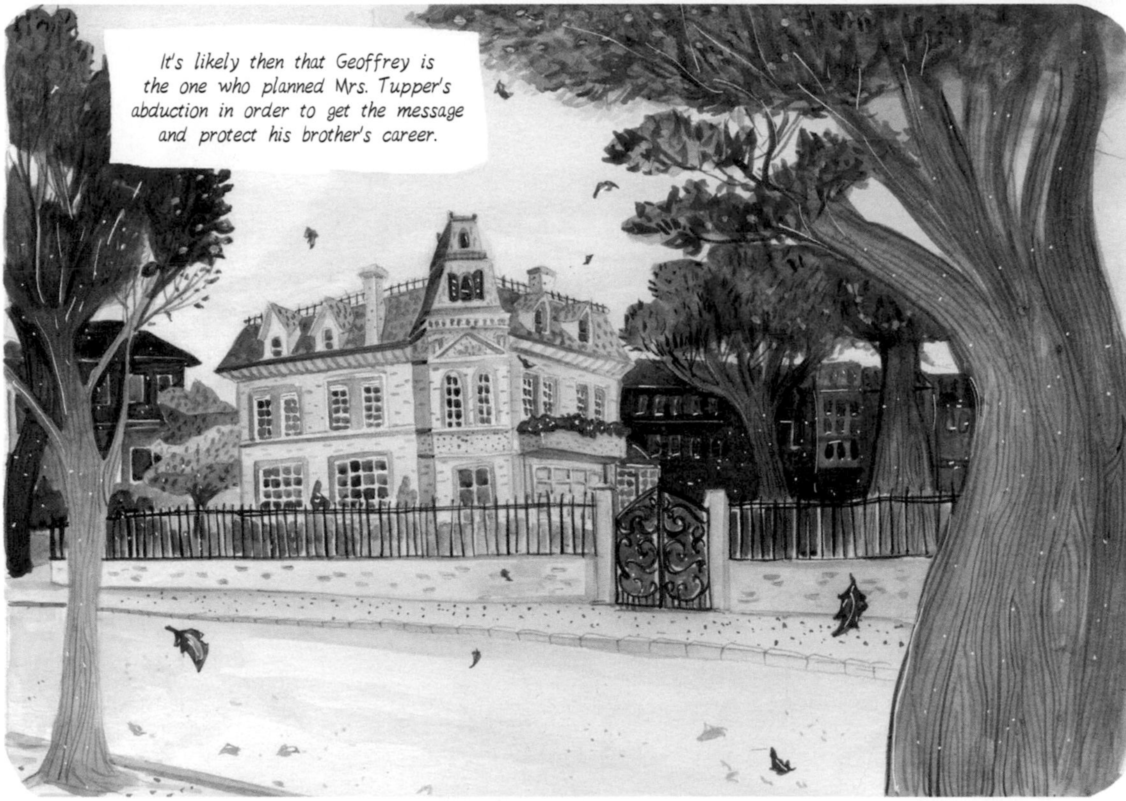
It's likely then that Geoffrey is the one who planned Mrs. Tupper's abduction in order to get the message and protect his brother's career.

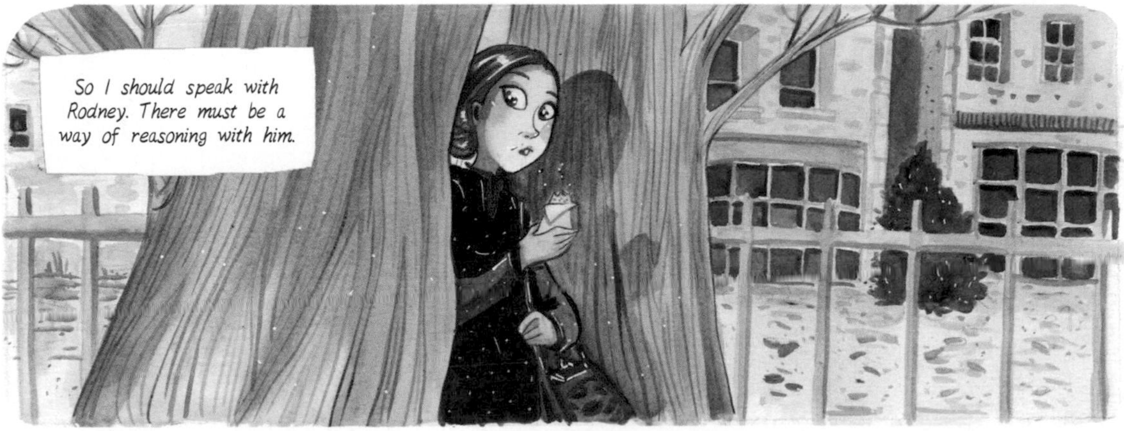
So I should speak with Rodney. There must be a way of reasoning with him.

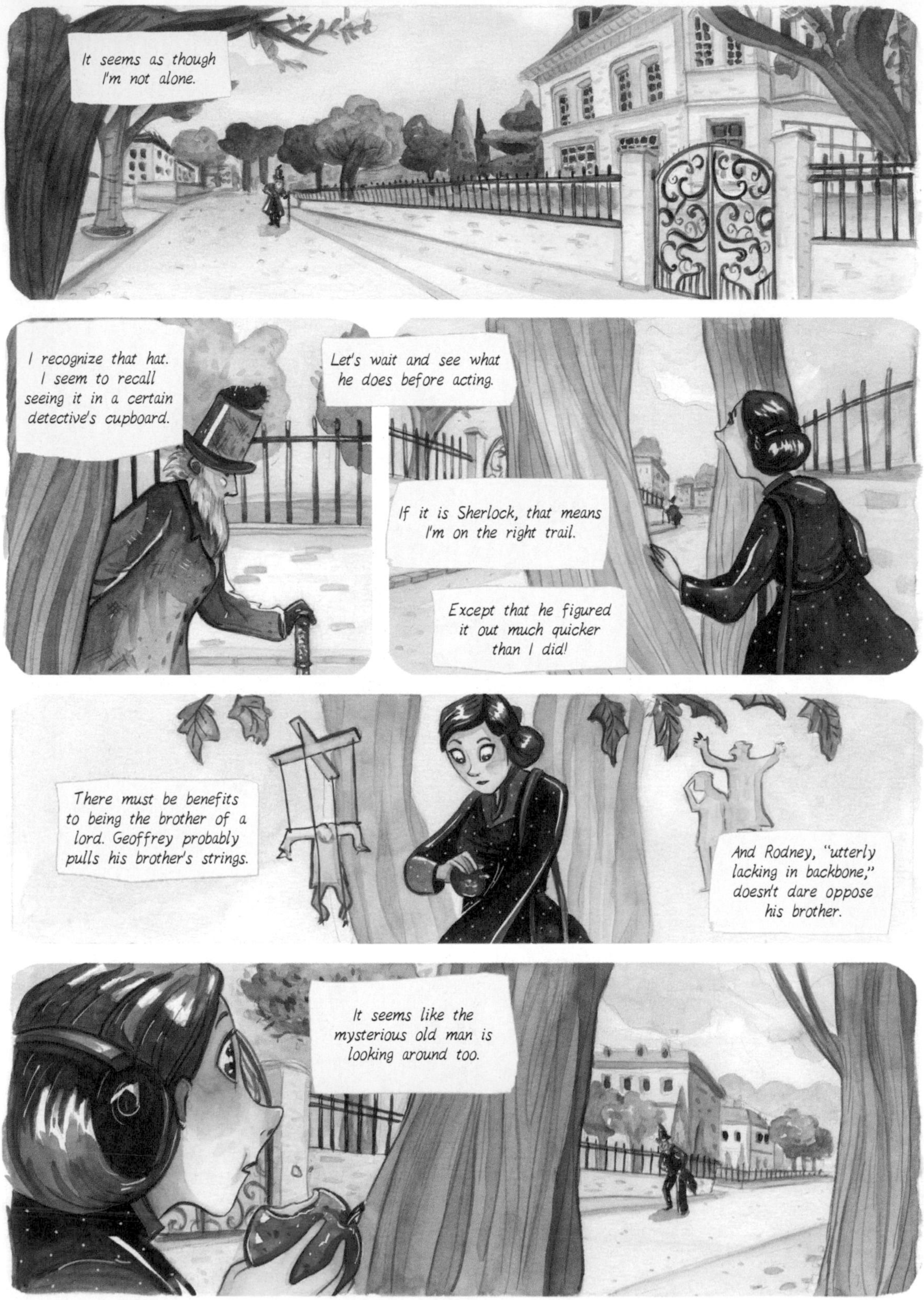
It seems as though I'm not alone.
I recognize that hat. I seem to recall seeing it in a certain detective's cupboard.
Let's wait and see what he does before acting.
If it is Sherlock, that means I'm on the right trail.
Except that he figured it out much quicker than I did!
There must be benefits to being the brother of a lord. Geoffrey probably pulls his brother's strings.
And Rodney, "utterly lacking in backbone," doesn't dare oppose his brother.
It seems like the mysterious old man is looking around too.

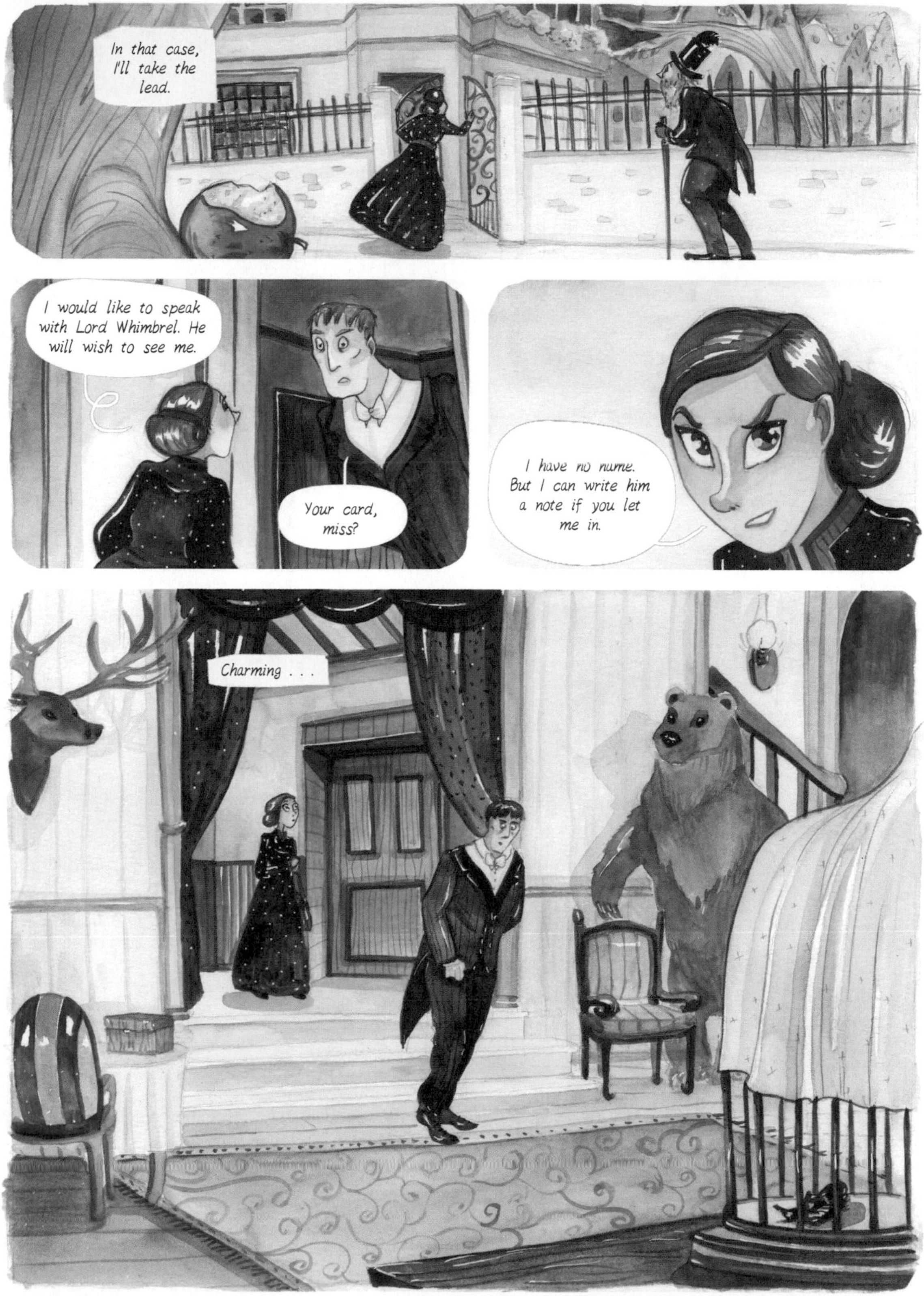
In that case, I'll take the lead.
I would like to speak with Lord Whimbrel. He will wish to see me.
Your card, miss?
I have no name. But I can write him a note if you let me in.
Charming . . .

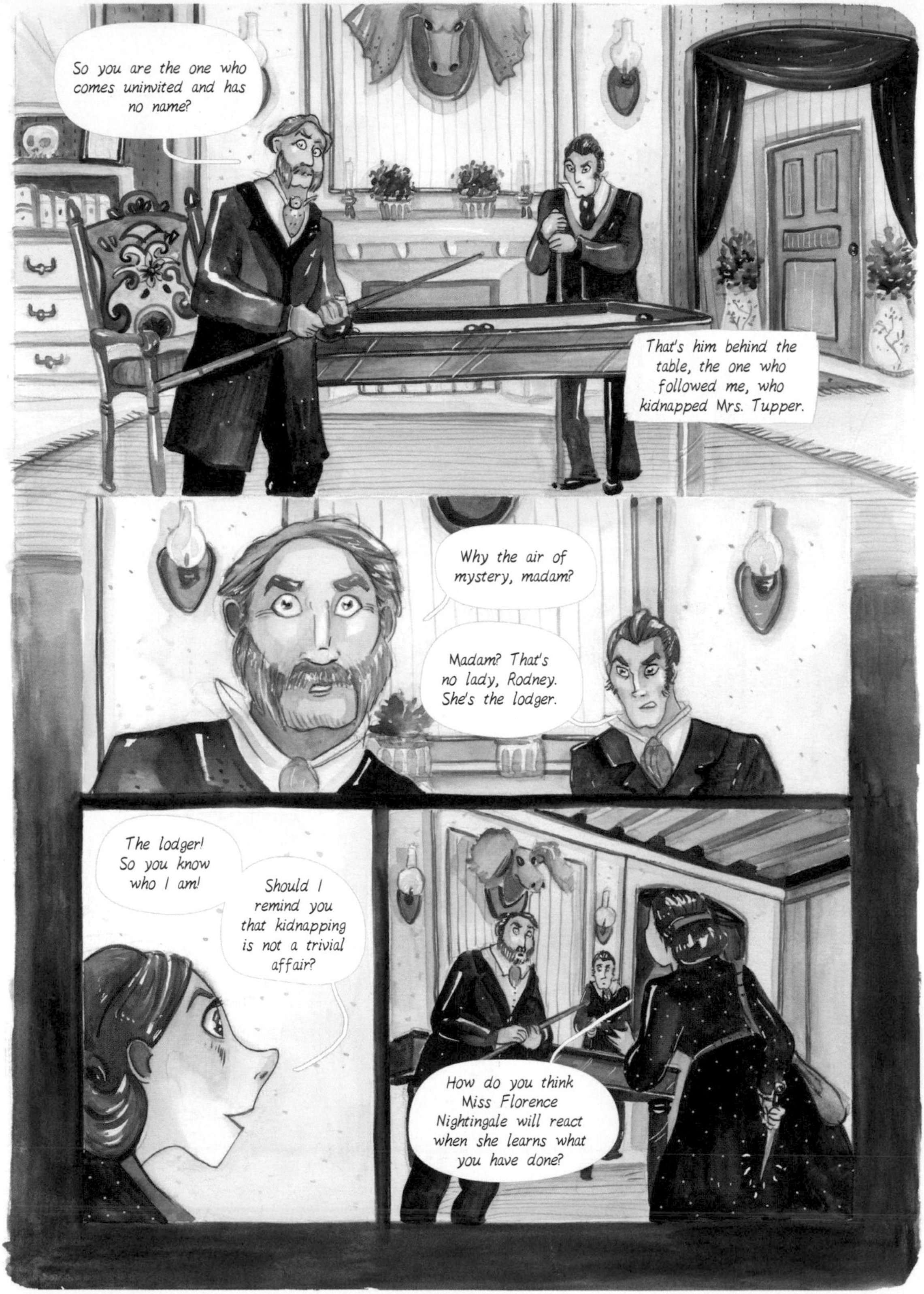
So you are the one who comes uninvited and has no name?
That's him behind the table, the one who followed me, who kidnapped Mrs. Tupper.
Why the air of mystery, madam?
Madam? That's no lady, Rodney. She's the lodger.
The lodger! So you know who I am!
Should I remind you that kidnapping is not a trivial affair?
How do you think Miss Florence Nightingale will react when she learns what you have done?

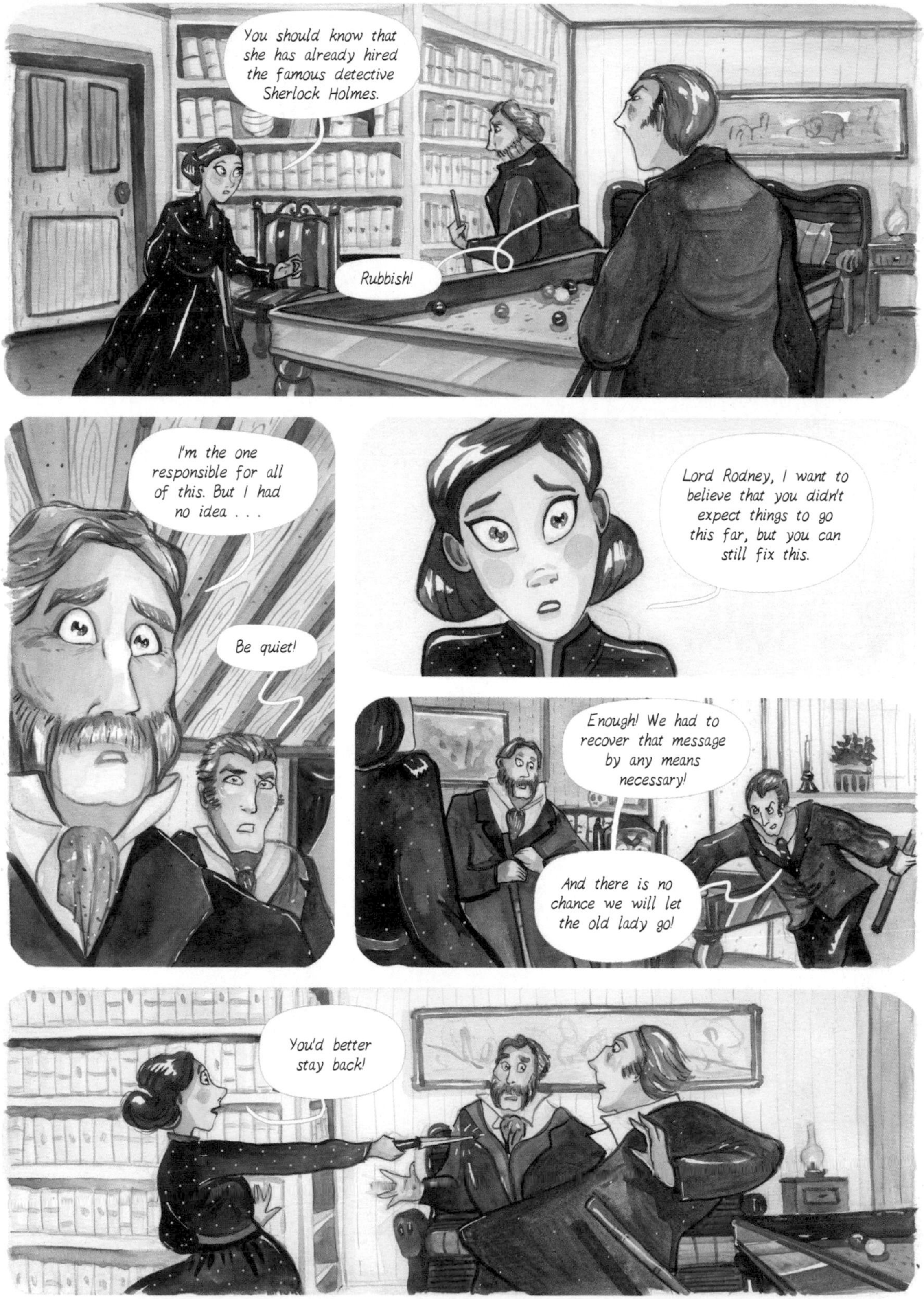
You should know that she has already hired the famous detective Sherlock Holmes.
Rubbish!
I'm the one responsible for all of this. But I had no idea . . .
Be quiet!
Lord Rodney, I want to believe that you didn't expect things to go this far, but you can still fix this.
Enough! We had to recover that message by any means necessary!
And there is no chance we will let the old lady go!
You'd better stay back!

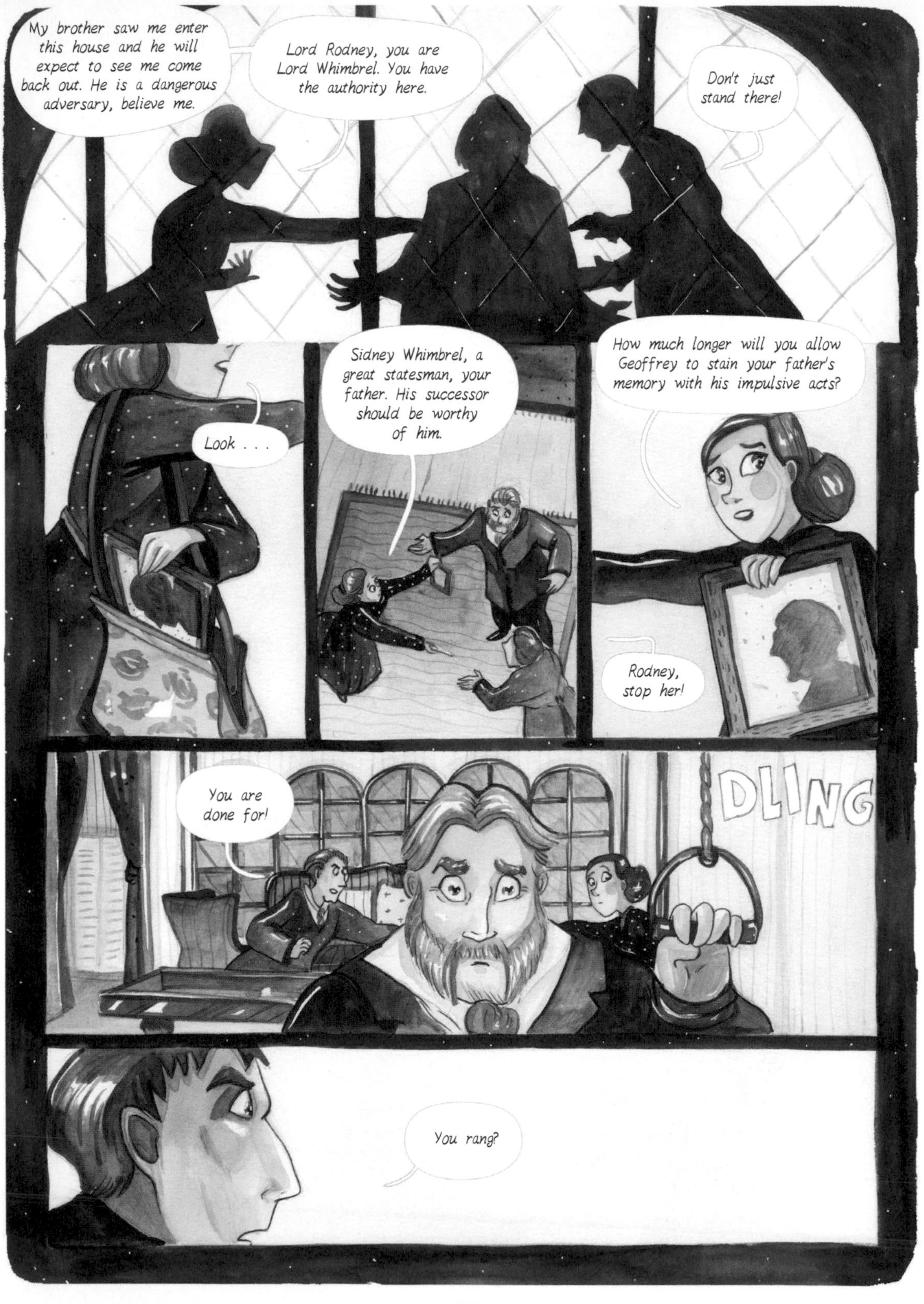
My brother saw me enter this house and he will expect to see me come back out. He is a dangerous adversary, believe me.
Lord Rodney, you are Lord Whimbrel. You have the authority here.
Don't just stand there!
Look . . .
Sidney Whimbrel, a great statesman, your father. His successor should be worthy of him.
How much longer will you allow Geoffrey to stain your father's memory with his impulsive acts?
Rodney, stop her!
You are done for!
DLING
You rang?

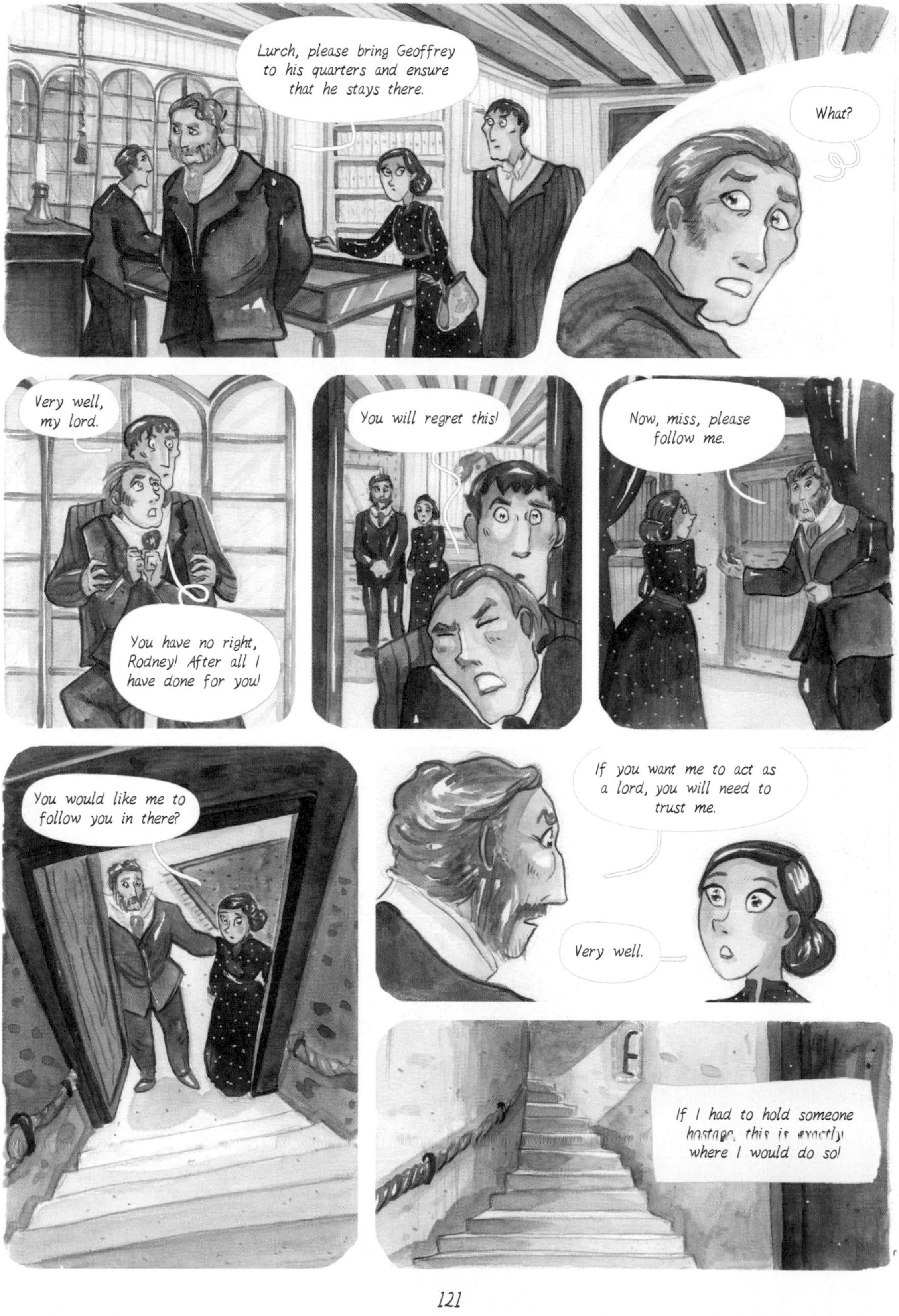
Lurch, please bring Geoffrey to his quarters and ensure that he stays there.
What?
Very well, my lord.
You have no right, Rodney! After all I have done for you!
You will regret this!
Now, miss, please follow me.
You would like me to follow you in there?
If you want me to act as a lord, you will need to trust me.
Very well.
If I had to hold someone hostage, this is exactly where I would do so!

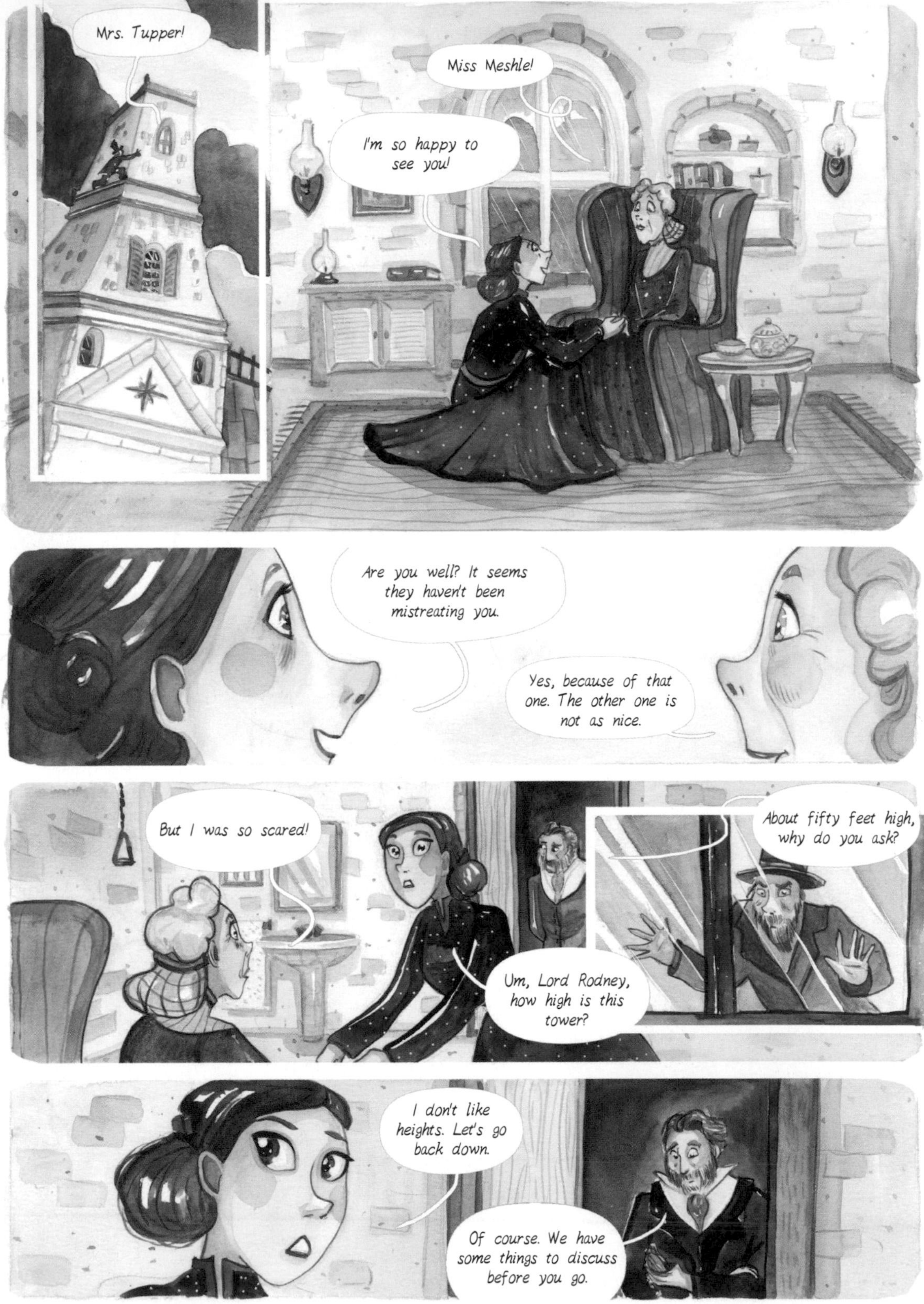
Mrs. Tupper!
Miss Meshle!
I'm so happy to see you!
Are you well? It seems they haven't been mistreating you.
Yes, because of that one. The other one is not as nice.
But I was so scared!
Um, Lord Rodney, how high is this tower?
About fifty feet high, why do you ask?
I don't like heights. Let's go back down.
Of course. We have some things to discuss before you go.

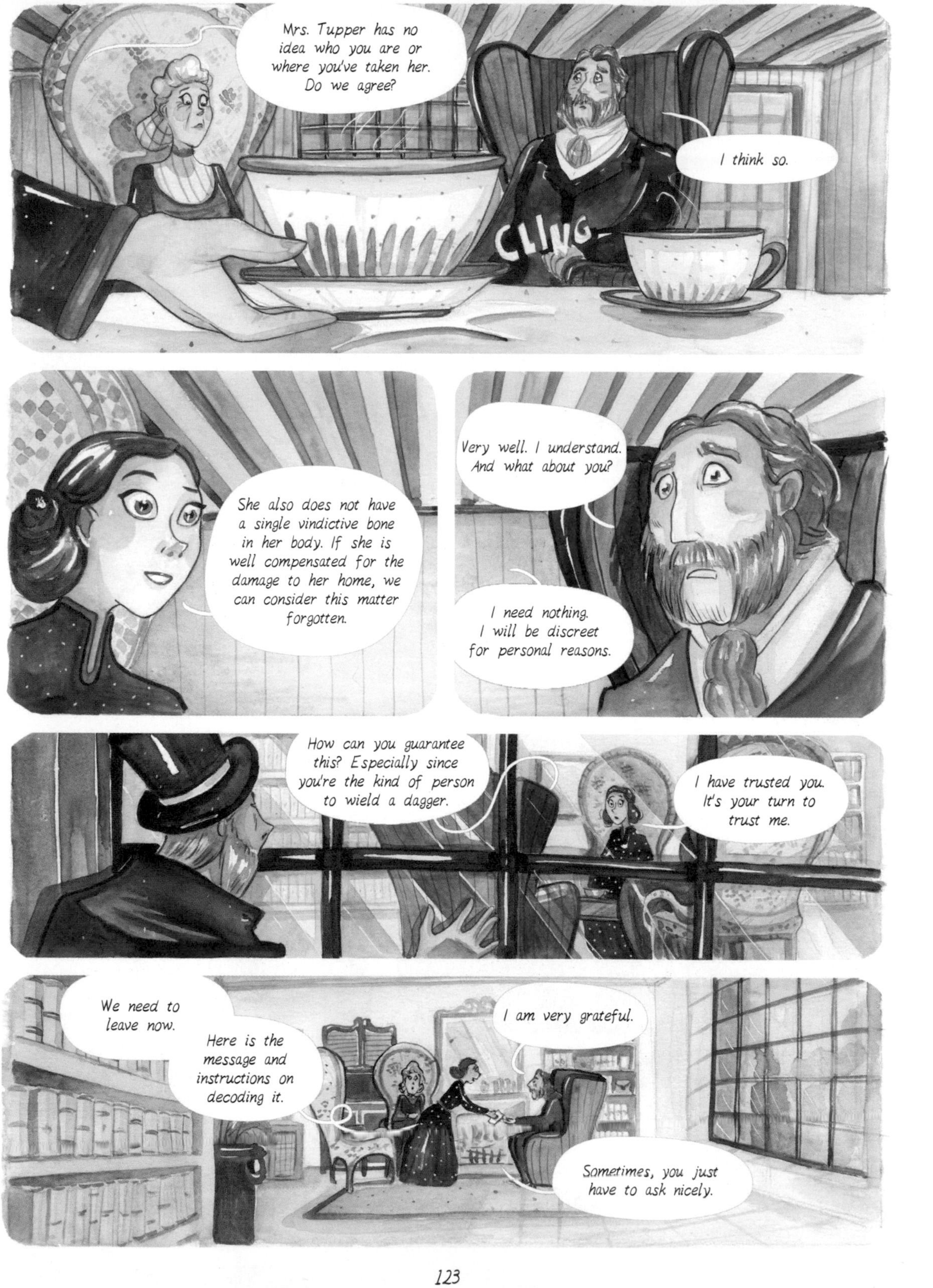
Mrs. Tupper has no idea who you are or where you've taken her. Do we agree?
I think so.
CLING
She also does not have a single vindictive bone in her body. If she is well compensated for the damage to her home, we can consider this matter forgotten.
Very well. I understand. And what about you?
I need nothing. I will be discreet for personal reasons.
How can you guarantee this? Especially since you're the kind of person to wield a dagger.
I have trusted you. It's your turn to trust me.
We need to leave now.
Here is the message and instructions on decoding it.
I am very grateful.
Sometimes, you just have to ask nicely.

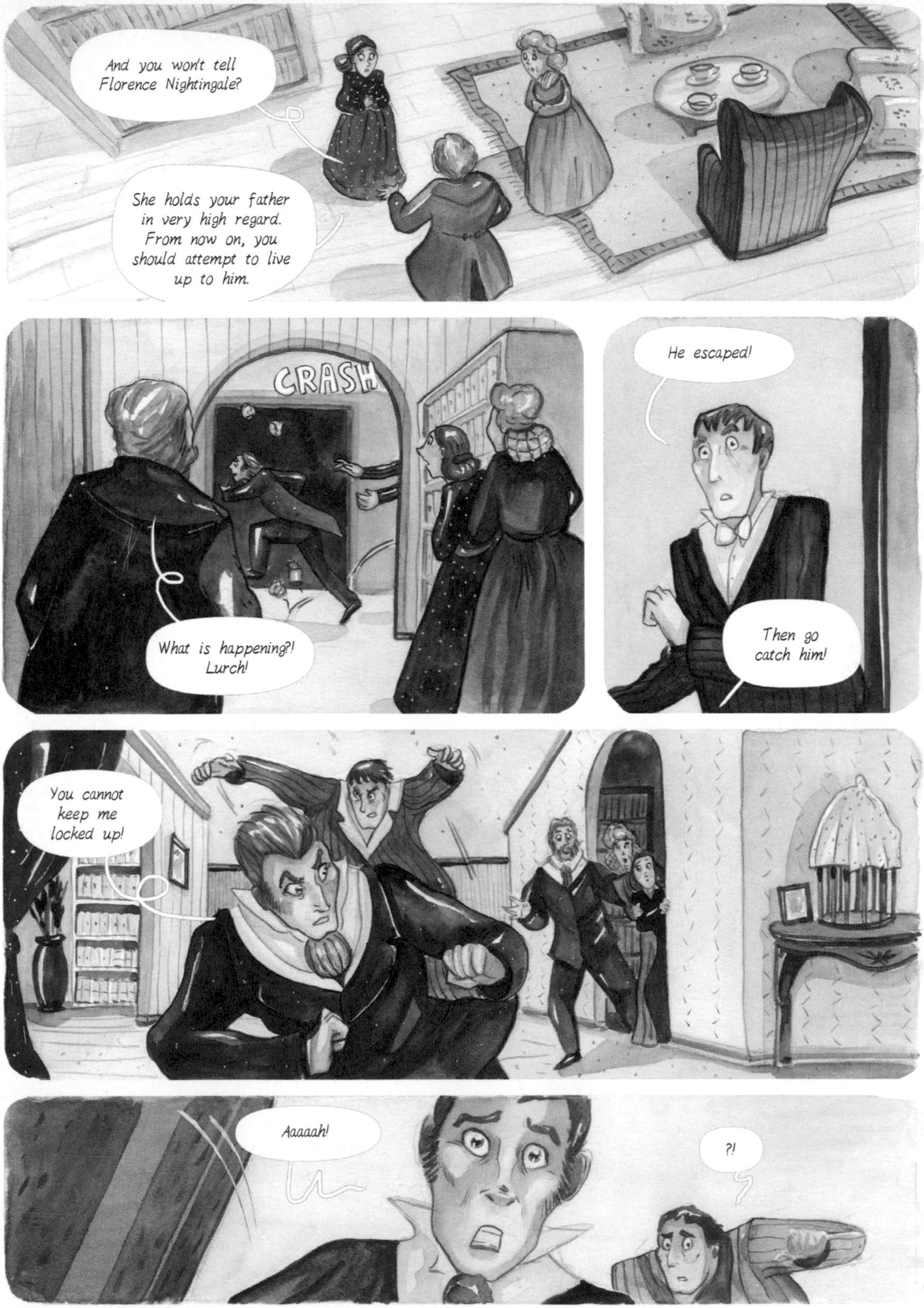
And you won't tell Florence Nightingale?
She holds your father in very high regard. From now on, you should attempt to live up to him.
CRASH
What is happening?! Lurch!
He escaped!
Then go catch him!
You cannot keep me locked up!
Aaaaah!
?!

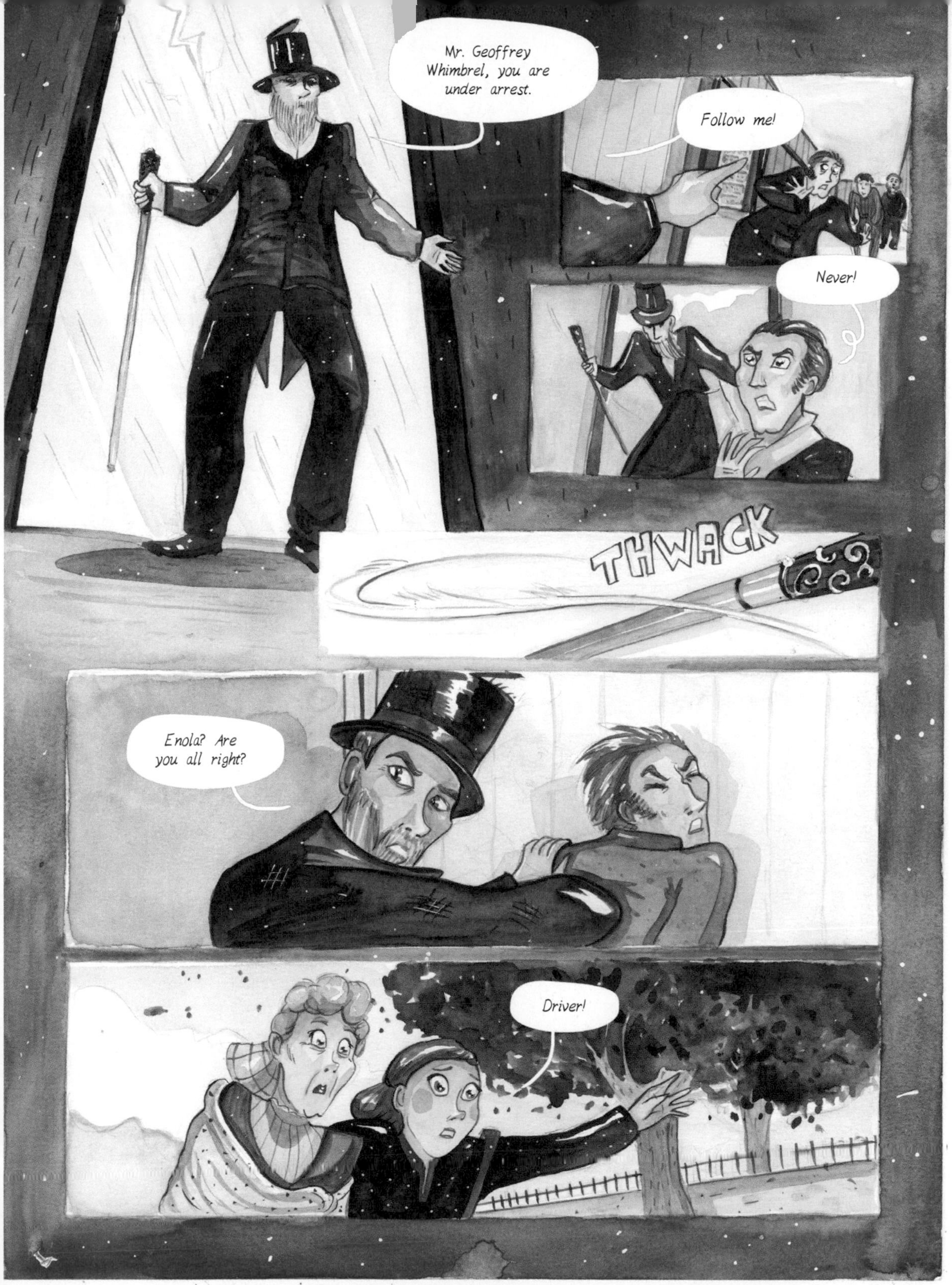
Mr. Geoffrey Whimbrel, you are under arrest.
Follow me!
Never!
THWACK
Enola? Are you all right?
Driver!

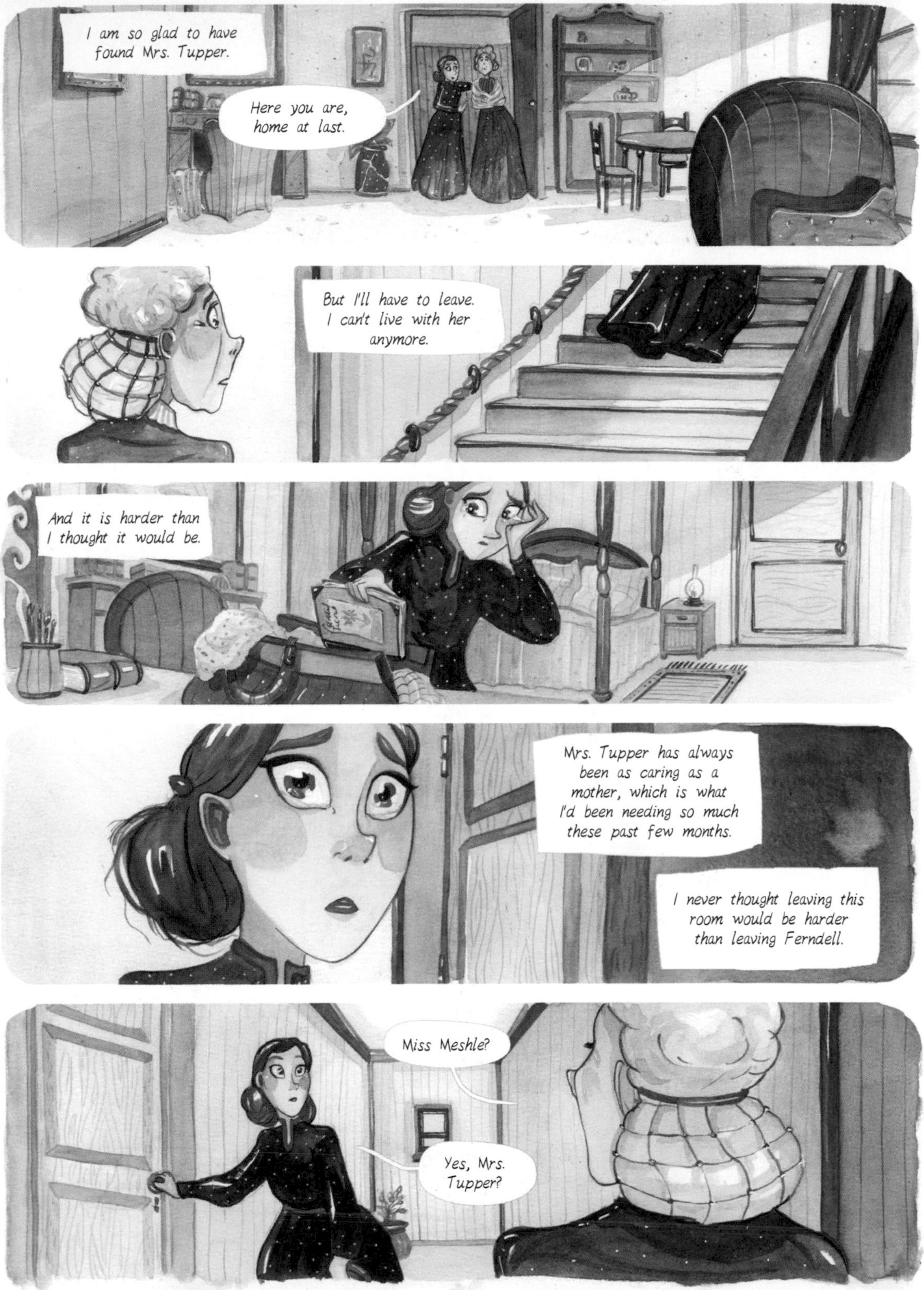
I am so glad to have found Mrs. Tupper.
Here you are, home at last.
But I'll have to leave. I can't live with her anymore.
And it is harder than I thought it would be.
Mrs. Tupper has always been as caring as a mother, which is what I'd been needing so much these past few months.
I never thought leaving this room would be harder than leaving Ferndell.
Miss Meshle?
Yes, Mrs. Tupper?

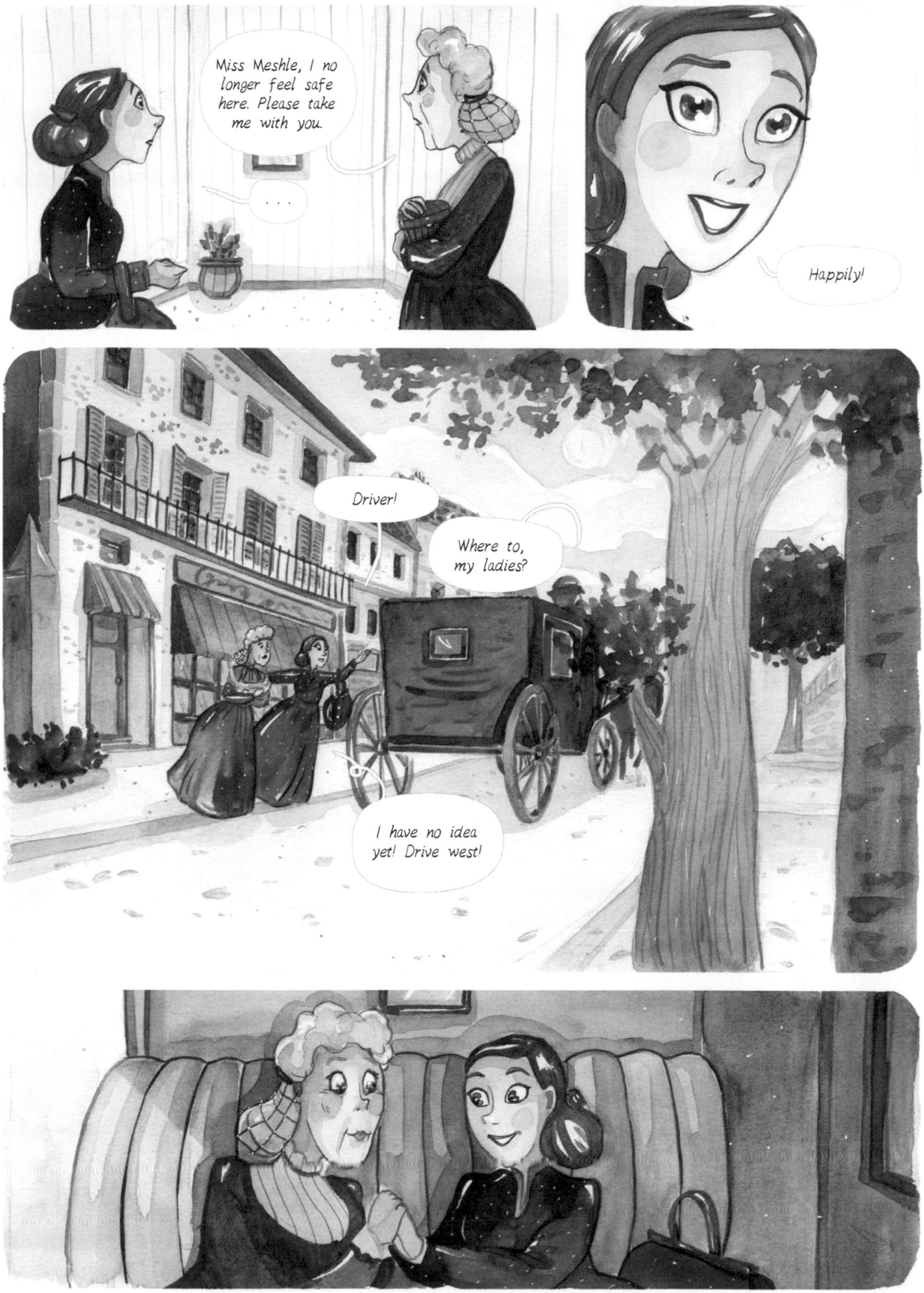
Miss Meshle, I no longer feel safe here. Please take me with you.
. . .
Happily!
Driver!
Where to, my ladies?
I have no idea yet! Drive west!

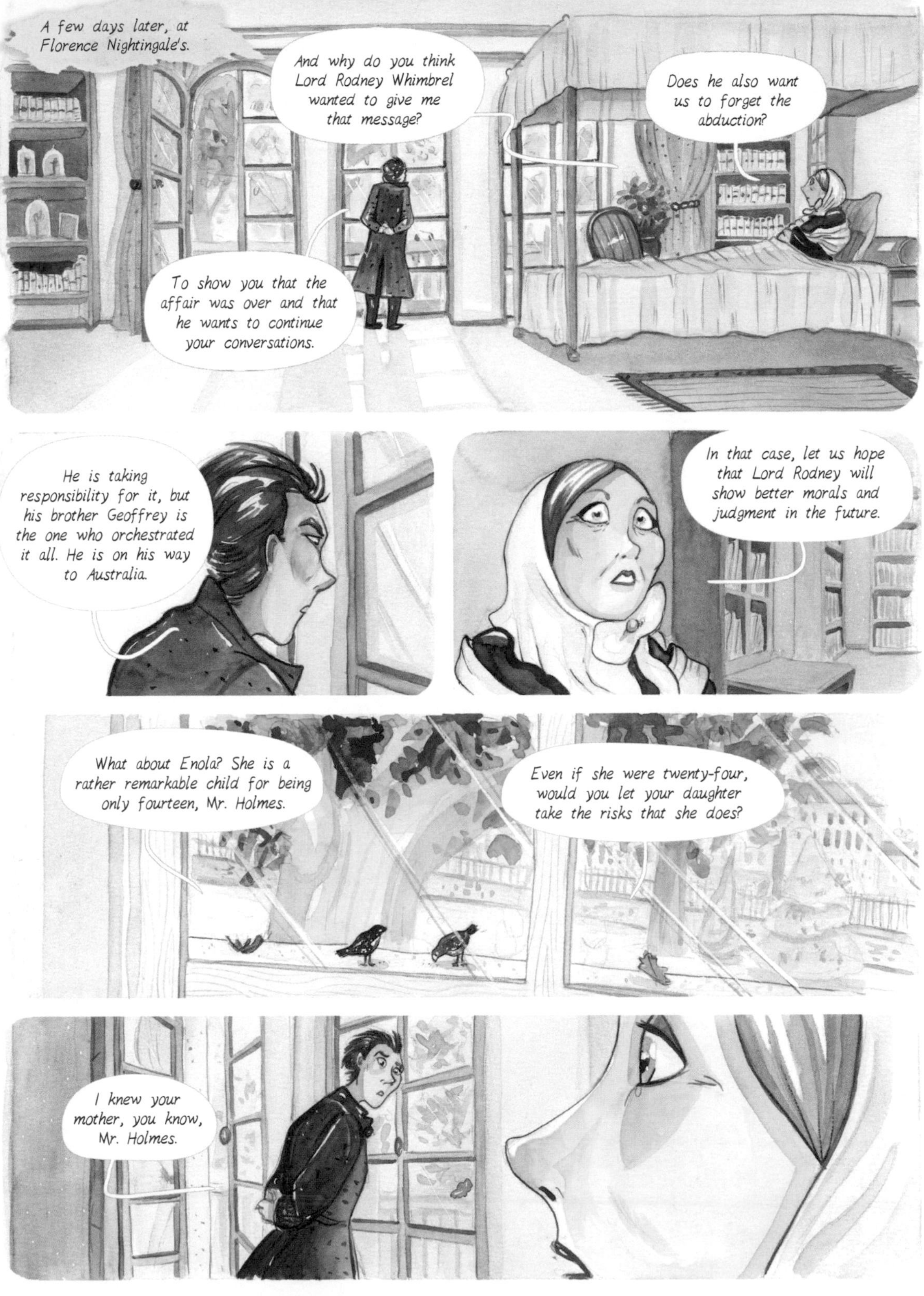
A few days later, at Florence Nightingale's.
And why do you think Lord Rodney Whimbrel wanted to give me that message?
Does he also want us to forget the abduction?
To show you that the affair was over and that he wants to continue your conversations.
He is taking responsibility for it, but his brother Geoffrey is the one who orchestrated it all. He is on his way to Australia.
In that case, let us hope that Lord Rodney will show better morals and judgment in the future.
What about Enola? She is a rather remarkable child for being only fourteen, Mr. Holmes.
Even if she were twenty-four, would you let your daughter take the risks that she does?
I knew your mother, you know, Mr. Holmes.

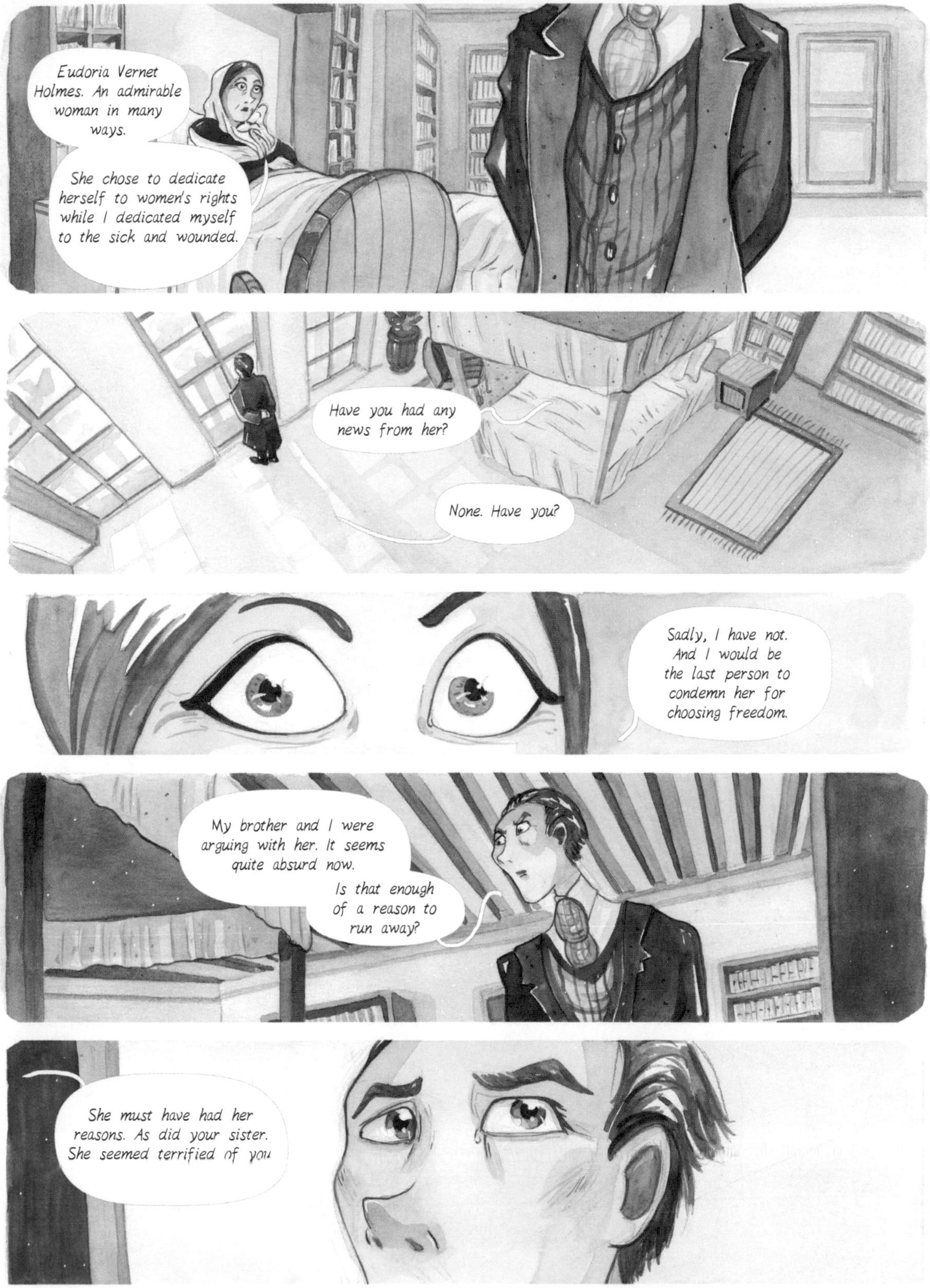
Eudoria Vernet Holmes. An admirable woman in many ways.
She chose to dedicate herself to women's rights while I dedicated myself to the sick and wounded.
Have you had any news from her?
None. Have you?
Sadly, I have not. And I would be the last person to condemn her for choosing freedom.
My brother and I were arguing with her. It seems quite absurd now.
Is that enough of a reason to run away?
She must have had her reasons. As did your sister. She seemed terrified of you

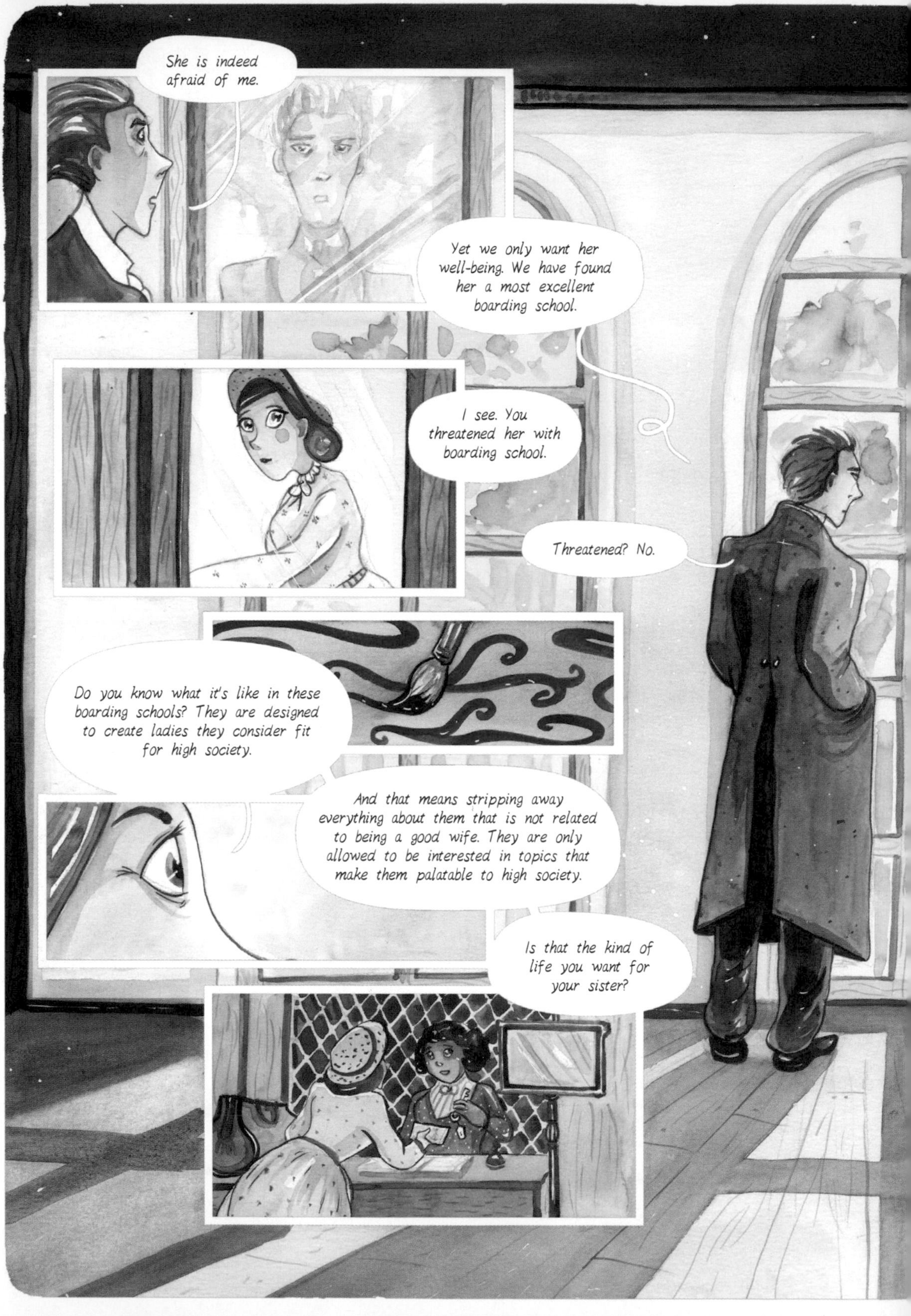
She is indeed afraid of me.
Yet we only want her well-being. We have found her a most excellent boarding school.
I see. You threatened her with boarding school.
Threatened? No.
Do you know what it's like in these boarding schools? They are designed to create ladies they consider fit for high society.
And that means stripping away everything about them that is not related to being a good wife. They are only allowed to be interested in topics that make them palatable to high society.
Is that the kind of life you want for your sister?

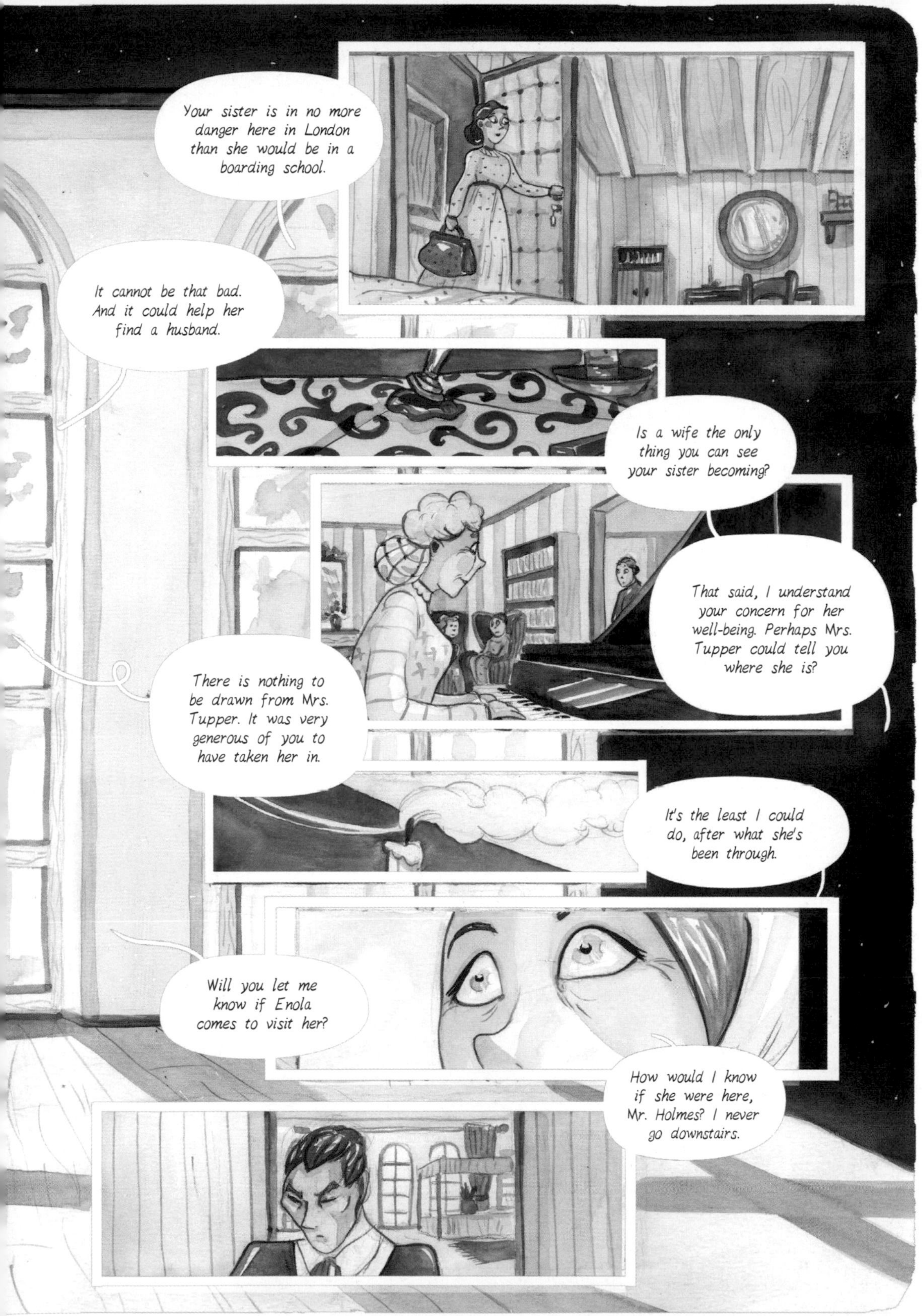
Your sister is in no more danger here in London than she would be in a boarding school.
It cannot be that bad. And it could help her find a husband.
Is a wife the only thing you can see your sister becoming?
That said, I understand your concern for her well-being. Perhaps Mrs. Tupper could tell you where she is?
There is nothing to be drawn from Mrs. Tupper. It was very generous of you to have taken her in.
It's the least I could do, after what she's been through.
Will you let me know if Enola comes to visit her?
How would I know if she were here, Mr. Holmes? I never go downstairs.

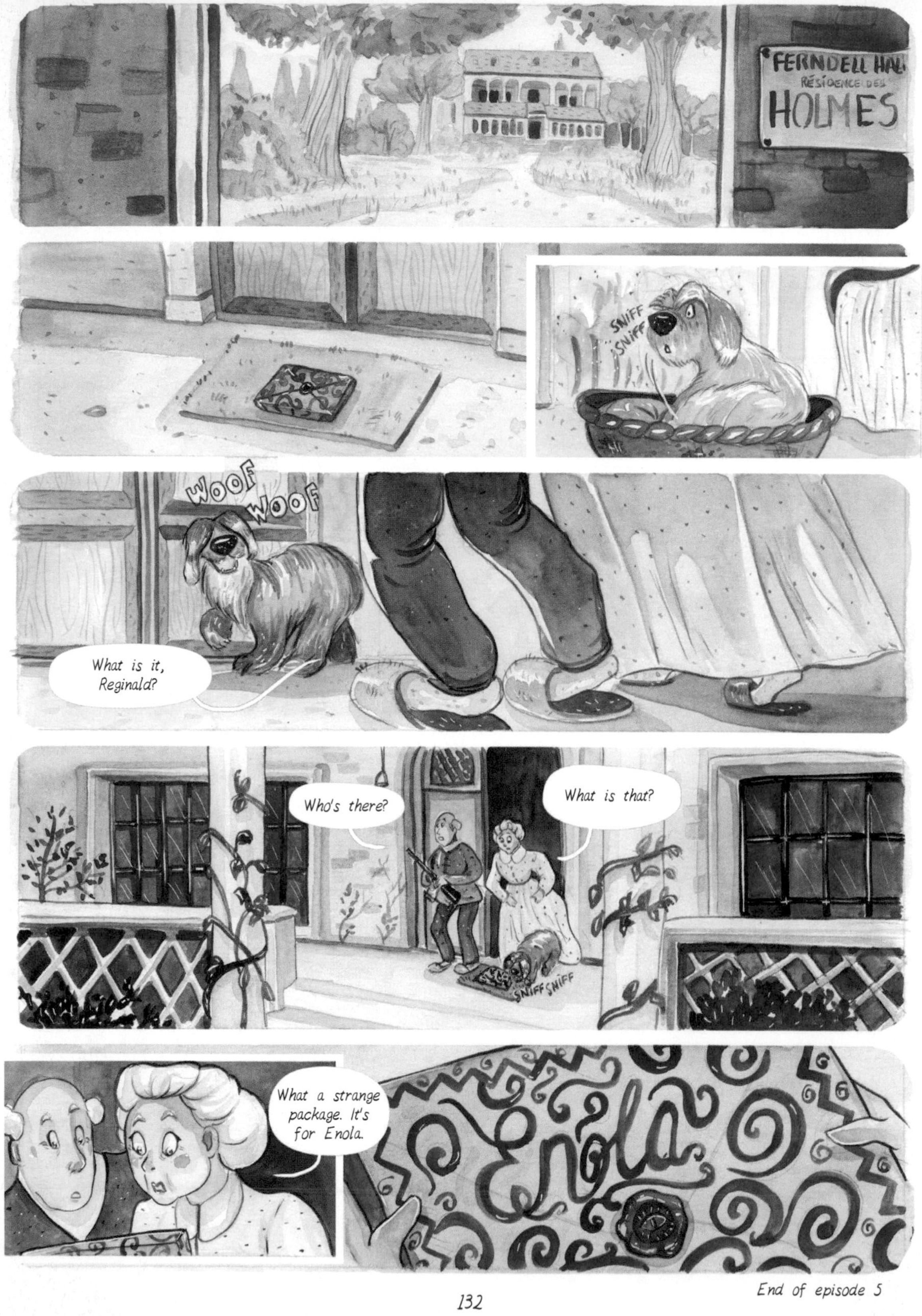
FERNDELL HALL
RÉSIDENCE DES
HOLMES
SNIFF
SNIFF
WOOF
WOOF
What is it, Reginald?
Who's there?
What is that?
SNIFF SNIFF
What a strange package. It's for Enola.
Enola

End of episode 5

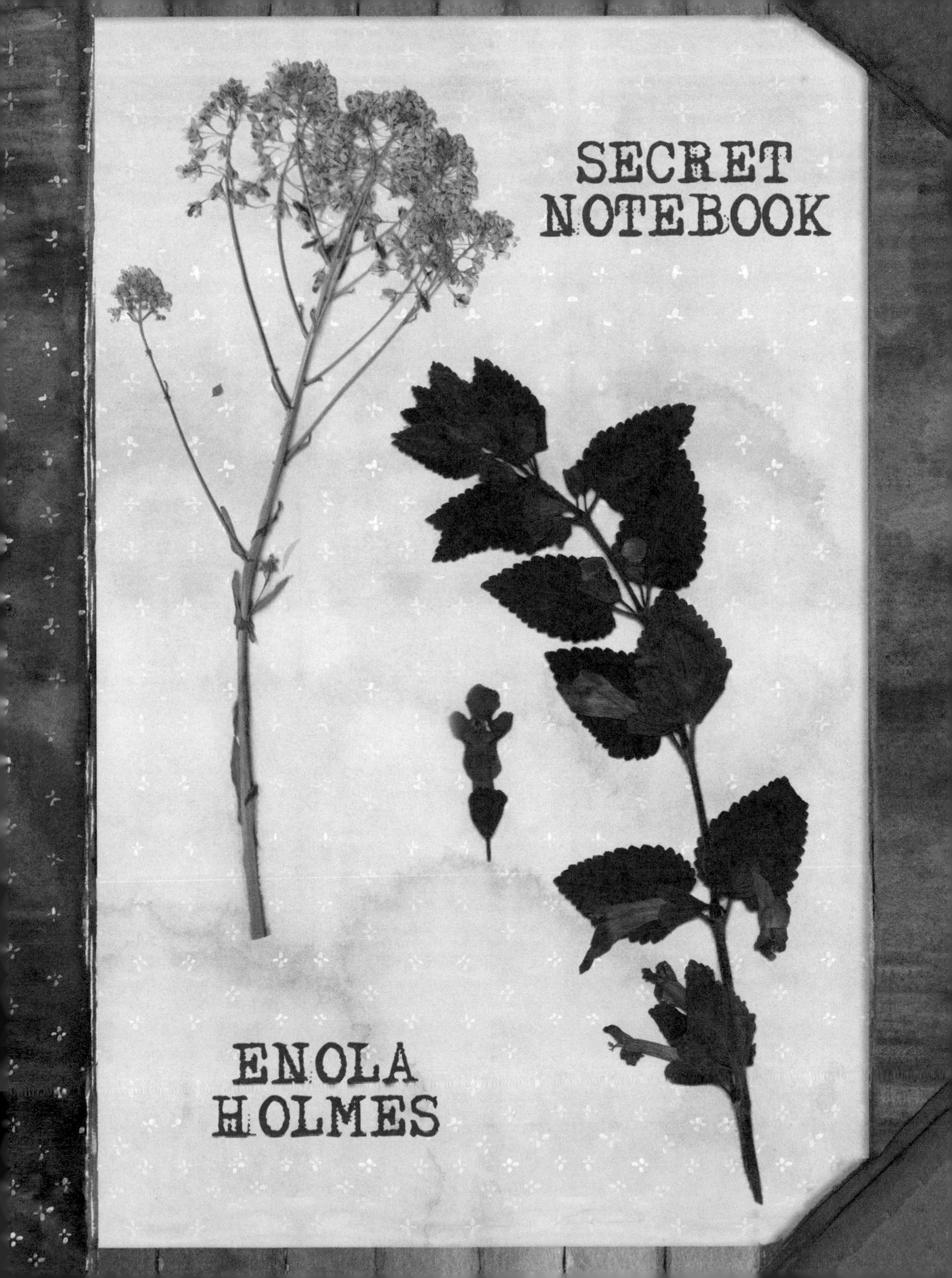
SECRET
NOTEBOOK
ENOLA
HOLMES

Florence Nightingale

Florence Nightingale was born on May 12, 1820, in Florence. She was a British nurse and is a pioneer of modern healthcare. She has fought to require military doctors to have medical training, which was not the case during the Crimean War. Most war surgeons had shockingly little experience.

She has also pushed for education for soldiers.

She has worked to make changes to poorly run hospitals with elevated mortality rates.

She has worked on reforms for medical care, for more hygienic conditions, and for better patient and staff accommodation.

She has worked on reforms to allow nurses access to medical education.

These changes have made waves because many surgeons and other doctors thought that nurses don't need more skills than maids.

Florence Nightingale has devoted her life to patients and hospitals, and many significant improvements in conditions are due to her efforts.

They said that she was constantly roaming hospital hallways to keep an eye on patients. Those who survived said they felt better just seeing the Lady with the Lamp's shadow when she passed by. Florence Nightingale was a symbol of hope during the entire horrific Crimean War.

Florence Nightingale is also well known as a feminist. She fought to free herself from her situation and her family's expectation to see her married well.

What luck to have met her! If only I could tell Mum all about it!

The Crimean War, 1853 to 1856

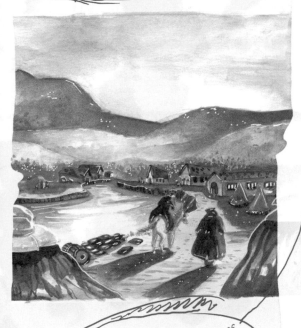

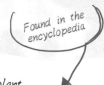

Found in the encyclopedia

Senseless and violent

The Crimean War was between the Russian Empire and a coalition composed of the Ottoman Empire, France, the United Kingdom, and Sardinia.

The siege was in Sevastopol.

The war was horrific. Russian winter could not be colder and disease was rampant, including typhus and cholera.

The conflict was not well planned and the distribution of supplies was a disaster. Since the sick were practically abandoned, Florence Nightingale went to Crimea to organize field hospitals. She took care of the sick and wounded there until the end of the war.

The war made no difference. The Russians ended up withdrawing.

The tsar requested a cease-fire. The Treaty of Paris was signed on March 30, 1856.

Let's hope it lasts . . .

The war was even worse because of disease. Deaths due to fevers or infection were two to three times higher than deaths in battle (according to Florence Nightingale's statistics).

SEA of AZOV.
BATSCHAI
SIMFEROPOL
SIEGE
S.
SEVASTOPOL
BALAKLAVA
BLACK SEA
1856–1853

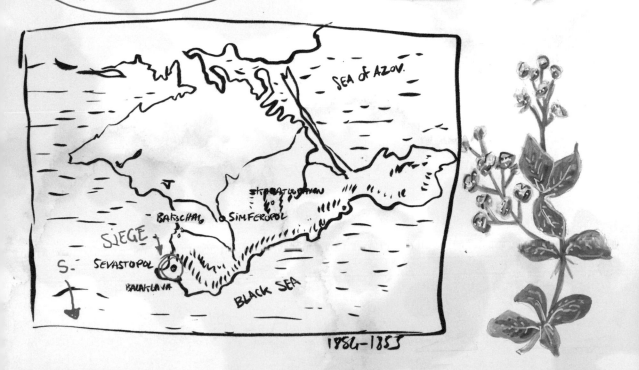

MORSE CODE

A •—
B —•••
C —•—•
D —••
E •
F ••—•
G ——•
H ••••
I ••
J •———
K —•—
L •—••
M ——
N —•
O ———
P •——•
Q ——•—
R •—•
S •••
T —
U ••—
V •••—
W •——
X —••—
Y —•——
Z ——••

1 •————
2 ••———
3 •••——
4 ••••—
5 •••••
6 —••••
7 ——•••
8 ———••
9 ————•
0 —————

A DASH IS AS WIDE AS THREE DOTS.

Flowers replace the dots and dashes.

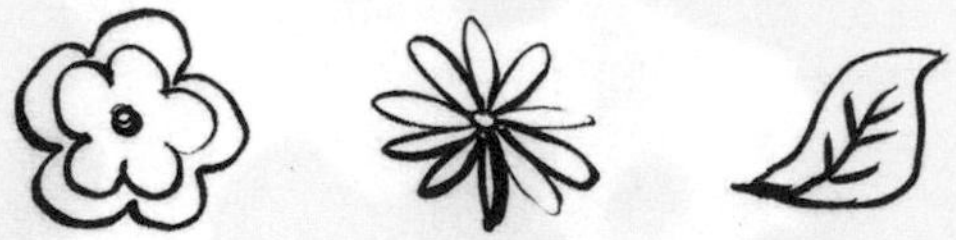

Dot — *Dash* — *End of letter*

• —

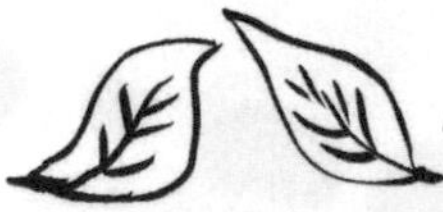

End of Word

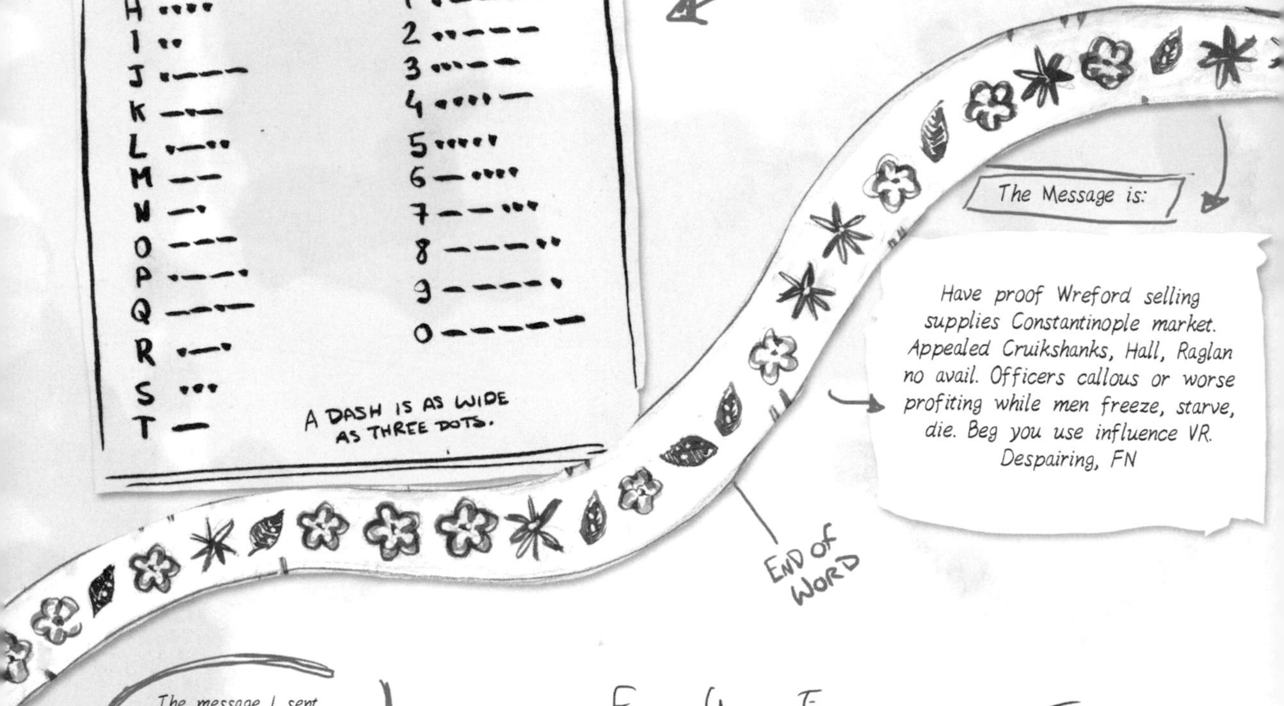

END OF WORD

The Message is:

Have proof Wreford selling supplies Constantinople market. Appealed Cruikshanks, Hall, Raglan no avail. Officers callous or worse profiting while men freeze, starve, die. Beg you use influence VR. Despairing, FN

The message I sent Florence Nightingale:

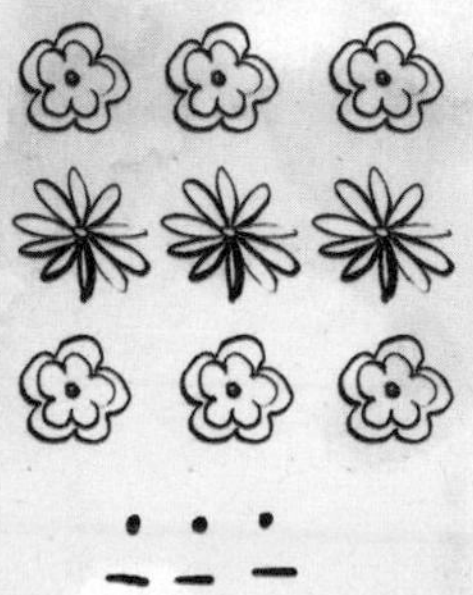

S.O.S

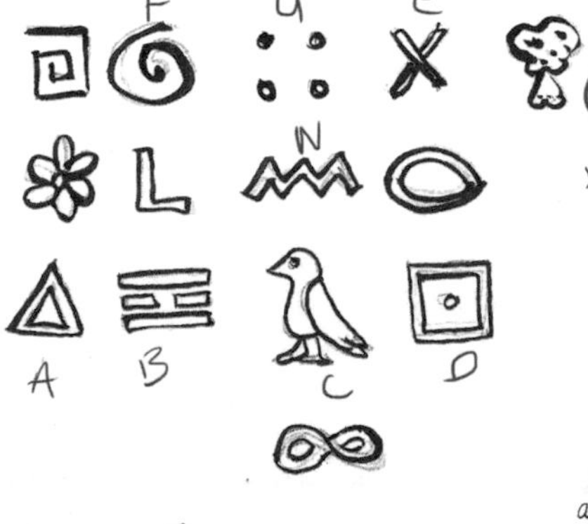
F
G
E
N
A
B
C
D

Creating one's own code

You can also create your own code by replacing letters with symbols.

...

Or even with little people. It could make a fun wallpaper frieze!

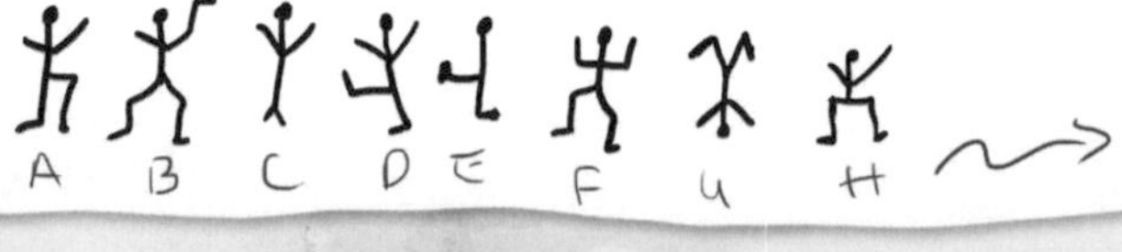
A
B
C
D
E
F
G
H

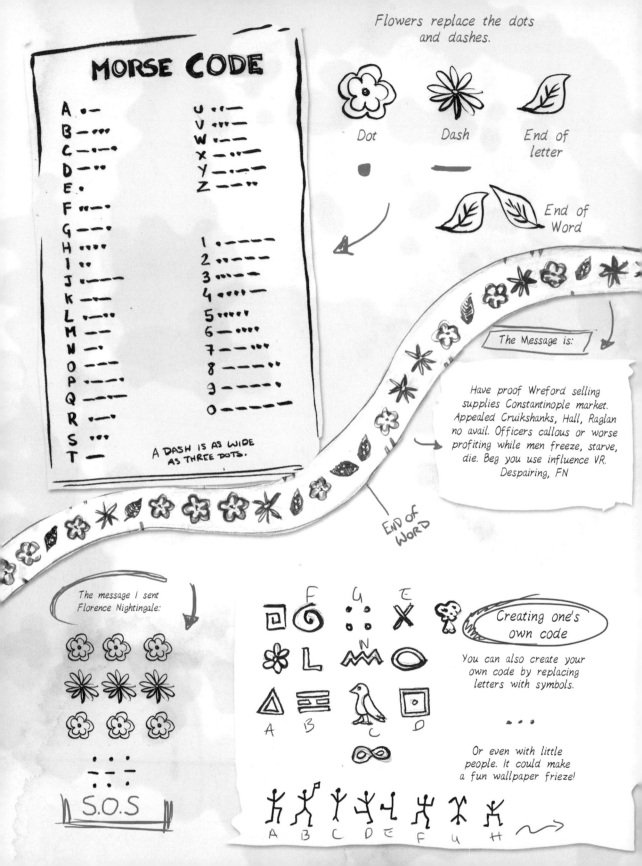

The Whimbrels' Manor

MRS. TUPPER

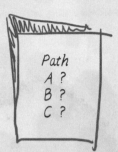

How did Sherlock make it up to the tower?

Path	
A	?
B	?
C	?

Sherlock's disguises don't fool me anymore.

When I spent the night at Sherlock's I riffled through his cupboards. I'm sure I saw that hat!

Old, damaged hat

Makeup, dark circles, and pale skin to make him look older

Gray-and-white beard

Second- or third-hand suit

PROFESSIONAL WOMEN'S CLUB

Mum's club!

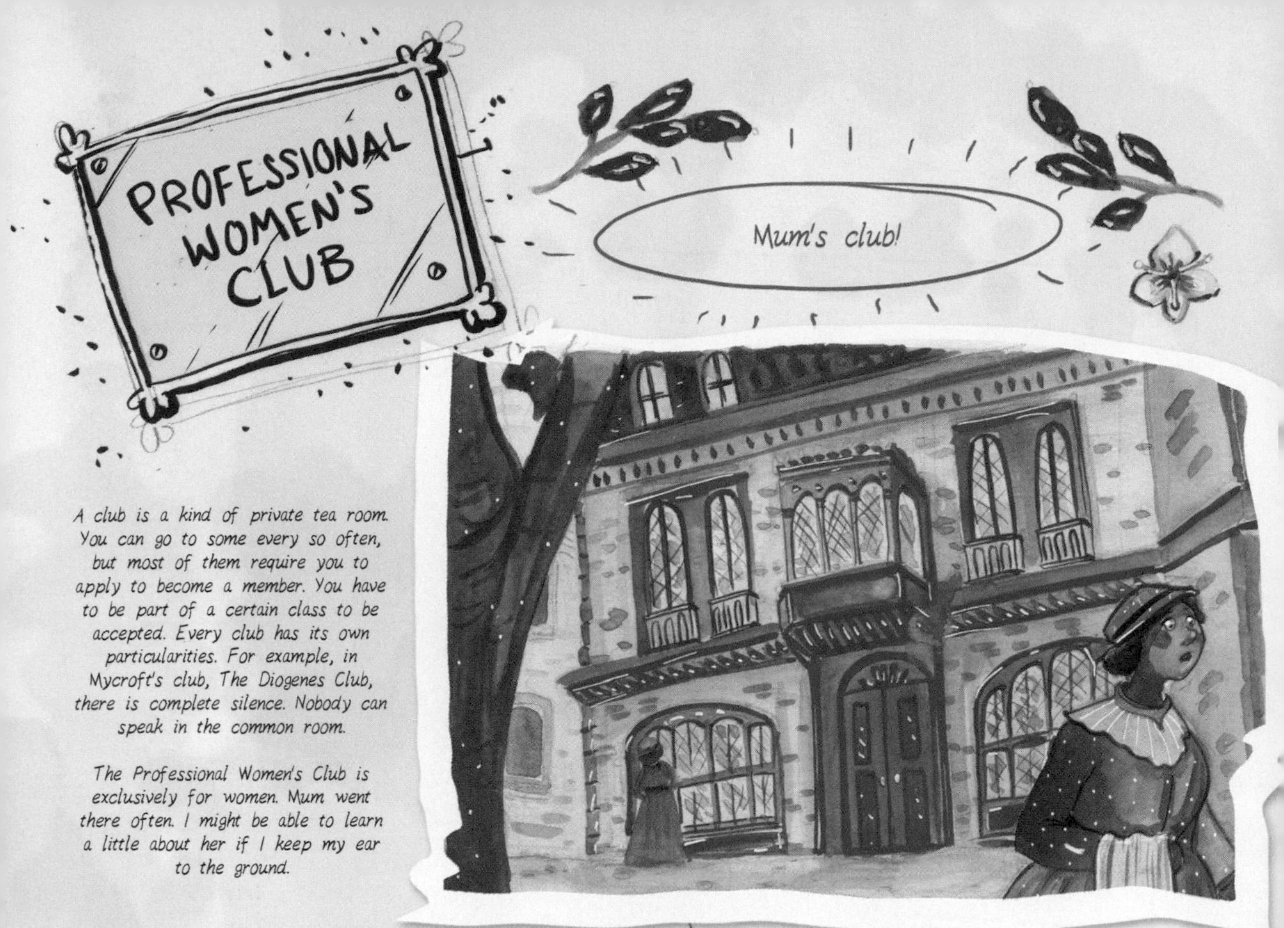

A club is a kind of private tea room. You can go to some every so often, but most of them require you to apply to become a member. You have to be part of a certain class to be accepted. Every club has its own particularities. For example, in Mycroft's club, The Diogenes Club, there is complete silence. Nobody can speak in the common room.

The Professional Women's Club is exclusively for women. Mum went there often. I might be able to learn a little about her if I keep my ear to the ground.

You find everything you need there: tea, books, soft pillows.

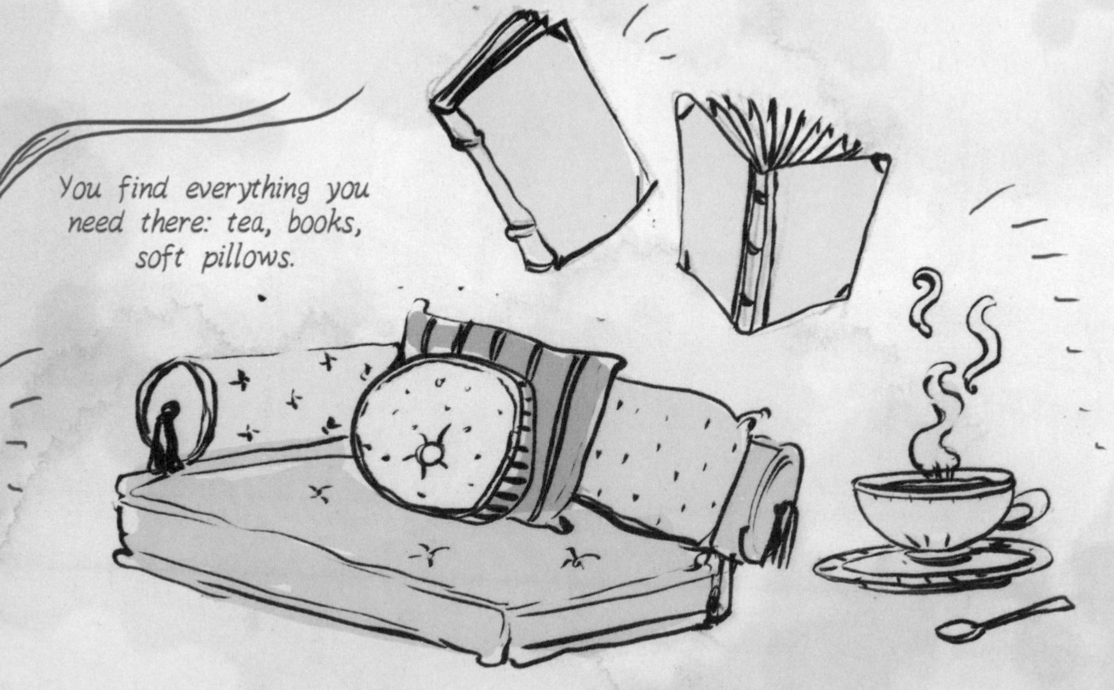

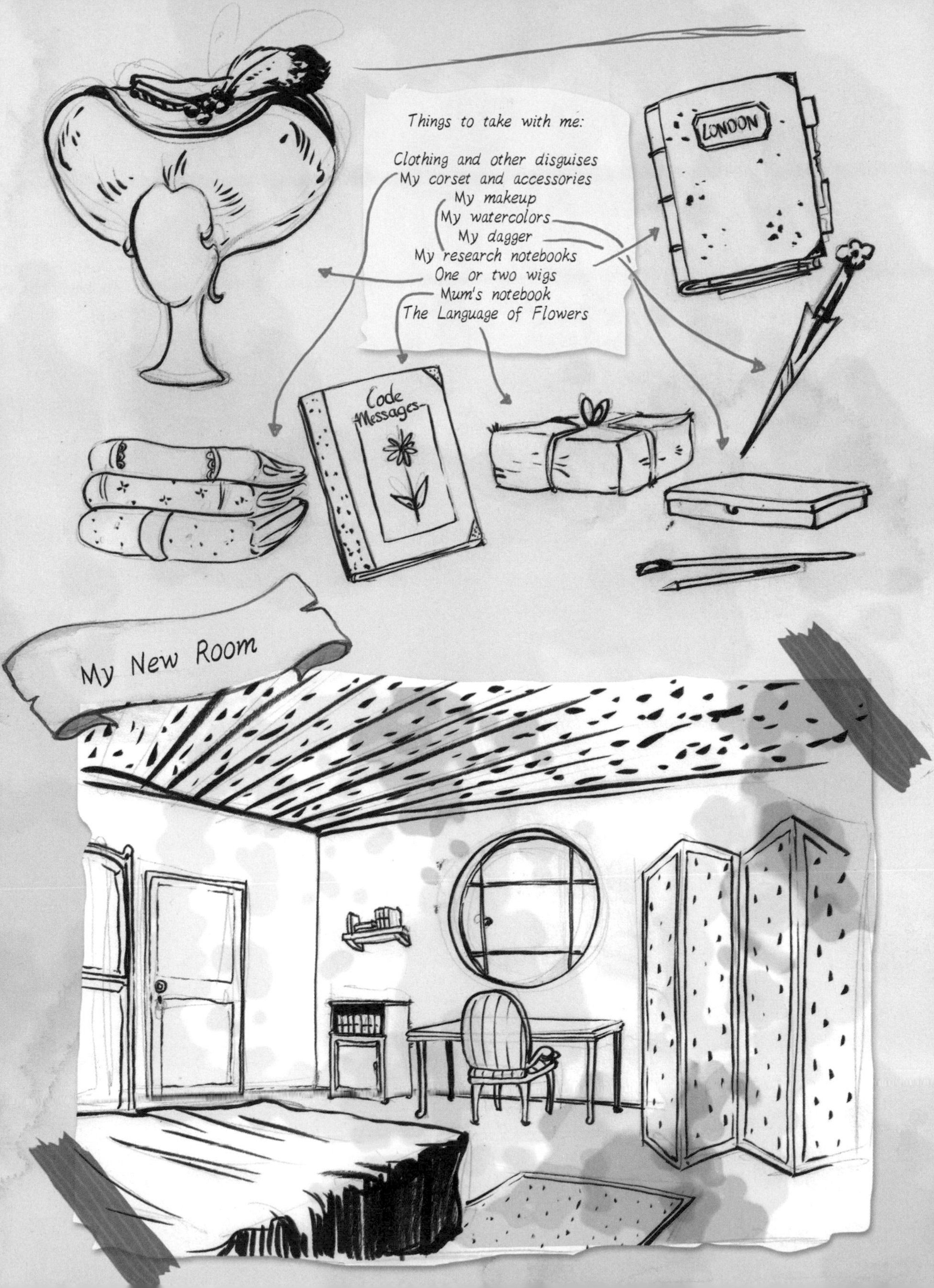
Things to take with me:
Clothing and other disguises
My corset and accessories
My makeup
My watercolors
My dagger
My research notebooks
One or two wigs
Mum's notebook
The Language of Flowers
LONDON
Code Messages
My New Room

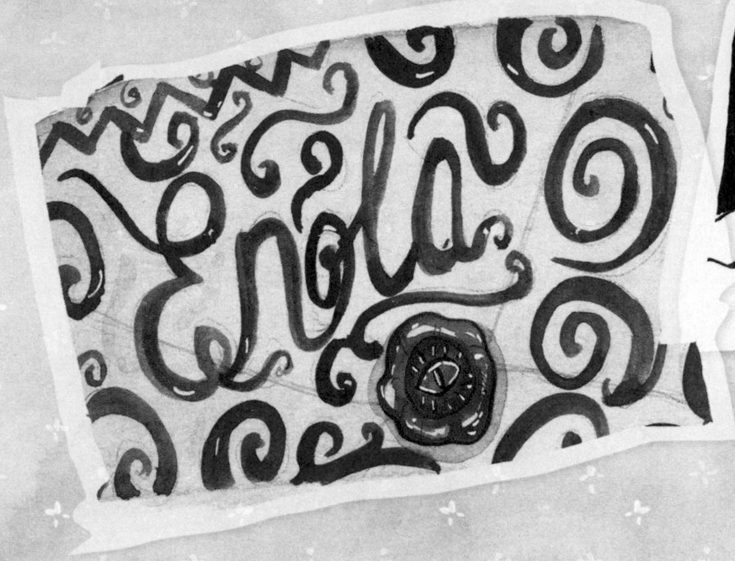
Enola

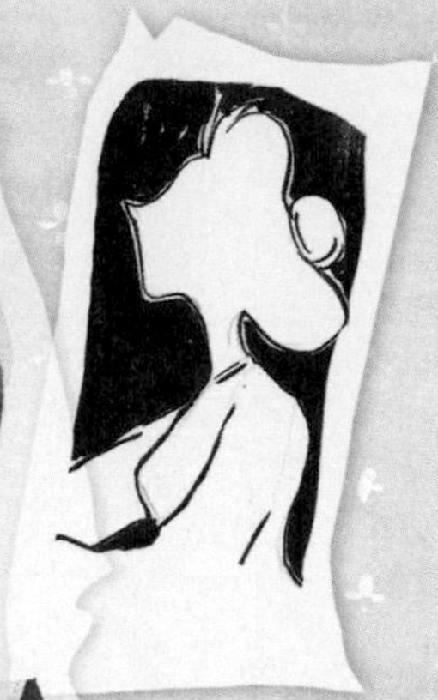

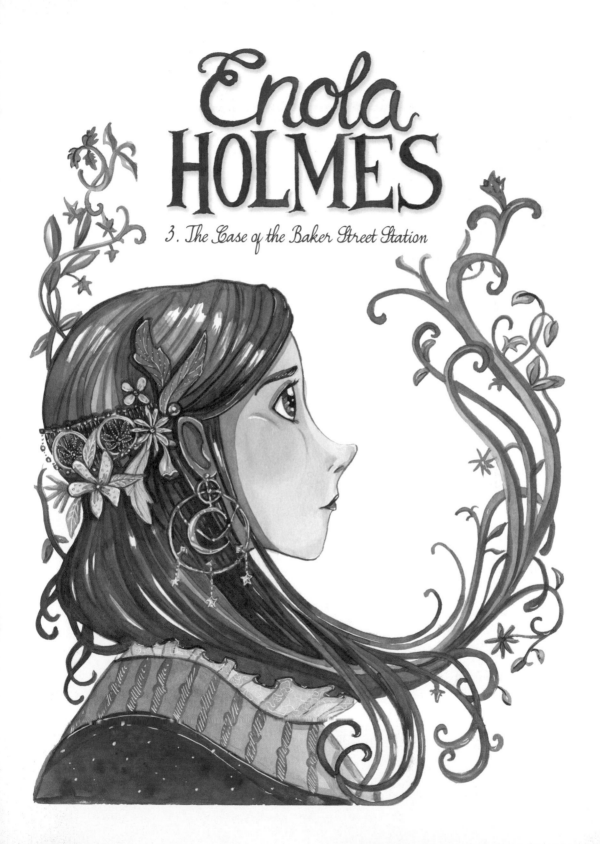

Enola
HOLMES

3. The Case of the Baker Street Station

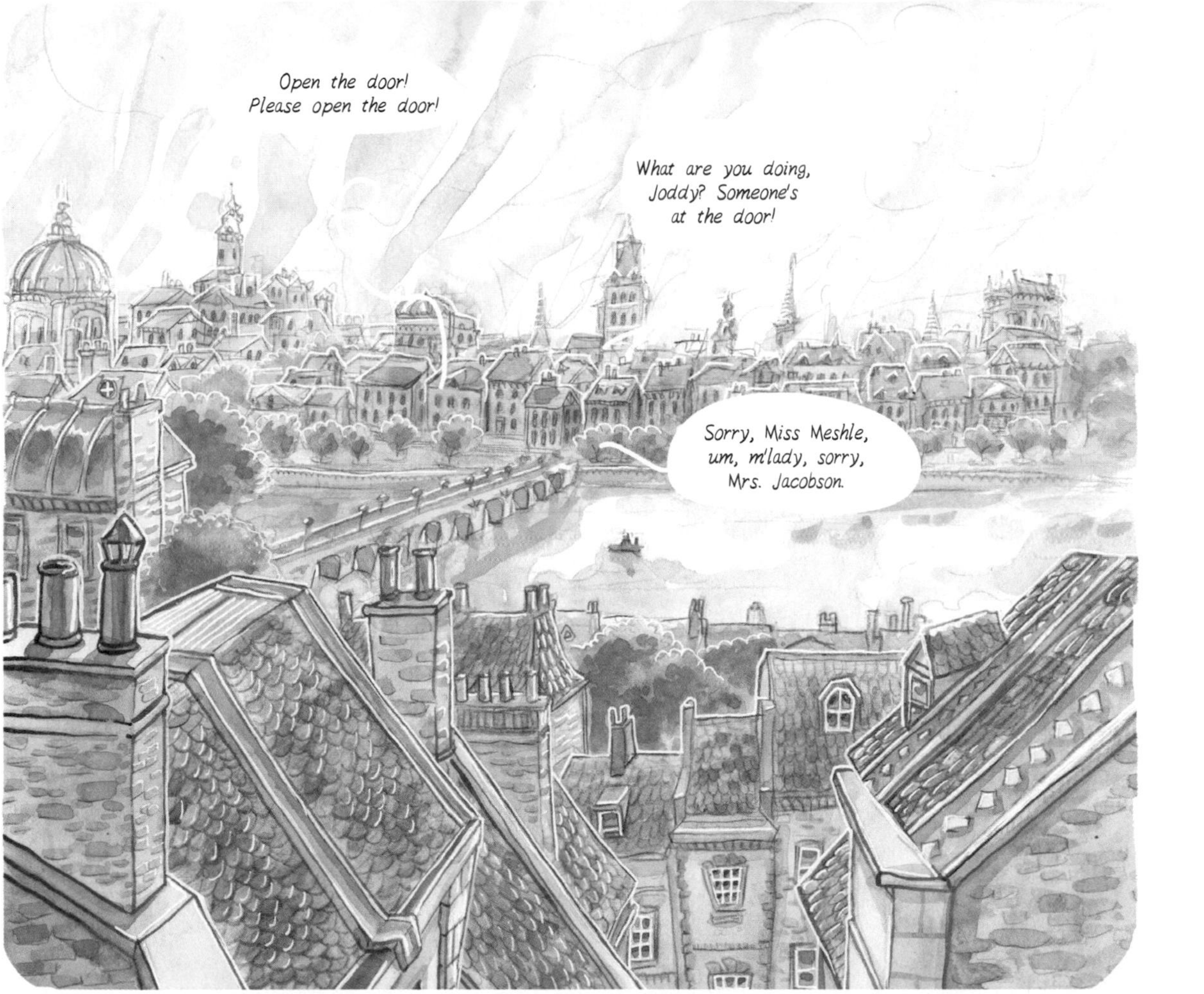
Open the door!
Please open the door!
What are you doing, Joddy? Someone's at the door!
Sorry, Miss Meshle, um, m'lady, sorry, Mrs. Jacobson.

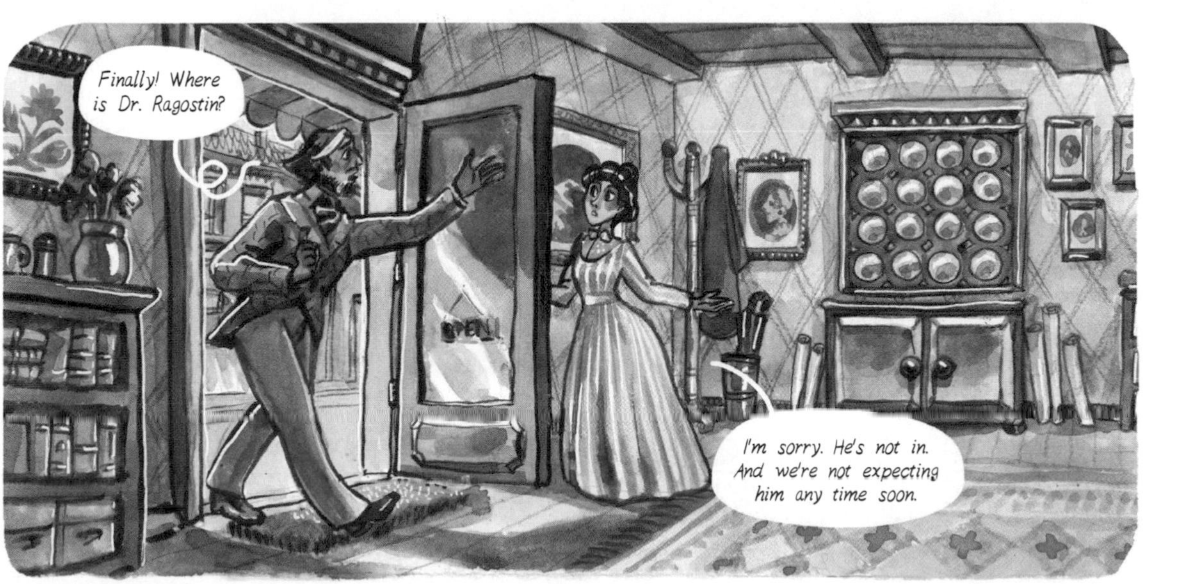
Finally! Where is Dr. Ragostin?
OPEN
I'm sorry. He's not in. And we're not expecting him any time soon.

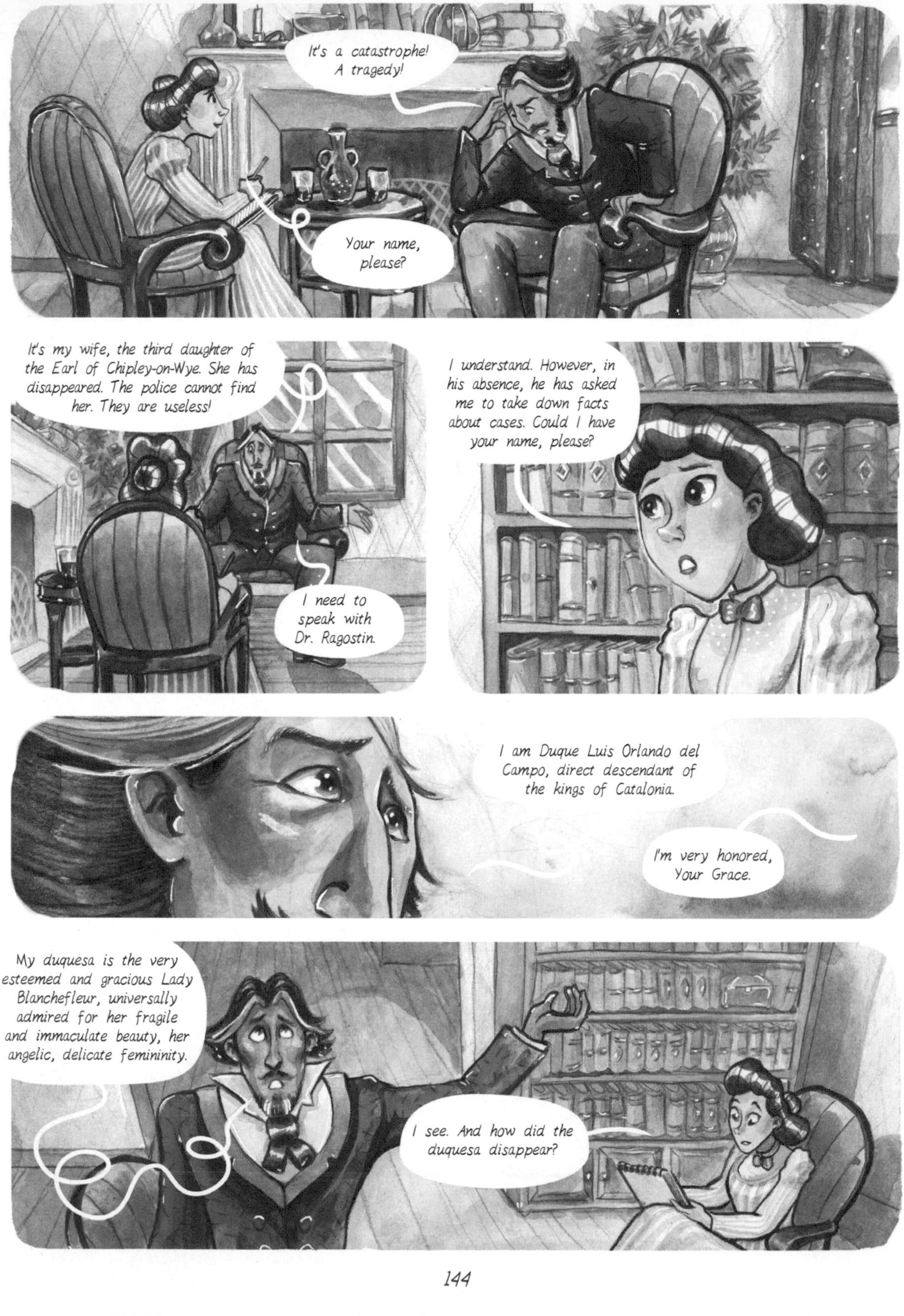
It's a catastrophe! A tragedy!
Your name, please?
It's my wife, the third daughter of the Earl of Chipley-on-Wye. She has disappeared. The police cannot find her. They are useless!
I need to speak with Dr. Ragostin.
I understand. However, in his absence, he has asked me to take down facts about cases. Could I have your name, please?
I am Duque Luis Orlando del Campo, direct descendant of the kings of Catalonia.
I'm very honored, Your Grace.
My duquesa is the very esteemed and gracious Lady Blanchefleur, universally admired for her fragile and immaculate beauty, her angelic, delicate femininity.
I see. And how did the duquesa disappear?

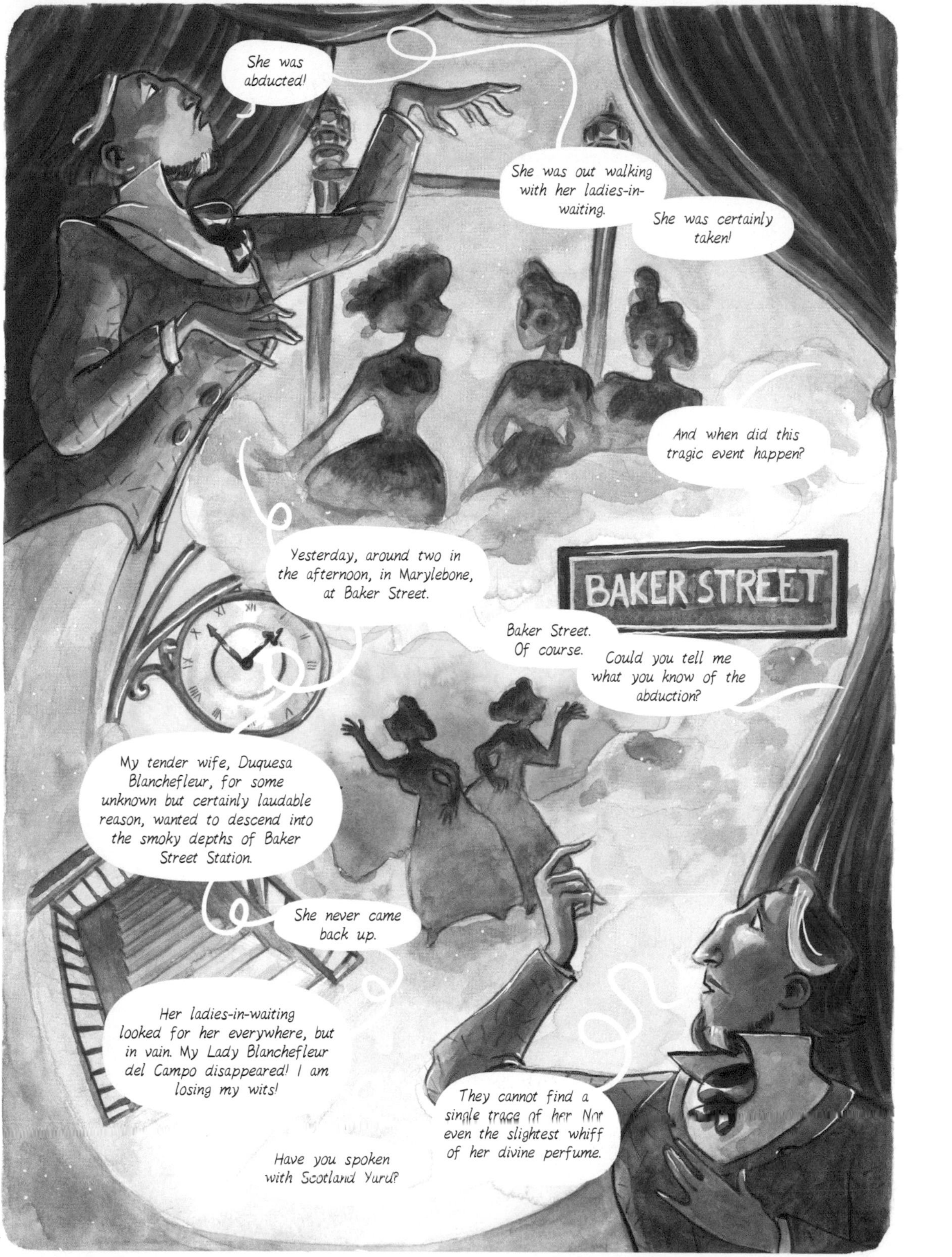
She was abducted!
She was out walking with her ladies-in-waiting.
She was certainly taken!
And when did this tragic event happen?
Yesterday, around two in the afternoon, in Marylebone, at Baker Street.
BAKER STREET
Baker Street. Of course.
Could you tell me what you know of the abduction?
My tender wife, Duquesa Blanchefleur, for some unknown but certainly laudable reason, wanted to descend into the smoky depths of Baker Street Station.
She never came back up.
Her ladies-in-waiting looked for her everywhere, but in vain. My Lady Blanchefleur del Campo disappeared! I am losing my wits!
They cannot find a single trace of her Not even the slightest whiff of her divine perfume.
Have you spoken with Scotland Yard?

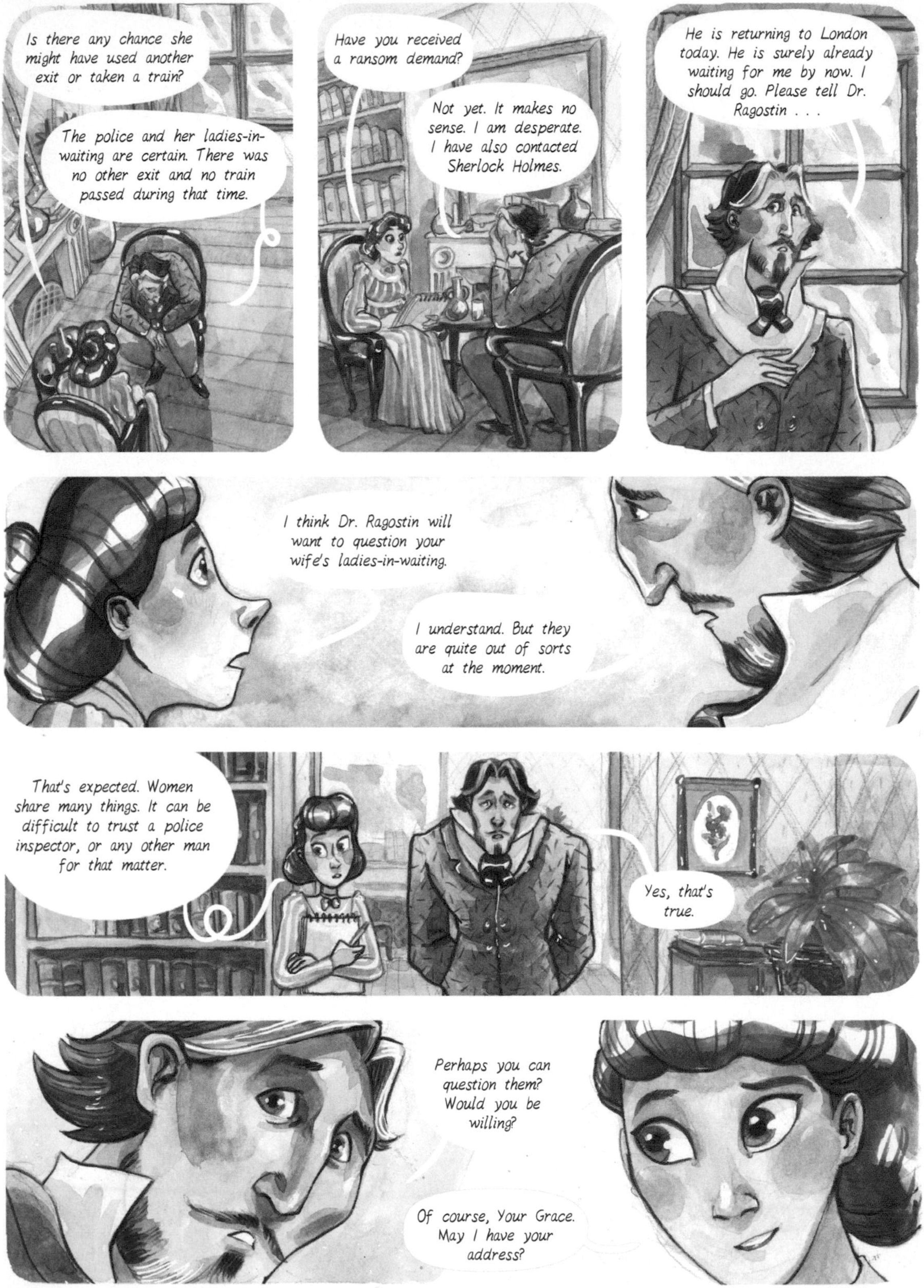
Is there any chance she might have used another exit or taken a train?
The police and her ladies-in-waiting are certain. There was no other exit and no train passed during that time.
Have you received a ransom demand?
Not yet. It makes no sense. I am desperate. I have also contacted Sherlock Holmes.
He is returning to London today. He is surely already waiting for me by now. I should go. Please tell Dr. Ragostin . . .
I think Dr. Ragostin will want to question your wife's ladies-in-waiting.
I understand. But they are quite out of sorts at the moment.
That's expected. Women share many things. It can be difficult to trust a police inspector, or any other man for that matter.
Yes, that's true.
Perhaps you can question them? Would you be willing?
Of course, Your Grace. May I have your address?

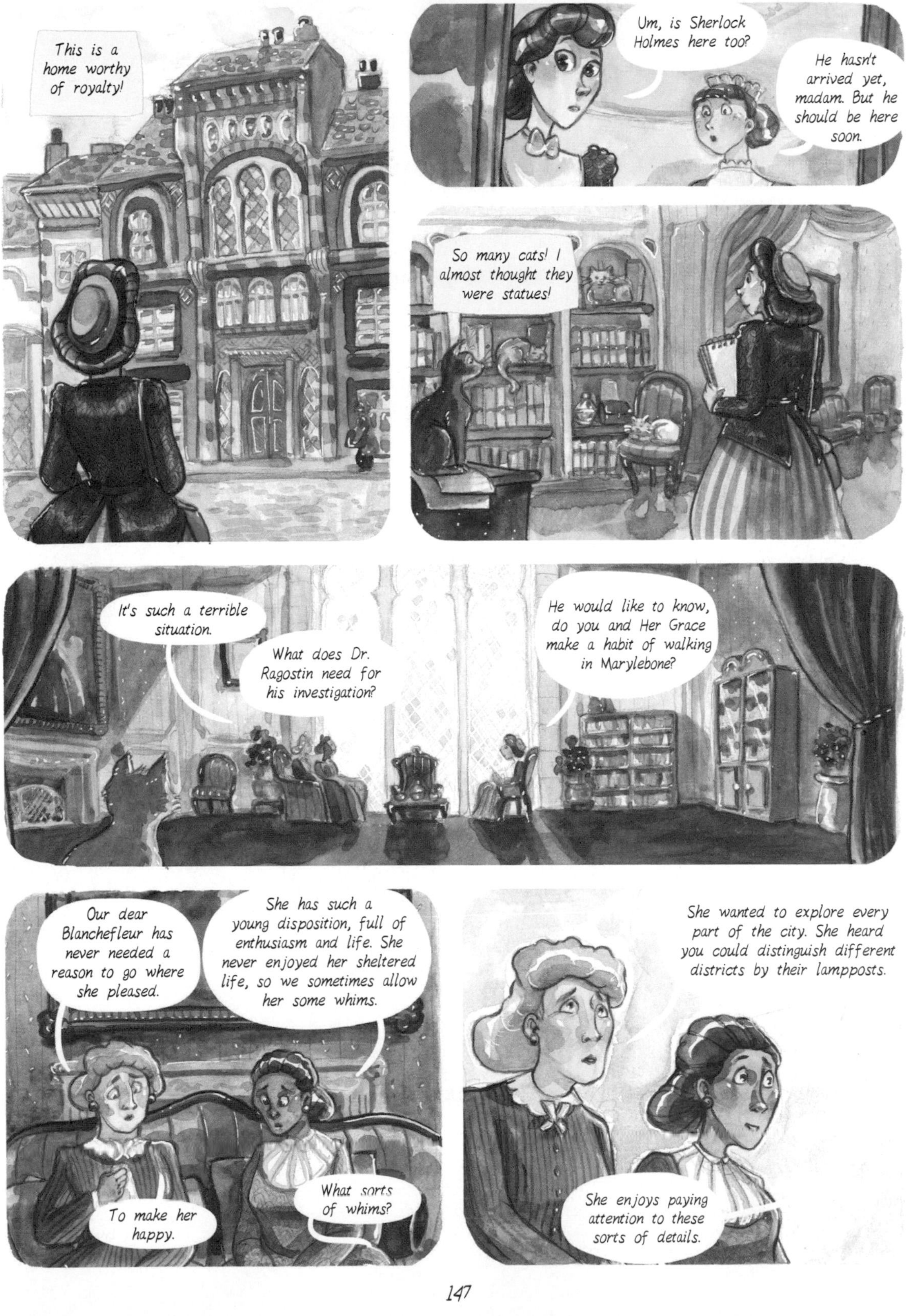
This is a home worthy of royalty!
Um, is Sherlock Holmes here too?
He hasn't arrived yet, madam. But he should be here soon.
So many cats! I almost thought they were statues!
It's such a terrible situation.
What does Dr. Ragostin need for his investigation?
He would like to know, do you and Her Grace make a habit of walking in Marylebone?
Our dear Blanchefleur has never needed a reason to go where she pleased.
She has such a young disposition, full of enthusiasm and life. She never enjoyed her sheltered life, so we sometimes allow her some whims.
To make her happy.
What sorts of whims?
She wanted to explore every part of the city. She heard you could distinguish different districts by their lampposts.
She enjoys paying attention to these sorts of details.

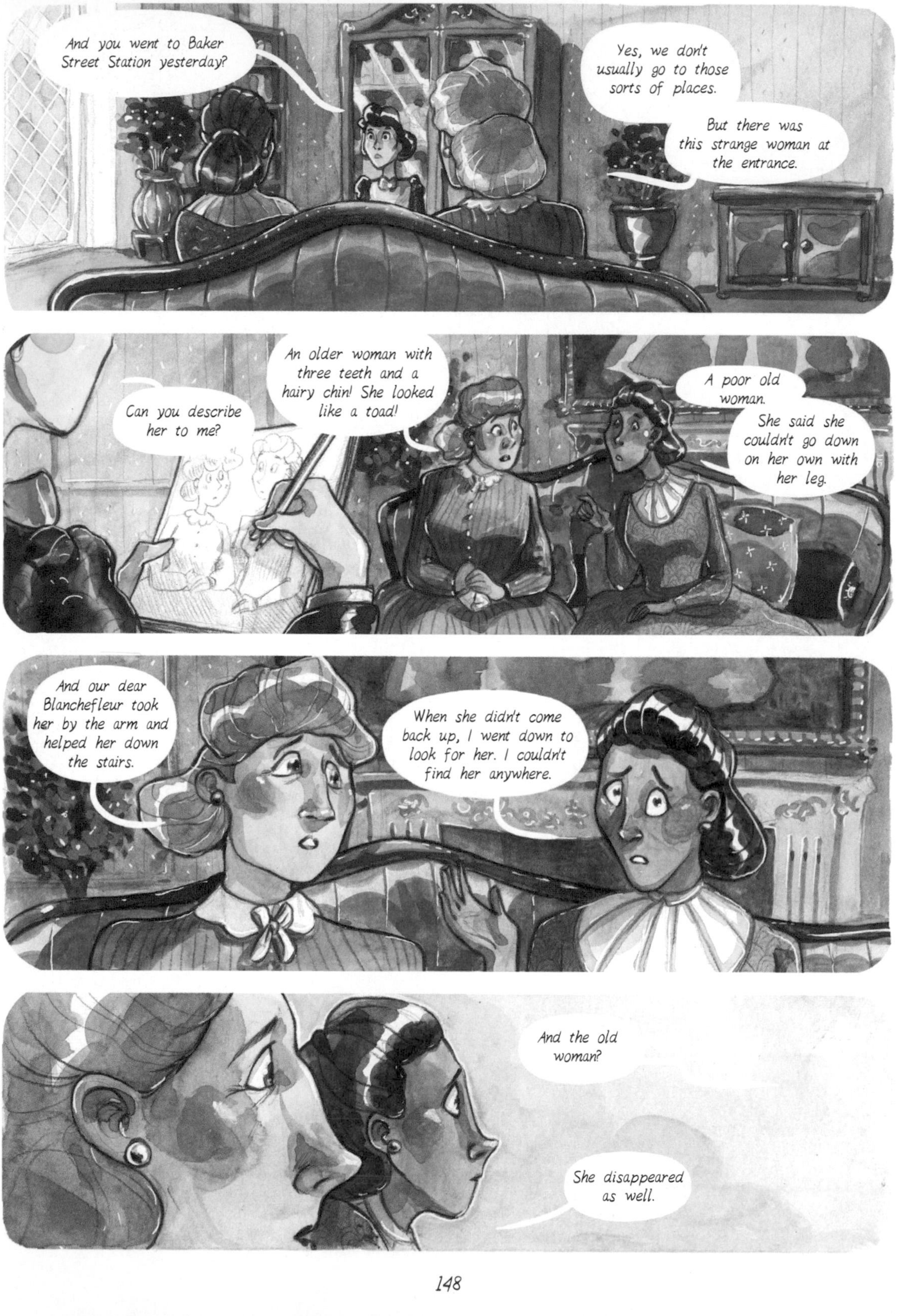
And you went to Baker Street Station yesterday?
Yes, we don't usually go to those sorts of places.
But there was this strange woman at the entrance.
Can you describe her to me?
An older woman with three teeth and a hairy chin! She looked like a toad!
A poor old woman.
She said she couldn't go down on her own with her leg.
And our dear Blanchefleur took her by the arm and helped her down the stairs.
When she didn't come back up, I went down to look for her. I couldn't find her anywhere.
And the old woman?
She disappeared as well.

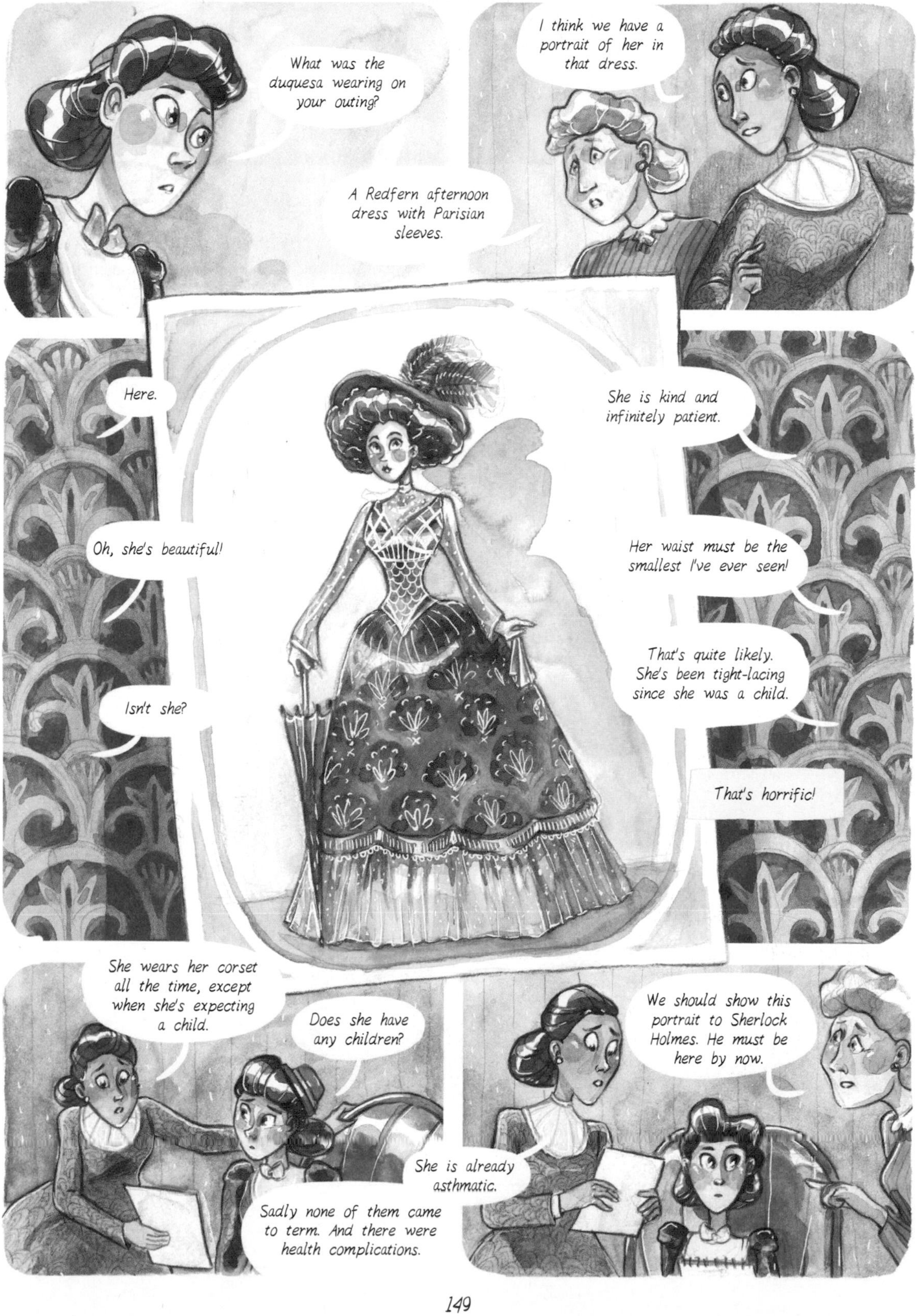
What was the duquesa wearing on your outing?
I think we have a portrait of her in that dress.
A Redfern afternoon dress with Parisian sleeves.
Here.
Oh, she's beautiful!
Isn't she?
She is kind and infinitely patient.
Her waist must be the smallest I've ever seen!
That's quite likely. She's been tight-lacing since she was a child.
That's horrific!
She wears her corset all the time, except when she's expecting a child.
Does she have any children?
Sadly none of them came to term. And there were health complications.
She is already asthmatic.
We should show this portrait to Sherlock Holmes. He must be here by now.

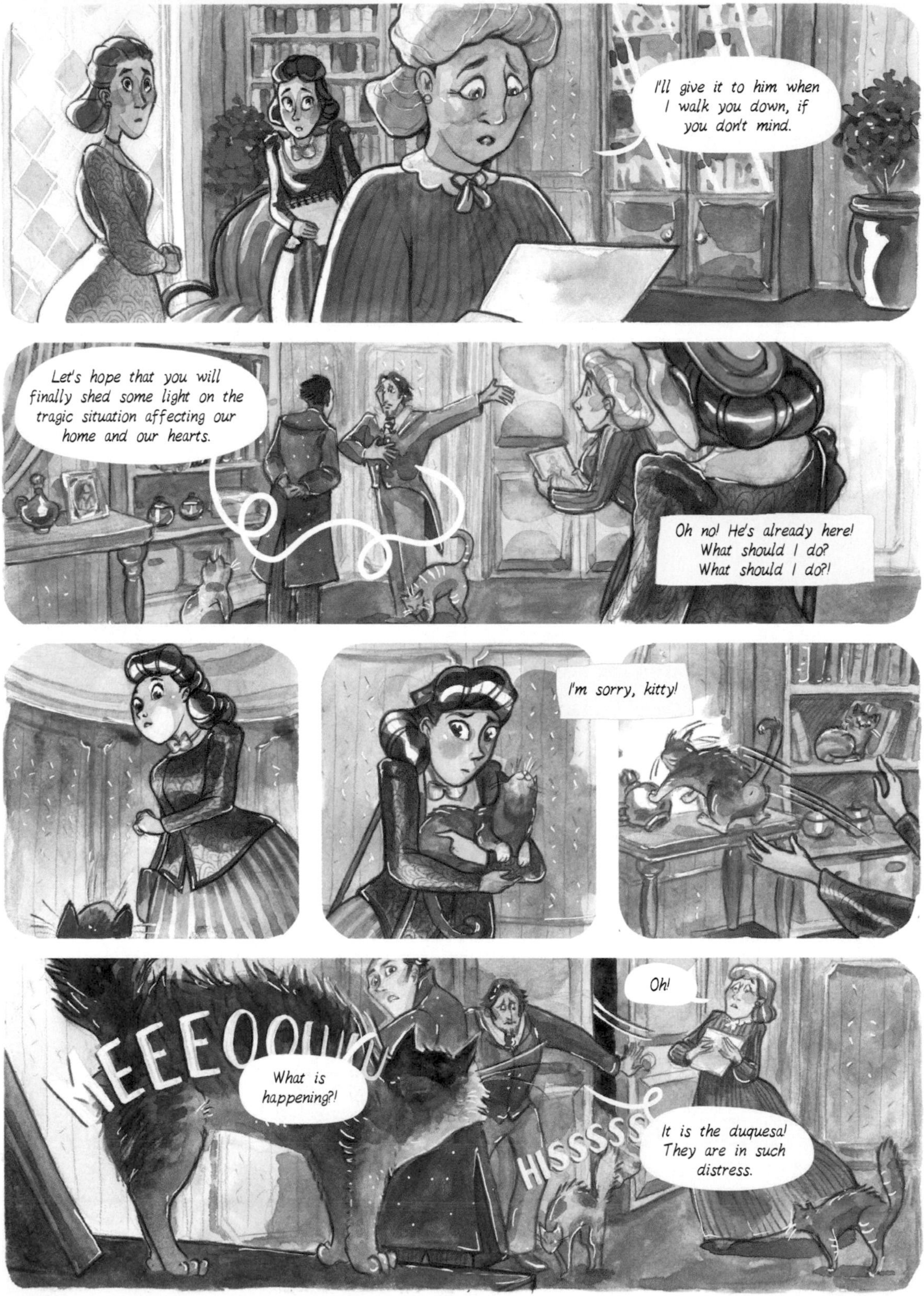
I'll give it to him when I walk you down, if you don't mind.
Let's hope that you will finally shed some light on the tragic situation affecting our home and our hearts.
Oh no! He's already here! What should I do? What should I do?!
I'm sorry, kitty!
Oh!
MEEEOOUU
What is happening?!
HISSSSS
It is the duquesa! They are in such distress.

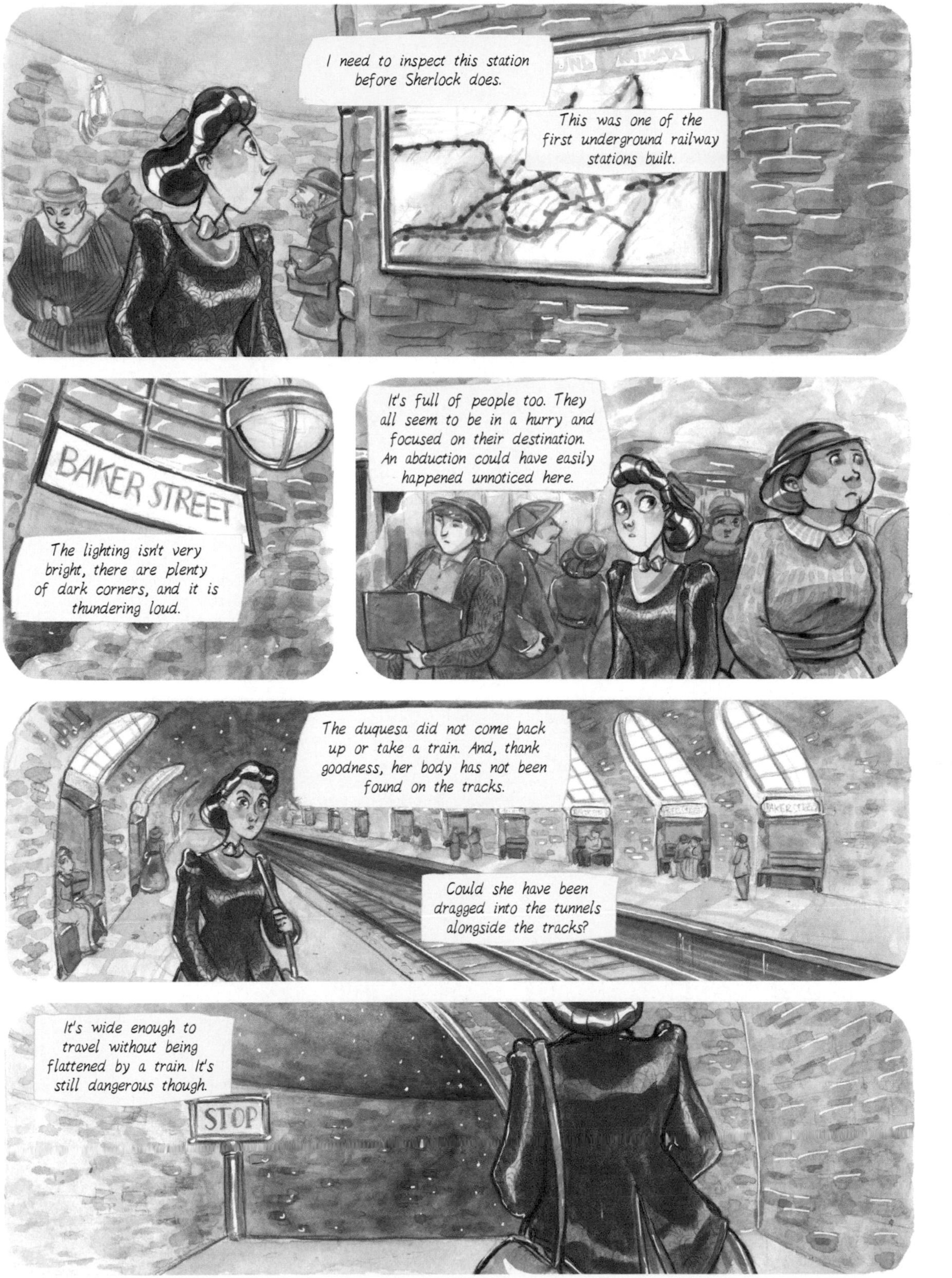
I need to inspect this station before Sherlock does.
This was one of the first underground railway stations built.
BAKER STREET
The lighting isn't very bright, there are plenty of dark corners, and it is thundering loud.
It's full of people too. They all seem to be in a hurry and focused on their destination. An abduction could have easily happened unnoticed here.
The duquesa did not come back up or take a train. And, thank goodness, her body has not been found on the tracks.
Could she have been dragged into the tunnels alongside the tracks?
It's wide enough to travel without being flattened by a train. It's still dangerous though.
STOP

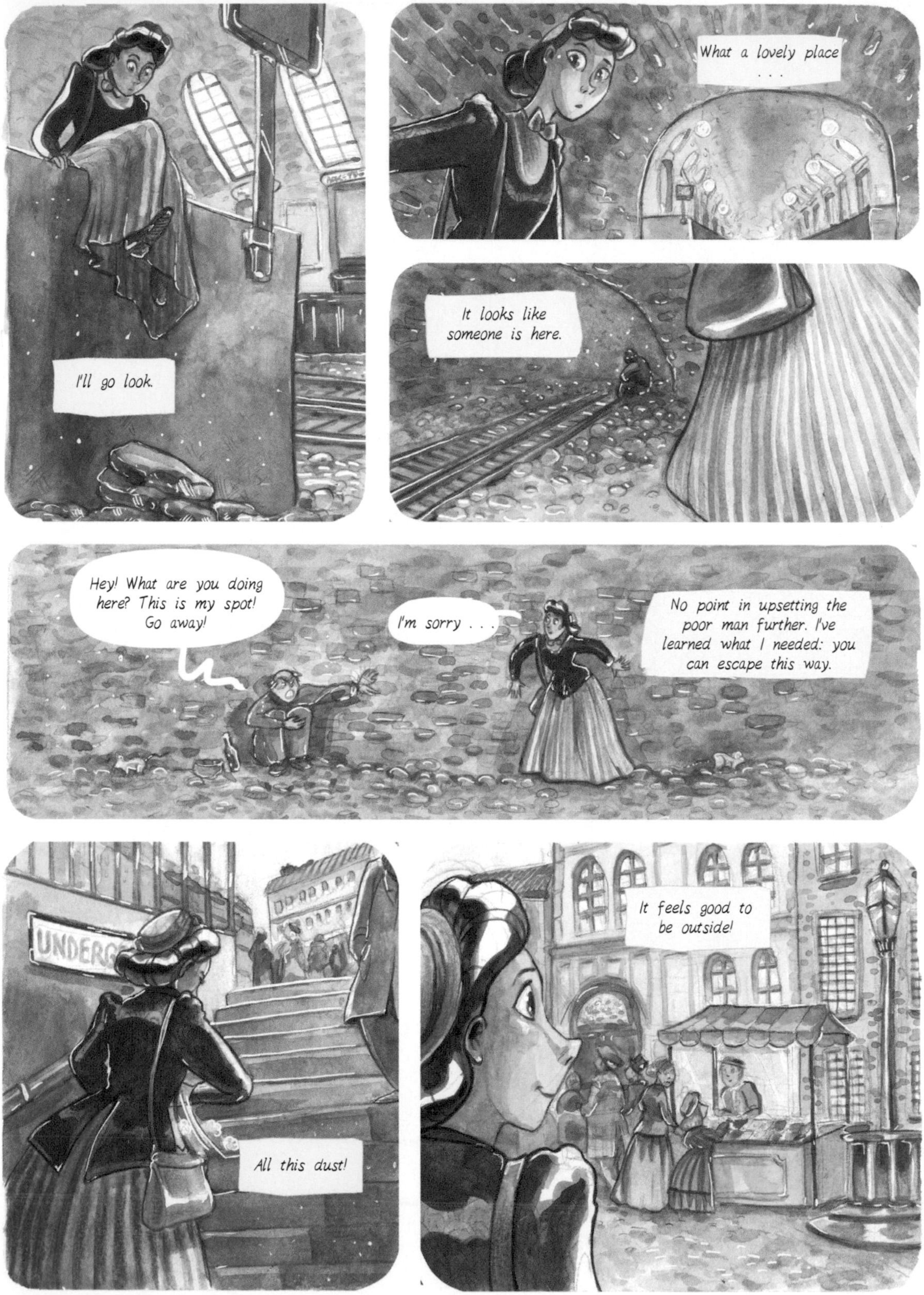
I'll go look.
What a lovely place . . .
It looks like someone is here.
Hey! What are you doing here? This is my spot! Go away!
I'm sorry . . .
No point in upsetting the poor man further. I've learned what I needed: you can escape this way.
UNDERG
All this dust!
It feels good to be outside!

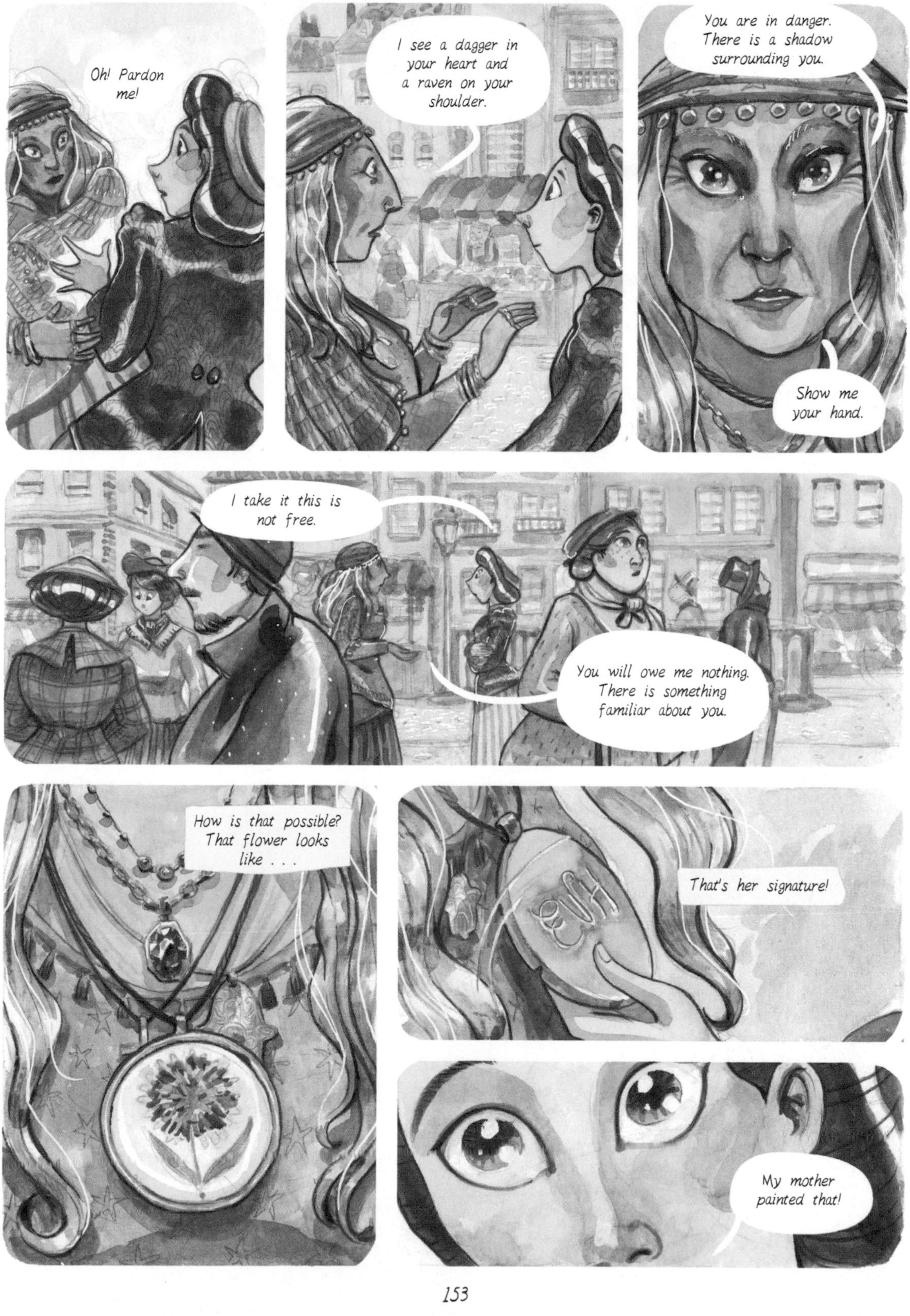
Oh! Pardon me!
I see a dagger in your heart and a raven on your shoulder.
You are in danger. There is a shadow surrounding you.
Show me your hand.
I take it this is not free.
You will owe me nothing. There is something familiar about you.
How is that possible? That flower looks like . . .
That's her signature!
My mother painted that!

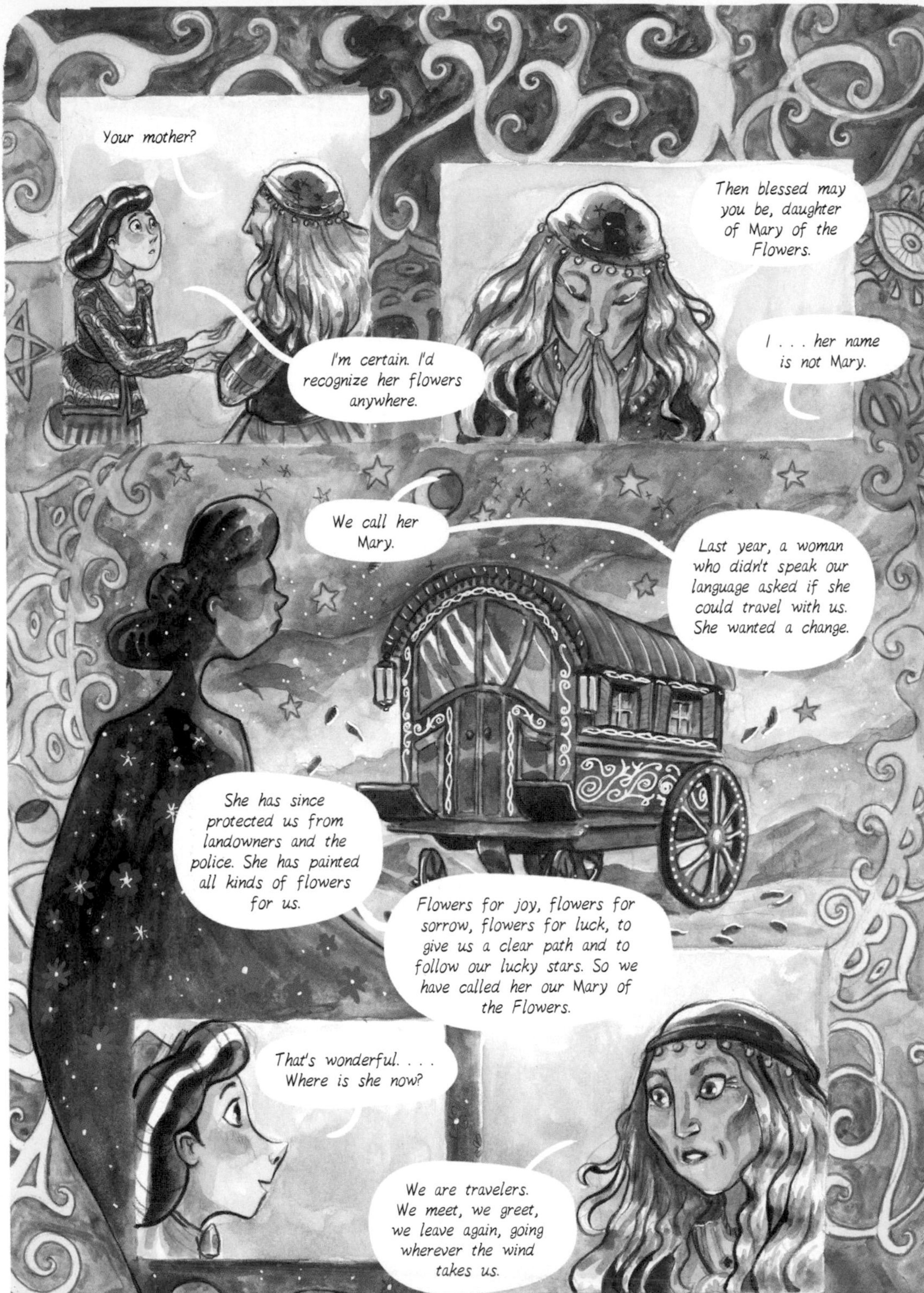
Your mother?
I'm certain. I'd recognize her flowers anywhere.
Then blessed may you be, daughter of Mary of the Flowers.
I . . . her name is not Mary.
We call her Mary.
Last year, a woman who didn't speak our language asked if she could travel with us. She wanted a change.
She has since protected us from landowners and the police. She has painted all kinds of flowers for us.
Flowers for joy, flowers for sorrow, flowers for luck, to give us a clear path and to follow our lucky stars. So we have called her our Mary of the Flowers.
That's wonderful. . . . Where is she now?
We are travelers. We meet, we greet, we leave again, going wherever the wind takes us.

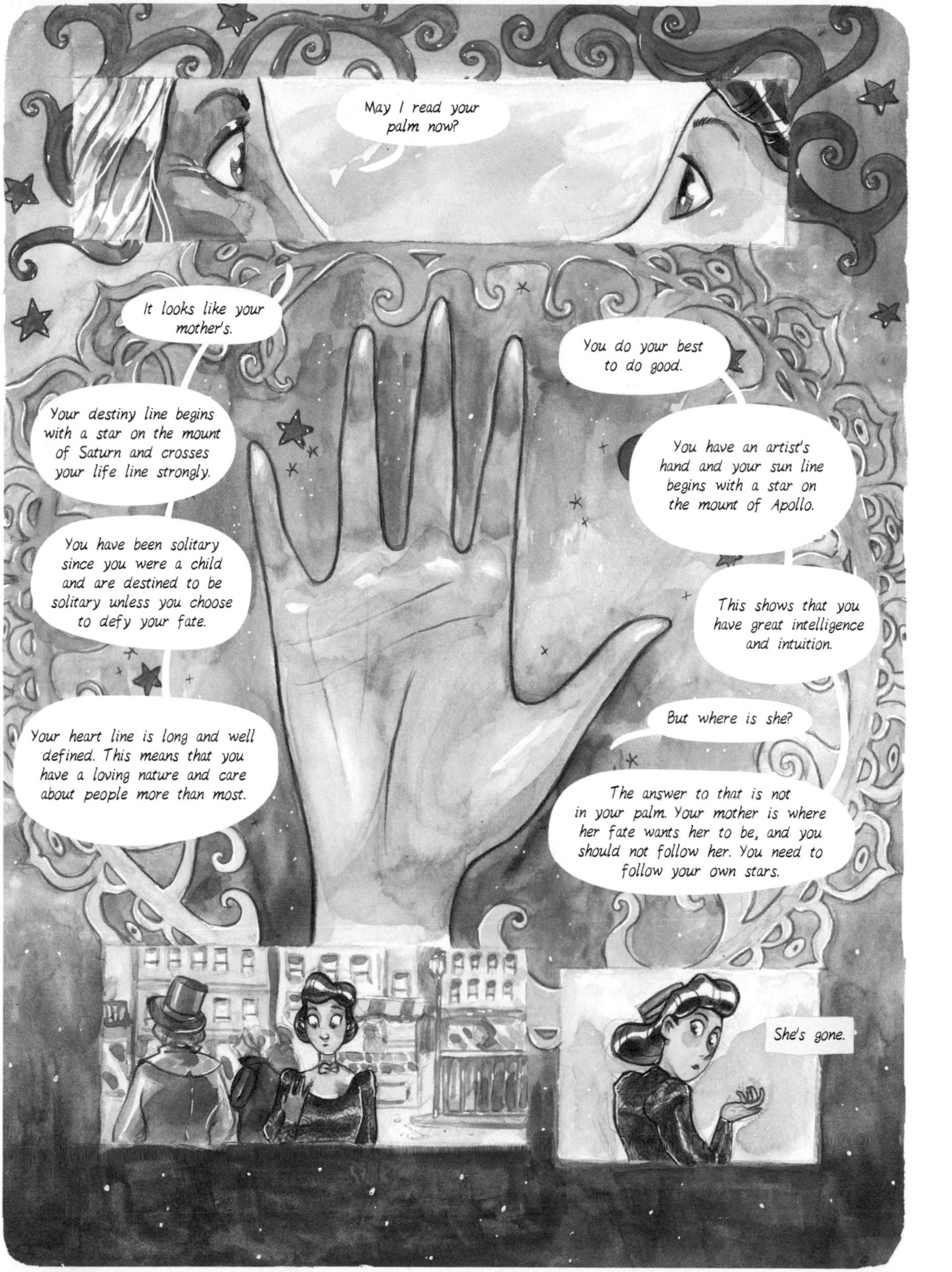
May I read your palm now?
It looks like your mother's.
Your destiny line begins with a star on the mount of Saturn and crosses your life line strongly.
You have been solitary since you were a child and are destined to be solitary unless you choose to defy your fate.
Your heart line is long and well defined. This means that you have a loving nature and care about people more than most.
You do your best to do good.
You have an artist's hand and your sun line begins with a star on the mount of Apollo.
This shows that you have great intelligence and intuition.
But where is she?
The answer to that is not in your palm. Your mother is where her fate wants her to be, and you should not follow her. You need to follow your own stars.
She's gone.

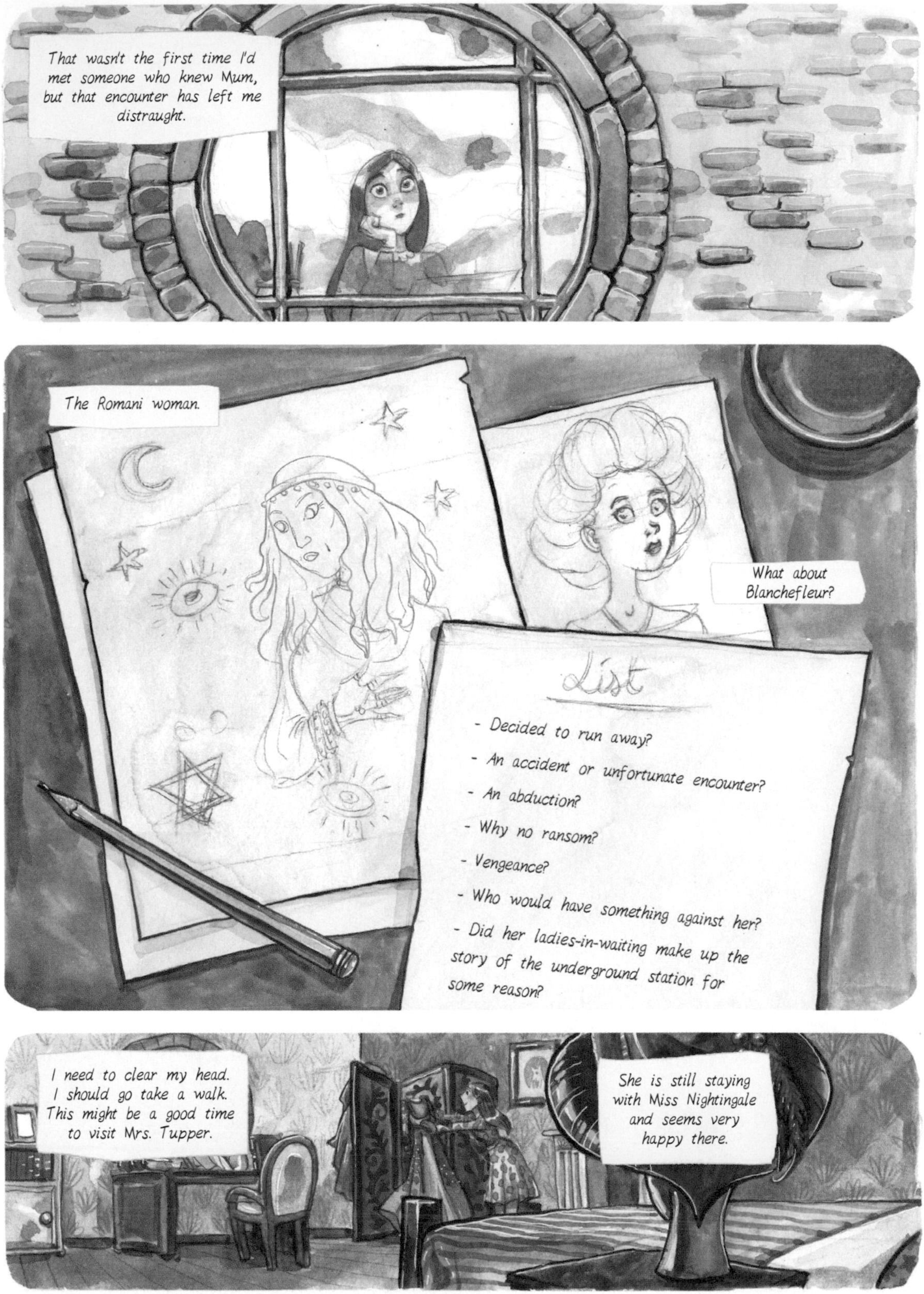
That wasn't the first time I'd met someone who knew Mum, but that encounter has left me distraught.
The Romani woman.
What about Blanchefleur?
List
- Decided to run away?
- An accident or unfortunate encounter?
- An abduction?
- Why no ransom?
- Vengeance?
- Who would have something against her?
- Did her ladies-in-waiting make up the story of the underground station for some reason?
I need to clear my head. I should go take a walk. This might be a good time to visit Mrs. Tupper.
She is still staying with Miss Nightingale and seems very happy there.

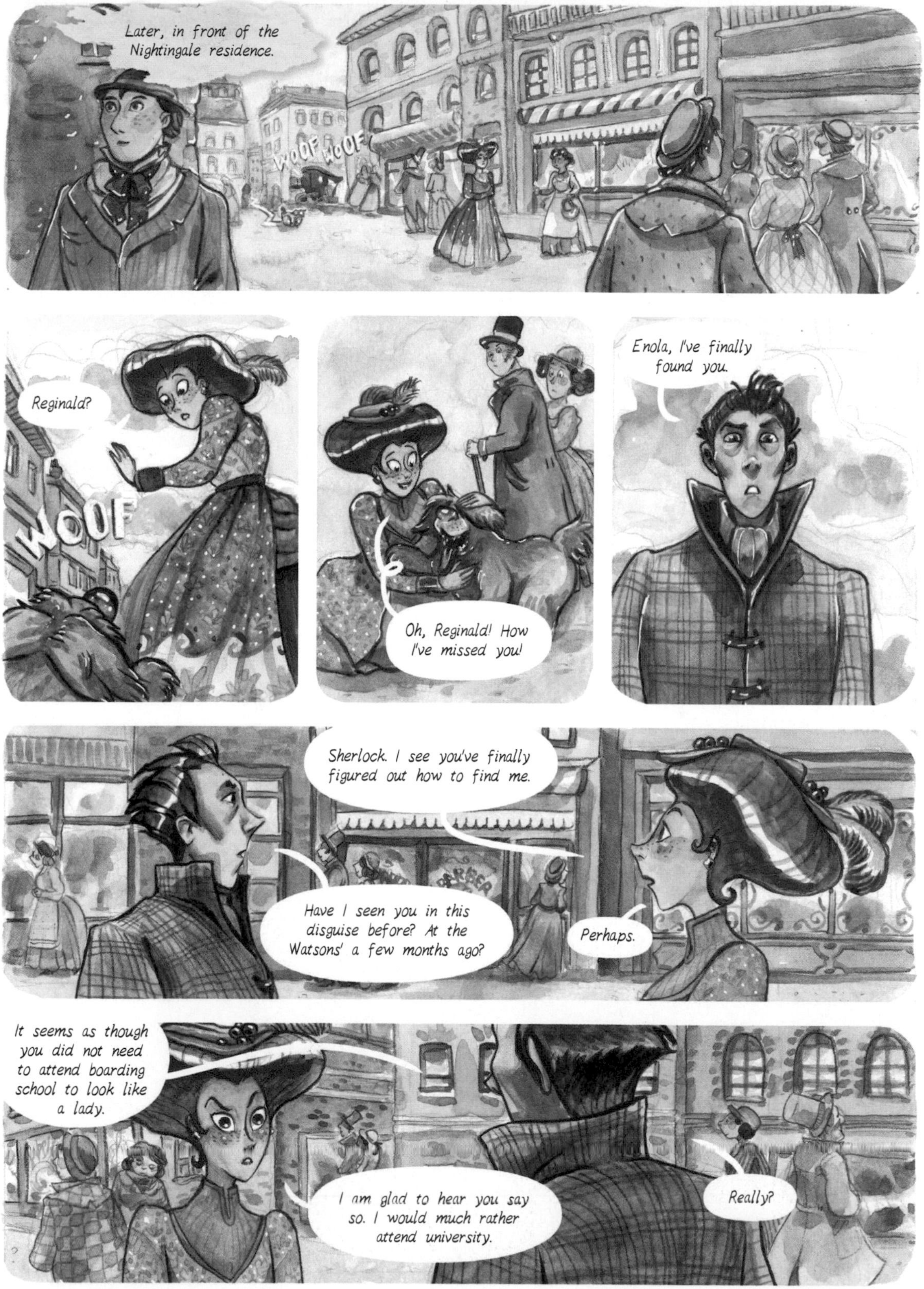
Later, in front of the Nightingale residence.
WOOF WOOF
Reginald?
WOOF
Oh, Reginald! How I've missed you!
Enola, I've finally found you.
Sherlock. I see you've finally figured out how to find me.
Have I seen you in this disguise before? At the Watsons' a few months ago?
Perhaps.
It seems as though you did not need to attend boarding school to look like a lady.
I am glad to hear you say so. I would much rather attend university.
Really?

Enola, I came to find you to share something strange. It's something from our mother.

What is it?

We should go in so I can show you.

Miss Meshle!

Mrs. Tupper! I'm so happy to see you. You look well.

Let's take a seat.

What a handsome dog!

Don't worry about Mrs. Tupper. She already knows a good many of my secrets.

As you wish.

Mr. and Mrs. Lane asked me to come urgently. There was a very strange package left at the door of Ferndell in the middle of the night.

I think it's from our mother. It's for you.

Enola

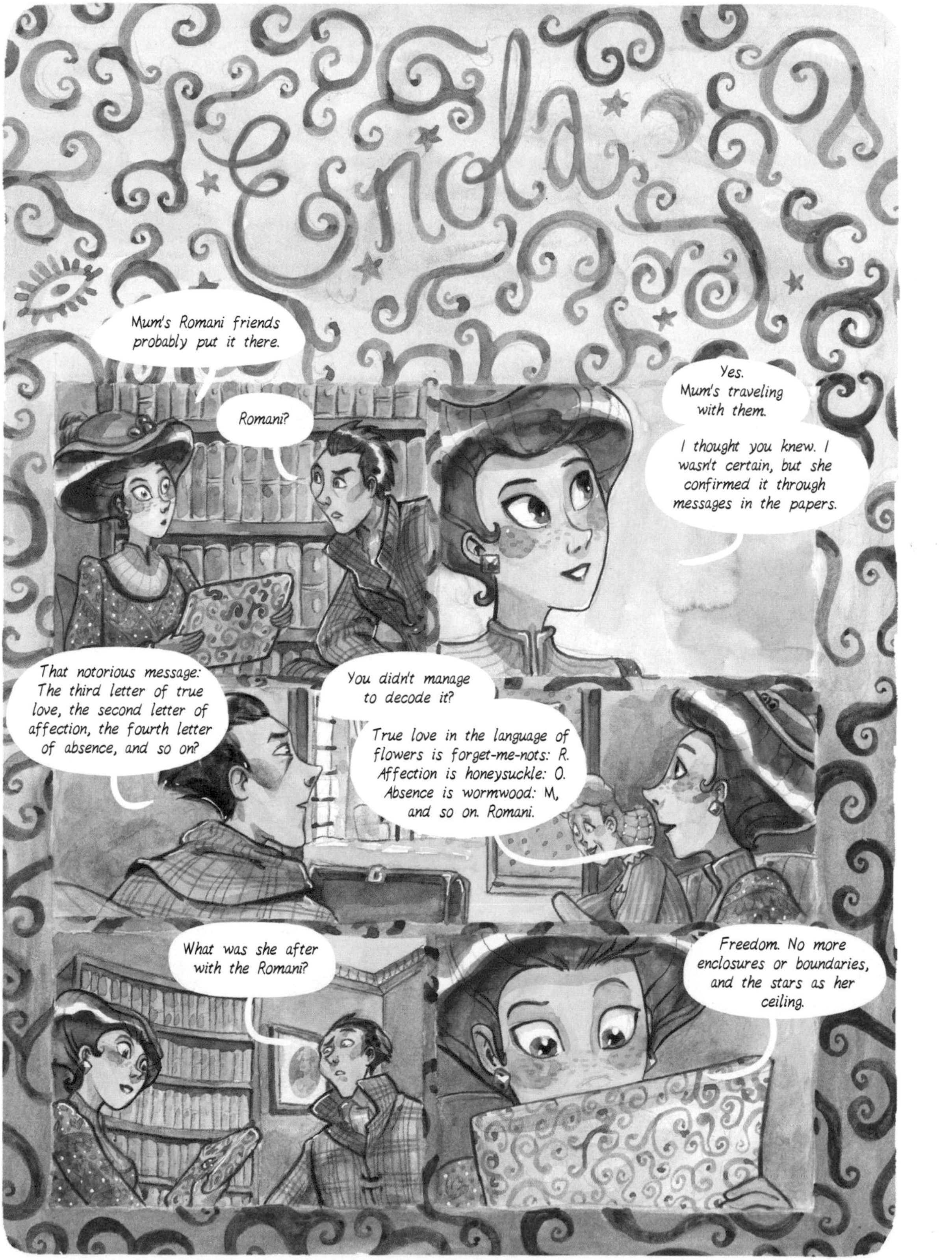
Enola
Mum's Romani friends probably put it there.
Romani?
Yes. Mum's traveling with them.
I thought you knew. I wasn't certain, but she confirmed it through messages in the papers.
That notorious message: The third letter of true love, the second letter of affection, the fourth letter of absence, and so on?
You didn't manage to decode it?
True love in the language of flowers is forget-me-nots: R. Affection is honeysuckle: O. Absence is wormwood: M, and so on. Romani.
What was she after with the Romani?
Freedom. No more enclosures or boundaries, and the stars as her ceiling.

I believe that the eye is a symbol of protection. The contents must be important.

What is it?

That's what we're about to find out!

Here comes Excalibur.

A scytale!

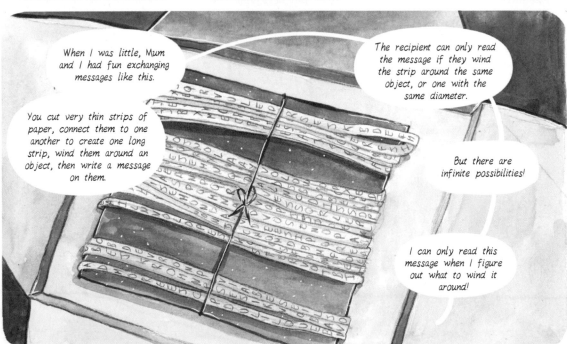

When I was little, Mum and I had fun exchanging messages like this.

You cut very thin strips of paper, connect them to one another to create one long strip, wind them around an object, then write a message on them.

The recipient can only read the message if they wind the strip around the same object, or one with the same diameter.

But there are infinite possibilities!

I can only read this message when I figure out what to wind it around!

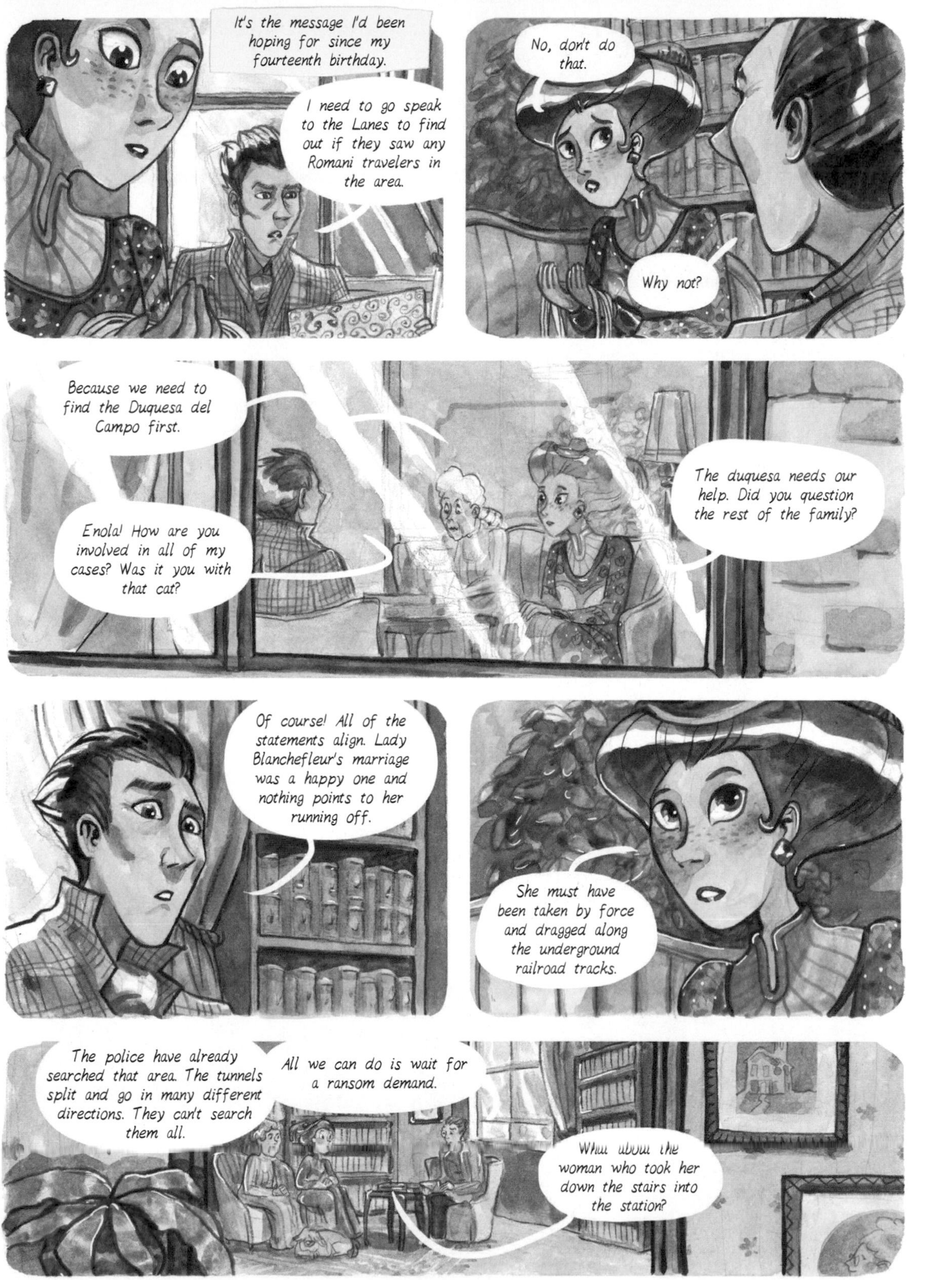
It's the message I'd been hoping for since my fourteenth birthday.
I need to go speak to the Lanes to find out if they saw any Romani travelers in the area.
No, don't do that.
Why not?
Because we need to find the Duquesa del Campo first.
Enola! How are you involved in all of my cases? Was it you with that cat?
The duquesa needs our help. Did you question the rest of the family?
Of course! All of the statements align. Lady Blanchefleur's marriage was a happy one and nothing points to her running off.
She must have been taken by force and dragged along the underground railroad tracks.
The police have already searched that area. The tunnels split and go in many different directions. They can't search them all.
All we can do is wait for a ransom demand.
What about the woman who took her down the stairs into the station?

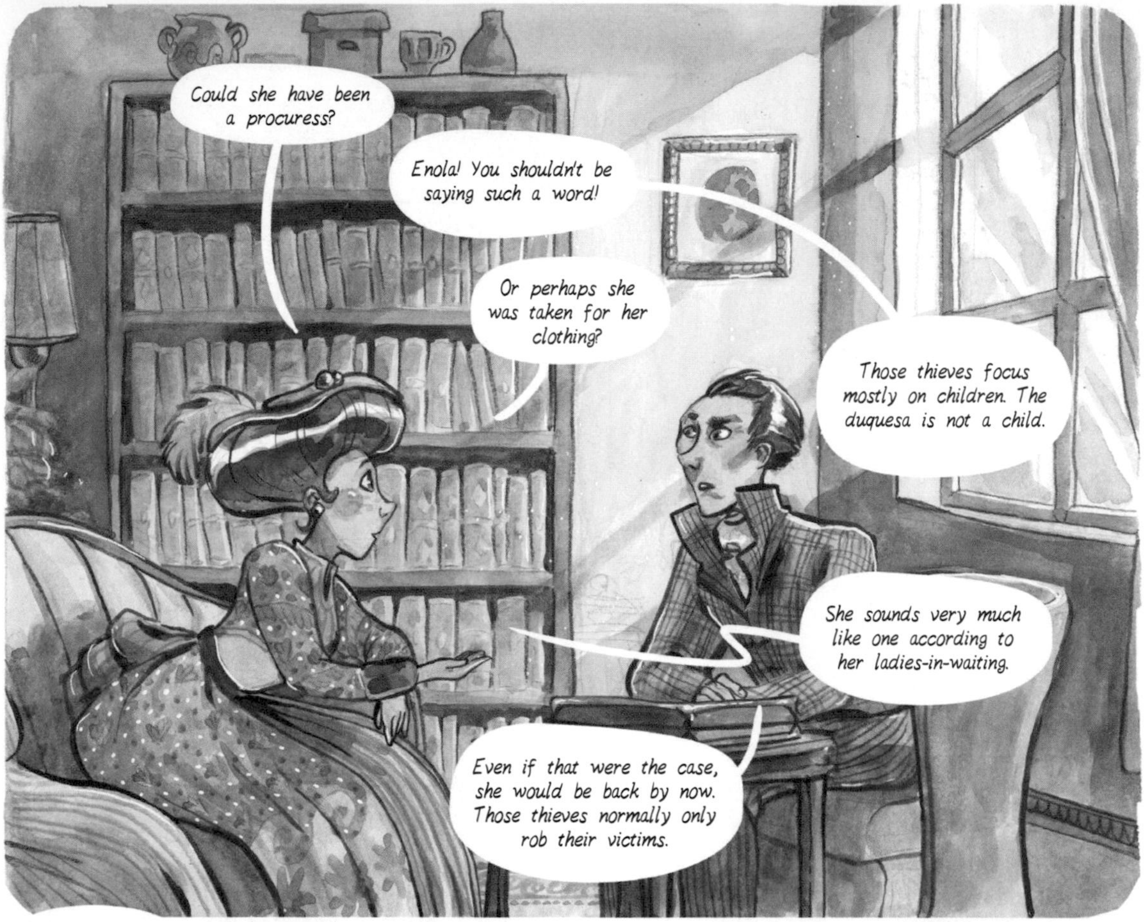
Could she have been a procuress?
Enola! You shouldn't be saying such a word!
Or perhaps she was taken for her clothing?
Those thieves focus mostly on children. The duquesa is not a child.
She sounds very much like one according to her ladies-in-waiting.
Even if that were the case, she would be back by now. Those thieves normally only rob their victims.
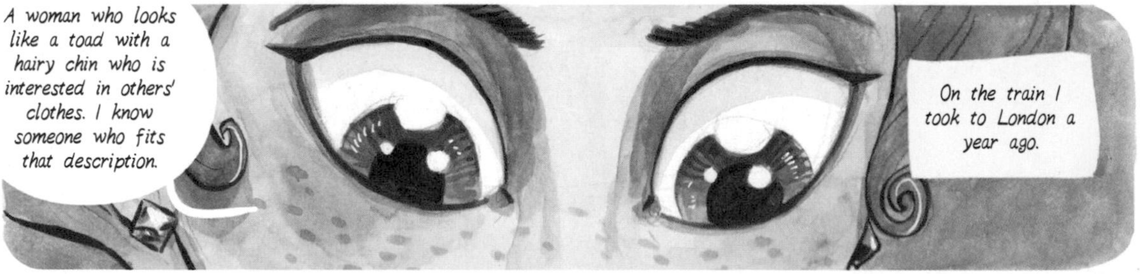
A woman who looks like a toad with a hairy chin who is interested in others' clothes. I know someone who fits that description.
On the train I took to London a year ago.
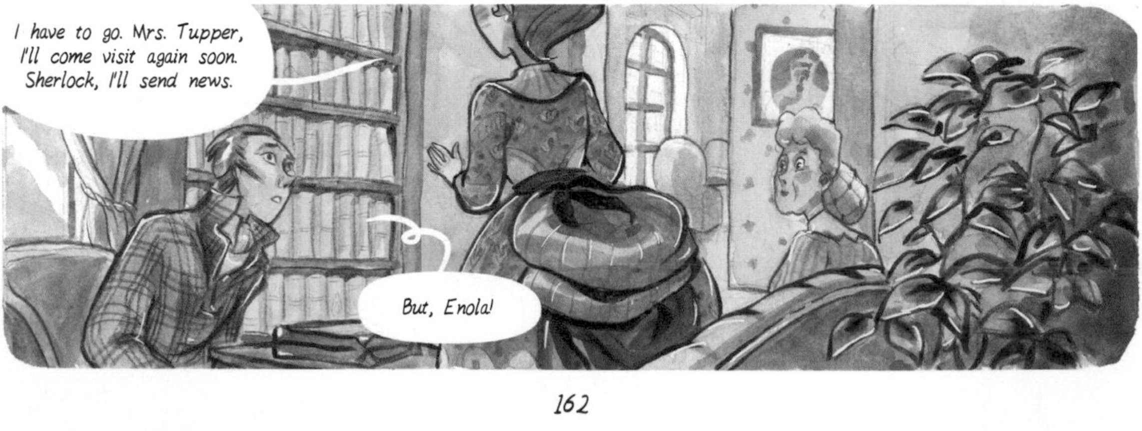
I have to go. Mrs. Tupper, I'll come visit again soon. Sherlock, I'll send news.
But, Enola!

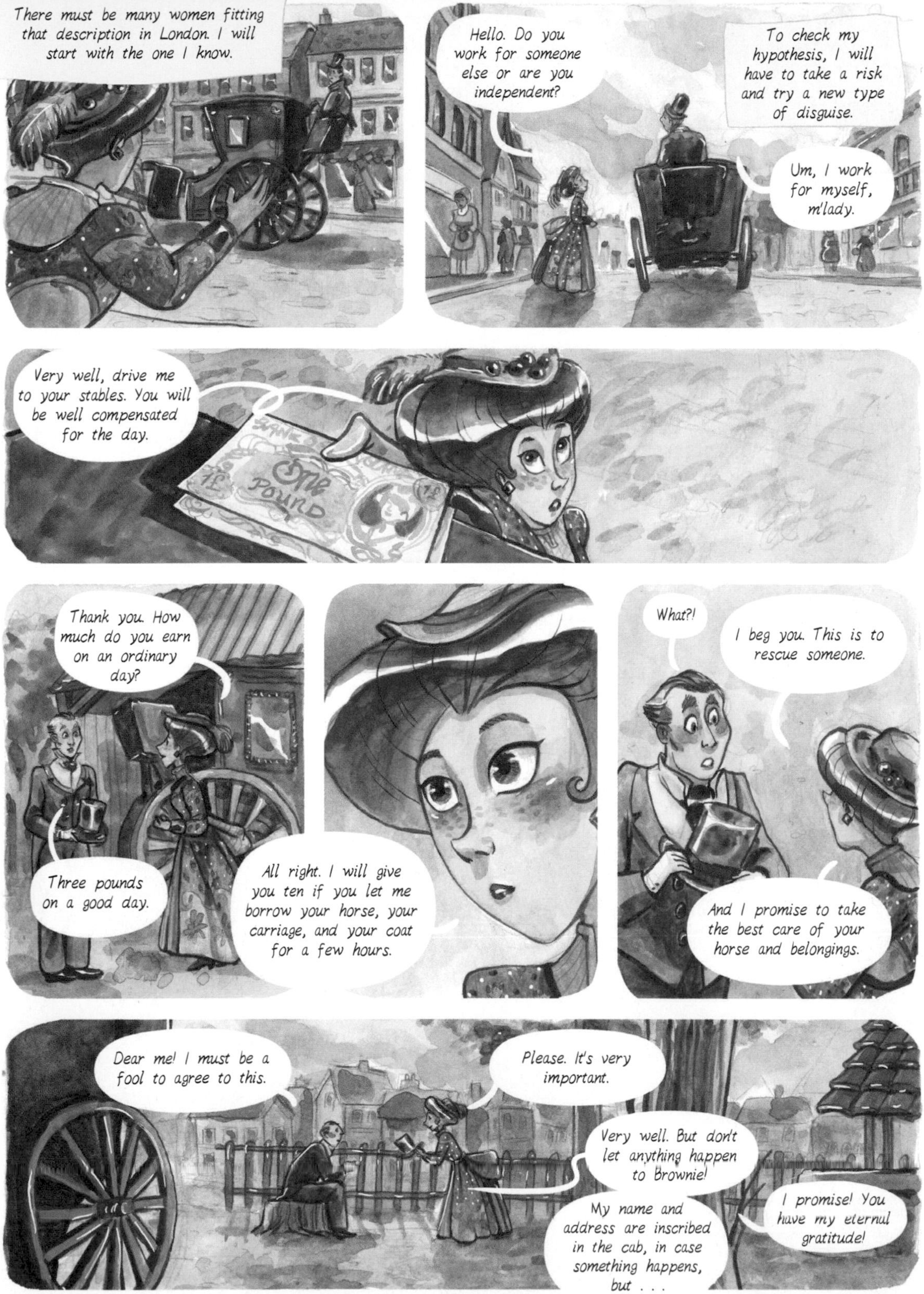
There must be many women fitting that description in London. I will start with the one I know.
Hello. Do you work for someone else or are you independent?
To check my hypothesis, I will have to take a risk and try a new type of disguise.
Um, I work for myself, m'lady.
Very well, drive me to your stables. You will be well compensated for the day.
ONE POUND
Thank you. How much do you earn on an ordinary day?
Three pounds on a good day.
All right. I will give you ten if you let me borrow your horse, your carriage, and your coat for a few hours.
What?!
I beg you. This is to rescue someone.
And I promise to take the best care of your horse and belongings.
Dear me! I must be a fool to agree to this.
Please. It's very important.
Very well. But don't let anything happen to Brownie!
My name and address are inscribed in the cab, in case something happens, but . . .
I promise! You have my eternal gratitude!

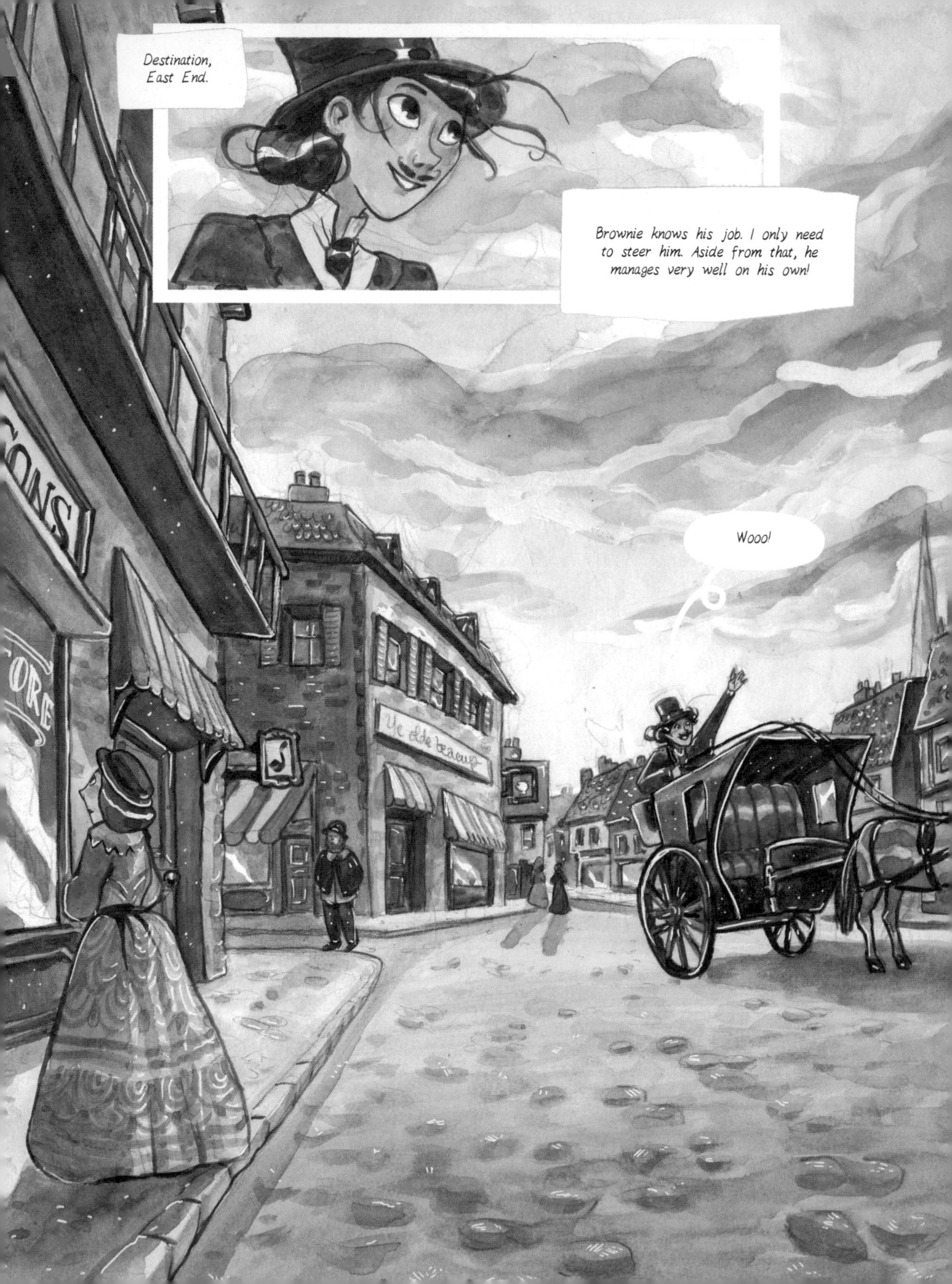
Destination, East End.
Brownie knows his job. I only need to steer him. Aside from that, he manages very well on his own!
Wooo!

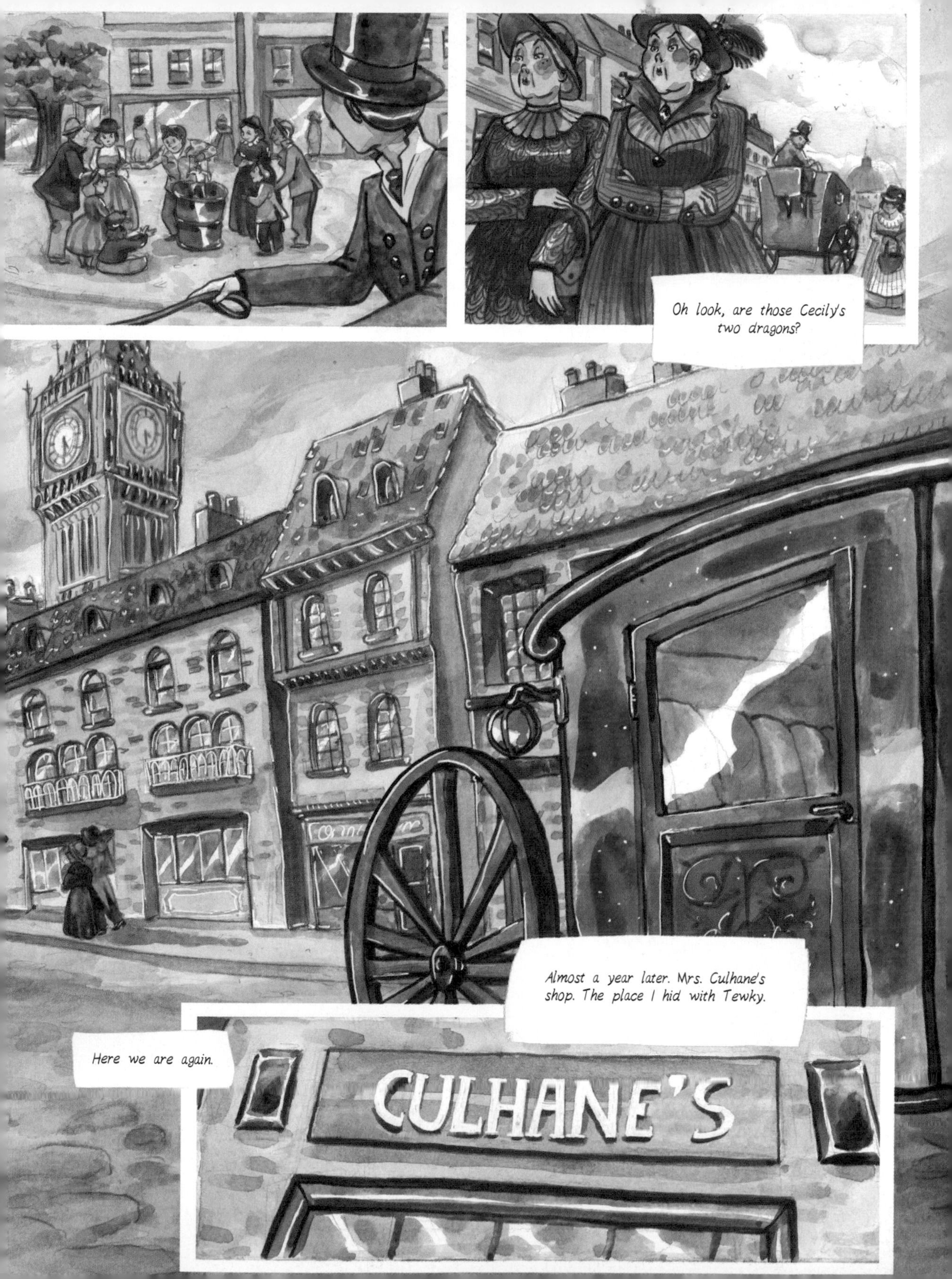

Oh look, are those Cecily's two dragons?
Almost a year later. Mrs. Culhane's shop. The place I hid with Tewky.
Here we are again.
CULHANE'S

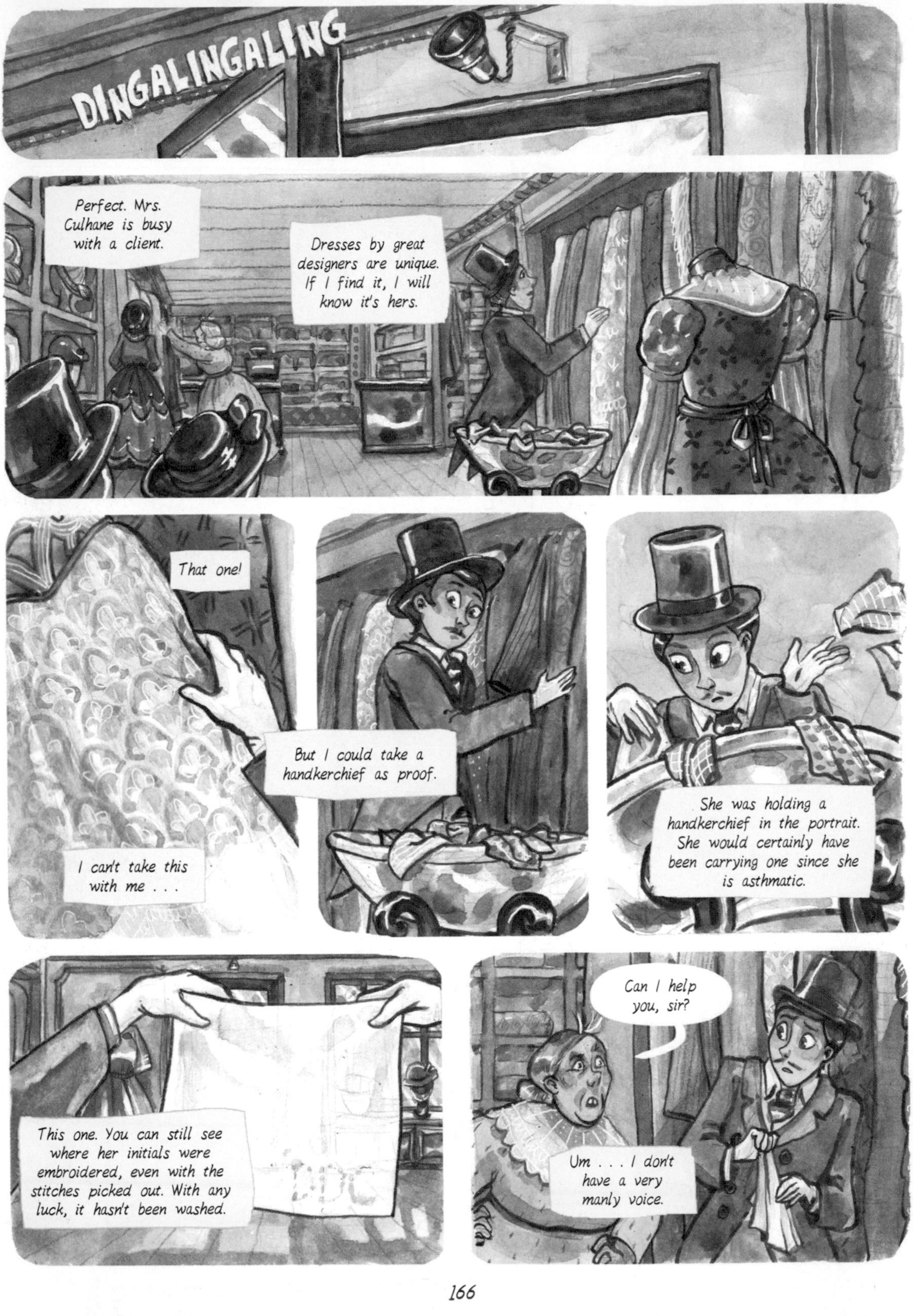
DINGALINGALING
Perfect. Mrs. Culhane is busy with a client.
Dresses by great designers are unique. If I find it, I will know it's hers.
That one!
I can't take this with me . . .
But I could take a handkerchief as proof.
She was holding a handkerchief in the portrait. She would certainly have been carrying one since she is asthmatic.
This one. You can still see where her initials were embroidered, even with the stitches picked out. With any luck, it hasn't been washed.
Can I help you, sir?
Um . . . I don't have a very manly voice.

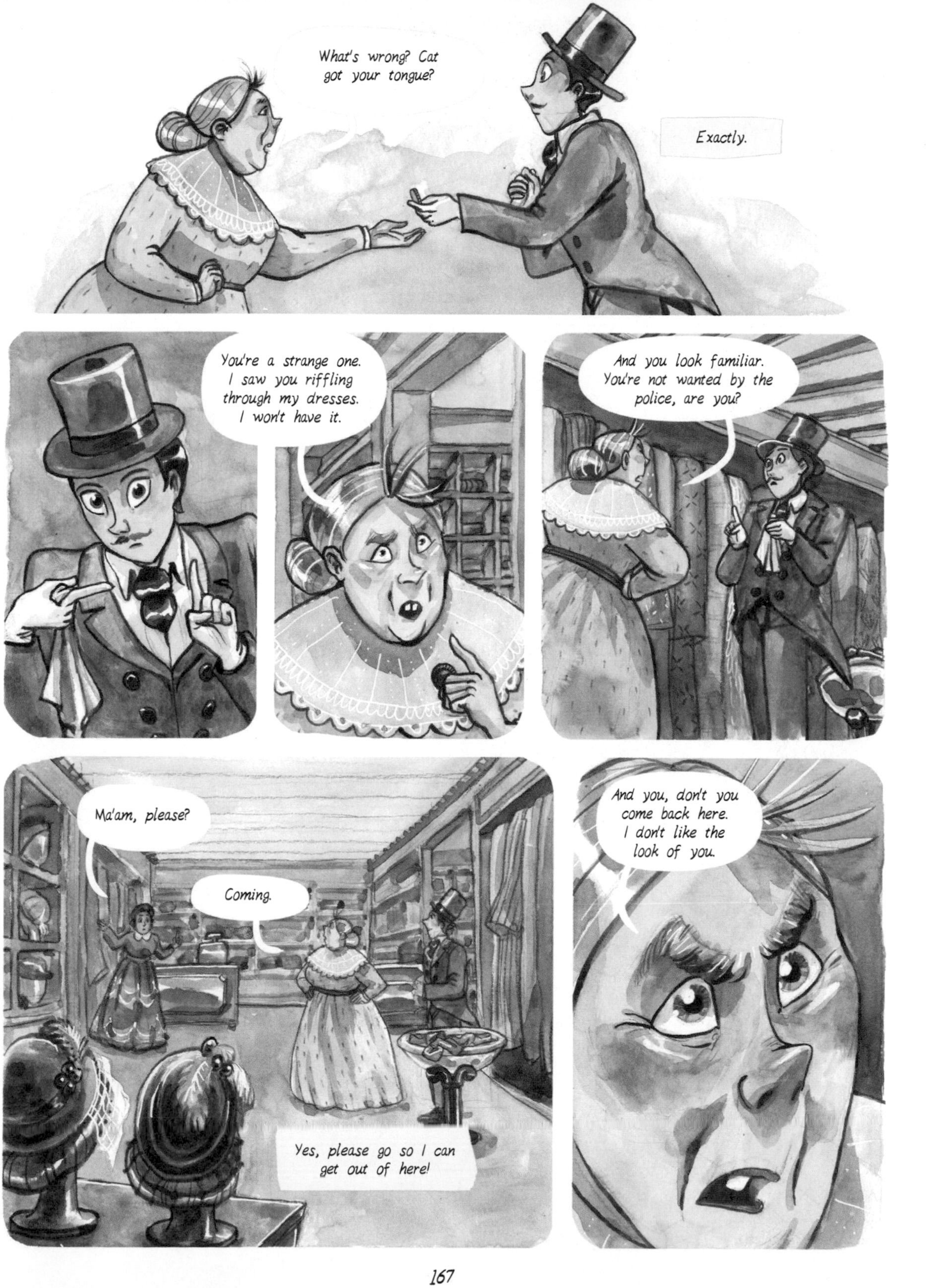
What's wrong? Cat got your tongue?
Exactly.
You're a strange one. I saw you riffling through my dresses. I won't have it.
And you look familiar. You're not wanted by the police, are you?
Ma'am, please?
Coming.
Yes, please go so I can get out of here!
And you, don't you come back here. I don't like the look of you.

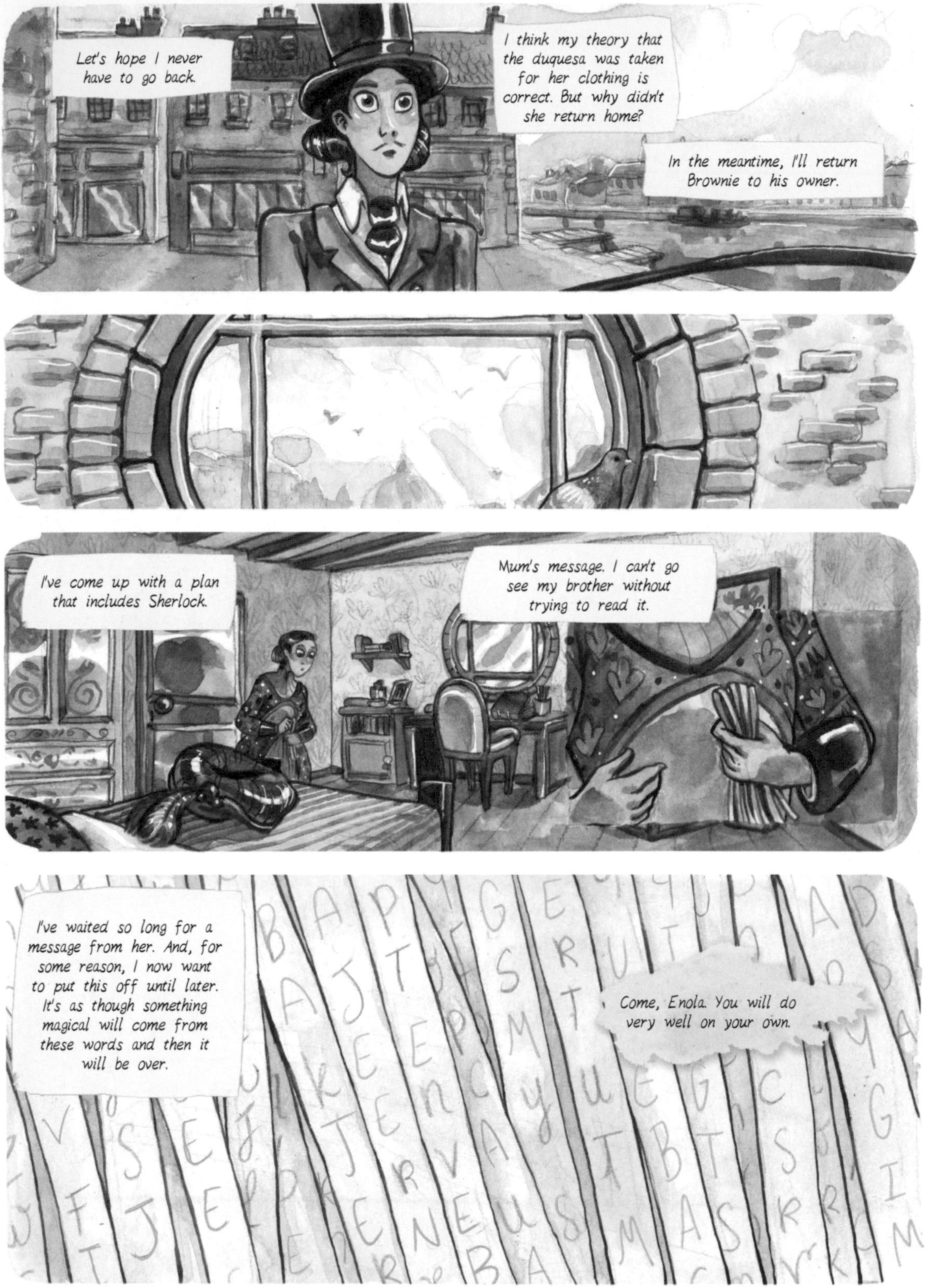
Let's hope I never have to go back.
I think my theory that the duquesa was taken for her clothing is correct. But why didn't she return home?
In the meantime, I'll return Brownie to his owner.
I've come up with a plan that includes Sherlock.
Mum's message. I can't go see my brother without trying to read it.
I've waited so long for a message from her. And, for some reason, I now want to put this off until later. It's as though something magical will come from these words and then it will be over.
Come, Enola. You will do very well on your own.

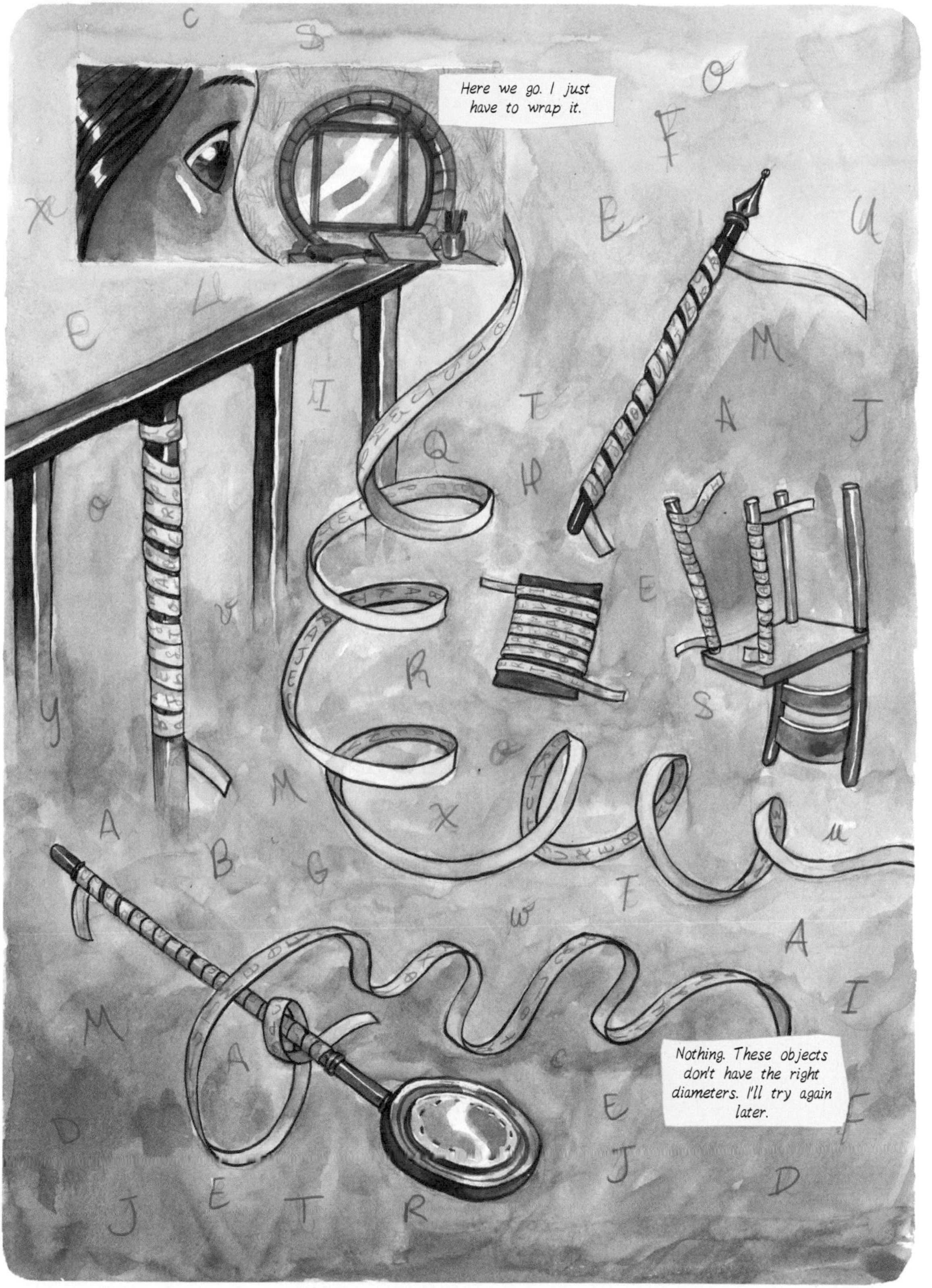
Here we go. I just have to wrap it.
Nothing. These objects don't have the right diameters. I'll try again later.

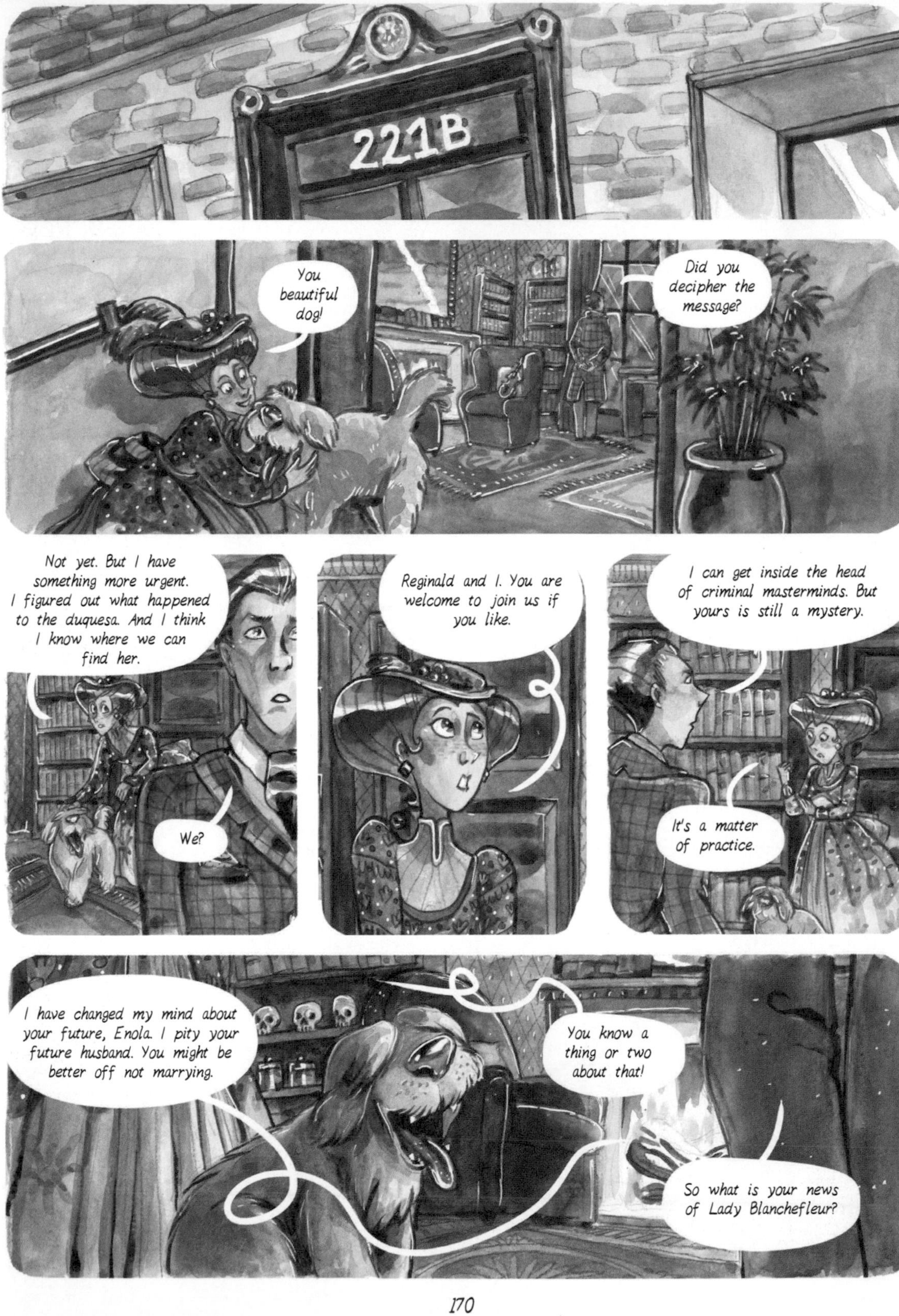
221B
You beautiful dog!
Did you decipher the message?
Not yet. But I have something more urgent. I figured out what happened to the duquesa. And I think I know where we can find her.
We?
Reginald and I. You are welcome to join us if you like.
I can get inside the head of criminal masterminds. But yours is still a mystery.
It's a matter of practice.
I have changed my mind about your future, Enola. I pity your future husband. You might be better off not marrying.
You know a thing or two about that!
So what is your news of Lady Blanchefleur?

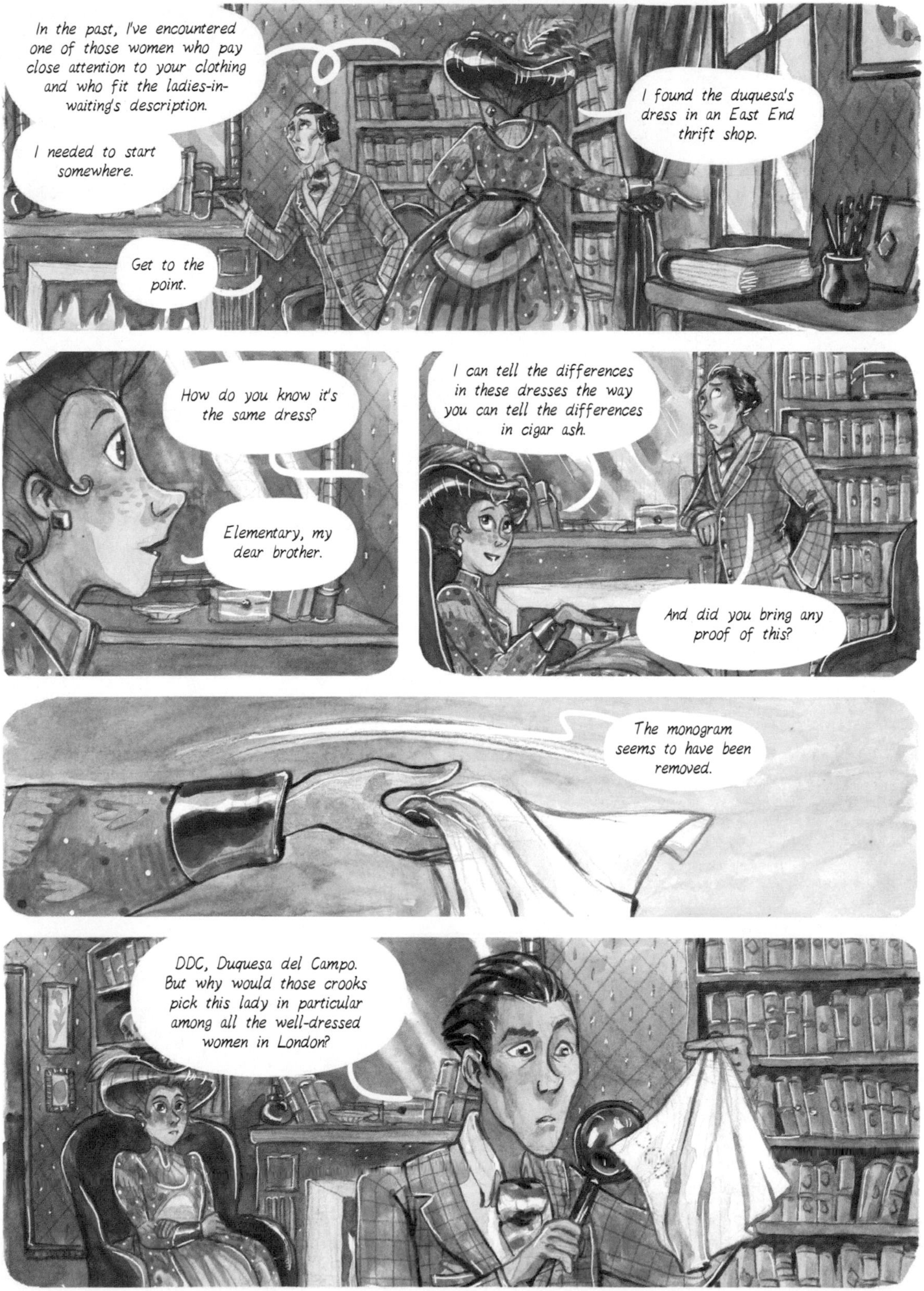
In the past, I've encountered one of those women who pay close attention to your clothing and who fit the ladies-in-waiting's description.
I needed to start somewhere.
Get to the point.
I found the duquesa's dress in an East End thrift shop.
How do you know it's the same dress?
Elementary, my dear brother.
I can tell the differences in these dresses the way you can tell the differences in cigar ash.
And did you bring any proof of this?
The monogram seems to have been removed.
DDC, Duquesa del Campo. But why would those crooks pick this lady in particular among all the well-dressed women in London?

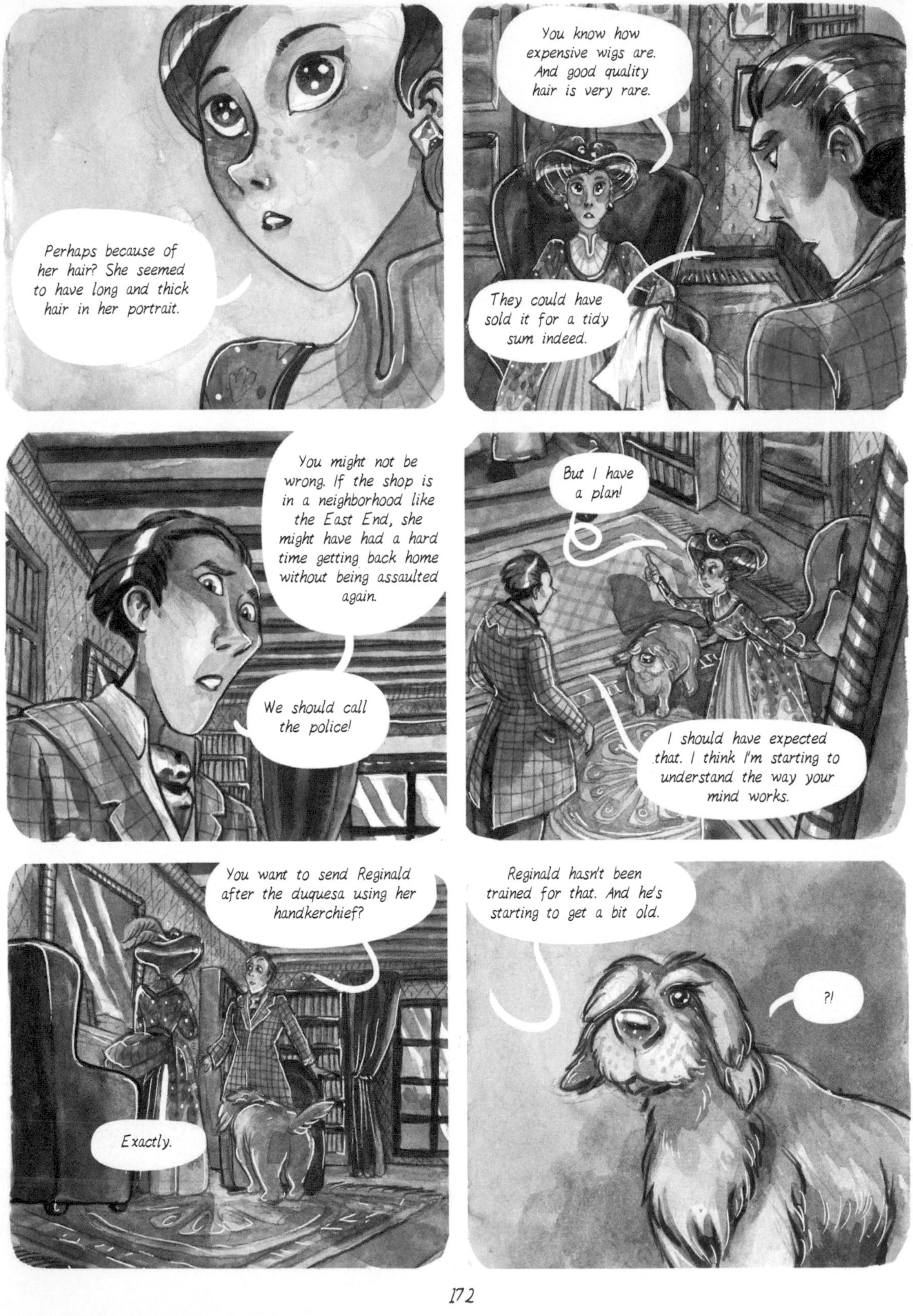
Perhaps because of her hair? She seemed to have long and thick hair in her portrait.
You know how expensive wigs are. And good quality hair is very rare.
They could have sold it for a tidy sum indeed.
You might not be wrong. If the shop is in a neighborhood like the East End, she might have had a hard time getting back home without being assaulted again.
We should call the police!
But I have a plan!
I should have expected that. I think I'm starting to understand the way your mind works.
You want to send Reginald after the duquesa using her handkerchief?
Exactly.
Reginald hasn't been trained for that. And he's starting to get a bit old.
?!

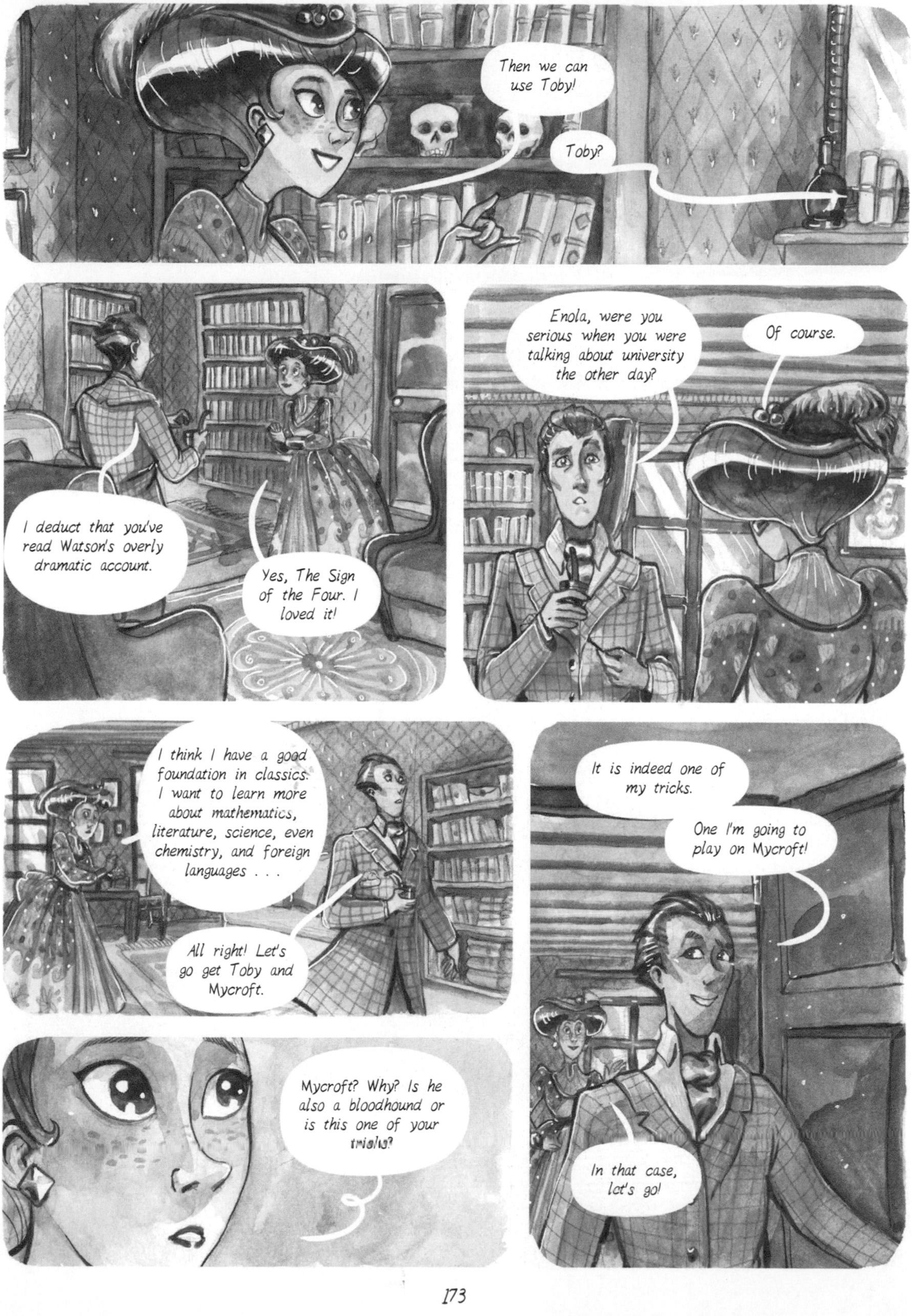
Then we can use Toby!
Toby?
I deduct that you've read Watson's overly dramatic account.
Yes, The Sign of the Four. I loved it!
Enola, were you serious when you were talking about university the other day?
Of course.
I think I have a good foundation in classics. I want to learn more about mathematics, literature, science, even chemistry, and foreign languages . . .
All right! Let's go get Toby and Mycroft.
Mycroft? Why? Is he also a bloodhound or is this one of your tricks?
It is indeed one of my tricks.
One I'm going to play on Mycroft!
In that case, let's go!

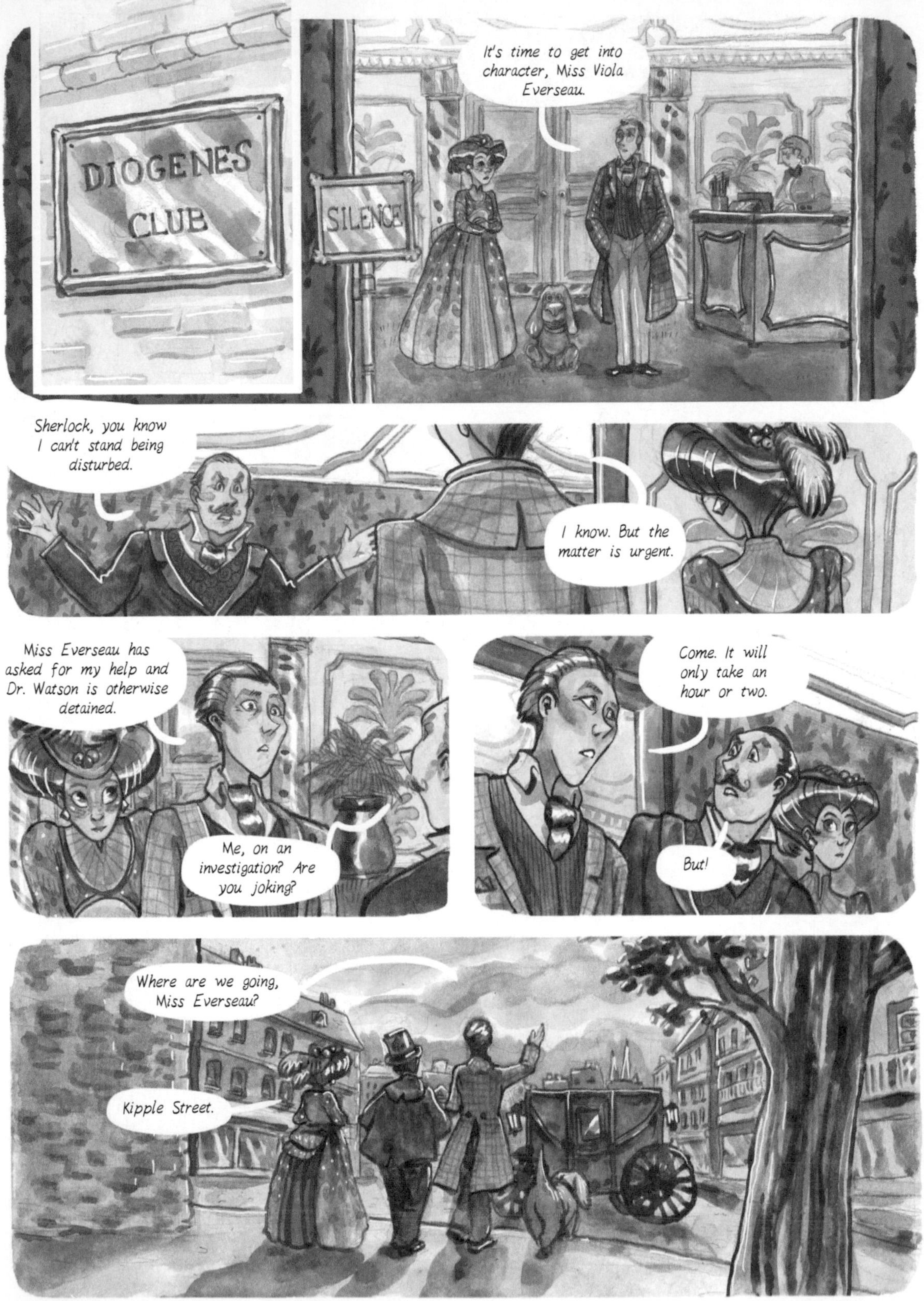
DIOGENES CLUB
SILENCE
It's time to get into character, Miss Viola Everseau.
Sherlock, you know I can't stand being disturbed.
I know. But the matter is urgent.
Miss Everseau has asked for my help and Dr. Watson is otherwise detained.
Me, on an investigation? Are you joking?
Come. It will only take an hour or two.
But!
Where are we going, Miss Everseau?
Kipple Street.

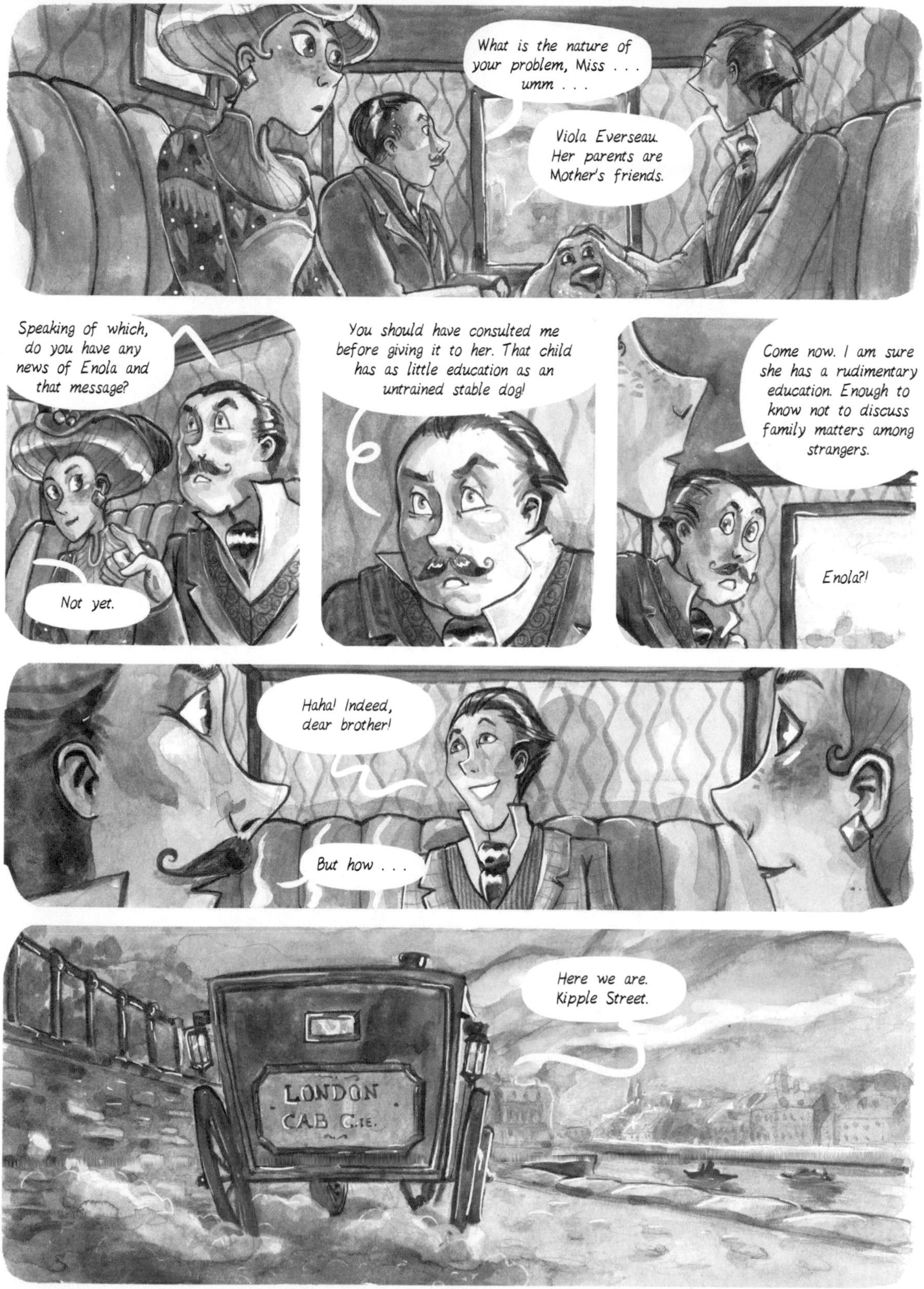
What is the nature of your problem, Miss . . . umm . . .
Viola Everseau. Her parents are Mother's friends.
Speaking of which, do you have any news of Enola and that message?
Not yet.
You should have consulted me before giving it to her. That child has as little education as an untrained stable dog!
Come now. I am sure she has a rudimentary education. Enough to know not to discuss family matters among strangers.
Enola?!
Haha! Indeed, dear brother!
But how . . .
Here we are. Kipple Street.
LONDON CAB C.ie

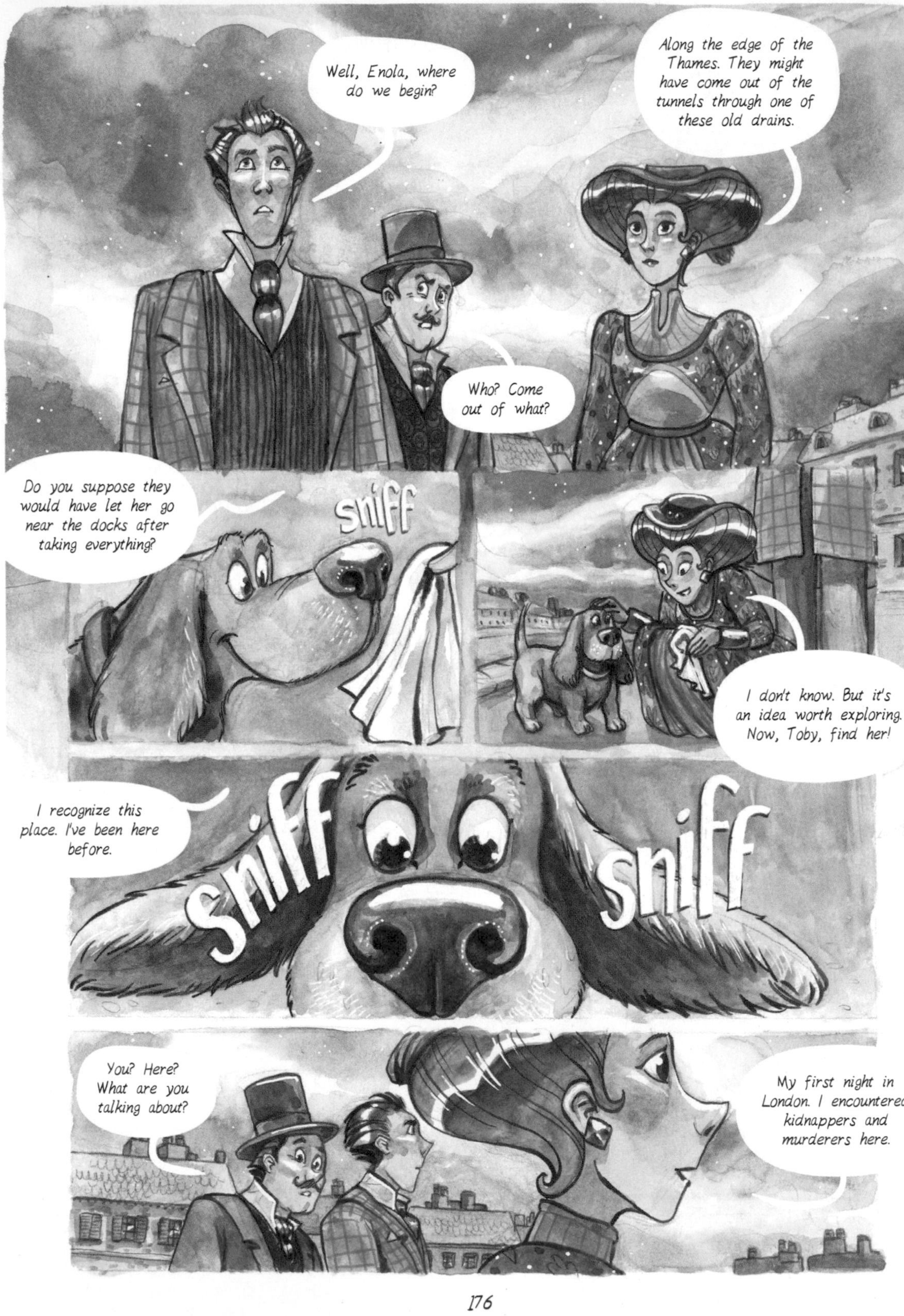
Well, Enola, where do we begin?
Along the edge of the Thames. They might have come out of the tunnels through one of these old drains.
Who? Come out of what?
Do you suppose they would have let her go near the docks after taking everything?
sniff
I don't know. But it's an idea worth exploring. Now, Toby, find her!
I recognize this place. I've been here before.
sniff
sniff
You? Here? What are you talking about?
My first night in London. I encountered kidnappers and murderers here.

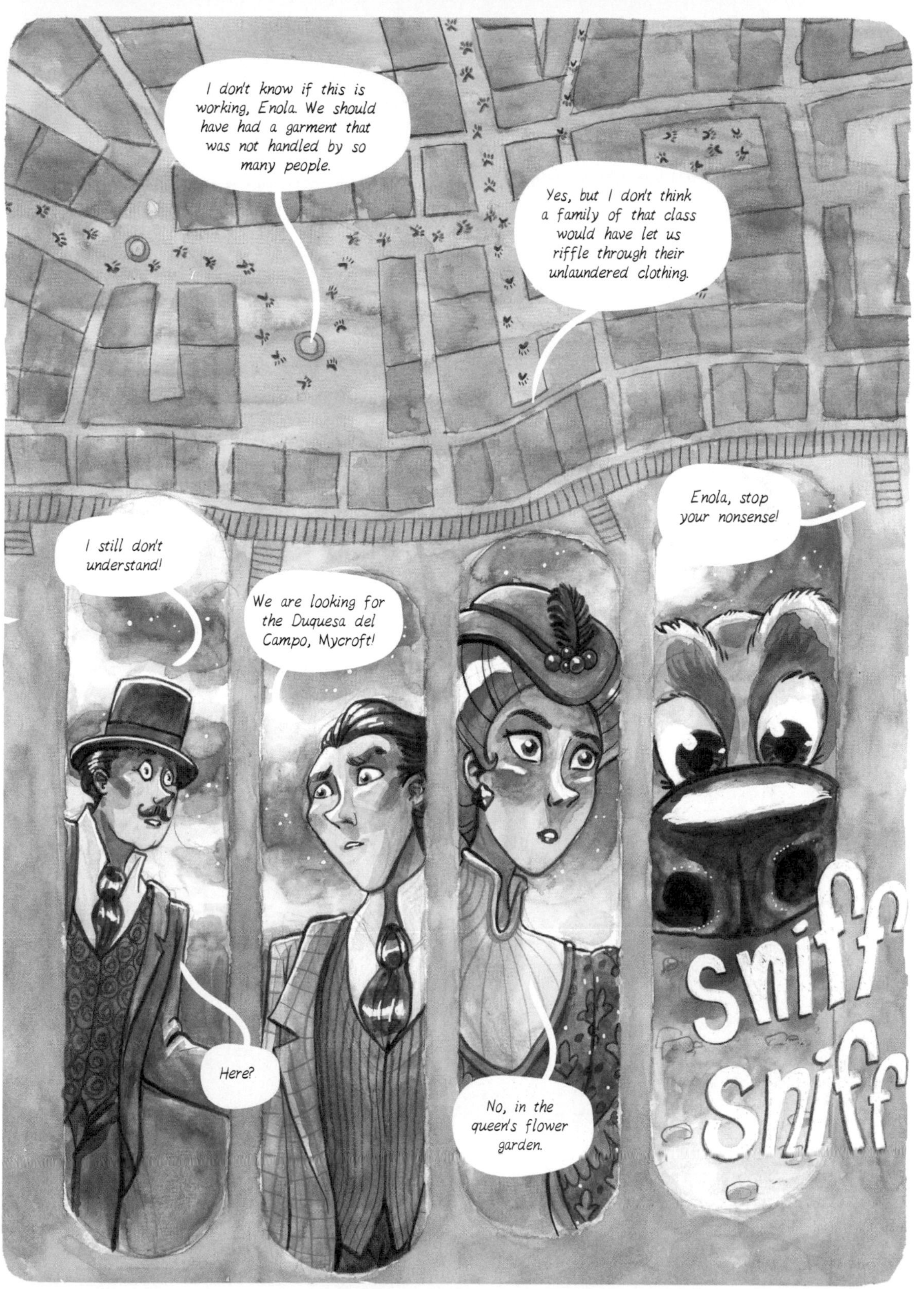
I don't know if this is working, Enola. We should have had a garment that was not handled by so many people.
Yes, but I don't think a family of that class would have let us riffle through their unlaundered clothing.
I still don't understand!
We are looking for the Duquesa del Campo, Mycroft!
Enola, stop your nonsense!
Here?
No, in the queen's flower garden.
sniff
sniff

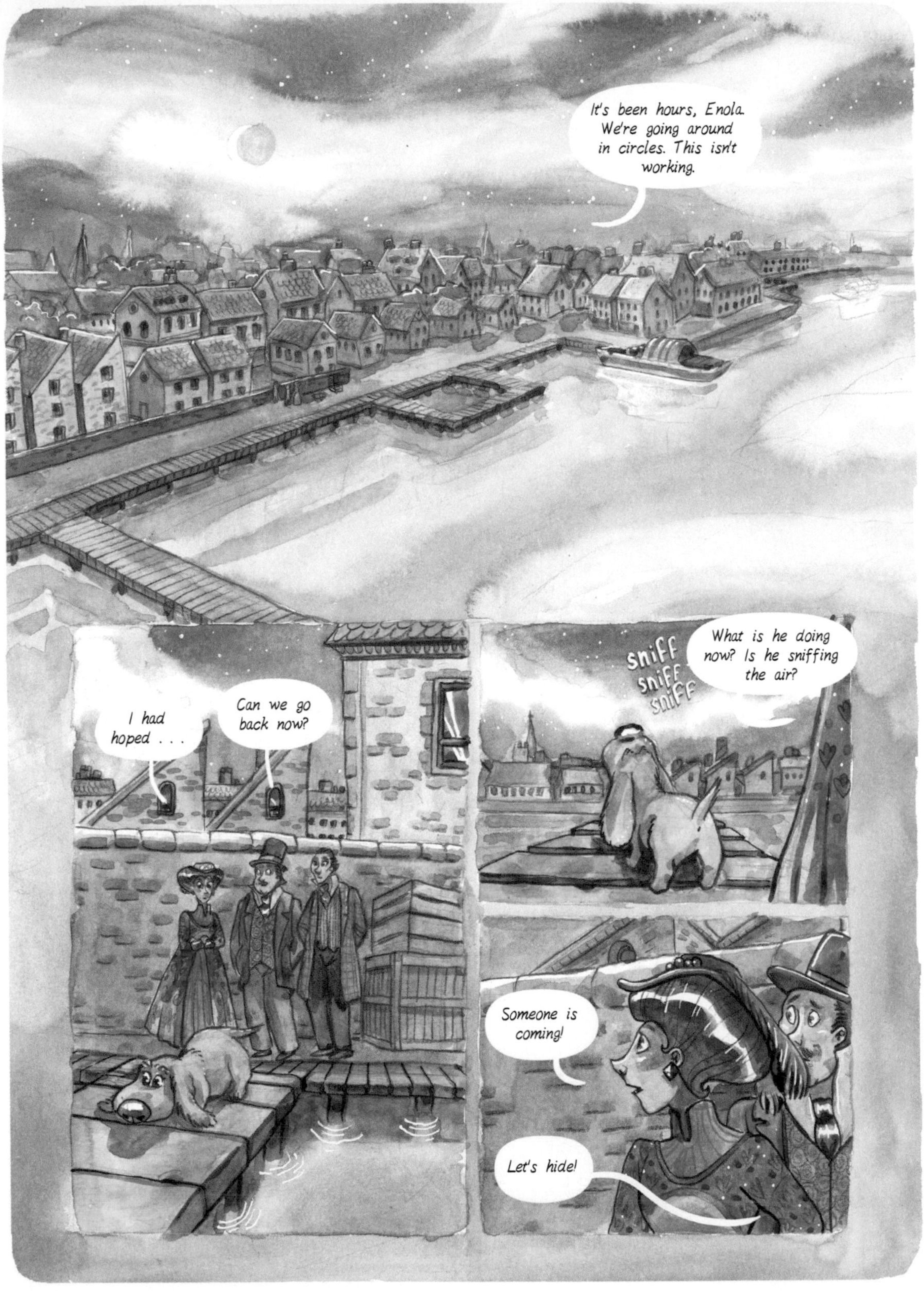
It's been hours, Enola. We're going around in circles. This isn't working.
I had hoped . . .
Can we go back now?
sniff sniff sniff
What is he doing now? Is he sniffing the air?
Someone is coming!
Let's hide!

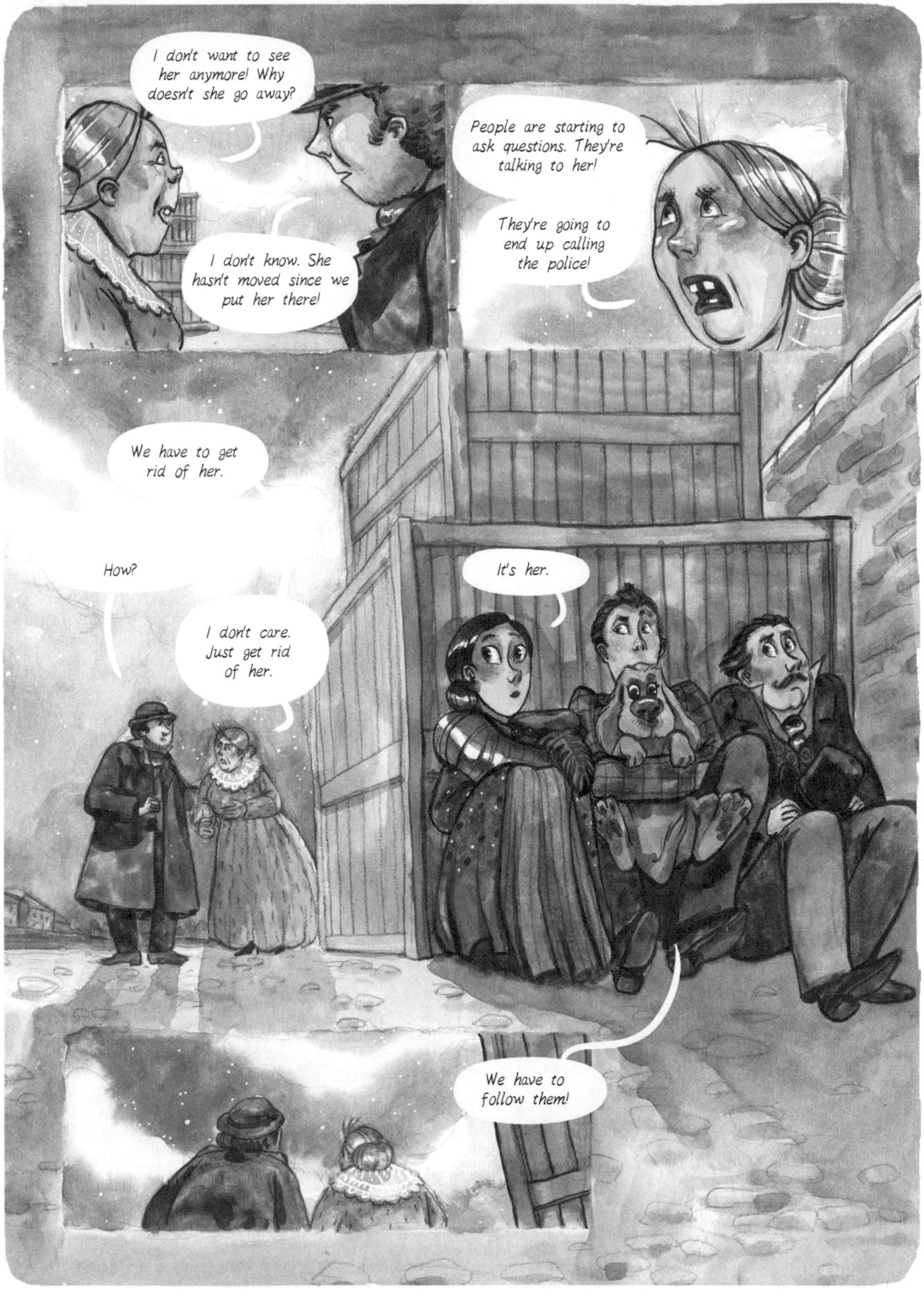
I don't want to see her anymore! Why doesn't she go away?
I don't know. She hasn't moved since we put her there!
People are starting to ask questions. They're talking to her!
They're going to end up calling the police!
We have to get rid of her.
How?
I don't care. Just get rid of her.
It's her.
We have to follow them!

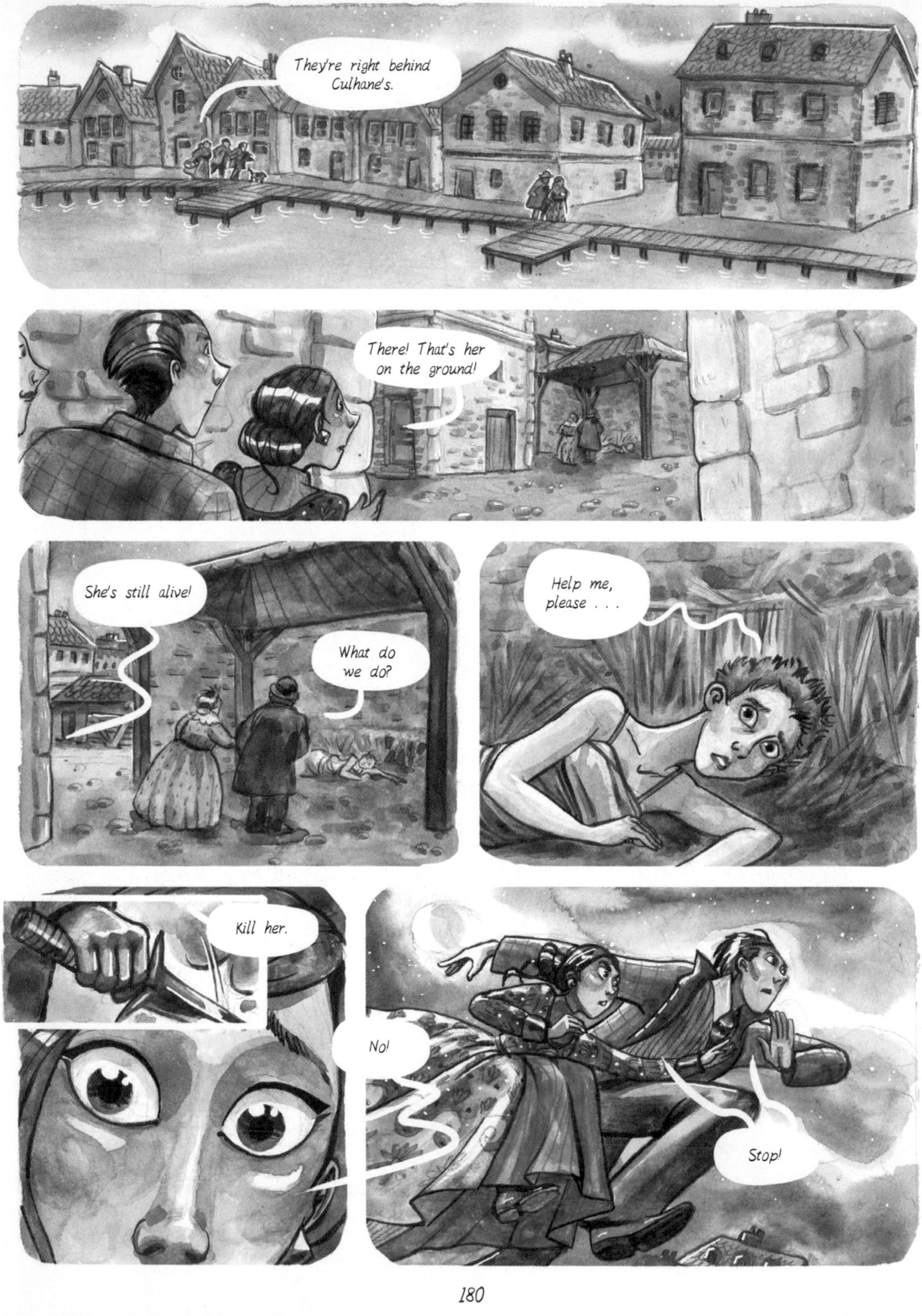
They're right behind Culhane's.
There! That's her on the ground!
She's still alive!
What do we do?
Help me, please . . .
Kill her.
No!
Stop!

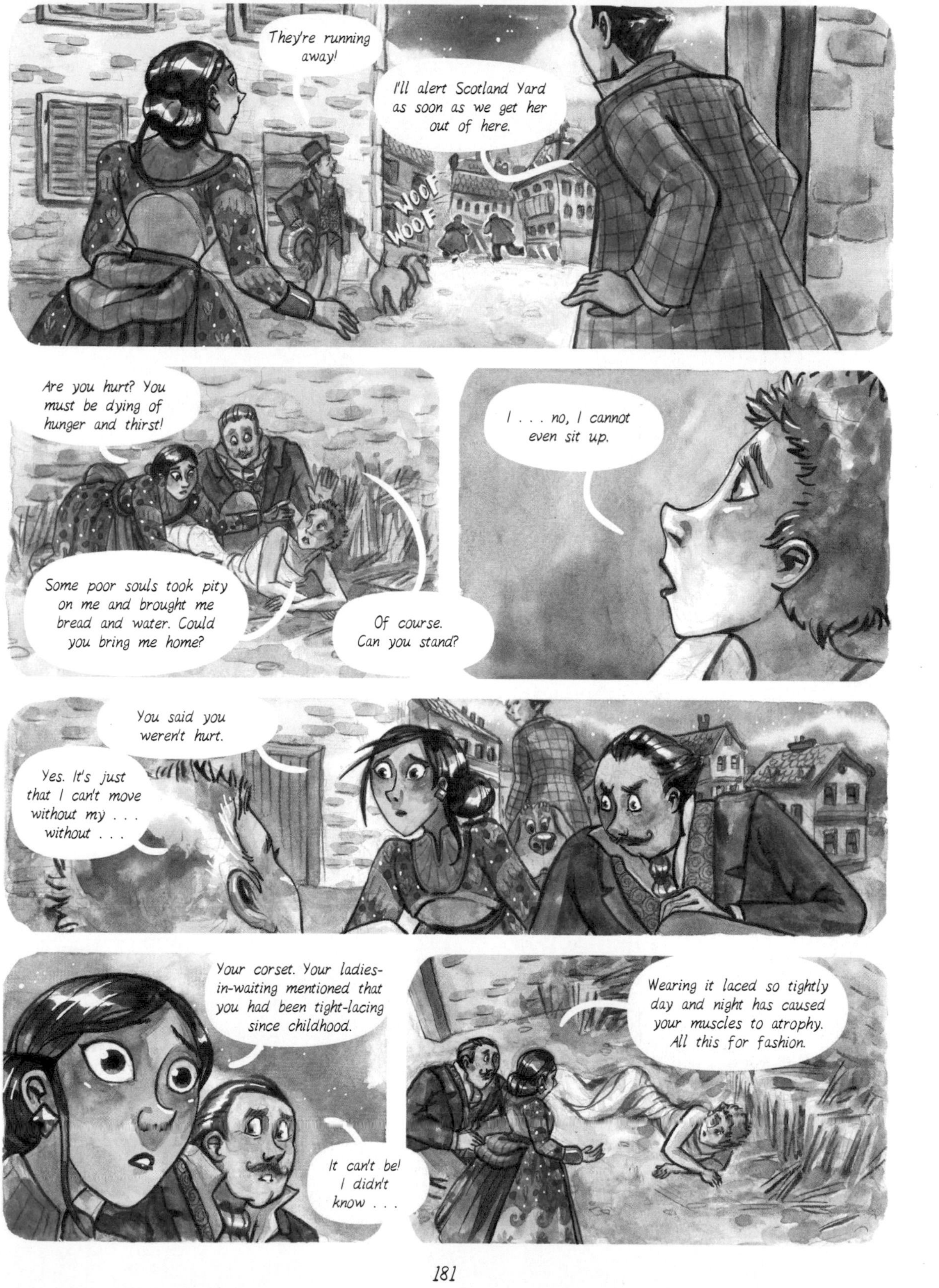
They're running away!
I'll alert Scotland Yard as soon as we get her out of here.
WOOF WOOF
Are you hurt? You must be dying of hunger and thirst!
Some poor souls took pity on me and brought me bread and water. Could you bring me home?
Of course. Can you stand?
I . . . no, I cannot even sit up.
You said you weren't hurt.
Yes. It's just that I can't move without my . . . without . . .
Your corset. Your ladies-in-waiting mentioned that you had been tight-lacing since childhood.
It can't be! I didn't know . . .
Wearing it laced so tightly day and night has caused your muscles to atrophy. All this for fashion.

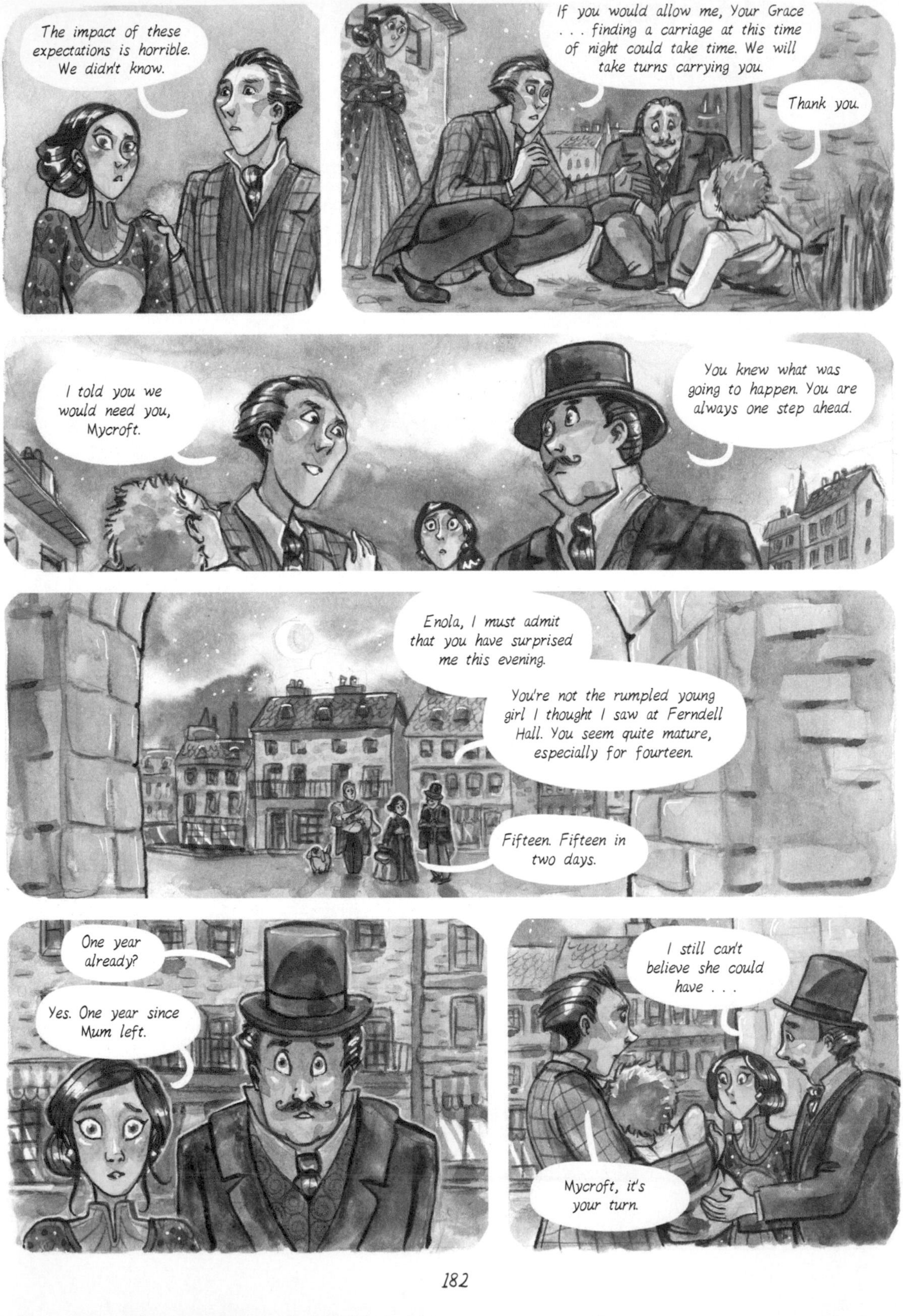

The impact of these expectations is horrible. We didn't know.
If you would allow me, Your Grace . . . finding a carriage at this time of night could take time. We will take turns carrying you.
Thank you.
I told you we would need you, Mycroft.
You knew what was going to happen. You are always one step ahead.
Enola, I must admit that you have surprised me this evening.
You're not the rumpled young girl I thought I saw at Ferndell Hall. You seem quite mature, especially for fourteen.
Fifteen. Fifteen in two days.
One year already?
Yes. One year since Mum left.
I still can't believe she could have . . .
Mycroft, it's your turn.

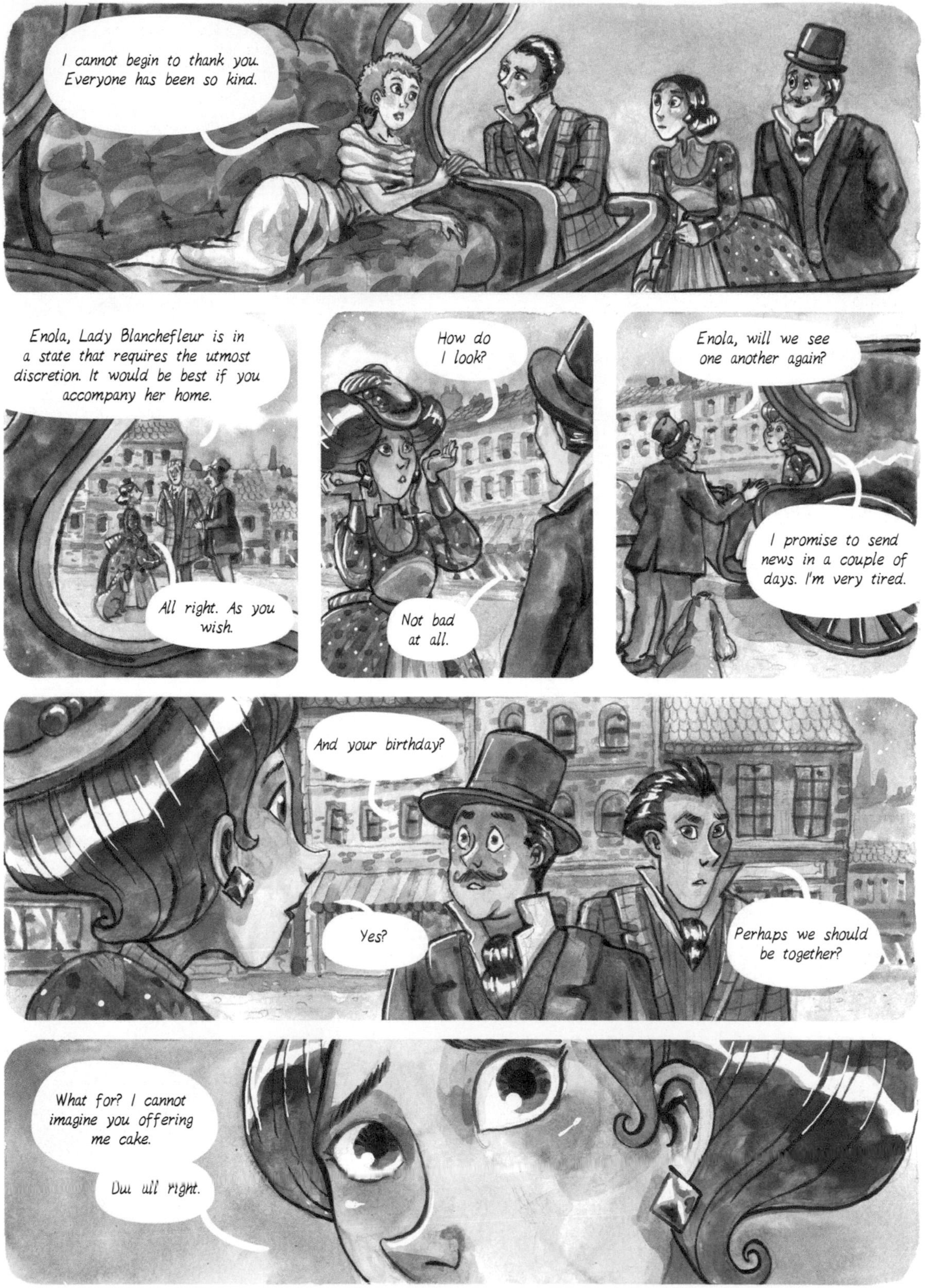

I cannot begin to thank you. Everyone has been so kind.
Enola, Lady Blanchefleur is in a state that requires the utmost discretion. It would be best if you accompany her home.
All right. As you wish.
How do I look?
Not bad at all.
Enola, will we see one another again?
I promise to send news in a couple of days. I'm very tired.
And your birthday?
Yes?
Perhaps we should be together?
What for? I cannot imagine you offering me cake.
But all right.

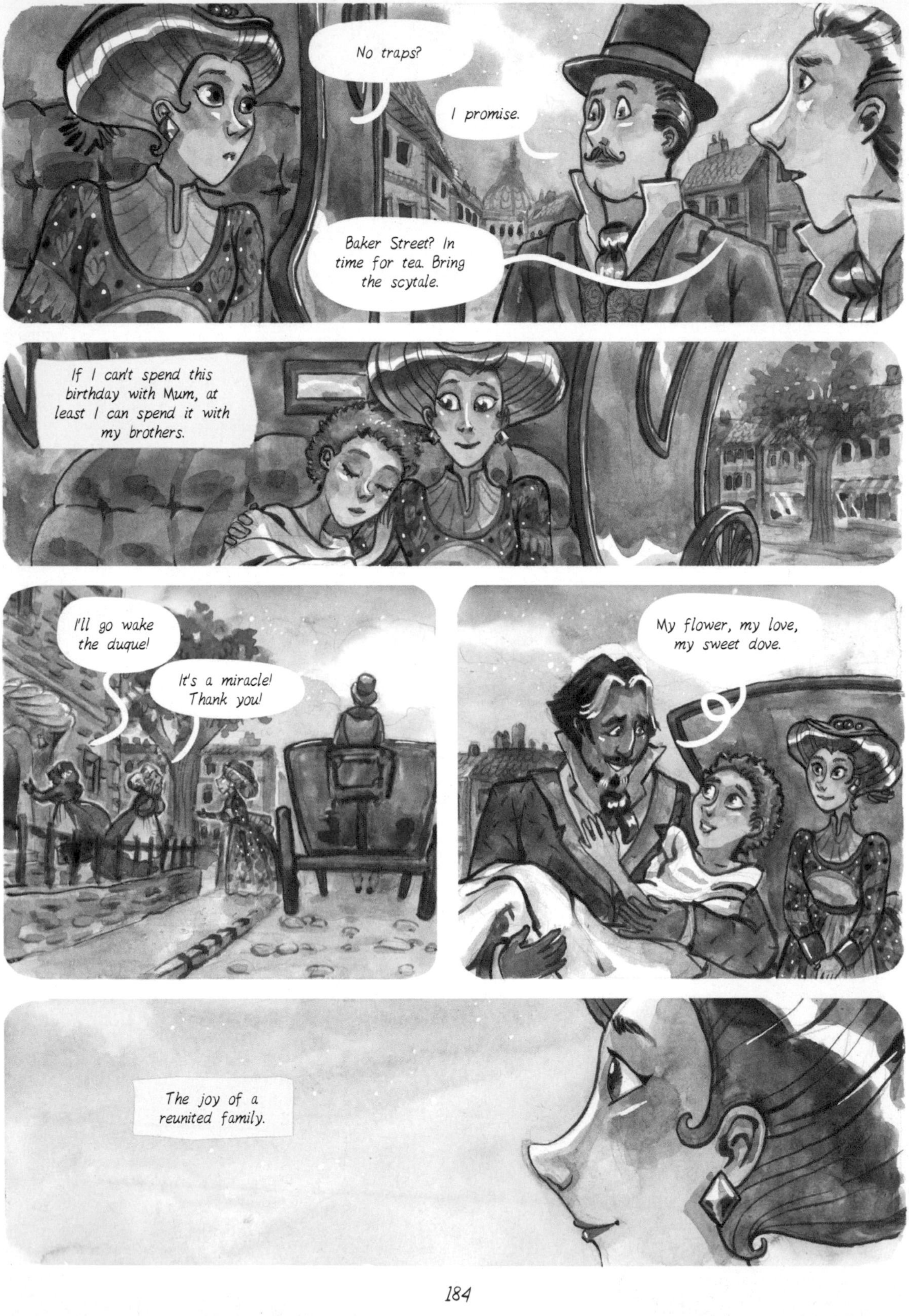
No traps?
I promise.
Baker Street? In time for tea. Bring the scytale.
If I can't spend this birthday with Mum, at least I can spend it with my brothers.
I'll go wake the duque!
It's a miracle! Thank you!
My flower, my love, my sweet dove.
The joy of a reunited family.

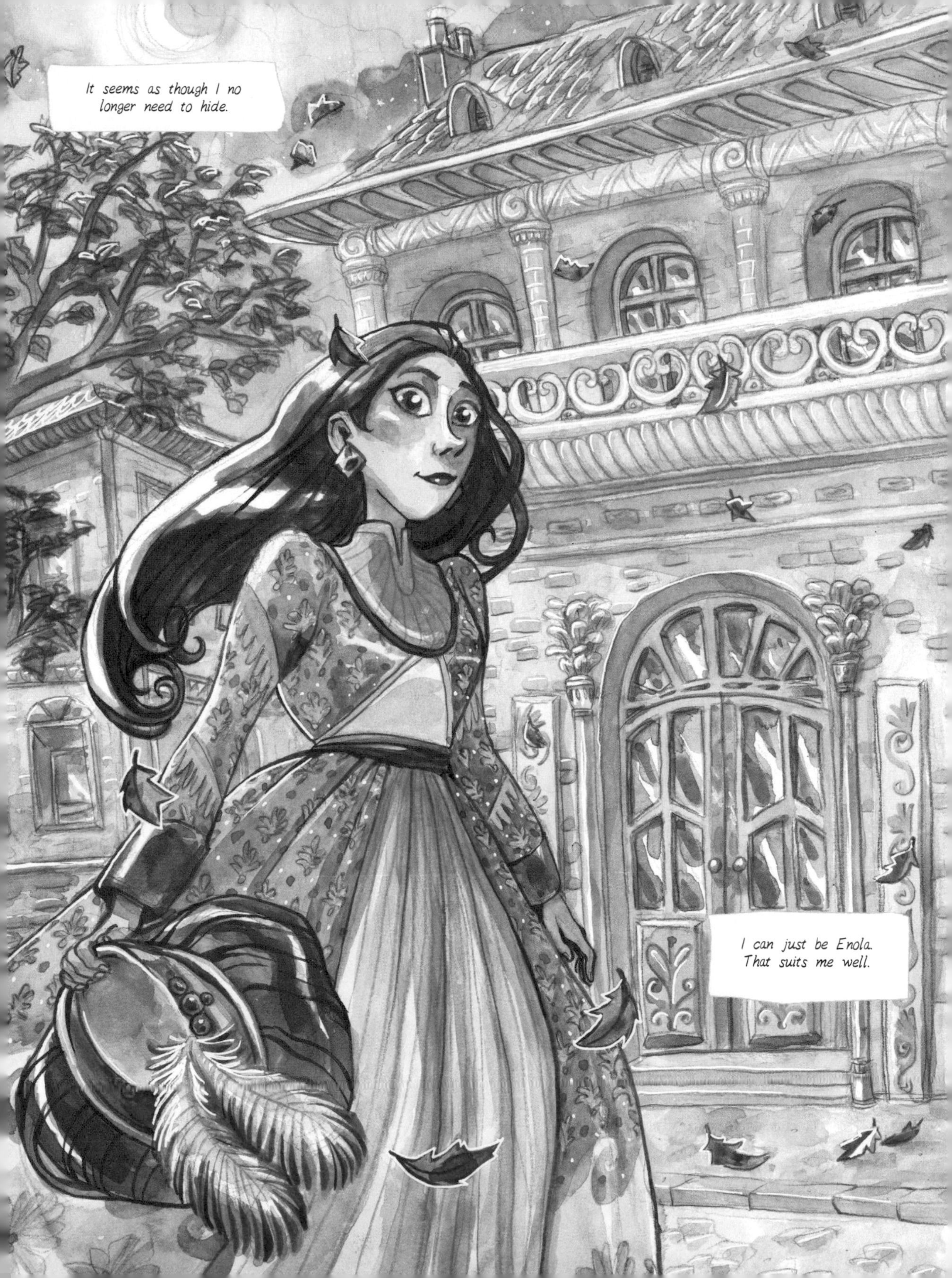
It seems as though I no longer need to hide.
I can just be Enola. That suits me well.

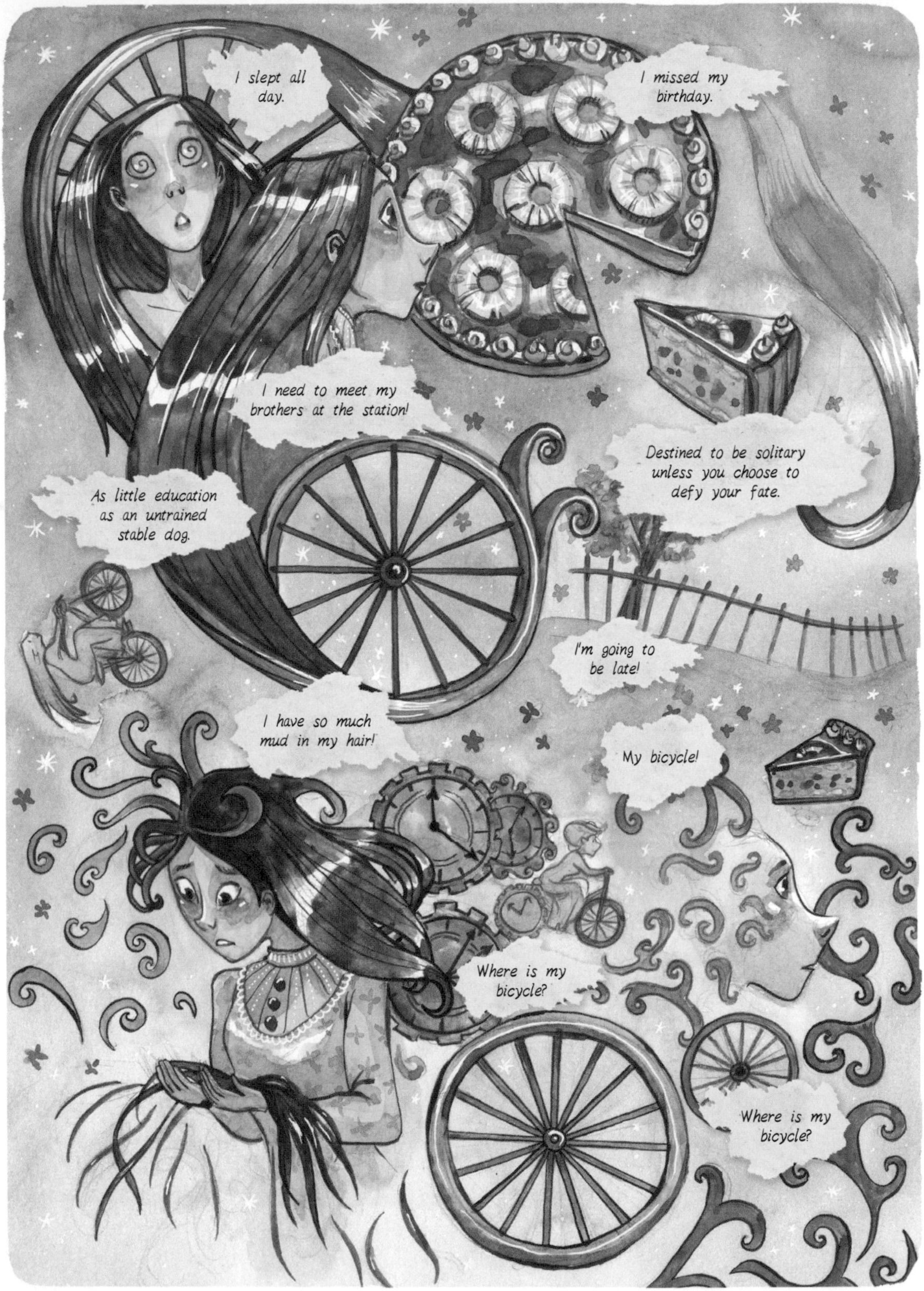
I slept all day.
I missed my birthday.
I need to meet my brothers at the station!
Destined to be solitary unless you choose to defy your fate.
As little education as an untrained stable dog.
I'm going to be late!
I have so much mud in my hair!
My bicycle!
Where is my bicycle?
Where is my bicycle?

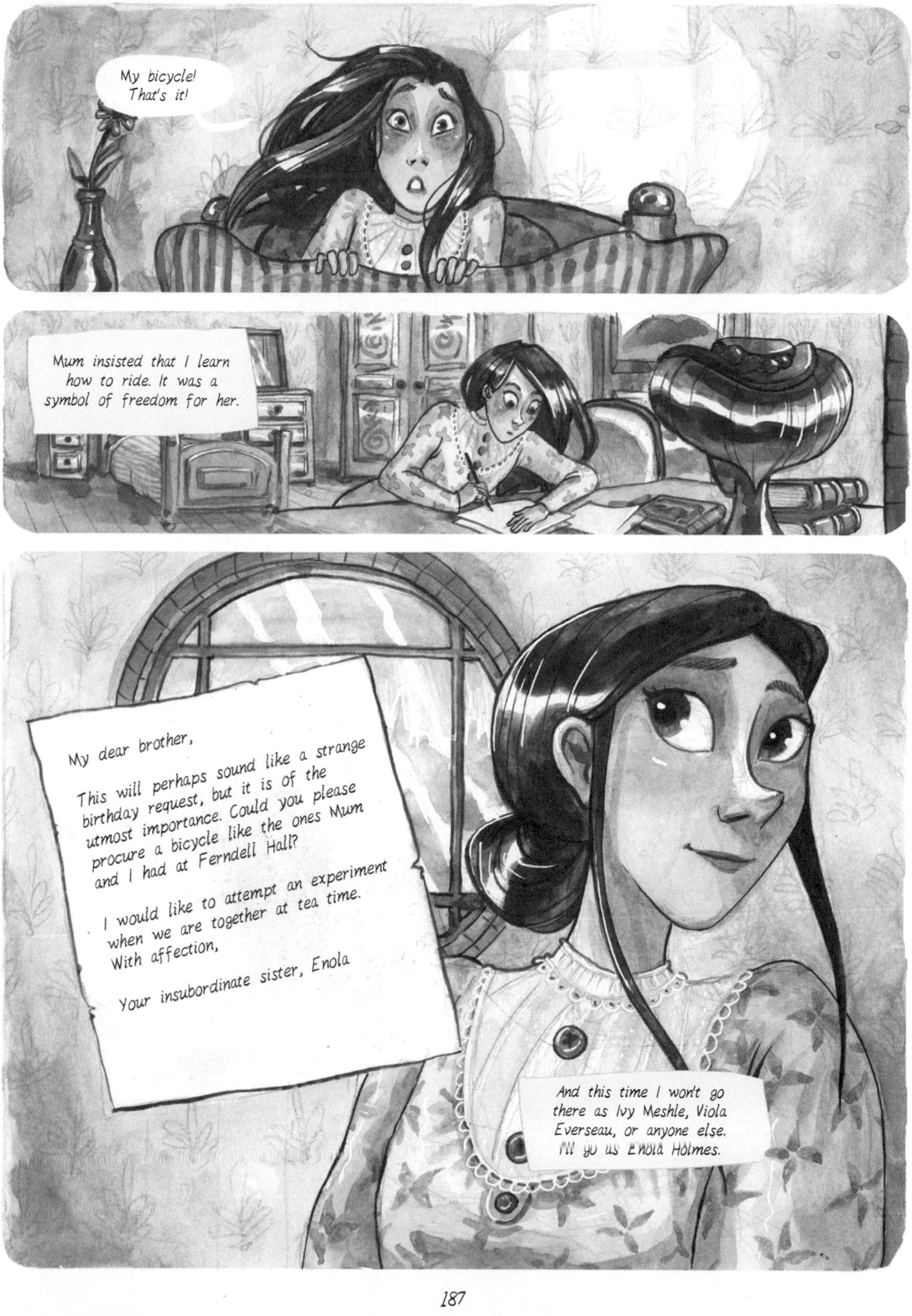
My bicycle! That's it!
Mum insisted that I learn how to ride. It was a symbol of freedom for her.
My dear brother,
This will perhaps sound like a strange birthday request, but it is of the utmost importance. Could you please procure a bicycle like the ones Mum and I had at Ferndell Hall?
I would like to attempt an experiment when we are together at tea time.
With affection,
Your insubordinate sister, Enola
And this time I won't go there as Ivy Meshle, Viola Everseau, or anyone else. I'll go as Enola Holmes.

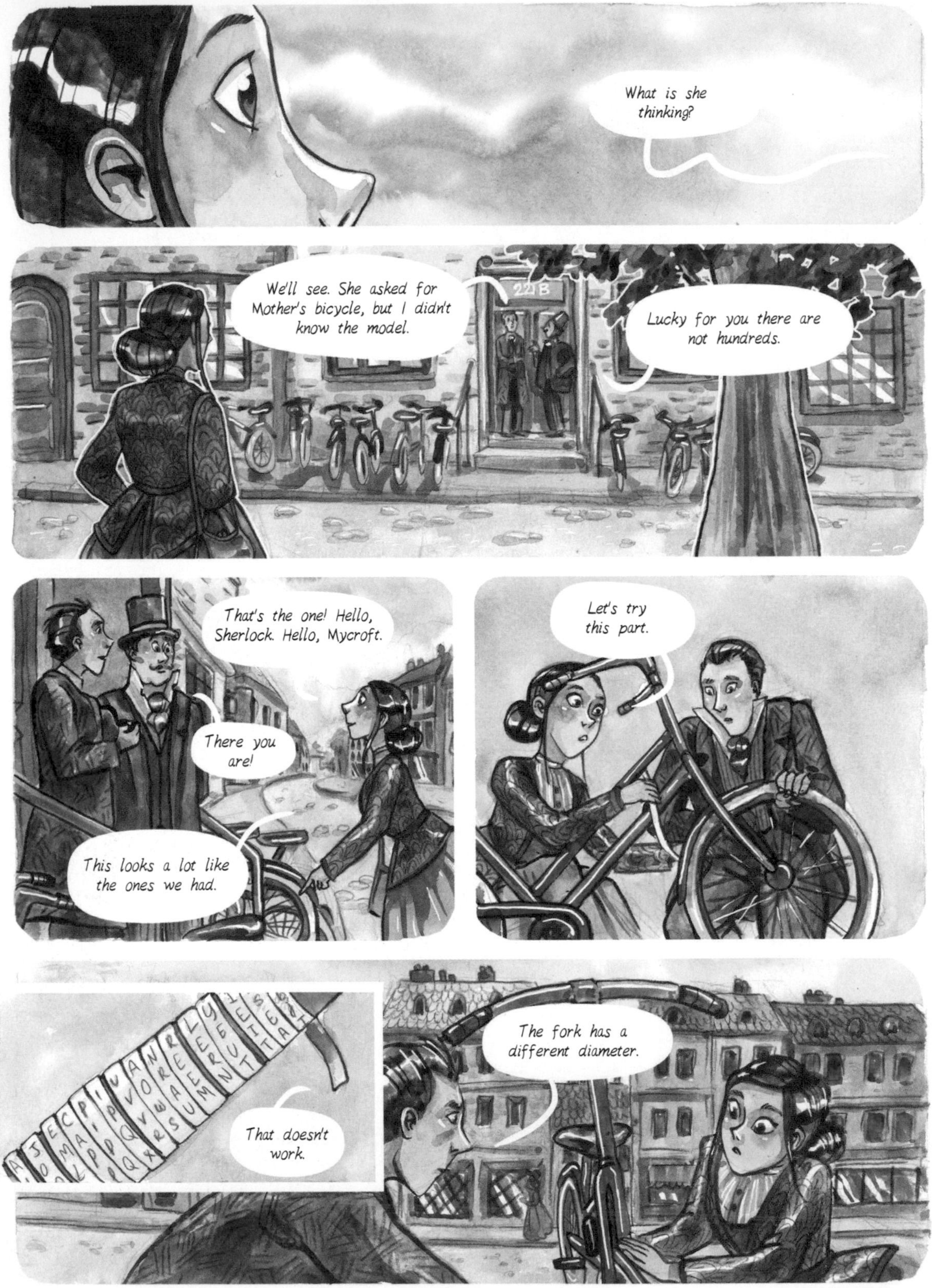
What is she thinking?
We'll see. She asked for Mother's bicycle, but I didn't know the model.
221B
Lucky for you there are not hundreds.
That's the one! Hello, Sherlock. Hello, Mycroft.
There you are!
This looks a lot like the ones we had.
Let's try this part.
The fork has a different diameter.
That doesn't work.

Here! I always thought that if I were not true to myself . . .

Therefore, it's not surprising that both your brothers are bachelors . . .

It seems as though we've started at the middle! We need to find the beginning.

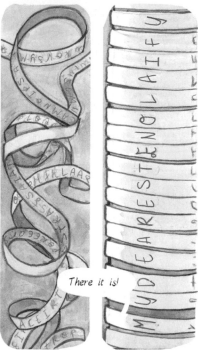

There it is!

My dearest Enola, if you have received this letter, it is because I am dead.

My dearest Enola,

If you have received this letter, it is because I am
dead. I know that these words are abrupt, but I refuse
to soften them by saying "gone to a better place" or
other such platitudes. You know that, as a free thinker,
I don't believe in one.

I always believed that this life is the only one we have
and that we each need to live it as fully as possible.
This is why I left you, or to put it plainly, abandoned
you in such a brutal way. Please know that I still
carry that guilt. I had hoped to wait a year or two,
but I sensed the cancerous growth in my abdomen
growing at an alarming rate. I knew I could not
put off leaving any longer.

Enola, you have always been wise and thoughtful for
your age. I hope you will understand that in addition to
being a mother, I was a person. None of us should give
up on our dreams, not even for our family. I always
thought that if I were not true to myself, everything I
taught you would be worth nothing. I cannot be
different to who I am, and perhaps I should not
have been a mother. Therefore, it's not surprising
that both your brothers are bachelors.

In any case, all my life, since childhood, I have
dreamed to taste the simple freedom of traveler life. I
love their colorful, comfortable clothing, the sound of
their violins, their horses with their heads held high,
their laughter, their life by different rules.

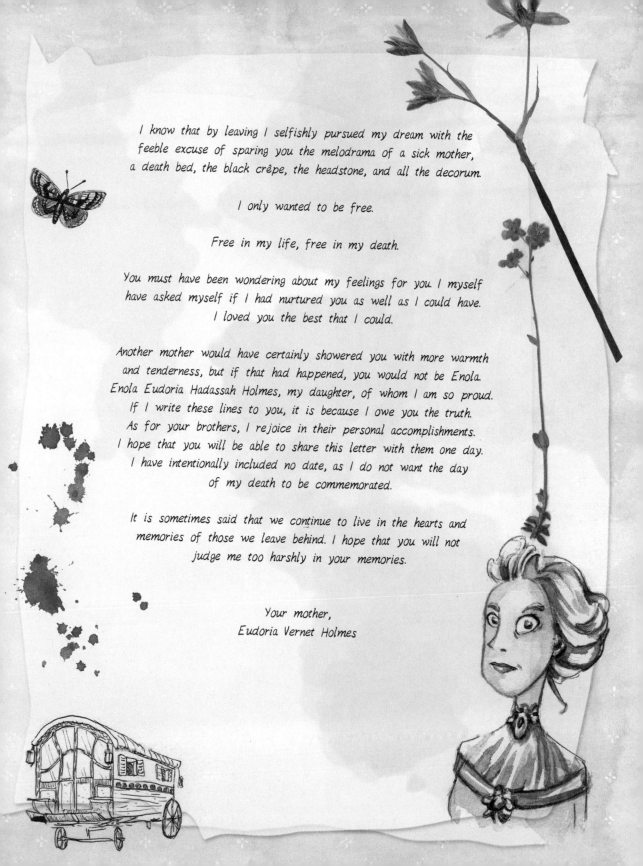

I know that by leaving I selfishly pursued my dream with the feeble excuse of sparing you the melodrama of a sick mother, a death bed, the black crêpe, the headstone, and all the decorum.

I only wanted to be free.

Free in my life, free in my death.

You must have been wondering about my feelings for you. I myself have asked myself if I had nurtured you as well as I could have. I loved you the best that I could.

Another mother would have certainly showered you with more warmth and tenderness, but if that had happened, you would not be Enola. Enola Eudoria Hadassah Holmes, my daughter, of whom I am so proud. If I write these lines to you, it is because I owe you the truth. As for your brothers, I rejoice in their personal accomplishments. I hope that you will be able to share this letter with them one day. I have intentionally included no date, as I do not want the day of my death to be commemorated.

It is sometimes said that we continue to live in the hearts and memories of those we leave behind. I hope that you will not judge me too harshly in your memories.

Your mother,
Eudoria Vernet Holmes

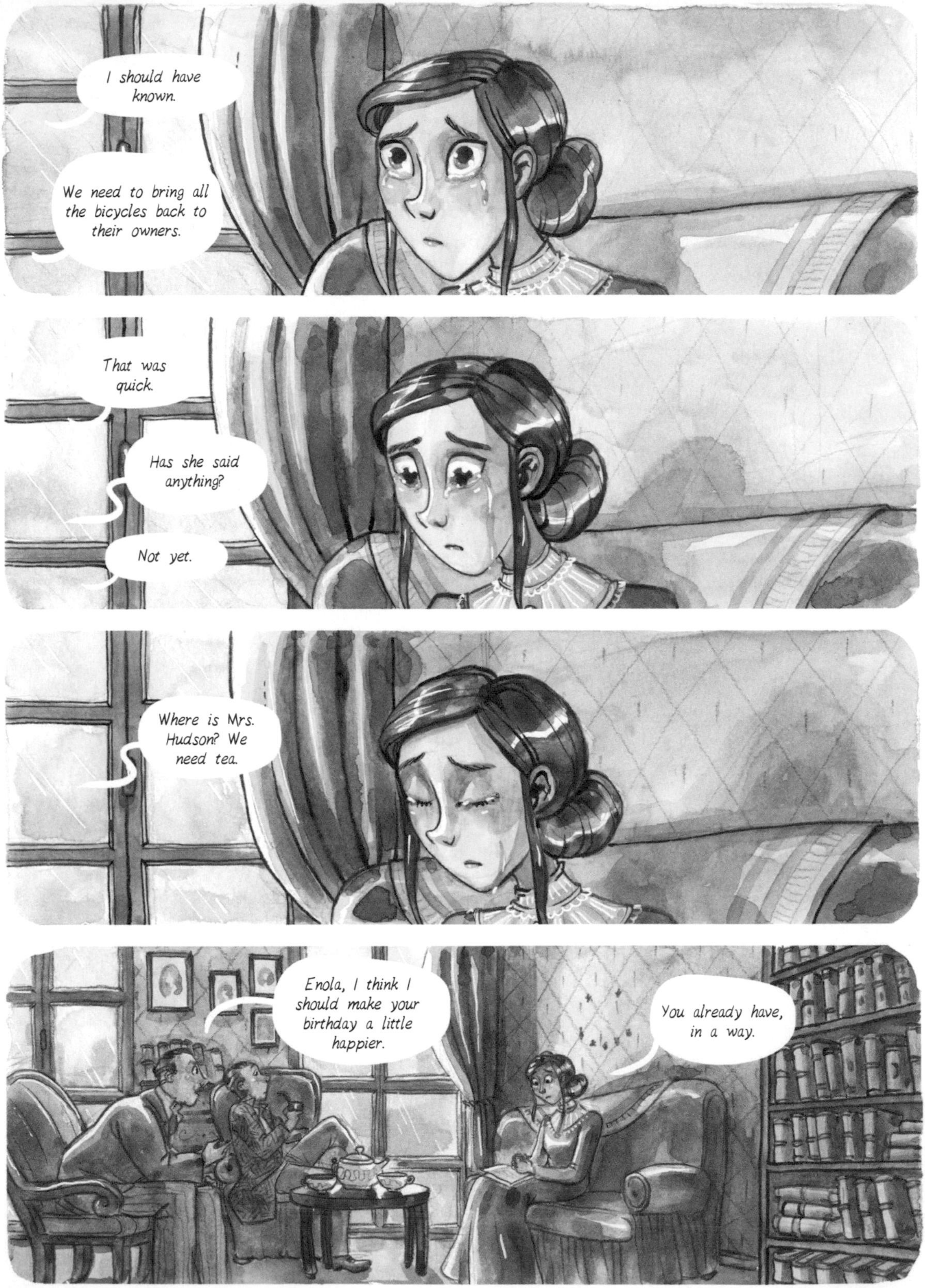

I should have known.
We need to bring all the bicycles back to their owners.
That was quick.
Has she said anything?
Not yet.
Where is Mrs. Hudson? We need tea.
Enola, I think I should make your birthday a little happier.
You already have, in a way.

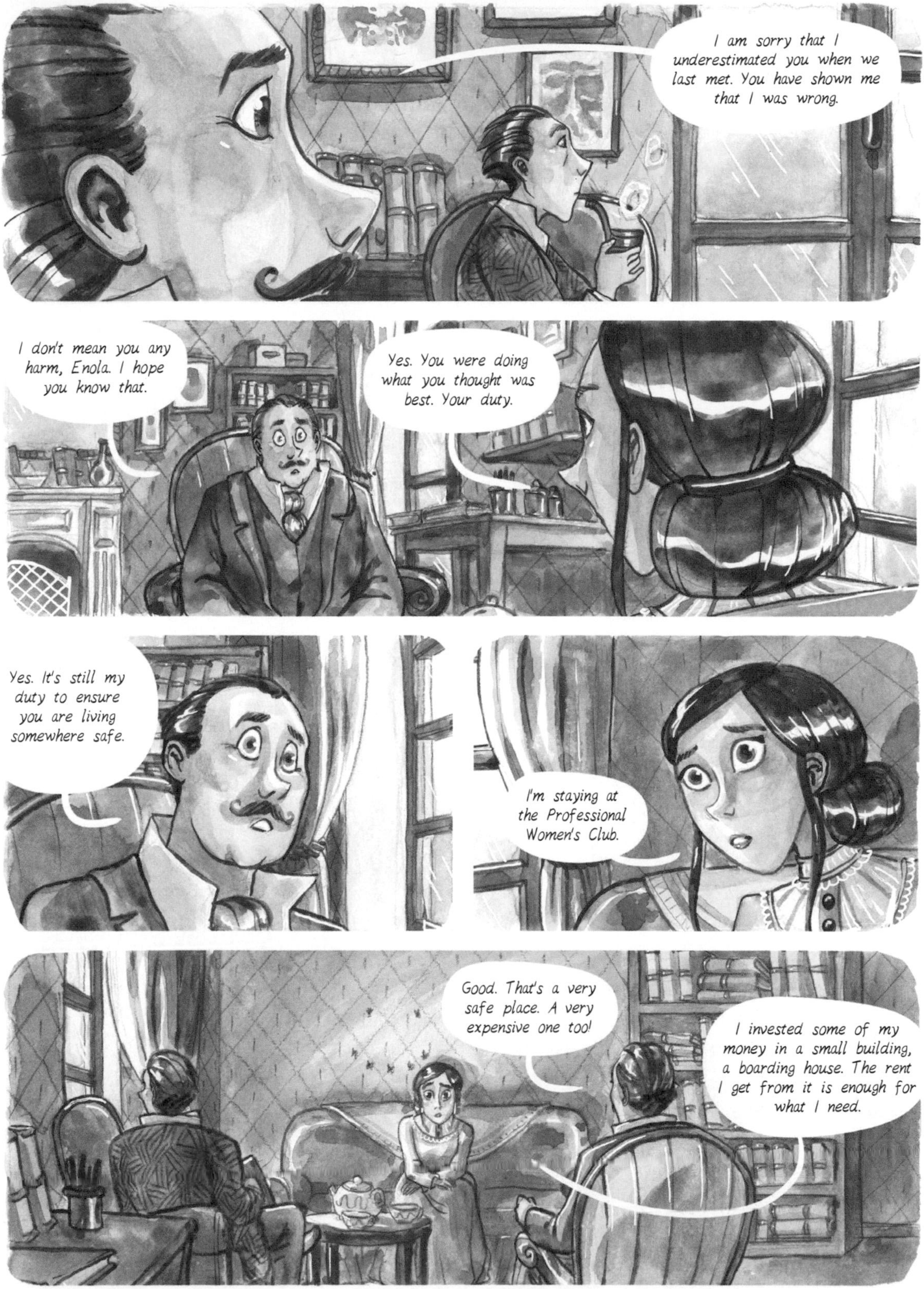
I am sorry that I underestimated you when we last met. You have shown me that I was wrong.
I don't mean you any harm, Enola. I hope you know that.
Yes. You were doing what you thought was best. Your duty.
Yes. It's still my duty to ensure you are living somewhere safe.
I'm staying at the Professional Women's Club.
Good. That's a very safe place. A very expensive one too!
I invested some of my money in a small building, a boarding house. The rent I get from it is enough for what I need.

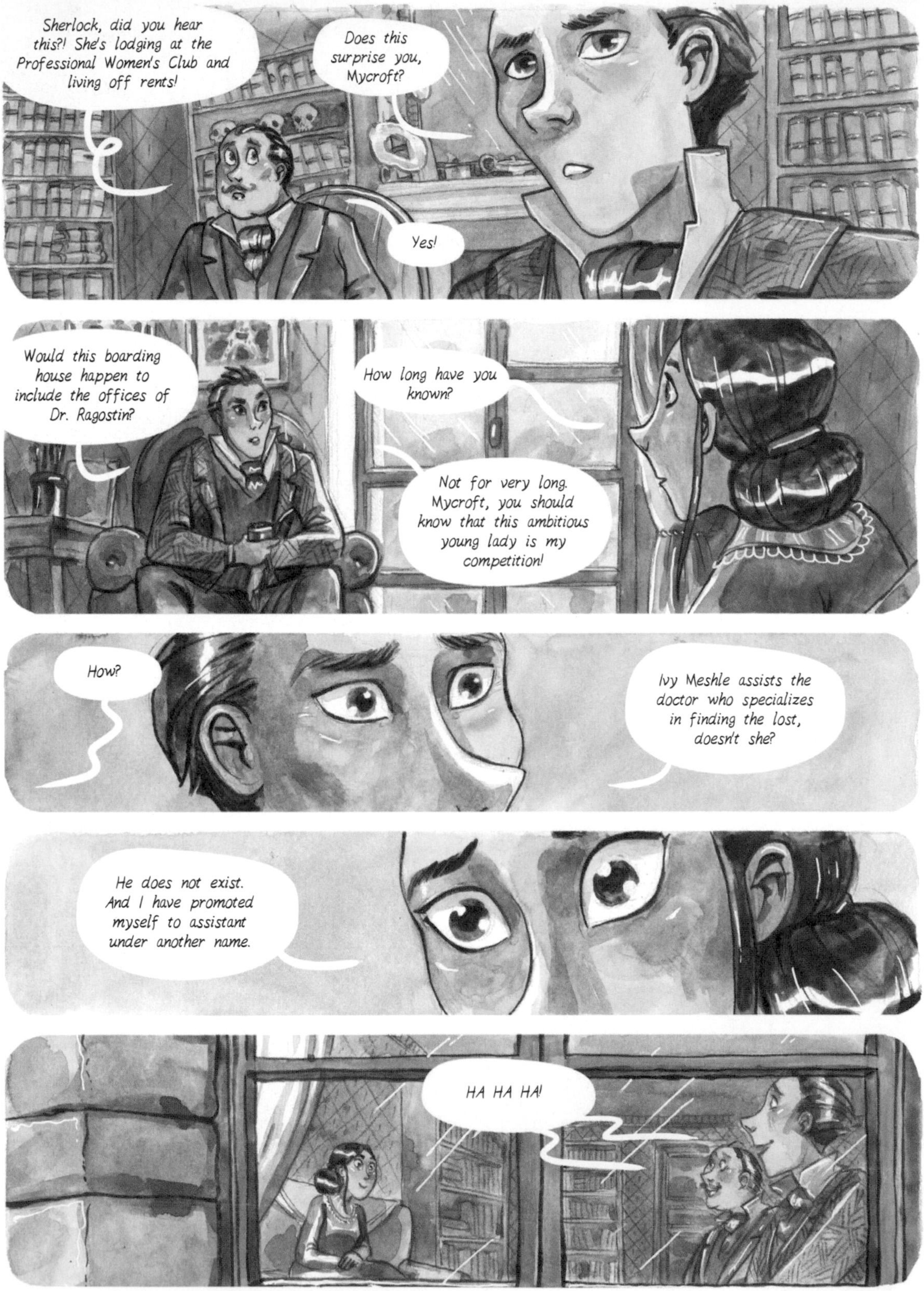
Sherlock, did you hear this?! She's lodging at the Professional Women's Club and living off rents!
Does this surprise you, Mycroft?
Yes!
Would this boarding house happen to include the offices of Dr. Ragostin?
How long have you known?
Not for very long. Mycroft, you should know that this ambitious young lady is my competition!
How?
Ivy Meshle assists the doctor who specializes in finding the lost, doesn't she?
He does not exist. And I have promoted myself to assistant under another name.
HA HA HA!

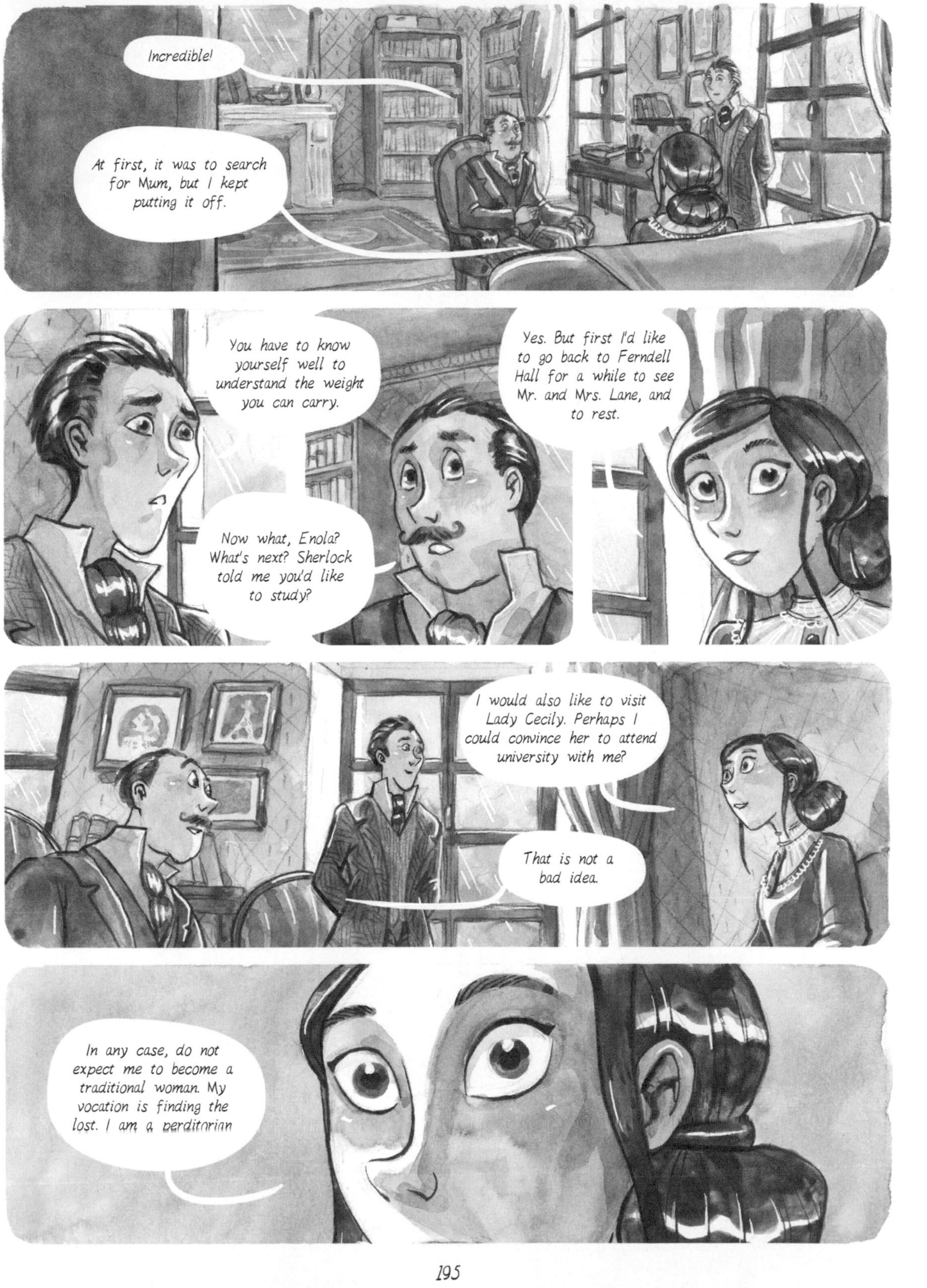
Incredible!
At first, it was to search for Mum, but I kept putting it off.
You have to know yourself well to understand the weight you can carry.
Now what, Enola? What's next? Sherlock told me you'd like to study?
Yes. But first I'd like to go back to Ferndell Hall for a while to see Mr. and Mrs. Lane, and to rest.
I would also like to visit Lady Cecily. Perhaps I could convince her to attend university with me?
That is not a bad idea.
In any case, do not expect me to become a traditional woman. My vocation is finding the lost. I am a perditorian

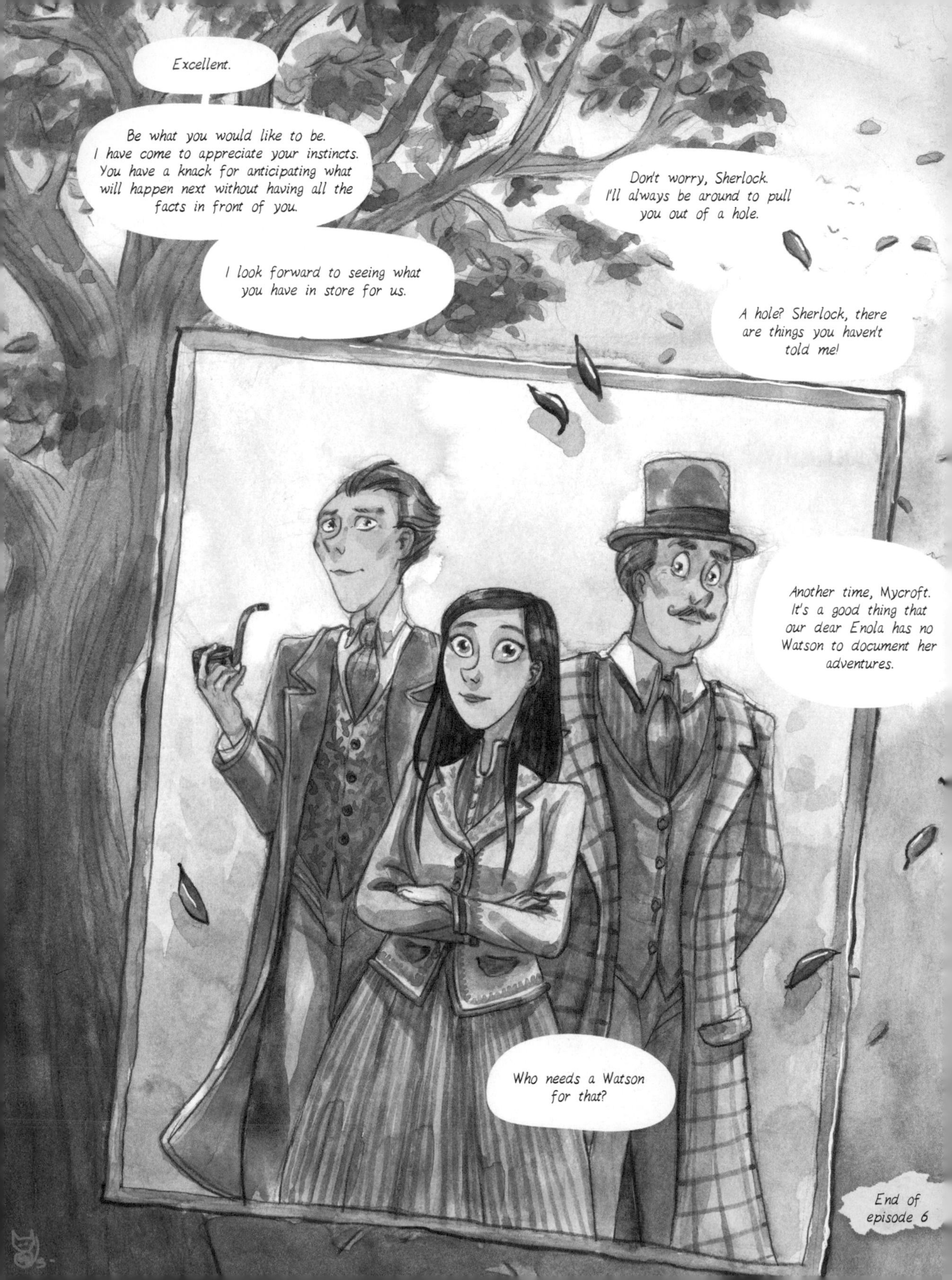
Excellent.
Be what you would like to be. I have come to appreciate your instincts. You have a knack for anticipating what will happen next without having all the facts in front of you.
I look forward to seeing what you have in store for us.
Don't worry, Sherlock. I'll always be around to pull you out of a hole.
A hole? Sherlock, there are things you haven't told me!
Another time, Mycroft. It's a good thing that our dear Enola has no Watson to document her adventures.
Who needs a Watson for that?
End of episode 6

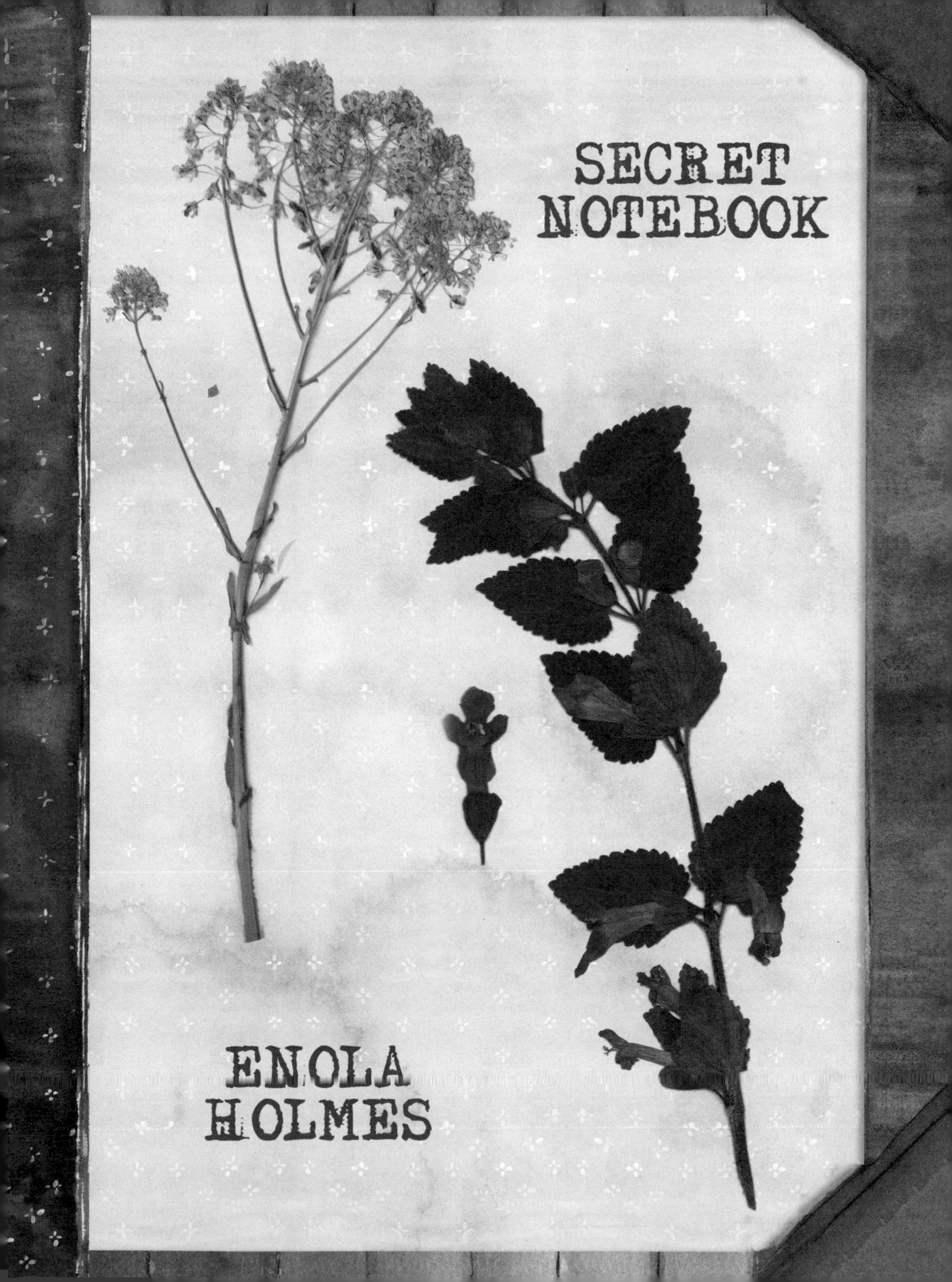
SECRET
NOTEBOOK
ENOLA
HOLMES

The Duquesa

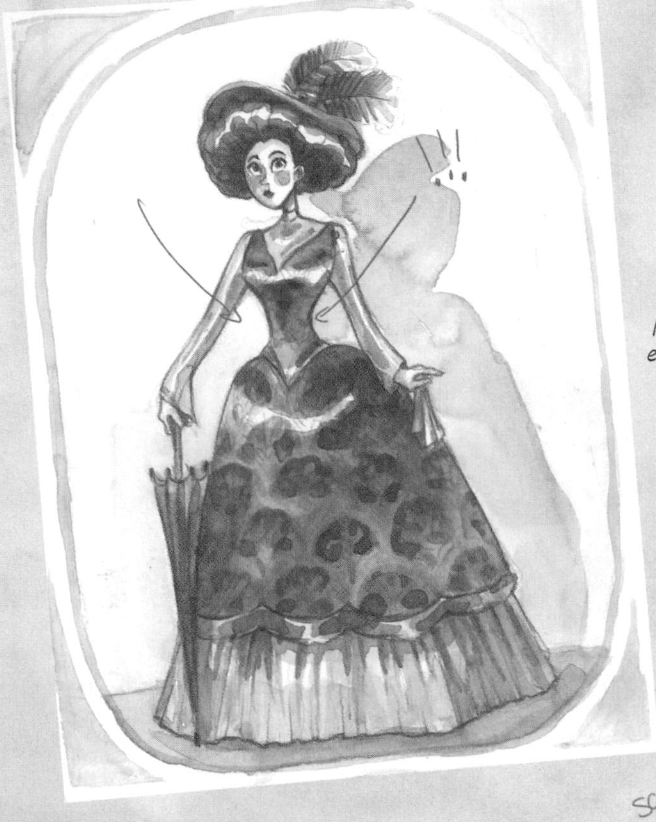

Poor duquesa. She was made to tight-lace her corset day and night since childhood. The muscles in her back and abdomen atrophied. Without her corset, she cannot stand or walk.

I can't thank mother enough for saving me from this!

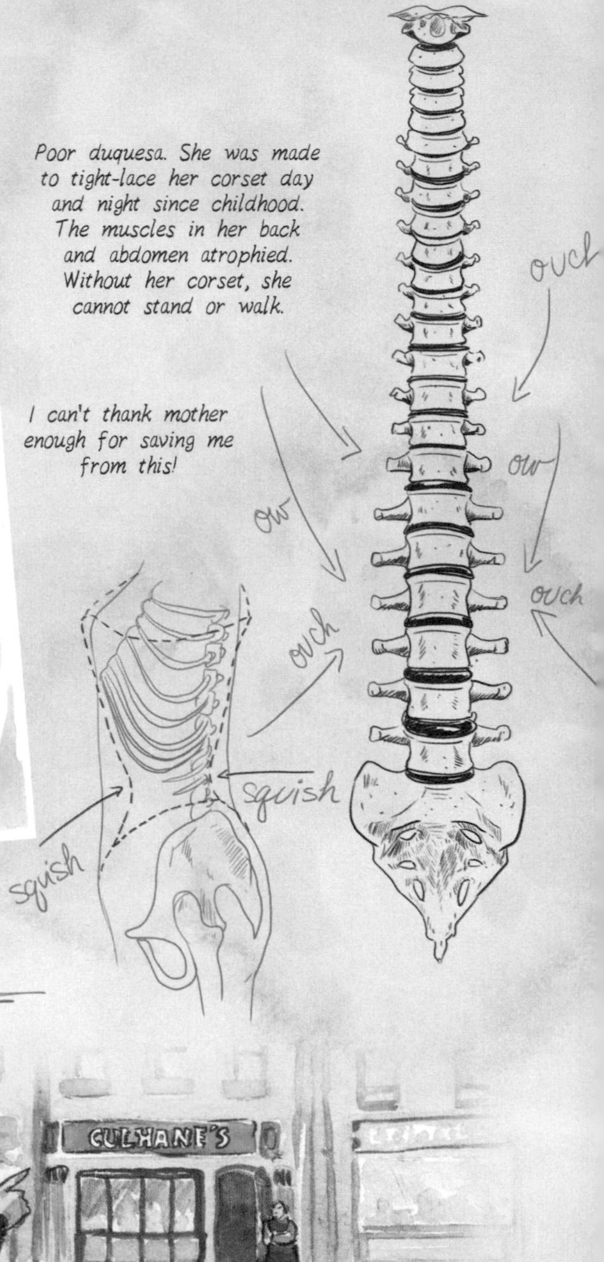
ouch
ow
ow
ouch
ouch
squish
squish

Culhane's

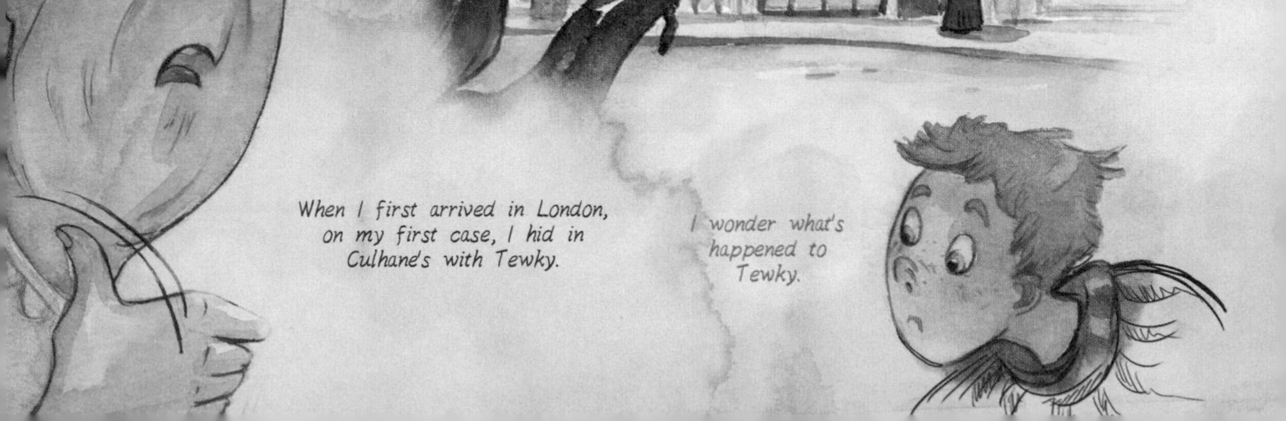
CULHANE'S

When I first arrived in London, on my first case, I hid in Culhane's with Tewky.

I wonder what's happened to Tewky.

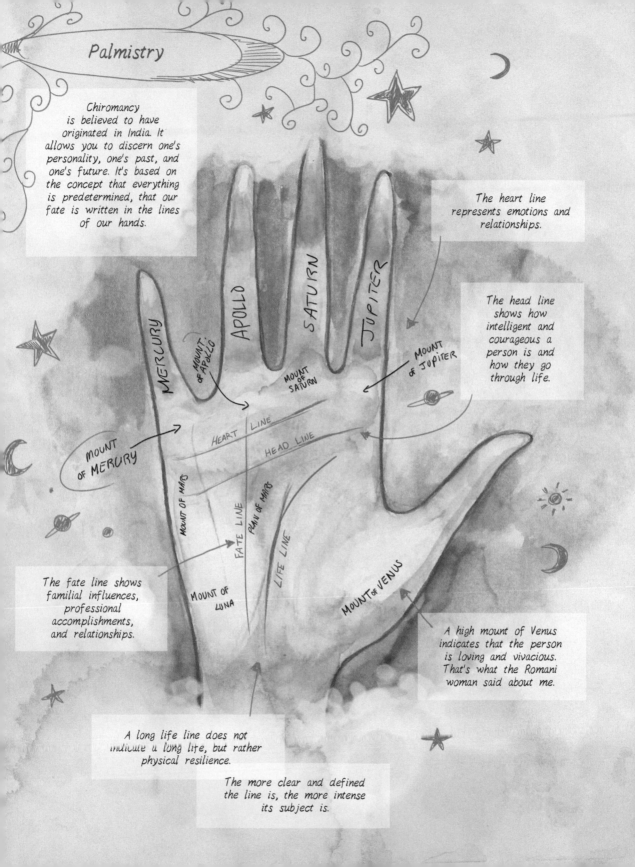

Palmistry

Chiromancy is believed to have originated in India. It allows you to discern one's personality, one's past, and one's future. It's based on the concept that everything is predetermined, that our fate is written in the lines of our hands.

The heart line represents emotions and relationships.

The head line shows how intelligent and courageous a person is and how they go through life.

MERCURY

APOLLO

SATURN

JUPITER

MOUNT OF APOLLO

MOUNT OF SATURN

MOUNT OF JUPITER

MOUNT OF MERCURY

HEART LINE

HEAD LINE

MOUNT OF MARS

PLAIN OF MARS

FATE LINE

LIFE LINE

MOUNT OF LUNA

MOUNT OF VENUS

The fate line shows familial influences, professional accomplishments, and relationships.

A high mount of Venus indicates that the person is loving and vivacious. That's what the Romani woman said about me.

A long life line does not indicate a long life, but rather physical resilience.

The more clear and defined the line is, the more intense its subject is.

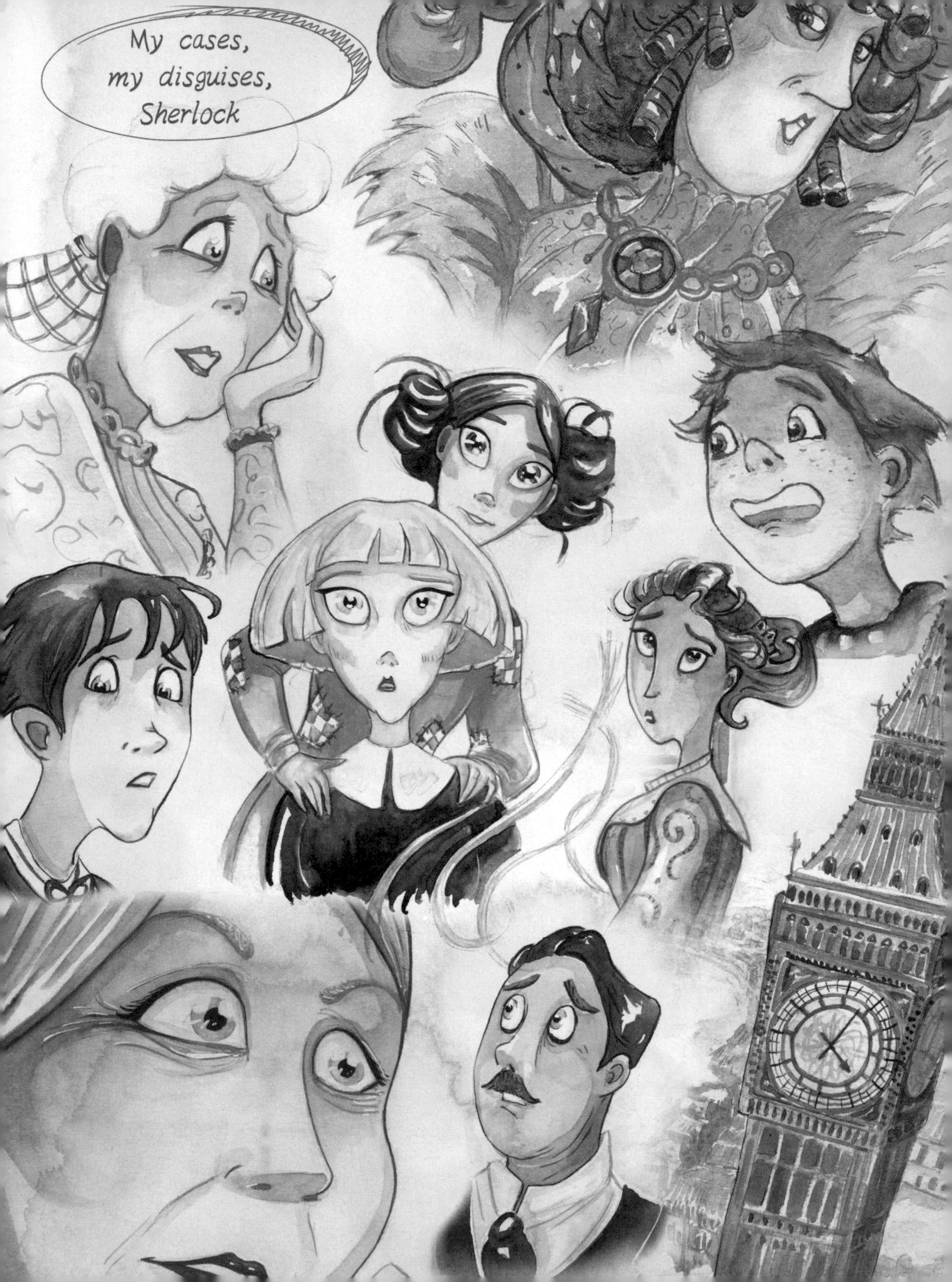
My cases,
my disguises,
Sherlock

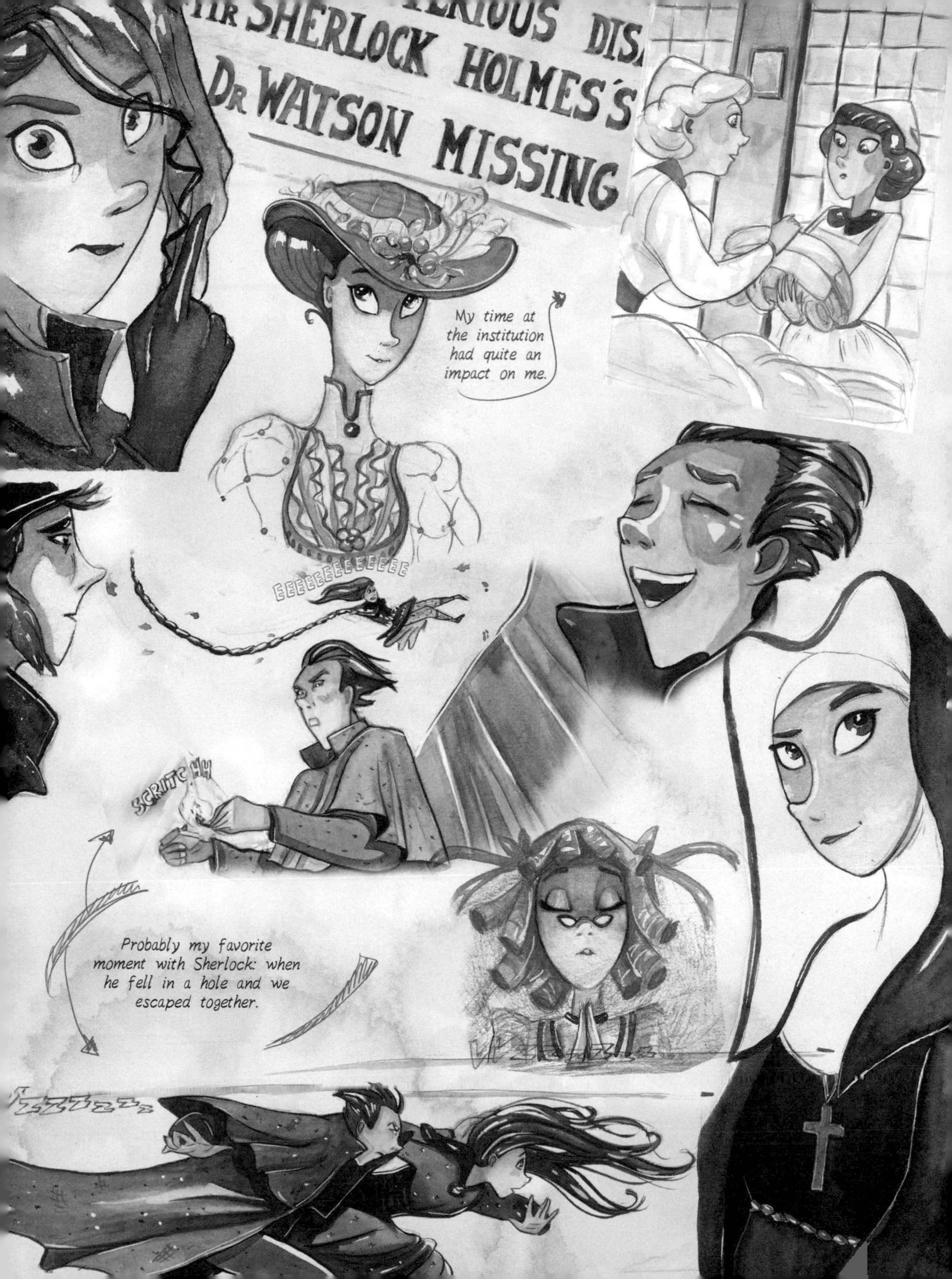
SHERLOCK HOLMES´S
DR WATSON MISSING
My time at the institution had quite an impact on me.
EEEEEEEEEEEEE
SCRITCHH
Probably my favorite moment with Sherlock: when he fell in a hole and we escaped together.

Mum
In my heart, always.